Hawley Smart

Hard Lines - A Novel

Hawley Smart

Hard Lines - A Novel

ISBN/EAN: 9783337031633

Printed in Europe, USA, Canada, Australia, Japan

Cover: Foto ©Andreas Hilbeck / pixelio.de

More available books at **www.hansebooks.com**

HARD LINES

A Novel

BY

HAWLEY SMART

AUTHOR OF

"BREEZIE LANGTON," "SOCIAL SINNERS," "THE GREAT TONTINE,"
"AT FAULT," ETC. ETC.

> "Of all the barbarous middle ages, that
> Which is most barbarous is the middle age
> Of man ; it is—I really scarce know what ;
> But when we hover between fool and sage,
> And don't know justly what we would be at—
> A period something like a printed page,
> Black letter upon foolscap, while our hair
> Grows grizzled, and we are not what we were."

"The greatest miracle of love is the reformation of a coquette."

New Edition

LONDON : CHAPMAN AND HALL

LIMITED

1884

CONTENTS.

CONTENTS.

HARD LINES

HARD LINES.

CHAPTER I.

THE CID.

York! Most of us know the pleasant, dreamy old northern capital on the banks of the Ouse, with its quaint narrow streets, lofty embattlements, massive gates, and grand old cathedral. Except London itself, there is not a town in England that can conjure up so many memories of the past. Stroll home from the Knavesmire in August, and muse over the famous equine battles that have been fought out over that deadly galloping course for a half-trained one; we remember the scene when the mighty Blair Athol went down there before a commoner, and caused the hearts of his St. Leger backers to sink into their very boots. As we rise the Mount fancy carries us back a century, and we picture to ourselves the feeling of exultation with which the travellers from the metropolis must have viewed the pinnacles of the Minster, and realized that their three days' journey was safely sped, despite accident of flood and field or reckless assault of highwayman. As Micklegate Bar comes before us it is hard not to recall the terrible rout of Marston Moor, and the scene of slaughter and confusion which occurred at the great southern gate of the city, and as we pass beneath the massive archway the grim remembrance of the display of heads on its summit which so speedily followed shoots athwart our brain, and inspires a vindictive feeling that heads lately used to our detriment would be more satisfactory to view there than on their owners' shoulders.

Next to Lewis Carroll's 'Queen of Hearts,' I have always regarded Richard III. as the greatest of historical characters from that one famous speech so poetically reported—

"Off with his head, so much for Buckingham ! "

Henry the Eighth was very fair in this way, and his Royal daughter, the last of the Tudors, had a very pretty knack of shortening men's stature in this wise also, but they lacked the cynical brevity and quick decision of the last scion of the House of York.

What a wonderful old town it is ! I could muse over it for weeks, and should then leave with a most unhallowed desire to dig it all up and look at those two or three other cities that lie buried beneath it. One looks up at the snow-white walls and fancies the steel morions and halberds gleaming above the parapet, and then remembers grimly what a mess the devil's dust, as used by modern artillery, would make of them in these days. Rare times must those have been when York held command of the Great North Road, and kept watch and ward at Bootham Bar over the restless reivers of the border on the one side, and a vigilant eye on southern treason from Micklegate Bar on the other.

Some thirty years ago, if you had left the city by Fishergate, near the Cattle Market, and made your way towards the cavalry barracks, you would have found shortly after clearing the city walls that the suburb ceased. Scarcely a house occurred till you arrived at the celebrated Light Horseman, a roadside tavern about half way between the city and the barracks, much patronized by the military, and celebrated as the place at which Turpin's Black Bess died. I am quite aware that it is the fashion of this day to deny that famous ride altogether. I make answer that, in these times of unbelief, we must remain faithful to some of the old legends, and this I have seen with mine own eyes performed often—on the Surrey side. At the bend of the road, a little after you passed the Light Horseman, lay to your right an old-fashioned country house, its gables wreathed in ivy, and surrounded by three or four acres of ground prettily laid out in gardens and pleasaunce; the dwelling this of Julian Harperley, banker, who, head of a very profitable business in the city, bore the reputation of a strictly just and honourable man. He stood well with all classes. He was hospitable, reasonably free with his money, and especially accounted fair and liberal in all his dealings. If things had prospered with him there was no hint of sharp practice or of usurious interest ever breathed against his name. A moderate sportsman, as every Yorkshireman is bound to be, and a moderate *viveur*, as most men were in those days, Julian Harperley was the *beau idéal* of the prosperous country banker, popular in the city, and upon excellent terms with all the county magnates that resided within reasonable distance. Julian Harperley was a widower, and in his married life he had been sadly unfortunate. About twenty years previous to the commencement of this history a Mr. Aysgarth, one of his partners, had been thrown out of a dog-cart and killed upon the spot. Business required that he should have frequent interviews with the widow, and the forlorn condition of the sorrow-stricken woman filled Julian Harperley's soul with pity. She was young and she was pretty, and, as often happens, her mourning became her wonderfully. Niobe in sombre draperies, with Psyche, in the shape of a little girl of five years old, clinging to her skirts, is undeniably attractive, especially to men verging on middle age. Julian Harperley was smitten with the love fever, took heart of grace, proposed, was accepted, and married the winsome widow, with little Annie included. She made him an excellent wife, and this was, perhaps, the happiest time of his life; but, alas! ere little more than a year had sped she presented him with a son, whose birth cost her life. She confided her little girl to his care, whispered him a faint farewell, and was gone, leaving the stricken man to bear his burden as he best could.

Annie, who was six years old when her mother died, was speedily a great solace to him. He had always been fond of the child, and now the little motherless thing stole her way into his heart completely. Her first passionate burst of grief over, and she seemed not only to sympathize with him in their mutual loss, but to transfer the affection that she had borne for her mother to Julian Harperley. She would creep up to his side, and nestle her tiny hand into his, until he felt impelled to lift the little maiden on to his knee, and once she had gained that desired position she would be quiet as a mouse, never interfering with his perusal of book or paper, save by a mute caress. That as she grew up she should become more and more to him was only natural, and undoubtedly Julian Harperley was the more delighted of the twain when, her schooling finished, she was solemnly invested with the keys, and proclaimed mistress of "The Firs."

A tall, handsome brunette, with flashing blue eyes, and plenty of vitality, Miss Aysgarth had not lacked admirers during the six years she had ruled over "The Firs," but no one could as yet flatter himself that he had made any serious mark in her good graces. Favourites she had, of course ; but when man's vanity, as it occasionally did, prompted one of these to believe that he was valued above his fellows, he had been gently but speedily made aware of his mistake. A shrewd, clever girl, apt to fathom people's characters pretty accurately, and to appraise them at their fair value, and yet as she sits there this pleasant autumn afternoon, it may be doubted whether in her thoughts she is not putting a higher price on one person than he exactly merits.

It is a very pleasant place, that flower-gemmed garden in these September days—glorious days of a fine Yorkshire autumn. If they get their warm weather later in the Ridings than we do down south, it stays with them longer, and they are often having a gorgeous time of it when we are grimly contemplating the commencement of winter. The soft, velvety turf was bordered by old-fashioned shrubberies, through which trimly-kept gravel walks meandered in the direction of the road. Annie Aysgarth is seated in a trim rustic summer-house, kept with such evident care, as to betoken it a favourite place of resort. She is occupied in piecing together some gaily-coloured bits of silk, though with what design is not easy of understanding. The mystery of a lady's work is generally above masculine comprehension. A light step on one of the gravel-walks running down

to the road causes her to raise her head, put her work on one
side, and resume the book she had been reading.

"Ah! Annie," exclaimed the new-comer, as he emerged from
the shrubberies, "I thought I should very likely find you here."

"Then all I can say, Harry, is, you had no business to think
anything of the kind," replied Miss Aysgarth, laughing. "You
should know I ought to be at the Dowtons', six miles away, but
I felt idle, 'and so, somehow, you see, never made a start of it."

"Your besetting sin, my dear, is this want of energy," rejoined
the new-comer, with mock gravity. "Ever since I have devoted
my energies to the service of my country there has been nobody
to keep you up to the mark. Two or three years back, and I
should have decided that you required pinching, and—yes," he
added, slowly, "should probably have done it."

"Two or three years back," retorted Miss Aysgarth, laughing,
"you were an unbearable schoolboy, whose ears I never could
box sufficiently hard in return for your impertinence; but now,
sir, bear in mind, you are an officer of dragoons, and as a cornet
of horse are expected—"

"To behave as sich; quite so, Annie; but let's stroll up to
the house. I want to see the governor. Is he in?"

"Yes; and how's the regiment, Harry?" said Miss Aysgarth,
rising and collecting her properties.

"The regiment is getting on very well, though the Colonel
showed a painful want of appreciation as regards my military
knowledge yesterday morning. You see, Cis Calvert was away,
so was my brother sub, consequently the command of the troop
fell on me yesterday at our drill on the Knavesmire, and I certainly distinguished myself, while as for poor old Copplestone he
must have given the recording angel a hard time, and nearly used
up the ledger."

"But why don't you learn your drill?"

"So I have; but when on your first mistake the chief goes
off like a broadside of thirty-two pounders, who is to recollect
it all? I should like to see you manage your cross stitch with
a she-martinet invoking blessings on your head, and wondering
how such an incalculable idiot found his way into the world.
Smart commanding officer of the old school, Copplestone must

have learnt his drill with that famous army of Flanders, I fancy."

"What is it you want to see papa about?" asked Miss Aysgarth, as she passed her arm affectionately through her half-brother's.

"I want him to give me another horse," replied the boy, for in sooth, he was little more. A good-looking stripling of eighteen, Harry Harperley, to his great delight and glorification, had some six months before the commencement of this narrative been gazetted to a cornetcy in Her Majesty's —th Lancers. He was just one of those devil-may-care young gentlemen whom the public schools turned out in shoals in those days. In these times I fancy the affectation of the *nil admirari* rather spoils these frank-hearted youngsters; but I am writing, as may be remembered, of what has been jestingly termed the pre-educational period, when a knowledge of the 'ologies' was by no means imperative.

"You see," continued Harry, "we are not allowed to hunt our first chargers, much less race them. My second's in the school. I must have a horse I can do as I like with. It seems so deuced slow not to enter a horse for the Regimental Cup, too. I should like to have a shy at that, though I don't suppose I should have much chance against either Cis Calvert or Crymes."

"Major Crymes is no great friend of yours, is he, Harry?" inquired Miss Aysgarth a little anxiously.

"No, sister mine. He's a fine horseman, and a good fellow, no doubt, but somehow I don't take to him. He rather snubs us young ones, and, what's more, I don't think the seniors care much about him either."

"Well, I am glad to hear you are not intimate with Major Crymes. I can't tell you why. He is always pleasant and agreeable enough when he comes here, and, to tell the truth, Harry, talks better than most men I meet. But he is rather cynical, I fancy."

"Can't exactly say," responded the cornet curtly. "He is pretty good at everything all round, when he takes the trouble to try; but he rarely plays cards, billiards, or anything else;

hunting is the one thing he goes in for, and if he gets anything like a start he's bad to beat to hounds, even Cis Calvert acknowledges. But here comes the father," and as he spoke Julian Harperley sauntered on his hack slowly up the drive.

" Well, Harry," he exclaimed, as he shook hands with his son, " are you going to honour us with your company at dinner? No one but Annie and myself to-night. We shall feel proud at the mess being thrown over on our account."

" No, father, I'll not sail under false colours. I am come to dine, but I am come begging, to boot."

" Ah, well!" replied Julian Harperley, laughing, " keep the petition till after dinner. Men's purse-strings, like their tongues, loosen more readily when that meal has been satisfactorily accomplished. If your request be not out of all bounds, and the housekeeper has not failed in her duties, I dare say you'll go back to barracks happy."

As the three gathered round the fire after dinner, Mr. Harperley pushed the claret across to his son, and said, " Now, Harry, what is it?"

" Well, the fact is, I want you to buy me another horse. I have only one I can hunt, you know, and two will be little enough to begin the season with."

" I make no objection to that; I always intended to give you a third. There will, I am afraid, be some trouble in getting hold of what you want just now. There are a good many men wanting hunters at this season of the year always."

" Ah, but I happen to know of one. You know Mappin, the dealer, who has the farm just off the old North road? I was out at his place the other day with Cis Calvert to look at a horse called The Cid—a clipper, a dark iron-grey, with black points. Such a fencer, for we had him out, and Cis schooled him a bit. As he said, he's good enough to win the Regimental Cup."

" But if we bid for this paragon we shall be interfering with Captain Calvert, surely."

" No, no, father; you know I wouldn't do that. Cis liked the horse, and admired him immensely; but he said he couldn't afford him. He bought an old screw for a trifle, and said he must see as much of the fun as he could with that on the off days."

"It strikes me, Master Harry, I shall perhaps find the same objection to this grey that Captain Calvert did; the price is beyond me.   What is Mappin asking?"

"Two hundred," replied Harry, "but he is well worth it."

"It's a stiffish figure, but I'll ride out there to-morrow afternoon after I get away from the bank, and if I am as much impressed with the horse as you and Captain Calvert seem to have been, I'll see if Mappin and I can deal."

"Hurrah!" exclaimed Harry. "We'll have the Regimental Cup on the sideboard before Christmas," and it was in a very jubilant frame of mind that he wended his way back to barracks shortly afterwards.

"You have sent Harry to bed in the seventh heaven," said Miss Aysgarth, laughing, as she bade her father good night.

"I always meant to give the boy another horse, as I said before, but they're always a little difficult to pick up when you want them.   However, he seems to have found one for himself, so that problem's solved.   Good night, my dear."

The following afternoon saw Julian Harperley riding leisurely along the North road, on his way to Mr. Mappin's, the dealer. That gentleman received him cordially, for the banker was an old and valued customer. Few men are more keenly alive to the infinite superiority of a cheque at sight to a bill at three months than those connected with the horse trade. Mr. Harperley's draft was as good as bank-notes; no wonder that he stood high in Mr. Mappin's regard.

"Very glad, indeed, to see you, sir," said the dealer, as raising his hat he emerged from a small counting-house in the yard, and advanced to welcome his visitor.   "Here, Sam! take this gentleman's horse.   You'll come in and have a glass of sherry and a biscuit, Mr. Harperley, before having a look round. I don't suppose you want one, but you like to look at a good horse, I know.   I've one or two just now I'd like you to see."

Mr. Mappin inhabited a comfortable farm-house at Askham, about four miles from York—a low, one-storied dwelling, with thatched, sharp-pointed gables and latticed windows; roomy and commodious within, and boasting floors and staircase of blackest oak.   The parlour, too, was wainscoted with the same material,

polished till the panels reflected the gleam of fire or candle almost
like looking-glasses. Adjoining the house was a large yard, surrounded on three sides by stabling. On the fourth was a large
paddock, in the midst of which leaping bars and other artificial
fences had been set up, while around the margin of the field a
miniature steeple-chase course had been laid out.

Mr. Mappin was a well-known character for many miles round
York. A lithe, wiry man of medium height, always scrupulous-
ly neat and quiet in his attire and manner, you might never
have suspected him of being a horse-dealer; but you would have
felt intuitively that he was an enthusiastic lover of the horse,
and would have felt not a whit surprised at hearing there was
no neater seat nor lighter hand in the East or West Riding.
He had acquired a very high reputation in his vocation; those
who had dealings with him were wont to speak of him as one
does of the leading magnates of the wine trade, " You paid very
dear, but you could depend upon what you got." He bought of
course horses of all kinds, but his dealings were principally in
connection with high class animals, and if a man wanted to pick
up a good hunter in a hurry, and was good to write a stiffish
cheque for the same, the sporting community round the metropolis of the north would have said unanimously, " Go to
Mappin." Another thing, too, that tended much to the horse-
dealer's popularity was the pertinacity with which he adhered to
his favourite maxim—" Have the best of its kind, or don't have
it at all." His wines and cigars were thoroughly in accordance
with this axiom, and when he modestly asked a customer to
share " his bit of fish and mutton," the salmon was fresh from
the Ouse, and the mutton was four-year-old Scotch. Mr. Mappin
was catholic in his hospitality, but at the same time he had all
a Yorkshireman's keen eye for the main chance, and would
laughingly say if reference was made to his prodigality, " Pooh !
man, we never deal in the North without ' the luck-penny,' and
a dinner or two is no great discount. That the wine is the best
I can buy is matter of calculation; bad liquor breeds bitterness
and mistrust, and might cost me many a customer."

" Well, Mappin," said the banker, after he had deliberately
disposed of a glass of Amontillado, " I hear you have a nicish

hunter on hand—an iron-grey, with black points. I have heard so much of him that I thought I'd just ride round and take a look at him."

" Ah ! it'd be Mr. Harry told you about him. Yes, 'tis a nice horse, but I have one would suit him quite as well for less money. That grey, Mr. Harperley, can carry fourteen stone to hounds, and Mr. Harry don't as yet want one within twenty-eight pounds of that. Were you thinking of buying for him, sir ? "

" I am thinking no more at present," replied the banker laughing, " than that I should like to see this grey horse."

" Very good," replied Mr. Mappin. " Try one of these cigars. If you'll excuse me for one moment I'll just tell the lads to bring him and two others down to the paddock. See 'em on the grass, sir, and you see what they are, and what they can do. These are all clever, put 'em where you like."

A few minutes more, and Mr. Harperley and the dealer were leisurely strolling through the paddock.

" You can tell a horse very fairly here," observed Mr. Mappin ; " if there is nothing very big the jumps are of all sorts, and one that will school freely here in cold blood will cover anything his rider has nerve to put him at when hounds are running. If he don't, the odds are it's the man's fault ; but here come the nags."

Mr. Harperley was fain to admit that the three horses that walked slowly past them in Indian file were all of good class ; there was quality and breeding about every one of them, but there could be little doubt that

" The pick of the basket, the show of the shop,"

was that grand iron-grey with black points. Standing sixteen hands, with plenty of substance, he looked a weight-carrier all over. With those loins and quarters an extra stone or so should make little difference to him, and with thighs let down like that he was bound to gallop. Mr. Harperley fell almost as much in love with the horse as his son, and as he walked up to him and patted his neck, and looked at the small lean head and mild steady eye, he determined if the grey could only jump, and the price was not outrageous, that the graceless cornet should have the wish of his heart, and become the proud possessor of The Cid. But the banker had bought many a horse of Mr. Mappin, and was conversant with the wiles of that eminent dealer, and he noticed that the head lad of the establishment, the one usually employed to show off a horse, was riding not The Cid but a brown.

"I see you have got Sam up on the brown; the grey was the horse, remember, I particularly wished to see."

"Yes, sir, but The Cid don't want any showing off, and I wanted you to see that brown horse. He'd just suit Mr. Harry. Take him down over the hurdles, Sam, and bring him back over the water. Sweet, handy horse, Mr. Harperley, he'd carry a lady well."

In Sam's experienced hands the brown acquitted himself admirably, but the banker was totally unmoved by his performance.

"Let me see The Cid, I think you called him, Mappin. When a man gets a horse like that in his eye, it's useless to suppose he'll look at another."

"Excuse me, sir, but though he can jump like a bird, I don't like risking a valuable horse like that over bars, hurdles, or water. It isn't business."

"Not business!" rejoined the banker in astonishment. "Why, you don't suppose we buy horses without to some extent testing their capabilities. You never made such an objection before. However, we know each other. I will take your guarantee that he's a made hunter. Now, name his price."

"I'm very sorry, Mr. Harperley, more especially as you have taken such a fancy to the horse, but he's not for sale, sir. I parted with him this morning."

"The deuce you did! What, I'm too late, am I? I suppose Captain Calvert bought him?"

"No, he looked at him, but didn't take him. I sold him to Major Crymes."

CHAPTER II.

THERE was, perhaps, in the days of which I am writing, no
more prominent lady mixing in the society of York and its
vicinity than Mrs. Charrington. A slight mist hung over her
antecedents, but she was reputed to have been the daughter of
some Indian official; at all events, Charrington, a cadet, of a
well-known county family, who had been despatched by his
friends to shake the pagoda tree, while the golden pippins still
hung fairly thick upon its branches, had acquired both his
wife and his fortune in the East. He was reputed to have
had the ruling of a large tract of country, and to have squeezed
those committed to his charge in somewhat unorthodox fashion.
However, nobody could speak very clearly upon that point;
communication between our Eastern Empire and home at that
time was tedious and uncertain, and it was possible to deal out
a good deal of arbitrary legislation without anybody in England
being a bit the wiser. This, at all events, was certain, that ten
years ago Robert Charrington had come back to his native
country with a liberal pension, a very comfortable private
fortune, and a tall, good-looking wife, some score of years his
junior.

Mrs. Charrington had passed as a beauty in India, and it was
not likely that she would renounce such pretensions on making
her *début* in Yorkshire. Very much the reverse. If not quite
a beauty, she was at all events a fine woman, and still adhered
pertinaciously to the sceptre she had claimed on her first arrival
in the country. She was fairly popular. She had plenty of
energy and go, and though much addicted to flirtation, her
liaisons were all of the most innocent description, and if

sometimes evoking sarcastic remarks from her sisters, had never drawn forth the stern condemnation of the veteran brigade. Mrs. Charrington had, unfortunately, one weakness which had more than once brought her into hot water. That she did not speak the exact truth was nothing; very few of us do. It was not that she indulged in malicious representation; she never meant any harm, nor had she any design of making mischief, but she was naturally a talkative woman. She had picked up that habit of continually discussing her neighbours' affairs so easily acquired in an Indian cantonment or country town, and she had a natural talent for embroidering. Her too lively imagination impelled her always to embellish such little histories as she might have to recount, and such delicate enlargement of course at times puts a very different complexion on affairs, causing some perfectly innocent incident to assume sombre hues, and suggesting a very background of darkness.

Still, despite madam's treacherous tongue, and her husband's arbitrary manner, the Charringtons were fairly popular. They kept a good house about five miles from the city, entertained liberally, and, while Mr. Charrington, a noted pig-sticker and shikaree in his Indian days, could be relied on to promote all matters of sport in the neighbourhood, his wife was equally to be depended on as regarded balls, picnics, archery, &c. Mrs. Charrington had taken advantage of the fine autumn weather to issue invitations for a garden-party and dance. In these days lawn tennis would probably have taken the place of dancing, as in a previous generation the madness of croquet would have been the main object of such a gathering, but in fifty-two such things were not, and really an you disported not in valse, schottische, or polka there was nothing but bowls or sheer undisguised flirtation left with which to while away the time.

Mrs. Charrington's invitations had been numerous. It was currently reported that all the neighbourhood would be there, and, as we know, only let that rumour get about, and it fulfils its own prophecy just as a whisper of difficulty about obtaining cards or tickets for anything leads to every description of machination to procure them.

A showy, handsome woman looks Mrs. Charrington, as she receives her guests; though inclining to *embonpoint*, she still retains a good, if well-developed figure; the delicate bloom of her complexion may have vanished, and her face is, perhaps, somewhat florid; but the artifices of the toilet, and a profusion of fair hair, soften the slight encroachments of time, and she may still assert herself as a beauty, albeit a somewhat full-blown one. The neighbourhood has gathered in force; there are most of the dignitaries of the cathedral, besides a strong muster of the minor clerical lights of the city, the country people within a radius of some miles, to say nothing of that mysterious but inevitable cohort of strangers who are brought, as a rule, by those least entitled to claim the privilege. Byculla Grange had the reputation of being a pleasant house, and the hostess was famous, not only for knowing how such festivities should be conducted, but for possessing the subtle art of imparting go to anything of the kind she took in hand. At present she is radiant with smiles, for has she not been vouchsafed a glorious day for her party? and who that ever dabbled in out-of-door entertainment can fail to recall how animal spirits at such times are regulated by the barometer.

When Robert Charrington elected to settle in his native county he naturally cast about for a residence. To find such a home as met the requirements of himself and Mrs. Charrington, accustomed to the ample house room of India, proved difficult. He at last solved the question by the purchase of Topover Grange, a farm of some couple of hundred acres, and pulling down the old farm-house, proceeded to erect on his new acquisition a mansion in accordance with the somewhat Eastern tastes of himself and his wife. The new building might be somewhat irregular in elevation, as Mr. Charrington insisted on the designs being carried out more in accordance with his own views than those of his architect, but the interior was exceedingly comfortable, and it boasted what in those days was by no means common, a luxurious smoking room. Dr. Dasent in his *Annals of an Eventful Life* has drawn a very amusing comparison between the early Christians and the early smokers, recalling the times when the latter sacrificed to the shrine of their nicotian goddess in saddle-rooms, in out-houses, or it might be late at night in deserted kitchens, even as the early Christians had worshipped in caverns, ruins, &c.; and further carries on an analogy by pointing out what sumptuous temples are now dedicated to the followers of both the creed and the custom. But when Robert Charrington's new house was erected smoking was still pursued furtively, very few country houses boasted a smoking-room, and not even some London clubs. When the Charringtons inaugurated their new home by a series of dinners, offering beds as well to their more distant guests, Topover Grange was pronounced perfect, and an invitation thereto a thing by no means to be neglected. But there it was; that was the crinkle in the rose leaves, that was the spectre in the Elysian fields, the fatal flaw in the paradise. "Topover Grange!" as Mrs. Charrington said, "it made her feel like a farmer's wife. It was impossible," she declared, "to live in a place called Topover Grange." In vain did Robert Charrington curtly tell his better half not to make herself ridiculous, he might have known better than to provoke such a contest. If he had ruled several thousands of Hindoos in right royally despotic fashion, he might have remembered he had never been able to make the wife of his bosom obey. He might be arbitrary, but Mrs. Charrington was pertinacious. They did not often differ, but when they did it invariably ended in the lady obtaining her own way, and such was the case in this instance. Topover Grange, as a name, being doomed, it became necessary to rechristen it, and in memory of many pleasant days passed at the famous Bombay Club, Robert Charrington named his place Byculla Grange. I don't think to people generally the new nomenclature conveyed much meaning, nor did they as a rule deem it an improvement, but to Mrs. Charrington, with her Indian recollections, Byculla Grange conveyed the idea of much magnificence.

"I am delighted to see you, Annie," exclaimed Mrs. Charrington, as she shook hands with Miss Aysgarth. "I always pride myself upon collecting all the beauty of the country at my gatherings, you know, and in that simple muslin and straw hat you look as if you had stepped out of a Watteau picture. Yes, there's nothing like simplicity, my dear, as long as you can stand it; but alas! the time comes when we must dress," and the speaker glanced down at her own rich toilette with palpable satisfaction. "How do you do, Mr. Harperley, and where is Harry ?"

" Harry will be here very shortly. He is to come with some of his brother officers. You forget that he is a dragoon now."

" Ah, to be sure, it had slipped my memory. We must hardly expect him yet. The Lancers are always so shamefully late."

" Let me, in my character of the advanced guard, apologize for them," said a tall, dark, good-looking man, who smilingly advanced to do reverence to his hostess ; " there hasn't been witnessed, Mrs. Charrington, such hard riding since ' the good news was brought from Ghent ' long since—

> 'I sprang to the stirrup and Joris and he ;
> I galloped, Dirk galloped, we galloped all three.'

There's severe spurring to be seen between Byculla Grange and the barracks just now, believe me."

" Ever ready with an excuse, Major Crymes," retorted the lady, as she stretched forth her hand, "so ready, indeed, that had I dreamt you were within ear-shot I'd never have ventured the accusation."

" Hardly a fair charge that, Miss Aysgarth, is it ?" replied the dragoon. " I made no excuse. I simply grovelled on my knees and begged pardon."

" There's very little of that about you," rejoined Mrs. Charrington, drily ; " but now you are here you must do your duty. Take Miss Aysgarth, and get her some tea, please."

" With pleasure," replied Crymes. " One moment, Mrs. Charrington, first—" and he murmured something in such low tones that only the hostess could catch it.

" Yes," she replied, with a nod, delighted. " Only you must wait till I am ready. Come for me when you see me a little disengaged."

Major Crymes bowed, and offered his arm to Miss Aysgarth. There was no reason why he should drop his voice in speaking to Mrs. Charrington. He had only asked her to give him a dance, but this was a way Horace Crymes had, and more than one woman had found herself on confidential terms with the

Major without in the least intending it. He was one of those men to whom love-making seems a necessity, and he had left 'sair een' behind him upon more than one occasion, when too-credulous maidens had believed those low-toned whispers meant so much more than the actual words conveyed, and that the cool man of the world by their side was swayed by a genuine passion instead of merely seeking amusement.

"Are you fond of hunting, Miss Aysgarth?" asked the Major, having duly provided the young lady with some tea. "We shall be very soon beginning now in earnest."

"I am fond of it in my way, but I don't ride to hounds, if that is what you mean. I enjoy all the fun of a meet as much as any girl in the county, but I don't tax my male friends to either pilot or take care of me afterwards. I generally join what my brother irreverently calls 'the trotting brigade' for a while, and when the hounds go right away, come home."

"You have, perhaps, strong opinions on the subject, and don't think it right that ladies should ride."

"No, indeed, Major Crymes," laughed Miss Aysgarth merrily. "Fancy a Yorkshire girl seeing any harm in hunting! But though not surprised, I feel rather sorry just now that you are so devoted to it."

"I am very much flattered that you should take any interest in my pursuits," replied the dragoon; "but why, Miss Aysgarth, regret my weakness for fox-hunting?"

"Because it has led to your forestalling Harry, and buying a grey horse that he had set his heart upon."

"That, I am afraid, is more your brother's fault than mine. He saw it, as did Calvert and others, before myself; but I never heard any of them were in treaty for it. I possess one virtue, Miss Aysgarth, and it's not a very common one. I can make my mind up at once. It has long been a maxim of mine never to miss buying a good horse if I have the money, and half-an-hour after I first saw the grey I wrote a cheque for him. If I interfered with Harperley, I can only say I am sorry."

The Major spoke very prettily on the subject, but showed no signs of giving up his right to 'The Cid.' Indeed, it was hardly to be expected that he should, and yet Miss Aysgarth had mystily fancied that she might do her brother good service in this matter. She was a reasonable young woman in the main, but was accustomed to see men make such little sacrifices for her sake. She did not, moreover, quite see the thing in its true light. Had she wanted the horse for herself it was just possible the Major would have resigned in her favour, albeit, the yielding of anything he coveted to another was a weakness Horace Crymes was especially free from ; but the idea of yielding his new purchase to the last-joined cornet because his sister happened to be good-looking would have been simply derided had it ever crossed the Major's brain. He admired Miss Aysgarth, and wished to stand well with her, but nothing further as yet. He said no more than the truth when he boasted he could make up his mind quickly ; he could whenever the necessity arose, and, having done so, would carry his determination out with ruthless persistency.

"Have you settled yet when your regimental races are to be, Major Crymes ?" asked the young lady after a short pause. "It is whispered about that you intend to finish up with a ball at the barracks, and in that you know we are all much interested."

"The precise day is not fixed, but early in December, we think : we shall have fewer on leave before Christmas than after. May I have the pleasure of this dance ?"

"Our valse I think, Miss Aysgarth," interrupted a laughing voice. "I am desperately late I know, and don't deserve it, but I must throw myself on your infinite compassion, which, like the dew from heaven, &c. Please don't punish me."

The girl hesitated for a moment, then bowing to Crymes, she observed, "I am afraid I am engaged to Captain Calvert," and took the arm of the new-comer. An angry light gleamed momentarily in the Major's eyes, but was almost instantly succeeded by his habitual *insouciant* smile, as muttering something about being more fortunate on some future occasion, he turned away.

It is, I verily believe, in the trifles of life that we evoke the deadliest animosities. It is astonishing how some people will brood over an ill-timed jest at their expense, biding the time when they can retaliate for such pleasantry with all the patient vindictiveness of an Indian. We forgive veritable injuries, but we cannot get over the culprit not having answered our letter of upbraiding. He neglected to pen that soft word which, lie though we should have known it to be, would have turned away our wrath. Unanswered letters, perhaps, plunge us into as much hot water as anything, and yet, when the lengthy report of a 'breach of promise' case meets our eyes, we become aware that there is evil in too much letter-writing. Similarly, in the ball-room, it is quite possible to lay the foundation of a very healthy hatred—hatred which in the duelling days was promptly eased by a little blood, or it may be life, letting. In these more polished times we cherish it, and give more or less vent to it, according to the strength and malignancy of our natures.

Major Crymes up to this time had no feeling for Calvert either one way or the other, but this little episode converted indifference into active dislike. He was much too practised a man of the world not to see that Calvert had taken the advantage of being *au mieux* with Miss Aysgarth to improvise an engagement, and she had consented to his ruse. The Major had so far merely regarded the young lady as a pretty girl, and with no particular attention ; in fact, he was at present carrying on a pretty vigorous flirtation with Mrs. Charrington, and but for being thus piqued might never have troubled his head about Miss Aysgarth. Horace Crymes was a man whom difficulties always stimulated—a man for whom grapes out of reach, or forbidden fruit, had special attractions, and the quiet way in which, to use his own phrase, ' he had been jockeyed out of that dance ' put two ideas into his head, to wit, a determination to be quits with Cis Calvert in some fashion, and that it was possible, perhaps, to accomplish that through the medium of Miss Aysgarth.

" I hope you will pardon my impertinence," said Cis Calvert to his companion as they took their place amongst the valsers, " but I wanted to talk to you so much, that I risked being properly snubbed sooner than forego the chance."

" And found me," interposed the girl laughing, " so utterly taken aback by your audacity or mendacity—which ought I to call it?—that I had not the presence of mind to rebuke it as it deserved."

"It was very good of you," replied Cis, "and your conscience may rest quite easy. I don't think Crymes had any idea that I was not really engaged to you. Let's have another turn."

"There you mistake," rejoined Miss Aysgarth, as she yielded to his encircling arm. "I don't fancy Major Crymes was in the least blinded by your bold assertion, and shall expect to find myself in his bad books for the future."

"A matter which will not concern you much," said Calvert.

"Who knows?" replied his partner, smiling. "He might get me struck off Mrs. Charrington's visiting-list. His influence here is supposed to be paramount, you know. Stop, there is Harry, and I want to speak to him for a moment."

"What? to comfort him for his loss?" rejoined Calvert, smiling. "It is rather rough on the boy, but to hear him make moan over it is too absurd. If he had bought the horse and found it dead in the stable next morning, he couldn't be sorrier for himself."

"But, Captain Calvert, that is just what it represents to Harry. Papa would have bought the grey for him, and but for the unlucky intervention of Major Crymes the horse would have been now in Harry's stables."

"And it is a nag to sorrow after, Miss Aysgarth. I could have shed tears myself when I saw it, and found I couldn't pay for it; then," continued Cis, with mock solemnity, "I reflected in my wisdom what a mildewed existence mine would become if I cried because I couldn't pay people, and what a vale of tears the British cavalry generally would be involved in; but, come, let us go and comfort the bereaved one."

"How dare you laugh at me?" cried the young lady, smiling; "but take me across to Harry."

"Surely, Mrs. Charrington, you must have at last finished playing hostess," murmured the Major into that buxom lady's ear, "and have leisure to grant the dance you promised me?"

"Willingly. I am quite tired of making pretty speeches. I hunger to speak ill of my neighbours. Let us bury ourselves in the crowd, where I may give free vent to malice and bitterness.

Ah! yes, I will valse, and you shall tell me all the gossip of the country."

" Ah, story, like the knife-grinder, I have none to tell; but that does not hinder our dancing—indeed, when one's tongue fails it is good policy to fall back on one's legs on these occasions. You paired me off unluckily, to start with."

" Unluckily!   Why I sent you off with the banker's daughter, one of the best-looking girls in our parts, and this is your gratitude.   I am a good-natured woman, Major Crymes, and, like certain royal ladies one has read of, always endeavour to provide for my admirers.   If ever I did my duty for an adorer it was to you on this occasion.   I paired you off with Julian Harperley's heiress, what more could you ask?   It was a piece of self-sacrifice that should have ever remained embalmed in your memory, if a man ever does recognize self-sacrifice on the part of a woman."

" You are making too much of it.   I only said ' unluckily,' because the young lady and myself were not exactly in accord; besides, I don't appreciate being provided for.   I prefer serving on your staff as yet.   The royal ladies you quote so glibly, remember, only provided for an admirer when they had satisfactorily replaced him."

" True," responded Mrs. Charrington, with a coquettish glance, " and that is very far from my meaning, but you soldiers come and go, and it would be better to settle you amongst us than lose you altogether."

There was no great danger to the pair in this sort of flirtation. Mrs. Charrington had been engaged in these airy love triflings since her school-girl days, and, despite proverbs anent playing with fire and pitchers going too often to the well, had not scorched her wings as yet; love triflings that consisted of

" A little glow, a little shiver."

Horace Crymes on his side had passed a life of intrigue and flirtation.   No woman's smile had quickened his pulse for many a day, but he still, from sheer habit, let him be where he would, was invariably engaged in a love-affair of some kind.   There are men to whom such philandering seems a necessity, as

essential to their comfort as tobacco, and having a similar soothing influence on their feelings.

"It is very good of you, but I had no idea Miss Aysgarth
was looked upon as an heiress."

"Of course she is. She inherits all her mother's property, to
say nothing of what Julian Harperley may choose to leave her.
He is a wealthy man, and has only the two of them to take care
of. Annie Aysgarth will come to her husband with her hands
full."

This was a fair specimen of Mrs. Charrington's embroidery.
Julian Harperley's brief married life had been long a thing of
the past when she made her appearance in Yorkshire. She
knew nothing of the late Mrs. Aysgarth's affairs, but chose to
assume she had brought her second husband a fortune. Mrs.
Charrington, as a rule, invented biography for her acquaintances
sooner than confess ignorance of their antecedents, which, as may
be supposed, led at times to some asperity and confusion ; but a
taste for gossip or the *cacoethes scribendi* are no more to be
grappled with than a passion for alcoholic drinks.

CHAPTER III.

SMOKE WREATHS.

HORACE CRYMES could hardly be pronounced a popular man in his regiment, and yet beyond a cynicism, by no means offensively obtrusive, there was nothing to be alleged against him. He was known to be devoted to the Turf, and believed by his brother officers to be a heavy speculator, but there was not a man in the corps who talked so little about racing as the Major. While beardless cornets discussed the respective chances of the Derby cracks, pronouncing judgment thereon with a confidence proportionate to their ignorance, Horace Crymes usually sat silent, as if the subject had no interest for him. The most direct appeal had never extorted more from him than he had been told such a horse would run well, and on the rare occasions he had so far abandoned his habitual reticence there had been found good reason for what he had said. He was, as Harry Harperley told his sister, one of those men who are ' good all round,' and it was whispered played very high when in London, but he never showed the slightest indication of a taste for gambling amongst his comrades. He seldom touched a card, and when to make up a rubber he sat down to whist, seemed perfectly contented with the usual regimental points. It was known, too, that he had three or four horses in training, but with these he pursued the same policy, never entering them in any races got up by the corps, or even by the garrison in which he might be quartered, but leaving them to pursue their chequered career on country race-courses, where in Tally-Ho stakes and Goneaway Plates they were all more or less known. The Major had, however, one peculiarity quite sufficient to account for his not being exactly popular with his brother officers—he lived his own life. He would contribute handsomely to anything they might wish to get up, such

as balls or other festivals; he was courteous and on good terms
with them all, but he was intimate with none. He went his
own way, and was rarely seen either walking or riding with his
comrades. He was a man, moreover, about whom little was
known; no one in the regiment could tell anything about his
friends, nor even about his means, further than that he seemed
to spend a good bit of money. In short, what little they did
know about him had come principally from the outside world,
for Horace Crymes was singularly free from that every-day weakness—the narration of his own doings. It was not that he
affected any secrecy, but he was habitually reserved and silent
with men. With women it was different; beneath their influence the frost-bound springs of his conversation seemed to
thaw, and those of them who had known him well were wont to
observe that he was not only well read, but could be excessively
entertaining. It seemed as if he did not consider it worth while
to exert himself to titillate masculine understanding.

And yet people who thus judged Horace Crymes made a great
mistake. There were few moves in his game of life that were
not the result of cool calculation, and at times men had found him
equally as fascinating as their wives or daughters, but such
occasions were rare. He liked society. Society he held to be
ruled by the women, if you wish to get on in it pay your court
to them, and don't trouble your head about the men. They have
little to give except shooting, and your fair friends will usually
see you get a sufficiency of that.

It is the evening of Mrs. Charrington's garden-party, and the
Major is sitting over the fire in his own quarters lost in thought.
He has dined at mess, and it is needless to say has made no
allusion to Calvert's rather impertinent ruse, not that he has at
all forgotten it; there never was a man less likely to forget anything of the kind, but the Major holds that such social amenities
should be reciprocated in similar fashion, and even amongst ladies
Horace Crymes is considered a dangerous man to play tricks with,
he having more than once displayed a most unforgiving memory
for former slights when his opportunity came. But at present
he is turning over a much more elaborate scheme in his mind,
wherein vengeance on the two culprits is a very minor detail.

"Yes," he muttered, pulling rather hard at his cigar, as men are wont when solving some of those abstruse problems anent 'ways and means,' which are the lot of most of us, "I suppose it must come to that pretty speedily—a little sooner or later won't make much difference. I've one pull, thanks to having learnt to hold my tongue early in life; nobody has an idea of what difficulties I am in. It's bad enough to be hard up, but only let *your* world know it too, and you're dead broke before you can turn round. It's a pity these fellows (he meant his brother officers) know anything about my connection with the Turf. When you contemplate matrimony it goes against you; fathers-in-law never appreciate that connection. I kept it as dark as I could, too, but it's a babbling world we live in, and men don't wait for their death-beds 'to babble of green fields' that grow white rails and a winning-post.

"Hum! now to reckon things up; first, is Mrs. Charrington right about that Aysgarth girl? Is she a prize worth laying siege to? secondly, how far would she herself really help me? A woman's co-operation is valuable if you can trust her; the danger in my case is when it comes to the point Mrs. Charrington may regard me as somewhat too much her own property to resign, and if she takes that view, well," and here he emitted a cloud of smoke from under his moustache, "it will be deuced awkward. She's safe to know more about me than I think, and will invent it if she doesn't. A woman always does under such circumstances. Lastly, I wonder how far Miss Aysgarth is interested in that fellow Calvert; that there is some sort of understanding between them that dance business this afternoon showed; however, that don't go for much. It only means he has got the best of the start."

A knock at the door interrupted his reverie, and in obedience to his sharp "Come in," a wiry, hard-featured little man entered the room, closed the door behind him, and made a respectful bow.

"Well, Tom, what is it?" inquired the Major. "I suppose you have fetched the grey horse home. How do you like him?"

"He's a good-looking nag enough," replied the new-comer. "We've had better, although I'll not deny we've had worse. I thought, sir, you'd like to know he'd arrived all right, and I wanted to see you about what sort of work I'm to give him."

Mr. Thomas Blundell conceived it his duty to disparage any horse, with the buying of which he had not been in some way concerned. Crymes had picked him up in a racing stable, from which he was on the verge of being discharged, on account of some suspicion as to his honesty, and appointed him his stud groom. A dangerous experiment that would probably have resulted in failure with most men, but in the Major's hands had turned out well so far. In the first place, there was no such temptation to turn rogue as there had been in his former situation, and in the second, Mr. Blundell had a wholesome appreciation of his new master's astuteness, and a strong conviction that he was dangerous to play tricks with.

"We may have had better, no doubt," returned the Major, "because at present I can't say I know much about The Cid, but I rather fancy we shall find him a pretty good horse. Put him in training at once. I mean to run him in the Regimental Cup just to see what he's like. I shall be disappointed if he's not good enough for the Grand Military in the spring."

"We can very soon see what chance this Cid has for the Regimental Cup, sir. Old Cockatoo can tell us all about that. He won it two years ago, and there's not likely, as I've heard of, to be anything much better in the field than what he beat then. None of the gentlemen have been buying anything of much account. That second charger of Mr. Harperley's is smart, but they've had him fiddling about so long in the school, he's most likely forgot how to gallop."

"You're right, Tom, the school may make 'em handy, but it don't make them quick. He'll not be dangerous this year."

Although Mr. Blundell at present had simply the care of his master's chargers and hunters, he still hankered after his old vocation. As Chrysippus considered the cause of cocks was cock-fighting, so Mr. Blundell apprehended the cause of horses was horse-racing. To get a horse into condition, and then not at least match him against something or other, was, in his eyes, a lamentable waste of oats, time, and talent. Hunting was all very well, but only as a means to an end; useful for schooling, and also for obtaining the necessary qualifications to run in stakes fictitiously supposed to be designed for horses habitually ridden to hounds; but the real salt of existence, the acme of human felicity, was in Mr. Blundell's eyes a big match, with about 10lb. the best of your opponent. His being allowed to train Cockatoo, a *bonâ fide* hunter, was the one white stone in his career since he had entered the Major's service, some five years back, so that the prospect of once more preparing two or three horses for a race of any sort was excessively exhilarating to Mr. Blundell.

"And you'll put them together—I mean old Cockatoo and this Cid—before the race, I suppose, sir? As likely as not the old horse will prove the best of the two," added Tom, in tones of disparagement.

"Certainly! I shall enter the pair, try them, and may be run both."

"Run both, sir?"

"I shall, perhaps, do so; and now, Tom, you've got your orders, and know as much as I mean to tell you at present."

Mr. Blundell took the hint, and with a respectful "Good night, sir," made his exit. "The Major's clever," he muttered, as he descended the stairs; "but he's hard, ay, hard as Brazilian nuts. He'll give me my orders, but never show me a bit of his hand. What does he want to run two for? What's his little game in that? Means to gammon them, I suppose, as to which is the genuine pea. It will go hard if I don't know before the day, and if I don't, why, I'll perhaps choose it for him. It's to be hoped our interests may be identical," and Mr. Blundell, as he emerged into the barrack square, winked confidentially at the gas-lamp, in due recognition of the comicality of his idea.

The Major took two or three rapid turns up and down the room as his servitor left him. "What has put it into my head to win this steeple-chase?" he exclaimed; "pique! by heavens, nothing else. I won it two years ago just to show that I could win it—that's all very well for once, but I don't habitually play for the gallery—there is no money to talk of to be made over it. Besides, to clean out one's own regiment don't sound well. It would be buying money too dear. No, it is pique, nothing else, that has determined me to take the Cup this year. Culvert shan't have it if I can prevent it. A few hours ago, and he was welcome to it as far as I was concerned. Now I have determined to cut his comb, and, if he is in earnest about Miss Aysgarth, so am I, and he need never count he has done with Horace Crymes till he has placed the ring on her finger. I'll not stand being thrown over by a country chit like that, more especially when she embodies money, which at this present moment it is my special vocation to wed. No, I am sorry to interfere with Pyramus and Thisbe; but, as I want Thisbe myself, I am afraid Pyramus must become the victim of circumstances."

*   *   *   *   *   *

Curiously enough, in another barrack room, not very far off, a somewhat similar scene was being enacted. Cis Calvert had, after the manner of his rival, left mess early, and strolled back to his quarters to indulge in day-dreams, visions of brighter hue than those which had mingled with the smoke wreaths around the Major's head. Never had Miss Aysgarth been so gracious to him as this day, and Cis was conscious that he had no whit neglected the occasion. He had danced a good deal with her, he had sat out with her more than once, and had assumed an air of proprietorship that had been prettily submitted to on her part. He had cloaked her and put her into the carriage, and fancied when he pressed her hand warmly at saying adieu that it was faintly returned. He was quite aware that he had been making as fierce love to the girl all the afternoon as the opportunity admitted, and his heart swelled with triumph at the idea that his attentions had been in no wise rebuffed. Cis was very earnest in his wooing, and was now counting up the probabilities of his success. He had never been told that Miss Aysgarth was an heiress. He had not the advantage of Mrs. Charrington for a friend, and so was happily ignorant of what would have seemed to him only an extra obstacle to the fulfilment of his desires. Still he did know that the girl was the only daughter of a man reputed wealthy, and that it was quite likely he might regard a captain of dragoons, with only five hundred a-year besides his pay, as no fitting match for his daughter, and yet he felt no disposition to undervalue himself. Let him only win Annie Aysgarth herself, and he thought he would speedily succeed in wringing her father's consent.   Do not think that there was any tinge of conceit about Cis Calvert, though he had some of the swagger essential to the class he belonged to.   You cannot incite men to wear caps on one side and wax their moustaches without putting a certain amount of that into them, but Cis was by no means unduly confident about his present love-chase ; indeed, until to-day he had experienced dire misgivings as to what advance he had made in the lady's good graces.   In short, it was only the fortunate result of his first audacity that afternoon that had emboldened him to make such severe running as he had done.   But the thread of his meditations is cut short by a sharp tap at the door, and hardly waiting for his response, Harry Harperley enters.

For a minute or two Cis regrets bitterly he has neglected to slip down the latch, but to the brother of the object of our devotion much toleration is existent ; and then again, albeit he had not desired that his day-dreams should be broke in upon, Cis really likes the boy for his own sake.   Still, wrapped in his own ecstatic vision, he feels that he cannot quite sympathize with Harry's perpetual lament over *his* lost love, and he knows that the Cornet is about to indulge in jeremiads over the bad luck which has prevented his becoming the proprietor of The Cid. He noticed that night at dinner the boy's wine did him no good, his grievance was rankling in his breast, and he gulped down his liquor in saturnine fashion, and refused to be comforted, as men do under serious affliction, such as finding the bride they hope to win is engaged to somebody else, or that the bookmaker whom for once they have landed for ' a thousand to thirty ' is hopelessly insolvent.

" Sit down, young-un," exclaimed Cis ; " put one of those big cigars *in* your mouth, and for heaven's sake don't let anything concerning that grey horse *out* of it.   It's rough, I admit, and I heartily wish the governor had got there before Crymes, but he didn't.   So there's no more to be said about it."

" Ah, well ! you do admit it is an awful sell," exclaimed Harry. " I know that horse is safe to win the Regimental Cup.   He's about as handsome as any I ever saw, and Mappin declares that, to the best of his belief, he's as good as he looks."

"I don't say he won't, but remember, all racing is a game of great uncertainty, more especially steeple-chasing. I don't myself think if he finds him very good that Crymes will run him. We know he has horses with which he could probably beat anything the rest of us have, and he never spoils sport by running them. Last year, though of course he subscribed, he didn't even start one, and during the four that he has been in the regiment he has never won it but once, and then with a most legitimate hunter. His old white horse, Cockatoo, remember, cannot be counted more, though no doubt very good of his class. I am not quite convinced, indeed, that he can beat Red Lancer. I only bought him just before that race, and he was so utterly out of condition that it would have been absurd to start him. He'll go this year though, and settle that question."

"What do you think of that brown horse Mappin has?" added young Harperley, wriggling restlessly in his chair. "The governor says I may have him if I like, and recommends me to take him, as I can't have the grey."

"I agree with your father, and think you can't do better. Now, for heaven's sake, let us talk no more horse, I'm sick of it for the present."

Harry opened his eyes in wide amazement. The Regimental Cup was to him at present what the Derby was to the London world the week before Epsom in those days, an all-absorbing event, before which the upsetting of thrones on the Continent faded into utter insignificance. He could, as a schoolboy, recollect Surplice breaking the magic spell at Doncaster in '48 by winning the double event, and the enthusiasm it occasioned ; but I am afraid, like many of riper years, was hardly cognisant of Louis Philippe's precipitate arrival on our shores. What could Cis want to talk about ? Was there a nobler subject of conversation than the horse ? He had never read Pope, or he would have greatly derided the famous line, "The proper study for mankind is man," and pronounced authoritatively that the poet had never been in Yorkshire.

Still, whatever might be the subject his host wished to introduce, he certainly was in no hurry to begin, as can be well understood, for, in reality, he merely wished to continue the

love-musings which his self-invited guest had so rudely interrupted.

The Cornet, damped by Calvert's taciturnity and the embargo
on a monody, regarding the loss of 'The Cid,' was about to
exchange the dulness of his present situation for 'pastures new,'
when a tap at the door arrested his attention, and he sank back
in the chair from which he had half risen. The new-comer was
Trooper Timothy Murphy, bâtman and master of the horse to
Captain Cecil Calvert of her Majesty's —-th Lancers.

Tim, as he was familiarly called, was a thorough good specimen
of the Irish soldier. A spare, muscular man, standing somewhat
over 5ft. 9in. in his boots, with red hair, light grey eyes, upturned
nose, and somewhat large mouth ; he looked the very incarnation
of fun and good-humour, but there was a glint in the eye and a
twitch about the corners of the mouth at times that would have
told a physiognomist that Tim Murphy was no fool.

He had been Calvert's henchman now for some years, and his
faith in 'the masther' was as unbounded as his attachment to
him.

"Halloa, Murphy !" exclaimed young Harperley, welcoming
any relief to the oppressive silence into which they had subsided,
"what's the row ?"

"'Deed, there's nothing the matter, Misther Harperley. I just
looked in on the Masther for a moment, but, as I see yer honour's
engaged, I'll just come again in the morning."

"What is it ?" inquired Calvert, shortly. "You've been on
pass, of course, I know, but it is pretty well time you were over
at your barrack-room."

"I was going there straight, but I saw a light in your honour's
rooms, so I made bould to come up. It's about that black 'atomy
ye bought a fortnight ago, sir. There's been a fellow questioning
me about him in York to-day, and sorra a bit I can understand
his maning."

"What did he say ?" inquired Cis.

" 'Your name's Tim Murphy,' says he.

" 'They call me that mostly,' says I.

" 'Captain Calvert's groom,' says he.

" 'You're a divil at guessing,' says I.

"'Ah, 'twas your master, then, bought that half-ton of bones done up in horse-hair, old Mappin called a hunter.'

"'And why not?' says I, 'shure he's going into high farming, and it's bones they swear by just now.'

"'Bones are on the rise,' says he, grinning, 'may be he'd like to turn a five pound note on his bargain.'

"'Och, niver a one of me knows,' says I; 'but an' he wor wise he'd give you that just to take him off the premises.'

"'Well,' he says softly, 'you see he was sold out of a family in which he was a great favourite, under peculiar circumstances; they're a bit sore at his loss, and would give a thrifle to get him back.'

"'Just so; their grandmother's favourite hack, I understand. Troth I riverence the feeling; they don't like heirlooms like that going out of the family.'

"'That's it,' he said. 'Captain Calvert's a good man, no doubt; but the poor crather's too ould for hunting, and so is no use to him. It'd be murther to attempt it.'

"'An' it's turning the poor baste out to end his days in pace, you'd be doing with him?' I asked.

"'My excellent friend, you've just hit it.' Those were his very words, your honour. 'He's past work, and we can't bear the idea of his being called on to do it.'

"'Ah! well. If the masther's willing to part with him, it'll be a proud day when I bring him back to ye. Where will I be inquiring after you?'

"'When your masther's tired of his bargain,' says he, 'you can just ask for Isham Boggs at the Punchbowl Tavern in Stonegate. They know me there, good day.' And off he walked with never another word."

"What sort of looking man was he?" inquired Calvert at the end of this history.

"'Deed he looked more like a Methody parson down on his luck than anything else. Most of the colour of his face had settled in his nose, and he'd a fair case for an action against his laundress av his linen went to the wash reg'lar."

"And what about the horse, Murphy?" inquired Harry

Harperley, who had listened to this conversation with the greatest interest.

"Well, sir, he's a good doer, but his oats seem to do him no good. I can't get him to carry any flesh. The boys down at Mappin's tould me he was a grate lepper, but I've never tried him meeself."

"All right, that'll do," said Calvert sharply, "good night." And in obedience to the mandate Mr. Murphy took his departure.

"What do you think of this?" inquired the Cornet eagerly as the door closed.

"Think, my dear Harry, that I have got an old horse worth rather more than I thought he was; that's all at present, but I think further that I am very tired, and it is high time to go to bed. So I exhort you to follow Tim's example and take your departure."

A request with which the Cornet immediately complied, walking back to his quarters much exercised in his understanding.

CHAPTER IV.

A DINNER AT THE FIRS.

MISS AYSGARTH was under no delusion as to what had taken place between herself and Cis Calvert at the garden-party. She was a young woman, remember, and not a girl; the distinction is really very great, although the terms are constantly looked upon as synonymous. At eighteen a girl *fancies* herself in love more often than not, but at twenty-four she should make no mistake on the subject. She knows thoroughly then, if she has any common sense in her, what she takes a man for—whether it is for position, a comfortable home, or from pure simple love of him. Annie Aysgarth was quite aware that Cis had shown her very marked attention, she was equally aware that she had deliberately encouraged him, and that the world generally were also cognisant of the fact. She was, as before said, a clear-headed young lady, whom flattery had never imposed upon; singularly free from coquetry, a weapon of her sex for which she had a supreme disdain, and, moreover, perfectly heart-free up to these last few days. Annie Aysgarth felt that it behoved her to think in sober earnest now whether she cared enough for this man to marry him. She never doubted but that he would ask her. Too proud to condescend to the game of flirtation herself, it never occurred to her that any man would dare play that with her, and in Cis Calvert's case, as we know, she was perfectly justified in this assumption.

It was the more imperative, she considered, because on the Friday, and it was now Wednesday, her father had a large dinner-party, intended to resolve itself into a small dance later on. Captain Calvert was amongst those invited, and Annie felt that she must be prepared to answer this question definitely at any moment. She had no idea of keeping any lover of hers shilly-shallying. She would place her hand in his, and own she loved him with all her heart, or gently tell him he was scarce justified in mistaking her kindly feeling towards him for more than friendliness. She knew she could not honestly say the latter now to Cis Calvert, but it was still possible to say him nay. She had after all seen but little of him when she came to think of it. He was not the ideal she had pictured to herself; no, Major Crymes, she was bound to confess, more represented that; but still, the fact remained—she rather disliked the Major, and had more than a suspicion that she cared for gay, light-hearted, *insouciant* Cis a great deal more than she ought. Miss Aysgarth had indulged in visions of a hero of god-like intellect and Apollo-like physique, such as is seldom to be met with in this work-a-day world, as the man she would bow down to and worship. Being in the main a sensible young woman, she never expected to meet him exactly, but she deemed that the man she married should be at all events a faint copy of that ideal. She could not delude herself into the idea that Cis Calvert represented him in any shape; he was only of medium height, instead of the six feet she had fixed upon as imperative. He was light in complexion, when he should have been dark; tolerably good-looking, but not at all suggestive of Apollo; a practical, sensible man, but showing no sign of high intellectual power, and yet she felt she loved him. Why? Ah, that will be a difficult question for woman, ay, or man too, for the matter of that, to answer till the hour-glass of this world is turned for the last time.

But did she love Cis well enough to leave her father for him? —that was now the great question in her mind. Very, very passionate was the love Annie bore her step-father, and none knew better than she what a terrible gap it would make in his life. Convinced that it was for her happiness that the man of her choice was an honourable, upright gentleman, and she knew that her father would smother his own feelings, nor permit her to feel by sign or word the wrench it was for him. She had done her duty by him, as he by her; she was loth to leave him, but Julian Harperley was, she felt, the last man to exact the sacrifice of her whole life to his comfort; she knew her step-father better than that. Did she love Cis Calvert well enough for this—to

to leave her own people for his sake?—and Annie felt that was
a question not to be determined lightly.   She knew that she
loved him, she thought that he loved her, but then did he?
Glance and gesture had told her so, but the avowal of his love was
as yet unspoken, and so, spite of her shrewd, clear understanding,
the girl was tossed here and there in her imaginings, like the
veriest love-lorn maiden of sweet seventeen.   In love-making, as
in racing, the fierce exultation of winning is as nothing to the
fervid excitement of the yet undecided contest.

Coming in from a ride with her father on the Thursday she
found Captain Calvert's card upon the table.   A slight tremour
ran through her frame at sight of it.   Men do not usually call at
a house the day before they are engaged to dine there, and she
thought had she been at home she might have been asked that
very question about which her mind was as yet undetermined.
More made up, perhaps, than she was aware of, as is the case with
most of us in our moments of indecision, demonstrated by our
weakness for begging that advice from our friends which we so
rarely follow.

In these more enlightened days, when people are told off to
their respective chairs, the hostess has a chance of mixing the
social salad to the best of her ability, which the old scramble for
seats utterly forbade.   Then various readjustment was often necessary to prevent all the vinegar collecting in one place, or in other
words, the more discordant elements finding themselves in closest
proximity.   But it also had this advantage—it offered great
opportunities to the audacious, who often succeeded in obtaining
the coveted position by a little readiness and *sang froid*.   Calvert,
on the eventful Friday, knew that he could not hope to take in
the lady of the house; there was sure to be some dignitary to
claim that privilege, but he was determined to be as close to her
as possible.   No sooner, then, was dinner announced than he
tucked the young lady committed to his charge under his arm,
silenced some faint remonstrances she made on the question of
precedence with the suave remark that he ' always went in with
the Dukes,' and promptly followed Julian Harperley's footsteps.
He was successful in his design, and found himself next Miss
Aysgarth when the party had finally settled down in their places.

He had no reason to complain of the manner in which that young lady received this arrangement; on the contrary, she smiled her approval of it; but the achievement of a *tête-à-tête* at a dinner-party must be always due to fortunate circumstances. The flaxen-haired young lady who was Calvert's temporary partner had a leaning for soldiers, and was not at all disposed to allow the light dragoon fate had consigned her to neglect his duty. Mr. Charrington, on the other hand, conceived it his duty to entertain Miss Aysgarth, so that Cis had little chance of pleading his cause.

It was a largish dinner-party, and casting his eye down the table, somewhat to his astonishment, Calvert saw that Major Crymes was seated next Mrs. Charrington. There was nothing really odd in his being there; if not intimate he had certainly dined at 'The Firs' before; the only thing singular about it was that he had never mentioned he was invited when Cis had alluded to the party the night before at mess. Still, the Major was not given to publish his movements to the world he lived in, so there was not much in that, and yet Cis Calvert kept on wondering what the deuce Crymes was doing there. Once he saw Mrs. Charrington glance his way, and then turn and address some observation to her neighbour, to which the Major returned a negative shake of the head. What could Mrs. Charrington have to say about him, thought Cis, and his reply to an observation of his fair companion was so palpably at random, that the nymph of the flaxen locks momentarily doubted whether the champagne had not been too liberally handed about. Cis indeed was in a state of nervous excitability. His was one of those peculiarly high-strung temperaments to whom suspense is of all the most intolerable. These are the men who before the fight you foretell will utterly lose their heads, and who, the fray once commenced, display a coolness and presence of mind perfectly marvellous. Cis had made up his mind to put his fate to the test this night, and chafed at everything that delayed the desired explanation. This reckless dragoon deemed apparently that love speeches with the soup, a proposal with the *entrées*, bless you my children with the cheese, and the health of the bride and bridegroom as the decanters made their first circuit, was the way the giving in marriage was ordinarily conducted in this country.   No man ever was more destined to be corrected on this point, or have the story of Jacob's servitude more pointedly recalled to his memory.

Miss Aysgarth bends her head, the ladies rise, and as he holds the door open Cis reflects ruefully that he has exchanged barely a dozen sentences with the enchantress, despite the audacious *coup de main* that had placed him near her. He turns him again moodily to the table, and becomes speedily involved in that all-absorbing topic to a Yorkshireman in September, 't Leger. The first half of the month they discuss fiercely what is to win it, during the second they are wont to argue with no little asperity as to what ought to have won it.   Nearly every man at the table had seen it run, and had had his bet upon the race, and there were those who still clung to the belief that the Whitewall horse was out of trim, refusing to recognize that his Epsom success was due to Frank Butler, the state of the ground, and luck, and that the king of the year was Lord Exeter's mighty chestnut, who, albeit ridden by ' the post-boy,' fairly smothered ' Daniel,' in spite of the assistance of the crack jockey of the day.   Others there were who shook their heads over Songstress, and muttered grimly she would run a very different mare when wanted, so that there was much Turf argument going on round the banker's table. Crymes sat, as was his custom, taciturn in the midst of all this racing talk, into which Cis Calvert had plunged wildly. A looker-on would have pronounced the one man devoted to the Turf, while he would have deemed the other a somewhat bored listener to a discussion which in no wise interested him, and this was precisely the conclusion Julian Harperley came to as he sat watching his guests in indolent fashion. No more erroneous deduction was of course ever drawn, as the two men's betting volumes would have shown, could the banker but have seen them. They had both lost their money ; but, whereas Calvert's cheque for a hundred would more than have covered his liabilities, the Major's were of a kind likely to necessitate intimate relations with the tribes, and heartfelt thanksgiving that they were not all lost.

' Still waters run deep,' is one of the aphorisms I believe in.

Your garrulous Don Juan has, usually, scarce courage to kiss his cousin under the mistletoe, and the way a man who has lost five pounds over an Ascot Meeting will fill the walls of his club with querulous and ear-piercing lamentation over his awful luck is a common, though sorry, sight to witness. Now those who are 'plungers,' either in love or racing are usually first heard of in the journals, and much to the surprise of their friends.

"You must excuse us, Major Crymes," remarked the banker at last, "but you know to us Yorkshiremen Doncaster races are a solemn festival, and to guard the Leger from the Southron the first duty of the many-acred county. This year we have been beaten on our own dunghill, we are all a little sore in consequence, and would fain explain away our defeat."

"Ah! I fancy the best horse won, though, from what I saw," replied Crymes, rousing himself from a reverie into which he had fallen. He had never taken very much notice of Miss Aysgarth before, but he had watched her pretty closely at dinner, and he was rather astonished to think so handsome a girl had not attracted his attention sooner. He was more determined than ever to win her for his wife if he could. He was *bonâ fide* struck with the girl. He wanted money; it was getting time to settle down and have done with soldiering, and then there was private pique. He detested Calvert—he could hardly have said why—still he did. Few of us can account for these instinctive dislikes. Then he could not forget the way Miss Aysgarth had thrown him over at the garden party. Absurd to think a girl's caprice could have such an effect on a man not even in love with her, but so it was. To paraphrase the words of the preacher, 'all is vanity;' 'master passion of mankind,' as Sheridan pronounced it.

"We are all looking forward with interest to your steeple-chases. My boy especially is enthusiastic about that grey you bought of Mappin, and declares the Regimental Cup is at your mercy. I presume you will run him?"

"Yes, I think so, Mr. Harperley. I don't know much about the horse as yet, and it will be an excellent opportunity to try him. By the way, next Wednesday is our nomination night, and we have got some men coming to dine. If you would give me the pleasure of your company I should be very pleased."

"I shall be delighted," rejoined the banker. "I've no doubt you will have a cheery party, and that there will be no end of chaff over the nominations. Pass the sherry, please. Any one down there for a white-wash?"

In the drawing-room Annie Aysgarth busies herself about her guests, flitting softly from one to another as the occasion prompted. She was making conversation with an old friend of her father's when Cis Calvert's name fell upon her ears.

"No, my dear," replied Mrs. Charrington, in answer to some question of Cis's flaxen-haired dinner partner, "I don't know much of Captain Calvert."

"Well, he can hardly be deaf at his age, but I declare he is the most absent man I ever encountered."

"Which means, Lottie, he wasn't thinking of you. Well, comfort yourself, he'd no business to. Let us hope his thoughts were where they ought to be."

"And where is that, I should like to know, Mrs. Charrington, unless with the lady he is taking care of?"

"Well, when he is going to take care of another for life, you must make allowances for his being a little distrait. If he was thinking of the cousin he is going to marry, you must not be hard upon him. Stupid, I admit, with you by his side, and shows a want of adaptability most unusual in a dragoon."

Not a word of this conversation was lost upon Miss Aysgarth, and she set her little white teeth hard, and her face flushed as she recalled how she had accustomed herself of late to think of this man. Was Mrs. Charrington's story true? She felt that she must get at the truth somehow before she slept. The sharp surgery of the truth was better than the incessant pin-pricks of suspicion. She was aware of Mrs. Charrington's besetting weakness, but she did not know that all the same we cannot help giving some credence to unreliable testimony when our feelings are concerned. Mrs. Charrington was not wilfully lying upon this occasion. She was only telling what she had heard after her own fashion. One of the stray guests at her garden party, brought there by one of her friends, had observed—"I see you have got a countryman of mine here, Cis Calvert. We used to think he would marry his cousin Kate, but he's still a bachelor."

Mrs. Charrington had retold this with unusual accuracy—that is, for her.

And now the gentlemen gradually stream in from the dining-room, and amongst the foremost was Cis Calvert, bent upon the achievement of that conversation which he had so failed to procure at dinner. But Miss Aysgarth was apparently in no mood to lend herself to this design. The sunshine of the dining-room had died away, and to his amazement Cis met with a somewhat chilly reception. The girl could not help it; she knew Mrs. Charrington's habit of exaggeration ; she did not in her heart believe that her lover could trifle with her in this fashion, and yet for the life of her she could not avoid showing in her manner that this story had laid hold of her imagination. To have taken offence on the one side about that which does not admit of explanation, and on the other to be conscious of the offending, but innocent of the manner of it, has resulted many times in a good lasting quarrel, but is sure to be productive of a game of cross purposes, to say the least of it. Cis felt that he had unexpectedly lost the key of the situation, and marvelled much as to what the arraignment against him might be, while Miss Aysgarth felt dissatisfied with herself, indignant with Mrs. Charrington, and angry with her lover for not at once vindicating himself in her eyes, regardless of the fact that he could by no possibility be aware of what had been alleged concerning him.

To one as well versed in the ways of women as Horace Crymes, it was little likely that Miss Aysgarth's change of manner should pass unnoticed. He had no idea of the cause, but it was plain to him that something had gone wrong between her and Calvert. That lovers' quarrels are rivals' opportunities no man knew better ; he was fairly in the field now, and determined to make the most of the chance with which fortune had favoured him. Should he only progress as far in the young lady's good graces as he had contrived to do in the good will of her father, he thought he should not be doing a very bad evening's work to begin upon. Acting upon this idea, the Major made his way at once to Miss Aysgarth's side, and at once engaged her in conversation. As she had herself said,

Horace Crymes was a good talker, but though he did his best to interest her, it was apparent that his fair companion's attention was somewhat astray. He understood all that, and was nothing daunted by it. She might not listen to him now, but that was no reason she should not do so a little later. A bad start he knew, from former experience, may be recovered, like most things, by patience and perseverance, and he possessed that great virtue of knowing how to wait. Not only did he succeed in somewhat monopolizing the young hostess, but when the dancing commenced he led her forth for the quadrille.

Exercised severely by the lady of their love, men either affect to console themselves with a counter-attraction or sulk. Cis was somewhat too hard hit for the former, so he betook himself to the latter line of conduct. He did not, of course, stalk about like a Manfred in private life, nor altogether drop the mask society demands of us all, but he wandered about rather vaguely, complained slightly of headache, and showed no disposition to dance with any one. Inwardly he was anathematizing Horace Crymes and woman's fickleness, with an intention that would have been highly estimated at Red Gulch or any other of the Colorado mining stations.

But Miss Aysgarth herself was not having altogether what is called a good time of it. No sooner was she conscious of the effect of her displeasure on her victim—and she watched him closely from those eyes at the back of her head which all women appear to possess—than she felt a little penitent for her behaviour, and remembered that she had pronounced sentence without waiting to hear if the culprit had anything to say in his defence. Then she reflected that she must at all events know whether Mrs. Charrington's statement had any foundation; and how was she to know that if she kept the only person from whom it was possible to learn the true state of the case at arm's length. Her resolve was speedily taken, and no sooner did the quadrille come to an end than, with her sweetest smile, she asked Major Crymes to take her across to Captain Calvert. "He is really neglecting his duties shamefully," she added, laughing, "and I must scold him." That done, and much more to the surprise of Cis than his rival, the Major was dismissed with a saucy little nod, and Miss Aysgarth and her lover were face to face.

"How is it you are not dancing, Captain Calvert? I really cannot allow you to remain idle. We are not, sad to say, so bountifully supplied with cavaliers that such a knight of the ball-room as yourself can be excused his devoir."

"I trust I am something better than that," rejoined Cis grimly, "but I did not know that my services were required. I am at your disposal, Miss Aysgarth; with whom shall I dance?"

"With me, I think, if it is not imposing too much on your good-nature," rejoined the young lady demurely. "You see," she continued, as she took his arm, "I should like to be one of the first to offer my congratulations."

"About what?" inquired Cis curtly.

"I am told you are engaged to be married."

"And is there any one in this room so capable of contradicting the report?" rejoined Cis, in a passionate whisper. "What nonsense you may have heard I can't tell; but that the question I tremble to put has yet to be answered you know as well as I do."

"But they say you're engaged to your cousin," faltered Miss Aysgarth.

"Do you suppose if there had been the faintest ground for such a report I should have dared to speak to you as I did at the Charringtons'? Do you hold me such a hound, Annie, that I could make love to you while I was engaged to another? If I don't rank higher in your esteem than that, I fear there is small hope for me."

"I didn't say I believed it," stammered Miss Aysgarth.

"Do you believe I love you?" whispered Cis. "You must have known that, Annie, for weeks. As for the story you have heard about my cousin—well—she and I have always been real good cousins, nothing more. I vowed when I came here to-night to ask you one question. You know what it is. What answer am I to take away with me? Am I to leave The Firs supremely happy, or sadly regret the day I first saw the walls of York."

The girl looked up into his face, inquiringly.

"Can you love me well enough to be my wife?" said Cis, in a low whisper.

Once more she looked him steadily in the face. Then a slight quiver played round her mouth, her eyes dropped, a little hand stole into his, and she answered softly, "Yes."

CHAPTER V.

THE NOMINATIONS FOR THE CUP.

It was a gala night at the mess of Her Majesty's —th Lancers, and the old room, scene of many a wild revel, glittered with plate and wax lights. These were the last days of the army of the great Duke, remember, of the veritable inheritors of the Peninsula traditions ; when the infantry had a quiet contempt for Brown Bess as a firearm, but a mighty belief in the efficacy of the bayonet ; when the cavalry held that any square of foot soldiers not British was to be broken ; when the joints were placed on the table in all their barbaric splendour, and dinners *à la Russe* were as yet in the womb of time ; when men not only could drink port, but did, by pailfuls, and toned it down afterwards with a grilled bone and a trifle of whisky punch. How they stood it is a mystery, but the veterans that are left should have some consolation in the gout that now mostly afflicts them when they reflect that they *did* earn it.

The nominations for the Regimental Cup are to be published to-night, and, although pretty well known already, still the —th have determined to have a party to give a little *éclat* to the official announcement. Julian Harperley is there by Major Crymes's invitation, not that Calvert troubles himself much on that point since his last evening at The Firs. He feels now that he is an accepted lover, and any transient uneasiness he might have felt about the Major is a thing of the past. Mr. Charrington is there—shrewd, sharp, and combative as ever. Many other guests are there besides these two, who, as they have no bearing on this narrative, it would be useless to particularize. In fact, it was a full house, and to those conversant with the habits of those apparently *nonchalant* light dragoons, there was presage of an

exceeding wet evening. It was the custom of the corps; they
were all so quiet and silky to start with that the stranger within
their gates could never dream of 'the high jinks' the evening
was destined to terminate in. So insidiously did they steal on
their victims as a rule, that temperate men found themselves
drinking burnt brandy punch and joining in tumultuous choruses
hours after the wives of their bosoms had expected them home,
and with no idea that they had exceeded a bottle of claret.

Dinner passed off pleasantly enough, as with good wine.
decent cooking, and cheery hosts, a dinner is bound to do, and
then having drunk 'the Queen,' there was a lull in the conversation while the pay-master, who took this duty upon himself,
proceeded to read out the entries for the regimental races; for,
besides the Cup, there was a Farmers' Plate and also a Challenge
Vase, open to all members of the York and Ainsty Hunt, but the
Cup was the event upon which interest chiefly centred. One
curious thing about such races as this is, that they are apt to look
a foregone conclusion and result in a most unexpected 'turn up.'
In a regiment every one knows, or fancies he knows, all about
everybody else's horses, and so imagines it is very easy to say what
will probably win, quite forgetting that amateur training and
amateur riding are apt to upset all calculations at times. Now
the Major's new purchase was of course no secret. They had all
seen and admired The Cid, and the prevalent belief was that there
was nothing in the regiment capable of beating that grand-looking
grey, therefore no little astonishment was manifested when it was
found that besides The Cid the Major had also nominated Cockatoo. Could it be that the new purchase was not quite so good
as he looked? but surely he must be better than old Cockatoo,
who, besides, had incurred a 10lb. penalty for having already
won the Cup, and who had won with not much in hand either.

"You don't seem to put quite so much faith in The Cid as
Mappin does," remarked Julian Harperley. "Running a second
string looks as if you—"

"Didn't know much about him," interposed Crymes; "just
so. I believe him to be the best of the pair considerably, but I
don't know as yet, and I have seen too many handsome impostors
in my time to trust to looks implicitly. All these fellows think

I am safe to win the Cup with him—why? because Mappin, who wanted to sell the horse, said so. They know nothing more than he is a good-looking one."

"Hallo!" suddenly exclaimed a vivacious subaltern, named Radcliffe, "here's another case of second string. Cis Calvert's named a couple; here's Captain Calvert's chestnut horse, Red Lancer, and Captain Calvert's black horse, The Mumper. What's that?"

"You don't mean to say you've entered that skeleton you bought out of the hounds' mouths?" laughed another. "Never were dogs more defrauded of their just due than when you interfered between Mappin and his good intentions. He picked up that horse with a view of presenting him to the kennel."

"Never you mind, Strangford; The Mumper will very likely beat more than beat him. He's a bit poor, perhaps, but he may mend of that."

Mixed with all the chaff was no little surprise as to what could have induced Calvert to enter this new purchase. Some of his brother officers had not even seen it, and those that had wondered not a little what had made him buy such an old screw, for it was palpably an old horse that had done a lot of work in its time— well-bred, no doubt, and not without some good points, but never likely to look like a gentleman's hunter, put what corn into him you would. Nobody was more astonished and excited about the entry of The Mumper than Harry Harperley. He had been present, as we know, in Calvert's room when Tim Murphy had reported his mysterious conversation with Isham Boggs. What had Cis found out about the horse since then that had determined him to run The Mumper for the Cup? He would have been much astonished if he had been told nothing; that the entering of The Mumper was due to the earnest entreaties of Tim Murphy, who had all an Irishman's passionate admiration for a grand jumper, and this he had ascertained the old horse to be; but then he had been sold to Cis with that character, and he could fairly have said with Crymes that his knowledge of his new purchase was simply what the horse-dealer had chosen to tell him.

As the claret circulated, discussion waxed warm about the various chances of the competitors for the Cup, and it speedily

came to pass that opinions were not only emphatically expressed,
but boldly backed by the disputants, until at last, amidst the
Babel of chaff, Strangford announced his intention of opening a
book on the forth-coming race, if only the owner of the favourite
would give him a start.

"Now, Major," he exclaimed, "set the market; they have
made The Cid first favourite down here. What shall I lay you?
Take my whole book, and let me lay you two hundred to one."

"No, thank you, Strangford. I'll take two ponies for fun if
you like; but I tell you all, that I believe The Cid to be a good
horse, but as yet know nothing about him."

"It's a bet," rejoined Strangford sententiously. "Now, gentlemen, who wants to back one? I keep my own course; Herodia
runs for me."

The amateur bookmaker got plenty of custom for the next
few minutes. All he had to lay about both The Cid and Red
Lancer was rapidly appropriated, and then there came a lull.

"Pass the decanters, Radcliffe," cried the layer of odds. "Tho'
business is slackening, thirst is on the increase. Won't anybody
else back one?"

"Yes, I will," exclaimed young Harperley. "What against
The Mumper?"

"Now look here, Cornet," retorted Strangford, with mock-
solemnity, "this touching loyalty to your Captain is a thing
beautiful to witness, and for which we must all both reverence
and pity you, but you don't mean in earnest that you want to
back that old plate-rack Cis found by the wayside the other day.
His story of buying it of Mappin is of course apocryphal."

"What will you lay against The Mumper?" replied the boy
doggedly.

"You can have two hundred to fifteen, if you really do wish
to make me a small present," was the reply.

"Done!" replied Harry Harperley. "I'll take that."

The other nodded assent, and noted it in his betting-book.

In the mean time an animated argument was going at the
other end of the table between Mr. Charrington and the Major.
The master of Byculla Grange was combative and dogmatic by
nature. It had struck him as singular that Crymes should have

entered two grey horses, although for the matter of that old Cockatoo was grey now only by courtesy, and perhaps more for the sake of saying something than aught else, he proceeded to state that in this country he never knew a good horse of that colour. With the Arab it was different, but the English thorough-bred of that colour was never good for anything.

But he had caught rather a tartar in the Major. Crymes pointed out that all tradition of ballad and poetry was rather in favour of greys. "Did not the old hunting song say

> ' And the best of the horses that galloped that day,
>   Was the Squire's Neck or Nothing, and that was a grey.'

"What about Chanticleer, did he not consider him a good horse?"

No, he did not. Chanticleer was much overrated, a mere handicap horse; and as for poetry, faugh! what did such men know about it? they put in whatever colour suited their rhyme.

"Well, you will see my greys run better than you give them credit for," replied Crymes, apparently wishing to drop the subject.

"Then I shall see what I don't in the least expect," rejoined Charrington testily. "Will you bet me fifty pounds that you win the Cup?"

"No, that would be to back my pair at evens against the field, and I should look for a better price than that."

Now there had been a good lot of wine drunk, and Mr. Charrington was one of those men whose wine does them no good. It is so at times, instead of growing genial under the influence of the rosy god, thawing to their fellow-creatures, and beaming with amiability, we meet cantankerous creatures who become more morose with every bumper, who become argumentative and obstinate, who once having started a topic that threatens to be disagreeable, pursue it with a pertinacity that sets one's teeth on edge.

He sat sipping his port and looking moodily at a written list of entries in front of him. "I don't like greys," he said, " I don't believe in them. Now, Crymes, I'll give you a chance to back your opinion. Captain Calvert's got a couple entered as well as yourself; only his are decent-coloured Christian horses,

not Pagan circus-looking animals like yours.   Will you back
your pair against his for fifty ? "

"Yes; or five hundred either," retorted the Major, contemptuously.

"You can put the remainder of the five hundred down to me
if you like," exclaimed Cis, no little nettled at the disparaging
tone assumed by the Major.

Crymes looked a little astonished for a second, then replied,
"As you like, Calvert.   You had better have an even monkey,
and I can bet Charrington an odd fifty, or a hundred besides, if
he likes."

"You shall bet me a hundred, then," said the latter; "I don't
believe in grey horses."

The Major nodded assent, and, having noted the two trans-
actions, turned quietly to his guest.   "I must apologize, Mr.
Harperley.   When I asked you to hear the nominations for our
races I had no idea these fellows would turn the mess-room into
a betting-ring.   Pray don't say I encouraged them because I have
been driven into backing my own horses.   My bets were put
down my throat, and my attempt to choke them off by offering
a big wager has only recoiled on my own head.   It is always a
mistake amongst brother officers, and I am surprised at Calvert
taking me up in that way."

Julian Harperley had heard vaguely that Crymes had a weakness for the Turf, still he knew from his son that the Major never
bet or played cards for more than nominal stakes in the regiment,
and he honestly considered that such wagering as had taken place
had been none of his seeking, but had been thrust upon him by
Charrington and Calvert.   It might be a mistaken mode of
putting an end to Charrington's persecution, but Julian Harperley
believed that Crymes had honestly meant no more than to extin-
guish his assailant when he proffered him a heavy bet, and he
did the Major no more than justice, he had never dreamt of
being taken up, much less by Calvert.   It did not much matter
to him, he meant winning the Cup this year, and he most
certainly meant also backing his horse to win him a good stake.
It might as well be won in one place as another, and then he felt
that there would be no little satisfaction in beating, and winning

money from, Cis Calvert. He had made up his mind, and intended to make defeating Cis for the Cup only the prelude to defeating him for a much bigger stake. He did not know that Cis had already proved successful in that other event, nor would that to a man of Crymes's persistency be deemed conclusive.

"And so you've been backing The Mumper, young un," said Cis, as Harry Harperley lounged up to him in the ante-room, dinner being brought to a termination, and coffee and cigars at length arrived at. "What made you do that?"

"I thought if it was worth your while to enter him, it was worth my while to take a long shot about him. You said the other night, you know, you fancied, from what Murphy told you, that you'd got hold of a better horse than you thought for."

"Yes; and I entered him to-night to gratify Murphy, who's sweet upon the horse, because he's discovered him to be 'a grand lepper.' I bought him on that account, thinking I might find him useful among those big fences up in the Ainsty country, but I know no more about him as yet. To-morrow I must ride over and see Mappin, and find out whether there's any history attached to the horse, where he picked him up, and whether he knew anything about him before he came into his hands."

By this time things had settled down into the ordinary groove of big mess parties. The elders and more decorous of those present were absorbed in a rubber, while the more tumultuous element had organized a loo, characterized chiefly by the boldness of the play. It is astonishing how keen men are to take 'miss,' who have the best part of a magnum of champagne inside them. When you begin ' unlimited' at a shilling it sounds playing for sugar-plums, but when the players take ' miss' freely it very soon becomes a considerably less innocent amusement. I don't mean that it quite means high play, but it is possible for people of moderate income to wake in the morning and feel they have been indulging in that diversion. Julian Harperley noticed that prominent at this table were his son and Cis Calvert. How they were faring he of course had no idea, as his whist engaged his attention for the most part. As for Mr. Charrington, who also formed one of the whist table, there was no getting him to abandon his crotchet. He had transferred his dislike to light

E 2

colour in horses to light colour in cards, and declared there was nothing to be done in the red suits. He played quite mechanically the good old-fashioned game he was accustomed to (asking for trumps was amongst the undiscovered blessings of the century as yet), uninfluenced by the wine he had swallowed, but turn him from his whim you could not. He refused to have a bet on the odd trick if a red suit was trumps, and even when he held four by honours in diamonds declared there was no trusting a deceitful light colour or a grey horse; if they did win it was always when no one had backed them. When between the deals it was suggested to him such a thing had been known at Baden or Homburg as a run on the red, he retorted angrily, " It might be, but he had never seen it," which, as he had never visited either of those places, was an answer hardly to the point. In fact, excess of wine had a very singular effect upon Mr. Charrington ; it always increased his natural obstinacy, and was very apt to find its outlet in leading him to take up some absurd idea. It was not often he trangressed, but this was generally the result of such transgression.

But the whist table breaks up, and it is time for the seniors to retire. As the Major bids his guest good night, he remarks in a low tone,

" Don't think, Mr. Harperley, we're a play regiment because you have seen a little betting amongst us to-night. I assure you we are nothing of the sort, and I have never seen the Cup call forth such wagering before. It's not our custom, believe me."

" No, no," replied the banker, " I don't think that. Charrington's obstinacy and Calvert's excitement were, I fancy, chiefly responsible for the events of the evening. Did you ever encounter such a mule as the former? Whenever he gets too much wine in him no idea is too preposterous for him to adopt, and you might as well try to dam Niagara as convince him that he is wrong."

" That I must endeavour to do on the 12th December," replied Crymes laughing. " Once more, good night."

" Fortune's rather favoured me to-night," mused the Major as he walked back to his quarters, " it's not much, but every point in the game counts, and I fancy in the eyes of our intended father-in-law Calvert and myself changed characters to-night. I think he would say if he was weighing us in the scales just now, Calvert's a gambler, Crymes is not. I wonder what made that old idiot Charrington make such a set at me; he surely cannot have the bad taste to be jealous!"

Now this was exactly, though unconscious of it, what Mr. Charrington was. As men often suffer from suppressed gout without understanding what is the matter with them, so Mr. Charrington had for years suffered from suppressed jealousy, and to a man of that temperament Mrs. Charrington gave much opportunity.

His theories read by this light, when wine threw the jealousy partially out, were not altogether so wild, being generally based on mad opposition to his wife's favourite at the time on some point or another. In this instance it had been grey horses.

"Get on your nag, Harry, as soon as this is over," said Cis Calvert the next day at morning stables, "and we'll ride over to Mappin's before lunch. I want to ask him whether he really does know anything about The Mumper more than he told me when I bought him. Don't fancy, please, I think I've got a phenomenon; but, as he is entered for the Cup, I should like to know if he's got any chance; more especially as I was fool enough to back him for a lot of money last night."

"What made you do that, Cis?" asked the boy.

"Because I was an ass, Harry; because Crymes's sneering manner made me lose my temper. However, I must hope Red Lancer will pull me through. The Cid may not be quite so good as he looks, and as for old Cockatoo, with 10lb. in hand, I fancy I hold him pretty safe."

Stables over, the pair were speedily cantering through the lanes towards the horse-dealer's. By good luck Mr. Mappin was at home, and welcomed the two officers cordially. He was always on good terms, as may be supposed, with the cavalry regiment quartered at York, and in Harry Harperley's case he had known him from a boy, and often lent him a clever pony in the Christmas holidays.

"Come in, gentlemen, and pick a bit. I've a cold round of

beef that is not bad to lunch off. Do me the honour to begin with it, and anything I can do for you afterwards, of course I will."

"Well, Mappin, if you will give us some lunch, we shall both be much obliged to you," rejoined Calvert, "and we can talk over what I've come to see you about while we have it."

The horses were put up, and the two quietly seated round the table in the oak-panelled parlour.

"Now, Mappin," said Cis, when he had assuaged a very healthy appetite with the cold beef, and a somewhat unquench-able thirst by a stupendous pull at a pitcher of home-brewed, "I want you to tell me all you know about the horse I bought of you the other day."

"Certainly, Captain Calvert. I picked him up for a song at a sheriff's sale of Dick Hunsley's horses. He was described as 'The Mumper,' a black hunter, aged, and, in that latter particular at all events, correctly, for I should think he's twelve or fourteen years old. I was told he was clever, but, further than he can jump like a deer, I know nothing. I had only had him a week when you took him. To the best of my belief he is what you wanted, a clever hunter, at a low price. I admit freely I turned my money over him. Of course I must, it's my business, but I don't think you paid a pound too much for him."

"You don't understand me, Mappin. Bless you, man! I'm not complaining, I'm quite content with my bargain. But what's the horse's history? that is what I want to get at. Who, for instance, is Dick Hunsley?"

"Dick Hunsley," returned Mr. Mappin, slowly. "Well, about ten years ago Dick Hunsley came by the death of his father into as good a farm as there is in all Yorkshire. The Hunsleys had been yeomen farmers for many generations, farming some two hundred acres of their own, and renting as much more under Sir Tatton, which lay next them. They had always been a straightfor'ard sporting lot, and this Dick was the first of the breed that took to running cunning. It don't pay mostly, and it hasn't with him. He's dead broke, had to sell every acre, every stick, and that's how The Mumper came into my hands."

"What sort of a sale was it?" inquired Calvert. "Had he a large stud?"

"No; they were a very mixed lot," returned the horse-dealer, laughing. "Three fourth-rate racers, a steeple-chase horse, a couple of hunters, and a trapper or two. The Mumper was one of the two hunters."

"Now, tell me this, Mappin. Do you know a man called Isham Boggs about here?"

"I never heard the name in my life, sir," replied the horse-dealer, in no little amazement, "and it is not a name one would be likely to forget either. Might I ask what he is?"

"That is just what I want to ascertain," replied Cis, "and as soon as I do I shall come to you again. And now, Harry, we must be off. Good-bye, Mappin; I've entered The Mumper for our Cup, so anything you can pick up about him I shall be glad to know."

"Entered that old black horse for the Cup! Well, I'm d—d?" muttered Mr. Mappin, as his guests rode away. "There's an awful fool about somewhere, and who is it? That's the question. Captain Calvert or Robert Mappin? Either I've sold the horse for a third of his value, or else the Captain's gone clean off his head."

CHAPTER VI.

AT THE LIGHT HORSEMAN.

"It's odd, deuced odd," said Cis, as they rode slowly back to barracks, "that Mappin should never have heard of this man Boggs. I should have thought Mappin would have known every one who had any connection with horseflesh through all Yorkshire."

"But," interposed young Harperley, "the gentleman with the sweetly euphonious patronymic may not be exactly in that way. Mightn't he be a friend of this Dick Hunsley's, who knows the horse, fancies him, and, thinking he was pretty well given away, is willing to make you a bid for your bargain?"

"I could have understood that if he had gone straight to Mappin, but Mr. Boggs don't suppose Mappin sold the horse to me without turning money over him. He don't even know what I gave for him. It looks to me as if Mr. Boggs was anxious to get back The Mumper at any price."

"Which must mean," exclaimed Harry, "that the old black is a great deal better than either you or Mappin had an idea of. I shall win Strangford's money after all."

"Well," rejoined Cis, laughing, "if The Mumper can get round the course about half as quick as you can arrive at a conclusion, I should say you would; but I've a good deal to learn about that horse, and, amongst other things, whether Red Lancer can't beat him easily."

"I suppose you'll send Murphy to see Isham Boggs?" remarked young Harperley.

"No, I think not. Tim is an excellent servant, but he has a slight weakness, and I don't consider a gentleman who lives at the Punch Bowl Tavern an eligible friend for him. No, I shall give him strict orders to avoid all acquaintance with Mr. Boggs, and to keep whisky at a distance till after the races; and I tell you what, Harry, you had better say nothing about the mysterious Boggs."

"All right," replied young Harperley, as they turned into the barracks; "but you'll let me know if you hear any more of that worthy, won't you?"

Cis nodded assent.

Now, there was no one connected with Her Majesty's —th Lancers so interested about the forthcoming races as Mr. Thomas Blundell; the idea of getting horses into condition for something like real business was to the ex-Newmarket stable-man quite exhilarating. He assumed an aspect of profound responsibility, and could not have looked more impressed with the cares of his position had he carried the key of West Australian's box in his pocket. As a matter of precaution, he knew the form of every horse in the regiment; who could say such knowledge might not some day be useful, and the Major recognize once more that the finality of horses was racing? Still, there was one of which Mr. Blundell considered he had never satisfactorily got the length, and that was Captain Calvert's chestnut horse, Red Lancer. Mr. Blundell was much exercised in his own mind as to how he might induce Tim Murphy to give him just a feeler with old Cockatoo as to Red Lancer's quality.

The proceedings of the mess-room are canvassed in the barrack-room more often than the denizens of the former imagine. Mess waiters, who are perpetually in and out, and whose presence is rarely noticed, are scarce likely to be miracles of discretion. Officers' servants, it stands to reason, must know a good deal of their masters' proceedings, and if master and man are of a sporting turn the chances are that the servitor is as well acquainted with the contents of the betting-book as the compiler. Men of the Crymes stamp may keep such volume under lock and key, but the majority leave it on the table when not likely to require it. There is nothing singular, therefore, in the barrack-room being tolerably well posted in what goes on in the mess-room. Mr. Blundell, prowling about in pursuit of information, is not long before he hears of the entry of the mysterious Mumper, and further, that Captain Calvert has backed his pair against those of the Major for a biggish bet. If the Newmarket ex-stableman is somewhat surprised, he is no whit dismayed, far from it, a racing mystery is to him what chess problems and double acrostics are to some people. It was a veritable duel then between him and Tim Murphy, and Mr. Blundell smacked his thigh and chuckled with delight at the idea of turning the Irishman inside out.

He was quite aware of Tim's amiable weakness; he knew that though he rarely got drunk in a military sense (it took a good deal to do that in those days), he was fond of a glass, and wont to be garrulous when his throat had been sufficiently lubricated. Other people might wonder what on earth could have induced Captain Calvert to enter that old black horse, but this merely aroused Mr. Blundell's suspicions. A regular plant he thought most likely arranged by Mappin and Captain Calvert; the two horses had been tried together, and 'the ugly duckling' had proved the better of the pair. Calvert immediately takes that, and the next thing is to stick the Major with the good-looking Cid. The grey is sure to be made first favourite for the Cup, as indeed Blundell has learnt he already is, which will enable the Captain and Mappin to back The Mumper for a nice little stake. Such was Mr. Blundell's theory of ' the little game,' as he called it, and it must be borne in mind that, from his stand-point, there was nothing wrong in all this. He didn't see that a piece of sharp practice such as this could be hardly stooped to among brother officers. No, it was smart, very; Captain Calvert had bought the best steeple-chaser Mappin had—all the more valuable because he didn't look it—and was doubtless grinning to think that the Major had bought one he knew he held safe.

Still, although Mr. Blundell, whose belief in his own acuteness was unbounded, made no doubt whatever that he had got to the bottom of things, yet he could not but acknowledge to himself that a little corroboration would be more satisfactory. When you do intend a *coup* it should be made as certain as lies within your power was Mr. Blundell's sentiment on all matters pertaining to the Turf, and he was wont to shake his head in doleful fashion over a certain Derby which had cost him dear some year or two before. The success of one of the Southern competitors had been carefully arranged for, but, alas! the manipulators had not thought it worth their while to trouble themselves about a North country outsider, and the result was discomfiture to the schemers and their friends.

In pursuance of this policy, Mr. Blundell took the readiest opportunity of suggesting an adjournment to the Light Horseman, after their horses were suppered up for the night, to his Hibernian compeer.

"A quiet pipe, just a moistening of our throttles, and perhaps a little palaver over the races. Mr. Murphy, I'd never refuse a hint to a pal myself, that is, one I could trust not to go gabbling about all over the place, and I think it's pretty plain either you or I'll take the Cup."

"Sorra a one of me knows," rejoined Tim. "Ye've a great horse in The Cid, there's no denying, and Old Cockatoo's useful, but I'm thinking Red Lancer 'll throuble yez something."

"All right, then we'll go down to the Light Horseman after we've done with the horses, and have a smoke and a talk over things."

"Faix and I'm agreeable," rejoined Mr. Murphy with a confidential wink. "May be, we might go near settling it to-night."

Tom Blundell was so pleased with the way in which his overtures had been met, that he already regarded the race for the Cup in his own hands; an affair of which the arrangement was to be quite at his disposal. It was such an opportunity as his heart had yearned for of late, the idea of winning money with cogged dice having always a peculiar fascination for some people. Still, Tom Blundell was essentially one of those to whom early information on either the Turf or Stock Exchange generally proves useless. There are men who can never make up their minds as to how to make the best of their opportunities; they are swayed this way and that, they listen to every one's advice, and are guided by none, and finally, when the *coup* comes off, win nothing, but sit down and anathematize their own want of decision. At least, that is what they really should do, but usually they put the result of their own miserable vacillation on the shoulders of a friend, and curse him freely through a far futurity.

The Light Horseman arrogated to itself the title of a snug tavern. It had perhaps been so some half-score years ago, when railways were struggling into existence, and the glories of the road, if on the wane, by no means a thing of the past. Although not on the great highway of the North, there was plenty of traffic through Fulford from Nottinghamshire and West Lincoln-shire into York that might have then warranted such *status*, but it had unmistakably now degenerated into a public-house depend-ing considerably upon the custom of the cavalry regiment stationed at the northern metropolis. Its situation, about half way between the barracks and the city, gave it an advantage not to be gainsaid, and the military were naturally much con-sidered at the Light Horseman. The landlord understood his customers and their requirements. There was the commodious taproom for the troopers, and the snug parlour at the back of the bar for the non-commissioned officers, to say nothing of a couple of small rooms at the back for gentlemen who had private business to transact. At the back of the house ran a long straggling garden, containing some two or three rather mouldy-looking summer-houses and a superior dry skittle-alley.

In this paradise Mr. Blundell was a man of mark ; free of the non-commissioned officers' parlour, and much respected therein as a great racing authority. He was in receipt of very liberal wages from the Major, and probably had more money to spend than any frequenter of the house, and was free with it. That he should rank high in the good graces of the landlord need scarcely be said ; consequently, when Mr. Blundell, accompanied by Tim, made his appearance, and demanded a private room and a bowl of whisky punch, he was met with obsequious smiles, and an immediate compliance with his request.

"Fair tipple, Tim, I think," remarked Blundell, as he put a steaming tumbler of the mixture to his lips. "A leetle too much of the sugar, perhaps, but they always overdo the syrup in the provinces."

"It's aisy suction," said Tim, smacking his lips, "and I'm thinking they'd mend it little in London."

"And who said a word about London?" rejoined Mr. Blundell, sharply. "A fig for London! the metropolis of the Turf is Newmarket. I don't believe breakfasts, punch, or pick-me-ups are properly understood anywhere else! and as for training—"

"Ah! well, they've a notion of it up here, the crathurs," interrupted Tim. "Maybe you've won the Leger with a south-country horse; but, bedad, ye'll admit ould John Scott made a mess of ye this year at Epsom."

"Ground upsets all calculations," muttered Blundell, a little discomfited, "but fill up your pipe, man; there's as good birdseye in that pouch as I can lay my hands on."

For a few seconds the pair smoked and sipped in silence. At last Blundell observed, imbibing confidence with the punch, "I want to be straight with you, Tim; we must put 'em together, but The Cid's our horse, you may depend on it."

"He's a raal beauty, and it isn't likely Cockatoo can give ten pounds to him is what they do be all saying—"

"Pooh! What do you and I care for the general opinion? I want to know what you're thinking," said Blundell meaningly.

"Is it me? Och troth, I'm of the same opinion meeself. It's beautiful punch—ah well, as you're so pressing, I'll just take another dandy," and Tim pushed his glass to his companion in admonitory fashion.

A savage expletive was smothered on Blundell's lips as he replenished his guest's tumbler. Mr. Murphy was displaying a want of confidence between man and man that was perfectly disgusting, or an amount of ignorance of the world that amounted to imbecility. Which was it? and Tom Blundell after a moment's reflection decided that *punch must show.* "It's a soothing mixture," he remarked, "and warms a man's heart. A queer start of your master, by the way, nominating that old black screw he bought the other day—"

"I'm thinking he's going on the off chance, like the man wo saw down at Carmarthen Steeple-Chases."

"Ah, what was that?" inquired Blundell.

"Well, you see, I was down visiting with the Captain in those parts a year or two back, and there was a gintleman who insisted upon putting a clever cob he had into a hunt race; the others all laughed at him, but although there was siven runners he finished second, d'ye see. 'Not quite such a fool as you thought me,' says he, as he weighed in. 'I got five of 'em down, and if I'd got one more I'd have won clever.' The black's a grate lepper, and maybe the Captain thinks most of them won't get round."

"I don't fancy that's quite the Captain's view," rejoined Mr. Blundell, eyeing his companion keenly. He could not quite make Tim out; was this pure simplicity, or was it affected stupidity assumed for the purpose of baffling inquiries. But the Irishman's face, though flushed with the punch, baffled all scrutiny as he pushed his tumbler significantly across the table. Blundell promptly replenished the glass, and then resolved to provoke Tim, if possible, to show his hand by depreciation of The Mumper. "I suppose," he continued, "he's made a bad buy of it, that's the fact; and thinks entering the black horse for the Cup will make people believe him better than he is, and so enable him to get out."

"Get out is it," rejoined Tim, upon whom the punch was telling, "it's mighty little throuble he'd have about that. Sure, the masther could turn his money to-morrow av he chose."

"That's easier to say than to do, Master Tim," laughed Blundell. "Some of our officers ain't very wise, but I don't think there's one of 'em fool enough to bid money for The Mumper."

"An' who said one of the gintlemen wanted him? Tho', per-haps, Major Crymes might lay out his money worse, as maybe he'll own when he finds himself at the bottom of a ditch, with The Cid on the top of him. It's a York gentleman who's so sweet. I suppose you've heard of Mr. Boggs in these parts? He's the boy for sport, whether it's cock-fighting or steeple-chasing. 'What's the Captain want for him?' says he to me the other day.

"'I don't know,' says I.

"'Just tell him to drop me a line,' says he, 'an' I'll take him off his hands at anything in reason.'"

Mr. Murphy was wont to be somewhat braggadocio when he had a little liquor in him.

"Why what does Mr. Boggs want with him?"

"'Deed I don't know, but from the look of him I'd think it's a team of hearse horses he's collecting."

Once more Mr. Blundell glanced keenly at his guest. Was there any grain of truth in his rodomontade, or was he playing a part? He came to the conclusion that Tim was at all events somewhat under the influence of drink. "And where does Mr. Boggs live?" he asked at length.

"I'm not just at liberty to mention," rejoined the other, with a sly leer. "Such a rale out-and-outer as he is there's no difficulty about coming across."

"It's no object to me," rejoined Blundell, carelessly, as he threw his tobacco-pouch across the table. "We don't trade in hearse horses ourselves."

Tim filled his pipe, and puffed savagely at it for a few moments in silence, and then growled out, "Maybe the hearse horse 'll astonish you before the year's out."

"Can't very much, when you're going to part with it to Mr. Boggs."

"Tear an ages, man! who tould you that? All I said was that he's mad to buy the horse; it isn't likely we'd part with a clipper like The Mumper."

"Do you mean that?" asked Blundell, eagerly.

"I mane that's what Mr. Boggs thinks him," replied Tim, rather taken aback.

"Ah, and he considers him a good horse, has known him before, and that's why he wants to buy him."

"Not at all, it's just funning I was. He's known the crathur a long while, and wants to buy him back bekase he's an ould favourite in the family."

Mr. Blundell experienced a considerable desire to punch his guest's head, but remembering that was the least likely way to get what he desired out of it, and that the experiment might possibly result in that operation being performed upon his own, he refrained.

"Did ye ever smoke a pipe at the Punchbowl?" suddenly inquired Tim.

"No. Where's that?" rejoined Blundell, no little astonished at the abrupt turn in the conversation.

"Troth, I'm tould it's one of the most elegant taverns in the city."

"But that don't tell me where it is?"

"Where is it?" replied Tim—with the tendency of an uneducated Irishman, to reply to one question by asking another—"It's in Stonegate; but it's getting late. I'm thinking it's time we were on the throt."

There was no denying it. Mr. Murphy was subject to military law as regarded his hours, and it was as well he should be on his way back to barracks again. As he settled for the punch Blundell reflected angrily that it was money clean thrown away unless Tim became communicative on the way home. He had brought this blethering Irishman down here and deluged him with punch for the express purpose of turning him inside out, and getting at all there was to tell about Captain Calvert's horses, and he was walking home with a dim consciousness that the Celt had proved too much for the Saxon. Especially did he intend to know Mr. Murphy's real opinion of that old black horse, and he was fain to own that Tim had not let the slightest hint of what he thought on that point escape him. All attempts at conversation on the way back to barracks proved futile. Tim was seized with an unconquerable fit of taciturnity, and responded to his companion's overtures with incoherent grunts and heavy clouds of smoke from his *brûle gueule*. In short, when they bade each other good night, Blundell felt that his hospitality had been obtained on the most fraudulent pretence, and felt as keenly anxious to be quits with Tim in some fashion as his master did with Captain Calvert.

But if not quite so clever as he deemed himself, the pupil of Newmarket had nibbled sufficiently of the fruit of the tree of roguery to be tolerably quick at putting two and two together. Racing men are wont to be rather rapid in their deductions at times, and don't feel it necessary to see the weathercock to tell which way the wind is blowing. When Mr. Blundell thought over the events of the evening next day, he gradually came to the conclusion that there was a pearl or two of useful information in that bushel of chaff to which Tim Murphy had treated him. First, Boggs was a most uncommon name, which it was hardly likely that Tim would have invented; it was probable, he thought, there really was a Boggs, and that, whether or no he wished to buy The Mumper back, he knew the horse's previous history. Secondly, what made him allude to the Punchbowl Tavern? Tom Blundell had never heard of this hostelry before, and he knew he thought pretty well what houses of call were patronized by the regiment from top to bottom; from the Black Swan in Coney-street, habitually used by the senior officers, to Harker's in Sampson-square, more confined to sporting subalterns, and so on through minor houses, till one arrived at the Light Horseman; but he had never heard any one mention the Punchbowl. Puzzling over these things he began gradually to connect them with each other, and slowly arrived at the conclusion that Mr. Boggs was not unlikely to be met with at that mysterious tavern in Stonegate. Once come to this conclusion, Blundell determined to take the earliest opportunity of inquiring for the shadowy Boggs, and ascertaining whether he had a palpable entity.

CHAPTER VII.

ASKHAM DOG.

THE Punchbowl, although unknown to Mr. Blundell, was in
those days a tavern very much in his line. What are called
sporting houses are now pretty well out of date; at all events it
is no longer the fashion for men about town to frequent them,
and the Castle, the Rising Sun, &c., are utterly unknown to the
golden youth of our time, favourite haunts as they were with
their progenitors. The particular pastimes which they nourished
and promoted have fallen into desuetude, and the noble science
of pugilism in these degenerate days are apt to bring fine and
imprisonment to its enthusiastic followers; ratting can hardly
be said to meet with encouragement, while cock-fighting is
pronounced decidedly unlawful, albeit no more cruel than
pigeon-shooting, and infinitely more sporting. Murder on a
large scale, under the name of war, or agrarian outrage, under
the name of agrarian agitation, seem to be the only two sports of
this description recognized in our advanced civilization. However, in '52 the prize ring, although in its decadence, was by no
means extinct, nor would the Coop week at Chester have been
deemed complete without a little cocking. To know the
whereabouts of such amusements men betook themselves to the
sporting houses, where they received what was technically
termed ' the office,' that is, were told the place of rendezvous,
and could then proceed to admire the dogged determination of
Portsmouth Jones, the amazing quickness and science of ' the
Spider,' or put their money on the famous ' white piles ' of the
Cholmondeleys in the Cestrian city. In a sporting county like
Yorkshire it followed of course that such things were, and for
information concerning such tournaments there was no better

place to look in at than the Punchbowl. More than one celebrity of 'Fancy land' was accustomed to make it his head-quarters during the race-week, and the then king of the billiard-table, the Great Jonathan himself, who did for billiards what Matthews did for whist, was a well-known frequenter when business or pleasure took him to the northern capital.

After this preamble it may be easily conceived that Blundell found no difficulty whatever in finding his way to the Punch-bowl, and his first feeling was one of no little amazement that so congenial a house should not have come to his knowledge before. A crisp October day was just coming to a close when the ex-Newmarket man stepped across the sill of the tavern in Stonegate. Three or four horsey-looking men were absorbing spirits and water in front of the bar, and carrying on a languid and desultory conversation; they took stock of Mr. Blundell in indolent manner, but when he inquired of the presiding goddess whether Mr. Boggs was staying there, Tom suddenly became aware that the conversation had ceased, and that he had become an object of considerable interest to these loungers.

"No, sir, he's not," replied the barmaid. "Who shall I say asked for him?"

"Never mind my name," rejoined Blundell. "He wouldn't know it if he heard it, but I want to see him badly all the same; when is he likely to be here?"

"Can't say, I'm sure," replied the young lady. "Mr. Boggs is very uncertain in his movements. If you left your name and address he'd perhaps make an appointment."

"Ah! thank you, miss, that's what I'll do. I'll just drop him a line here. I s'pose he'd be safe to get it."

"Sure to in the course of a day or two; he's mostly in three or four times a week."

As Blundell—having bade the barmaid good night—issued once more into the street, "Who is he, and what the devil does he want with Isham?" caught his quick ear, and he marvelled greatly who or what this mysterious Boggs might be.

But that was a point upon which he was not destined to be speedily enlightened. He wrote as he said he would do, and was assured, on calling at the Punchbowl, that Mr. Boggs had got his letter, but he received no reply. He had taken kindly to the house, and now often dropped in there of an afternoon, but never could succeed in meeting Boggs. He had got acquainted with some of the *habitués*, and soon discovered that Isham, as they called him, was well-known amongst them, but what his precise calling might be baffled him. If he inquired what he did? he was generally told " sometimes one thing and sometimes another—he's a many irons in the fire has Isham." Did he know anything about horses? " Well he did ought, he's had a mort to do wi 'un," and a general grin pervaded the company, as if much tickled at the suggestion. Equally indefinite was all information as to his whereabouts. " He was a deal about, was Isham, down South to-day, and up away North to-morrow; he's a busy man is Isham."

Weeks slipped by, and it is no secret by this time in the regiment that the derided Mumper has turned out a good deal better horse than either seller or purchaser had ever deemed him. Cis has been on him, and discovered that both Mappin and Tim are right on the one point—the horse is a magnificent fencer, without an idea of refusing. " He tucks his hind legs under him, and throws himself into the next field as if shot from a catapult; if he'll only face water," says Cis, " I've never owned such a jumper before." Calvert is fortunately possessed of a few common-sense ideas on the subject of training, and therefore orders that The Mumper shall do but very moderate work. He knows that old horses as a rule require much less work than young ones, and that, when you come to a really old horse, he will sometimes do his best thing when in the eyes of many people half-trained. The black, in his opinion, wanted rest, and, acting on this principle, he told Tim to give him plenty of oats and moderate exercise. The horse didn't put on flesh, but that he was improving was evident by the brightness of his eye and coat, and also by his gaining heart. Still there were many who agreed with Blundell that was no sort of preparation for a horse to go three miles across country, and that jump as he might The Mumper could never be dangerous after the first mile, on account of his want of condition.

Cis has never as yet ridden the black in the hunting-field, but

the York and Ainsty are advertised to meet at Askham Bog,
'the very best fox cover in all England,' as the enthusiasts of
those parts are wont to proclaim it, and Cis announces his intention of giving The Mumper a turn to Harry Harperley.

"What fun," rejoins that young gentleman. "I do believe
Crymes means to ride The Cid. It will be a sort of trial."

"I suppose your sister will be out ?"

"Of course, and the governor too ; neither he nor Annie ever
miss Askham Bog. It's your first season with us, and you don't
know what a festival the first meet at Askham Bog is. Why,
half York will be there on the Great North road to see us
throw off; always a fox, generally a run, and the only place
I should think where it is possible for a crowd not to spoil
sport."

Cis Calvert's engagement, though suspected, is not as yet a
published thing. Annie had told her story to her father, and
Julian Harperley had, as is mostly the case, listened to it with no
little surprise. A mother would have foreseen it, but to the
widower it came as a revelation. The Banker was not altogether
pleased. It was not that he thought his daughter ought to do
better ; he was perfectly satisfied with Calvert's position and
family; as for ways and means, he could afford to make Annie
such an allowance as would enable them to get along comfortably,
but the fact was he did not take to Cis exactly. He had liked
him to start with, his son, who was in Calvert's troop, was
enthusiastic in praise of his captain, regarding him with all that
hero-worship a boy of his age is capable of, but Julian Harperley
had of late got it into his head that Cis was something of a
gambler. The banker was no purist on this point, he was far too
much a man of the world and a Yorkshireman to boot to see
harm in betting on a horse-race, but when it came to betting
pretty well a year's income on the result he was somewhat
staggered by it. He had heard Cis's bet at the mess that night
of the nominations; his engagement to Annie had of course
involved a clear explanation of his means on Calvert's part. So
that Julian Harperley was aware that Cis on that occasion had
staked his whole private income on the result of the Cup. A
man who will bet so recklessly as that may love his wife very

dearly, but make life very hard to her all the same. Very pleasant-mannered are those young gentlemen—

> " *Whose fathers allow them two hundred a year,*
> *And who'll lay you a thousand to ten;* "

but they are usually viewed askance by the heads of the family, and the banker feared much that Cis Calvert was somewhat in that way.

"You must not think, my darling, that I am opposing your marriage when I tell you that I wish no positive engagement to exist between you for six months. I have told Calvert so, and he admits that I am not very unreasonable. The words spoken of course cannot be recalled, nor do I wish they should be, but I do want you to be quite sure you know each other. The regiment is not likely to be moved yet awhile, and, though when I gave it a son, I little thought it was to rob me of a daughter, yet I shall not complain if only it is for her happiness. What tacit understanding there may be between you I have nothing to say to, but I wish there to be no formal engagement for six months."

. "It shall be as you wish, father," replied the girl, smiling. "As I shall see Cis constantly it will not be very hard to keep our secret for six months."

"I am not so sure about that," said the banker. "It's a lynx-eyed neighbourhood, and much given to what Mrs. Charrington would call putting two and two together, though turning two into one would be the more correct expression in such cases."

This delay Julian Harperley thought would give him time to study Calvert's character, to ascertain whether he really was an inveterate gambler or whether he was merely a man who had made a rash bet in the excitement of the moment, for that it must be held regarded as relative to his income, and if he felt, at the expiration of the stipulated time, that his duty to his daughter required him to solemnly counsel her to break with Cis, well then, was it not better that their engagement should not have been formally promulgated.

Such was the state of affairs between Calvert and Miss Aysgarth on that soft November morning, when all York and its neighbourhood were gravitating up the great North road to

Askham Bog. There were sporting pedestrians; there were the mere loafing sight-seers; horsey men on foot, apparently breakfasting on ash plants. Carriages swept by, with delicate ladies swathed in fur and velvet; tax carts, crammed full of blooming rustic maidens, with rosy cheeks, sparkling eyes, and a perpetual giggle on their lips; solemn gigs, occupied by stout comfortable-looking men and their spouses; vehicles that defied nomenclature, that had started as something else near a century ago, and had been modified from time to time to meet the requirements of fashion, all jogged along midst joke and jollity to see the hounds throw off in the crack cover of the York and Ainsty.

The vendors of apples, oranges, and gingerbread had established their stalls, as usual, by the wayside, and were driving a roaring trade, while at the little inn on the opposite side the road to the famous fox cover, it was whispered the finest old crusted gingerbeer was on sale, a drink apparently highly popular and inspiriting, and known to many of the consumers by the presumably local appellation of 'jumping powder.'

That the hunting men should muster in great force was only natural, but besides these were that numerous contingent who take an occasional day; men who borrow or perhaps hire a horse for the occasion, and amongst these were undoubtedly some very rusty-looking customers, none more so perhaps than a bottle-nosed man, in seedy black, but who sat the sorry screw he was riding, nevertheless, like a workman. The soldiers paraded in considerable strength, and there was no little curiosity among the York and Ainsty men to see them perform. The regiment had only arrived in York from Newbridge in April, bringing with it the reputation of being a very hard-riding lot, and though, of course, this was not quite their first appearance, the hunt considered they had not really had an opportunity of taking stock of them as yet. Then the story of the big bet (I am speaking comparatively) had oozed out, and it was known that the Cup was considered to lie between Crymes and Calvert, who again were recognized by the regiment as the two best horsemen they had. Further, it had become known that each would be riding one of his nominations, and, therefore, it may well be conceived that the pair were the subject of no little scrutiny.

Miss Aysgarth, as she rode up to the cover-side under her father's escort, had quite a little staff around her. Calvert, Crymes, her brother, and one or two more of the Lancers were all of the party, and that the popular daughter of the popular banker should receive many cordial greetings was matter of course, but, sad to say, upon this occasion I am constrained to admit that The Cid attracted as much attention as Miss Aysgarth. A Yorkshireman has quite as appreciative an eye for a pretty woman as for a good-looking horse, but he is no more exempt from the worship of new gods than his neighbours. Miss Aysgarth was charming, but then they had never seen The Cid before.

"If that man and that horse can't go, then all I've got to say is looks go for nothing," remarked a veteran sportsman, after a lengthened contemplation of the grey. "We haven't seen much of the Major as yet, but if you chaps mean catching him to-day, you must be off in good time, mark my word."

The Mumper, on the other hand, attracts but little attention; he looks well, but is a plain horse, and never in his best day could have caught the eye like The Cid. The way, too, in which he is ticked with white hairs indicates that he is no chicken, and the general impression is that Calvert is not riding what will represent him in the Cup.

"Ah! Crymes, giving one of your greys an airing, eh?" said Mr. Charrington, as he rode up, and raised his hat to Miss Aysgarth, "a good-looking one, very, but it's a soft colour; yes, soft, sir, d—d soft!"

"Where's Mrs. Charrington; surely she's out?" asked Annie.

"Yes, but we've got a couple of nieces staying with us, so she drove them over to see the fun; however, she's got her horse here, too, so no doubt you will see her in a few minutes."

Muttering something about paying his respects, the Major moved quietly off on The Cid, but he had little thought of philandering at the bridle-rein of the fair mistress of Byculla Grange. He had a new, and, he firmly believed, a very first-class hunter under him, and Horace Crymes vowed two things to himself that day, that he would know what The Cid was like, and that the York and Ainsty should see whether he could ride or no. He stole quietly along the cover on the far side of the road, creeping up the rising ground a little as the hounds drew that way.

"Now, Cis, don't be absurd," said Miss Aysgarth, in a low tone. "Papa will take every care of me, and you know I never really ride to hounds. I won't hear of your missing the first day from Askham Bog on my account. I want to see if The Mumper can really jump as you say. Look at the little knot creeping up the slope, they are old hands, Cis, stealing forward for a start. Go, or I'll hold you the carpet knight I was once rude enough to call you."

Cis bowed low, and then pressing The Mumper into a smart canter, pushed up the cover-side in the direction indicated.

" How very much better that black of Calvert's looks when he is going," exclaimed Julian Harperley ; "but come, Annie, although we don't aspire to the first flight, it is getting time we also pushed a little forward."

The few preliminary whimpers that for the last three or four minutes had troubled the ear now swelled into a very babble of tongues, and Cis shook up his horse to catch that little knot of horsemen edging rapidly towards the end of the cover, and which he felt intuitively was composed of a cohort of the hard-riding division. He got there just in time to note that the group were well mounted, and looked like going all over, with the exception of a bulbous-nosed man in seedy black, riding a thorough-bred screw, with fore-legs that made one shudder for the owner's neck. Another minute and a cheery 'gone away' calls attention to the fox gallantly breasting the hill-side. The hounds crash out of cover, a faint roar is heard from the road, dimly recalling the tremendous diapason which announces the fall of the flag at Epsom, hats are jammed on, and catching their horses by the head, the little knot are racing up to the first fence, a somewhat hairy blackthorn, with a ditch on the take-off side, the hounds lying slightly to the left. Some of them charge it almost in line, but all are well over, including, no little to Calvert's surprise, the gentleman in seedy black. Cis looks back, and sees they have got a start for what threatens to be ' a cracker'; he is pleased with his position, and more especially is he pleased with the galloping power The Mumper develops. The old

black horse is sailing along with the low, sweeping stride
of a thorough-bred, little as he looks like one.   Crymes, on The
Cid, has settled down to his work just in front, while, odd to say,
Cis finds the bottle-nosed man on the cripply weed lying at his
quarters.   But—

"If ever they meant it, they meant it to-day,"

as White Melville sings, and racing over the crest of the hill
the hounds stream across towards Swann's Whin at a pace that
leaves short time for reflection.   "Well away," thinks Cis,
"with the pick of the York and Ainsty men, and in for a run.
I shall know all about The Mumper before this is over, and
be able to make a rough guess at what The Cid can do with
him.   By Jove, what a fencer he is!"
Whether he meant his own horse or the grey matters little—
the remark applied equally to both.   Making the very best of
a capital start, and riding as if he'd no doubts about his second
horse turning up, the Major had succeeded in leading the field,
and grimly swore to himself never a soul should pass him that
day.   If he had driven The Cid rather hard at first, he was
riding him coolly and steadily enough now, and no one knew
better than Cis how bad a man Crymes was to beat at any time,
much more when he had a bit the best of his field, as he had
at present.   For a moment, so well was The Mumper going, the
temptation to race up and really have a shy at The Cid was all
but irresistible.   Then Cis reflected that his horse was by no
means fit, that winning the Cup had now become a matter of no
little moment to him, both from pride and pecuniary motives.
"No," he muttered, "I'll not ride my horse's head off.   Second
string, indeed!   I shouldn't wonder if he turns out first fiddle
when I have to determine which is my best."
The pace was severe, and amongst the select few right up
with the hounds, the two dragoons occasioned no little curiosity.
New-comers with a reputation are always keenly scanned in the
hunting-field, and when the pair are supposed to be riding the
very horses on which they propose to shortly contest a race, the
interest of the lookers-on is, of course, heightened.   But there
was, perhaps, no one of that select band who watched the

relative going of The Cid and The Mumper so closely as the bottle-nosed gentleman in seedy black. How he kept with them at all was a mystery, as neither he nor his horse gave the faintest sign of such capability. A little under a mile and he began to tail; a couple of fields more, and the plucky screw he was riding galloped into a fence completely pumped, and desposited him on his back in the adjoining enclosure. The man picked himself leisurely up, bestowing in the first instance no manner of notice on his luckless steed, but gazing steadfastly after the receding horsemen.

"By G—d," he exclaimed, "the old horse has got back his form, and if these soldiers don't mess him about with too much work, that Cup's as good as on Captain Calvert's table. Poor Dick! I thought his break-up had put an end to the little game we meditated, but it looks as if other people were going to play it for me. I've not quite cyphered it out yet, but it strikes me I shall have a pretty good race over that Cup whatever wins."

And now occurred one of those distressing episodes so familiar to hunting men, when revelling in all the delights of a good start for a good thing. The hounds suddenly threw up their heads, and checked. What was it? Had they overrun it? It gradually became apparent that was just what had happened. The fox had been headed, and, after circling round to the right, had doubled back again to the friendly shelter from whence he came. Maledictions on their luck burst from the lips of the leading division of horsemen. It was disgusting; they were well away, riding delightfully jealous, and in a moment the cup was dashed from their lips. But to one of the cruelly-disappointed band there came balm speedily. A road ran adjacent to the scene of the disaster, and amongst the macadamite contingent that the check had permitted to come up Cis espied a certain riding-habit, which completely changed the current of his thoughts. Leaving the hounds to puzzle out the lost trail, he jumped his horse quietly into the road, and once more took his station by Miss Aysgarth's side.

"I tell you what, Calvert," exclaimed the banker, "they may laugh about the old black at the mess-table, but, by Jove, they'll none of them laugh much at him in the hunting-field. Why, he's a rare galloper as well as jumper. We've managed to keep you in view all the time, and you looked as if you'd take some beating to-day."

"Yes, I think I've picked up a cheap horse," replied Cis, laughing, "and feel that for once in a way I really have had the best of a deal with Mappin."

CHAPTER VIII.

A SUBLIME SACRIFICE.

"Only to think of The Mumper distinguishing himself in that fashion ! As Papa said, we could see you capitally all along, and you looked like being right in front all the way to Swann's Whin, which we all thought his destination," said Miss Aysgarth.

"It most probably was, but circumstances at times compel foxes to change their minds as well as human beings."

"A remark pregnant of meaning, no doubt, but I don't see how it particularly applies just now," rejoined the young lady demurely.

"In this way ; having been done out of my gallop, I decline to lay myself open to further caprice on the part of the fox family for to-day, and elect to ride with you instead."

"Nonsense ! see, they've hit it off again, and you're losing a start."

"Don't be sarcastic, Miss Aysgarth," returned Cis, laughing. "There's not much fun to be got out of muddling back with the pack to Askham Bog."

"But to think of a man dangling by a lady's rein when hounds are running, be it ever so slowly."

"I would willingly forego the best run of the season if I might linger at yours," replied Cis in a low tone.

"You don't really expect me to believe that, do you? Some one has said that 'all females love exaggeration,' but don't you think, Cis dear, you are carrying it just now a little too far ; and even if there be a wee bit of truth in it, tell it if you like in Gath, but for the sake of all you hold dear never whisper it in Yorkshire."

"I'd not shrink from proclaiming on the steps of the York Club that a ride with Annie Aysgarth was of better worth than the best run ever galloped from Askham Bog."

"Hush!" exclaimed the girl with a mock affectation of terror. "Cis, dearest, you are talking blasphemy; that exclusive body would cast you out from among them as a barbarian, and taboo me as the Circe who had ensnared Ulysses."

"Well then, we'll revert to the more worldly and cowardly policy, and vow we lost the hounds—must, you know, if we don't follow them?"

"And yet that is what we came out to do."

"In a qualified way. Please remember this ancient but valuable animal I am riding has an important engagement, and I am bound not to ride his head off. I wanted to give him a gallop, but not a hard day."

"Yes, and I am told you have got a terrible lot of money on it, Cis."

"Who told you? your father?"

"No, Harry. I wish you wouldn't bet, at least so high as you did the other night. It will do you harm with papa; he always looks rather askance at men who gamble."

"But, my dearest Annie, I don't. Crymes was speaking in such contemptuous terms of my horses the other night that I lost my temper, and made a foolish bet if you like, but I neither play nor bet as a rule, except in quite a modest way."

"I am afraid, from something papa said, he thinks otherwise. It was that made me question Harry, and so learn all about what took place at the mess. Harry, by the way, is immensely mysterious about The Mumper. He told me he had backed him, that nobody knew what he was, and that you had got some private information concerning him, and then," added the girl, laughing, "he seemed so swelling with irrepressible stable secrets that I maliciously declined to manifest further curiosity."

"Harry is foolish to talk so," replied Cis, smiling, "though, as far as I am concerned, secret he has none to divulge. What the mysteries of his own stable may be I can't say. We're as near the cover here as we want to be, and shall have a good chance to see them go away again, if they manage it."

"No fear but what they will do that," said Miss Aysgarth, "though, perhaps, not with the same fox."

She was right in her prognostications. A few minutes more, and once again re-echoed the many-throated chorus. Again the jealous riders with whom

" "While horses can wag it is never say die"

steal forward to the end of the cover. A crash, and the dapple-coated pack pour over the fence like a mill race. A melodious 'gone away' from their scarlet clad chiefs, faintly re-echoed from the Great North road, and the pageant streams along before their eyes, a repetition almost of the first burst.

"By heavens, what a glorious sight!" exclaimed Cis, as his eyes flash, and his cheeks flush; "and look, Annie, there's Crymes away well in front again; ha! the York and Ainsty men must ride to-day if they mean to take down our number. The best man we have leads them just now, and I verily believe on the best horse in the regiment."

"I'll not believe him the best man, nor The Cid the best horse, till a warrior I wot of has gone down before him in the Cup," cried Miss Aysgarth. "If a girl don't have faith in her lover, all creeds are torn up as far as she is concerned; but he can ride, Cis; just look at the way he's pulling his horse together over that awkward little bit of ridge and furrow."

"And if that isn't the way to hand one over post and rails, I never saw it done," cried Cis enthusiastically. "Belief in oneself is a good thing no doubt, but the way Crymes is leading the field to-day is somewhat calculated to shake it."

They were trotting and cantering briskly along the road all this time, with a very fair, though gradually decreasing, view of the hounds. Still, as long as they could see them that gallant grey held a commanding lead, which his rider looked resolute to maintain, riding straight as an arrow and indulging his horse with just what came in their way.

" I don't think we shall see much more of them," said Cis at last as he pulled up at the top of a small hill.

"No," said Miss Aysgarth, "they are vanishing fast in the distance, going where you should be going also—to Red House.

It's very sad, Cis, and I quite sympathize with you. Ah, why did you take charge of me instead of wooing fortune once more? You might have cut down Major Crymes, and made a name in Yorkshire story; who knows?"

"I do," replied Cis gaily. "And I'll make that name yet. When I've carried off the prettiest girl in the county, and disposed of Crymes in the Regimental Cup, even the club will admit my conduct to-day as madness with a purpose in it."

"Ah me! yes. 'Young Lochinvar has come out of the West,' but before he carries off his bride in old Border fashion will he permit her to give him some tea? Let's ride home to The Firs, Cis, and have a quiet gossip over the fire. I declare papa has abandoned me in shameful fashion; to leave his loved daughter in charge of a hard-riding dragoon, is equivalent to desertion of the most unpardonable description."

"Nothing of the sort," retorted Calvert, laughing. "It only shows the high estimate he places upon the sagacity and prudence of the horse-soldier. It's only young ladies, as a rule, who properly value the dragoon as a *chaperon*."

"Poor things," cried Miss Aysgarth, with a burst of merry laughter, "but here's a lovely stretch of turf for a canter, so let's make the most of it."

On arrival at The Firs they handed their horses over to the grooms, made their way to the drawing-room, and Annie rang for tea. Very pretty did the girl look in the brightly-flashing firelight that still gallantly held its own against the fast falling shadows of a November afternoon. She had thrown aside her hat, and the dusky tresses gathered into a knot behind the small, shapely head, and falling low over the broad forehead, glistened like a rook's wing in the flickering light of the flame. The dark blue eyes shone with marvellous softness as they glanced proudly on the man she loved, while the close-fitting habit showed off her lithe, supple figure to perfection. The gay badinage of the hunting-field had ceased, and the conversation carried on between them now was low of tone and earnest of purpose. Cis was mooting his plans for the future, telling her how, for the present, it was incumbent on him to stick to his profession. Would she mind following the steel scabbards about the United Kingdom? There was no chance of their being ordered abroad for years. Some of those Irish quarters were, he knew, deadly dull, certainly, but they had just finished their turn there, and had all England and Scotland before them.

"No, Cis," she gently replied, "I shouldn't like you to give up your profession. I think any woman whose love was worth having would never wish that, as long as her husband had health and strength. A man has his appointed work to do in this world, and it's more likely to be bad for his wife than anybody when he shirks it."

"I am a little afraid that your father will expect it."

"No, Cis, you don't know papa; he's the last man to expect it. No," she added, with a smile, " when he gives me to you it will be with full permission to enroll me in the D troop at once. And now, my own, I must send you away. It's long past five, and I have to clothe myself in splendour preparatory to driving over to dinner at Byculla Grange. Kiss me, Cis, and say good-bye."

He clasped her in his arms, and pressed his lips to the rosy upturned mouth so freely yielded to him, and then, with a whispered God bless you, darling, passed out into the dark November night. Cis Calvert was doomed to think over that day the hounds met at Askham Bog in many a far-away land before Annie stood at the altar with him, and little guessed as he rode gently home to barracks, musing over the roseate prospect before him, what pitiless buffets fate had in store. A run sacrificed, and a horse in training brought home like a common hack in this fashion; verily I think a Yorkshire jury would have found Cis guilty of being close bound to Miss Aysgarth's apron-strings.

There was much talk about Crymes and The Cid amongst the hunting-men as they jogged home after the day's work; both horse and man were honestly lauded, for there was no denying that the Major led the field from Askham Bog to Red House, and never a one could wrest the pride of place from him. Freely they admitted that he had shown himself both ' a customer ' and

a sportsman, but as far as this last goes, it happened to be just
one of those occasions when a master of hounds might have cried
gaily, "Now, gentlemen, ride over 'em if you can!"   Still,
Crymes was the undoubted hero of the day, and those who
did not see individually, concurred with those who did, anent
Rufforth drain, when, in the words of the late laureate of the
hunting-field—

> "They told me that night he went best through the run,
>   They told me he hung up a dozen to dry,
> When a brook at the bottom stopped most of their fun,
>   But I know that I never went near it—not I."

That there should be much converse about this at Byculla
Grange after the ladies left the table was only natural, and that
it should be talked about, as it related to the coming steeple-
chases of the Lancers, was merely what was to be expected.   The
rivalry between Crymes and Calvert had already attracted attention to the race for the Cup, and the way the grey has carried
him to-day undoubtedly prepossessed men in favour of the Major's
chance.   Still there were not wanting those who had seen the
first burst and recognized what a show Cis had made on the
black.

"Calvert went quite as well as Crymes in that first spin, and,"
added the host, oracularly airing that peculiarly conceived hobby
of his, "I've no belief in greys."

"Seeing is believing, Charrington," retorted a bluff hunting
squire opposite, as he tossed off a bumper of port. "I don't like
your gaudy-coloured ones myself, but I cave to public form when
I see it, and if Captain Calvert's got one in his stable better than
the one the Major showed us the way with to-day, all as I can
say is he's lucky."

"I agree with Charrington.   The Mumper went wonderfully
well till the check, and I don't think there was much to choose
between black and grey that time," said Julian Harperley
quietly.   "Why Captain Calvert didn't persevere, I can't say."

"Because he knew that old horse of his was about spun out;
they do for a spurt, but they can't stay when they are really
aged."

" No, I don't quite think that was his reason," rejoined the banker with an amused smile.

And then came much more discussion about the day's sport, and the *pros* and *cons* of black and grey were argued out with much intensity, fortified by that conclusive expression of opinion common to Englishmen, an offer to bet upon it. No little wagering in a mild way was the result of this after-dinner argument, and had it come to a poll there could be no doubt that the greys had it.

The sole representative of the —th Lancers present, as it happened, was young Harperley, and that he should ardently champion his captain, in whom his belief was unbounded, was quite in accordance with the natural hero-worship of boyhood. Chaffed and too closely pressed by those shrewd old sportsmen who surrounded him, what wonder he took refuge in the indefinite, and more than hinted that Cis had knowledge of The Mumper they little dreamed of, and that when the time came they were destined to be considerably astonished by that noble animal's capabilities. " Backed him ! of course he had," cried the boy, flushed with excitement. " Had he not taken Strangford's book about him ? Only let them wait and see what a mess Calvert would make of Crymes and The Cid when the day came."

If there was a man at that table this talk puzzled it was Julian Harperley. A few weeks back and his son had done nothing but dilate on the certainty this race was for The Cid ; that he had turned round and changed his opinion was nothing. Young people often do that, and, alas ! there are old ones, too, who when it comes to racing could tell sad stories of what vacillation has brought upon them ; but why should Harry so persistently contend that his owner knew The Mumper to be very different from what he was believed to be ? Calvert himself always declared he knew little about the horse, and Mappin less.

Was this misty, undefined knowledge he hinted at merely Harry's own particular opinion, and was he indulging freely in that dearly-loved weakness of youth—the backing of it ?

I always admire a man who has an opinion ; there are so many who have not, whatever they may think to the contrary ; specially

is this the case about Turf matters. When Jackson confides to
me that such a horse will win the Derby, I know that he means
such a sporting writer says he will, and when Clackson breathes
his views of the political situation into my ear I am also aware
that I am receiving an abstract of the leader in the *Standard*,
the *Times*, or it may be the *Daily News*. A friend of mine
some years ago declared his intention of listening to no advice
concerning a certain big race about to be run, but "to play off
his own bat," and have at least the satisfaction of losing his
money in his own way. Well, he lost his money by a head, and
subsequent running showed that he ought to have won it The
result was soothing, if not lucrative. Still satisfied vanity, with
pockets well emptied in sustentation of its opinion, is not, upon
the whole, a pleasant reminiscence, while, saddest of all, he has
held positive and of course expensive opinions ever since—
luxuries these to be indulged in only by the rich.

But nobody out had been so much impressed with The
Mumper's performance as the hero of the day himself. Crymes
had noticed with no little astonishment how well Cis Calvert had
gone up to that first check; he had noted that the black was a
remarkably fine galloper, as well as jumper, and had seen a great
deal too much of racing not to know that they run in all sorts of
shapes. He could call to mind, too, some big things done by
horses supposed past their prime, and especially in cross-country
conflicts had the equine veterans distinguished themselves. He
was perfectly well aware, too, why Cis had not persevered, and
could not disguise from himself that the Cup was not quite such
a certainty as he had booked it, and that his chance of winning
Miss Aysgarth looked woefully distant and dim. Difficulties never
discouraged Horace Crymes, and though he seldom fell into the
error of under-estimating an adversary's hand, it never cowed
him. He patted The Cid on his neck as they jogged home from
Red House, and muttered, " You're dirt cheap at the price I paid
for you, and, although that black of Calvert's is a good deal
better than I had any idea of, I think, my boy, we shall manage
to give a good account of him on the 12th." Then he fell to
musing over his chance with the banker's daughter, and was fain
to admit that unless something occasioned a breach between Miss

Aysgarth and her lover, their engagement would be a thing published to society before many weeks were run. That it already existed he thought probable, but still it was a little in his favour that it was not as yet announced. He held no frivolous scruples about being 'the something' himself, did he only see his way, but at present he most certainly did not. A man of a curious but by no means uncommon code of morality, Crymes held all fair in love, and a good deal fair in racing, that would hardly seem so to the uninitiated; that bets must be paid while debts were by no means obligatory, and that cheating in love was a thing to jest about, while cheating at cards put a man outside the pale of society. A singular creed, no doubt, but pray do not run away with the idea that it numbers a paucity of believers.

There had been two other lookers-on at Askham Bog that day, who had taken no little interest in the respective performances of The Cid and The Mumper, in the persons of Mr. Robert Blundell and Tim Murphy, and the way Cis had kept his place in the first burst clinched the former's original conclusion that the whole thing was a regular plant arranged between Mappin and Captain Calvert. Strongly imbued with this notion, he determined to once more pump Tim as they rode home together after the hounds had fairly gone away in the direction of Red House.

"Ah, well, the cat's out of the bag to-day, Tim," he observed, "and I don't want to be told you are just exercising the second string as well as myself. Red Lancer looks well," he continued, throwing a critical eye over his companion's horse, "but the Captain will no more want him on the 12th than my master will this old white beggar."

"Oh," rejoined Murphy. "Ye'd have to travel west of Athlone to pick up such a lovely lepper as that ould black. It's a murthering shame the master didn't have another go on him."

" Do you mean he's an Irish horse?" said Blundell, sharply.

"An' couldn't ye tell that by the ways of him?"

"No, nor you either! he jumped well, but so did The Cid, for the matter of that."

"You're a man of mighty little observation," rejoined Tim. "Didn't ye see the crathur wouldn't pass 'a habit.' It's a way they have, though they'll follow them annywhere, an' on mee sowl, the men are much the same when it comes to a petticoat."

"Pooh, what rubbish you talk," returned Blundell, angrily. "I thought, perhaps, your friend Mr. Boggs had told you how that old black is bred."

"My friend Mr. Boggs!" ejaculated Tim, uneasily. "Where did you hear anything about Mr. Boggs?" The Irishman had utterly forgotten his indiscretion that night at the Light Horseman.

Tim Murphy's uneasiness didn't escape Blundell. He leant forward in his saddle for a moment, as if adjusting the throat-lash, and then said, "How did I hear about Isham Boggs? Why at the Punchbowl Tavern in Stonegate, of course, he's always there, you know."

"No, I don't. Why should I?"

"I'm sure I can't say, but I suppose you'll admit you do know Isham Boggs? At least you said so that night we'd a pipe at the Light Horseman."

"Ah, shure! I remember, I've met a gentleman of that name," replied the sorely repentant Tim, now cognisant that his tongue had been running riot.

"And does he not know all about The Mumper, and what a great horse he is?" continued Blundell, marking the effects of his random shot. "Ah, well! my friend, don't confide in me, but I fancy you'll find more than one at the Punchbowl who knows the old black besides Isham Boggs."

Mr. Murphy vouchsafed no reply, but producing a short black pipe from his pocket, proceeded to leisurely illumine it, and puff away in moody silence.

"If you won't be sociable, you won't," said Blundell, at length, "and if you won't be confidential, you won't. I should like to have arranged things comfortable with a brother trainer," and tho scamp rolled the last words out with unctuous significance, "but if you won't, well, again, you won't. I shall likely know as much about your horse as you before the day, and mind you, Mr. Murphy, we win the Cup, and you don't, if your d—d old hearse horse can take the Shannon in his stride."

"Ye'd be mighty good at brag, an' it might take about two

days to skin you in the West ; but it's aisy to see why you left
Newmarket," remarked Tim, meditatively.

"And why, I should like to know ?" inquired Blundell, in
a voice hoarse with restrained anger.

" It's a cruel thing to say of 'em, but I'm thinking their ways
were a thrifle too straight for *a trainer* like you."

Mr. Blundell smothered a strong expression, and putting old
Cockatoo into a sharp trot, left his unsociable companion without
further remark.

CHAPTER IX.

ISHAM THE PROPHET.

In a bedroom on the first floor of the Punchbowl Tavern, overlooking Stonegate, on the evening of the meet at Askham Bog, sat a man, who looked for all the world like a dissolute undertaker. One who habitually drowned the grief of bidding adieu to his fellow-mortals in gin, and had gradually come to delight in such 'sweet pain.' He had drawn a small table in front of the fire, relieved himself of a well-splashed pair of antigropolos, and was leisurely consuming a decanter of spirits while he smoked a pipe.

On the table lay pens, ink, and paper, several letters, a *Ruff's Guide*, and a volume or two of the *Racing Calendar*, which latter rather tended to shake belief in the undertaker theory. What Isham Boggs had been originally sometimes puzzled his intimates. A hanger-on of the Turf, and consorting in great measure with that unscrupulous scum to whom racing is no matter of sport but a mere gambling on 'the colour,' he was remarkable, despite his disreputable appearance, for a softness of manner and correctness of speech, which showed that his bringing up had at all events been different to theirs. True when the drink took hold of him, as, sad to say, it too often did, he relapsed into the coarse language of his habitual companions, but otherwise he was

> "the mildest-mannered man
> That ever scuttled ship or cut a throat;
> With such true breeding of a gentleman,
> You never could divine his real thought;"

and if he didn't go quite that length he certainly indirectly made little scruple of slitting purses.

What was his business? Ah, what is the business of some of these turf parasites? I presume it might be designated as raging around and seeking whom they may devour, and a very poor living many of them seem to make of it, but Boggs was not of these. He had a business, and a very extensive business he might have made of it, but in consequence of that miserable failing no one could trust him. Was not one of the mightiest turf *coups* ever planned lost in this wise? There are magnates of the ring yet, I trow, who shake their heads over Blair Athol's year, and muse how wine will steal away the brains of men.

Mr. Boggs was a prophet, not of the sort that concern themselves about either the weather or the end of the world, but a genuine veiled prophet of Khorassan, who had visions of the finish of the Derby, and other important Turf contests. He had barked his opinion as 'Tom Todger's Terrier' in one paper, he had squeaked it as 'the Rat in the Cornbin' in another; but, alack! there were times when editors could get no opinion from either 'Rat' or 'Terrier,' and on non-fulfilment of contract editors are relentless. He was a good judge of racing, and perhaps had somewhat better luck than his brethren in the trade; but a prophet who won't prophesy can no more get a living than a cobbler who will not stick to his last. The oracles of Delphi, I take it, were always on sale, but we should hardly pay for such shadowy prophecy in these times, and the Turf vaticinator who gave the winner of the City and Suburban in a double acrostic would find trade slacken.

The prophetical business having somewhat fallen off after the manner of all neglected industries, and Isham Boggs's passion for strong waters having in like *ratio* improved by cultivation, it behoved that worthy to supplement his original trade by the addition of divers smaller callings, and he became Turf adviser for a consideration to various callow fledglings from the universities, in the army, &c. From that out, the decadence was rapid, and he was soon known as a clever man, who might be bought for the perpetration of any Turf iniquity. It was true that little matter of the wine cup still made against him, but he had a marvellous shrewd head, no scruples, and never babbled in his drink. He had by this time acquired a most undesirable notoriety, and, with the modesty of all great men, was reticent about obtruding either his name or his personality on those likely to recognize it. The fellow, indeed, had more than one alias, but, whatever they might do elsewhere, these stood him in little stead at Newmarket, where he was as well known as the Bushes, call himself what he might. At York it was different; although Isham Boggs was as sure to appear wherever there was horse-racing of sufficient magnitude, still he was more especially a fungus of south country growth, and a man like Mappin, whose race-going was limited to his own and the adjoining counties, was little likely to know anything about the redoubtable Isham.

"Ah!" he said, after a gulp from the tumbler at his elbow, "that spin to-day told me a lot. I wonder whether Captain Calvert had an idea he was in some measure riding a trial ; how astonished he'd have been to know that the old cripple racing alongside him would about sweep the board if hurdle-races were run one mile instead of two. Yes," he muttered, meditatively, "The Coiner would take a deal of doing even yet over four flights at that distance ; pity the beggar can't stay. Well, I've seen for myself, and my verdict is this—that the old black has come back to his old form, and, if he only keeps right, will win that race on the 12th of next month. If he's beat it'll be by that grey of the Major's. Good horse that, and good man, too, his owner; from all I hear, there's nothing else in it. Now, how am I to make a good thing of this? I must stand to win on both, and without risk. Oh dear no," he continued, smiling, as he took his pipe from his mouth, and addressed an imaginary audience. "What! lay odds on two! Fie, gentlemen! Poor patient sportsmen like me don't dash it down in that fashion. Our poor brains must serve us in lieu of your well-stuffed money-bags. I don't think it will be difficult for *me* to stand a pretty little stake, for a man in my humble sphere, on both The Cid and The Mumper.

Once more did Isham take counsel of his tumbler, and then proceed to smoke and stare into the fire with steady persistency. At last, knocking the ashes out of his pipe, he kicked the coals together with his boot, and, turning to the writing-table, drew a small note-book from his breast pocket, and said, "Now to look out the man I want. Ha! here we have 'em, bookmakers. I wonder what a publisher would give for this little volume? it would sell. 'A Book about Bookmakers,' how they began, broke, and were buried. Lord! the public would go wild about it. Fancy the biographies of B. Green and Davis; what's fiction compared to facts like that? and I could write it, I could. No," he muttered sadly, as his eye fell on the waning spirit decanter; "no, not now, I could have done, once. Ah, well, now to find the man I want. He should be a north countryman, or he may hardly think it good enough to come so far for, and then—yes, he must be one who doesn't know me too well. Nottingham, yes, there's plenty of good men there, but there's some I don't fancy, and there's some would hardly fancy me. Hah! here is the very man, Bilton of Leeds, new at it, only got into Tattersall's last year, and a dashing bettor. That settles it," and swinging his chair round to the table, Isham proceeded to write a couple of letters, one to the Leeds bookmaker, and the other was subscribed to Mr. Thomas Blundell, —th Lancers, Cavalry Barracks, Escrick Road, having accomplished which feat Boggs finished the gin, and went to bed.

Tom was not a little surprised and elated when he in due course received Isham's letter. The mystery that surrounded the man, the dark hints dropped by the frequenters of the Punchbowl concerning his business, and, above all, Isham's apparently supreme indifference about an interview with Mr. Blundell, had all impressed the ex-Newmarket man with a respect for the unknown Boggs difficult to imagine. The veneration for the unknown is a singular weakness of humanity. Heaven knows what the inhabitants of India thought John Company Bahadoor might be, but he was to them a magnificent myth, such as the Empress of India can never hope to become, and their veneration was in proportion. Japan the same; as soon as that mysterious sham, the Mikado, was exposed to the view of the multitude he perished. What respect can there be left for general officers in an age when they are as many as the sands of the sea-shore? The democratic wave of the day is quite possibly due to the excessive plenty of princes of the blood, for humanity in its foolishness is apt to hold cheap what becomes plentiful, and alack! the royalties recall the bygone ballad,

> "We very much winces, at this long list of princes,
> Which is longer than it ought for to be."

The eagles of the earth, like the eagles of the air, should be restricted by nature as to progeny.

Mr. Blundell lost little time in responding in person to Isham's summons. He was conscious of being under the protection of the redoubted Boggs the minute he crossed the Punchbowl's threshold. "Oh, yes, sir," exclaimed the barmaid with a smile, "Mr. Boggs is at home. Here, Sam, show the gentleman up to Mr. Boggs's room," which Sam—called by courtesy a waiter, but with an unmistakable look of potboy about him—proceeded to do.

The great Isham, in all the easy *deshabille* of shirt-sleeves, was busily engaged in writing letters when they entered.

"Sit down, please, Mr. Blundell, and excuse me for one moment. We'll have our talk as soon as I've finished this note."

Tom sat down, and very naturally fell to studying the queer figure seated at the table. A spare man, of medium stature, with a tallowy, sickly face, in the midst of which a bulbous nose glowed like the red light above the door of a chemist, close-cut grizzled hair, and clean-shaven cheeks made his age very difficult to define; he might have been anything between forty and fifty-five. He was habited, as far as he was habited, in the sable garments he usually affected, and his linen, as Tim Murphy had observed, was not suggestive of extravagance in the laundry line. But the thing that puzzled Blundell most was a hazy idea that he had somehow seen this man before, though when and under what circumstances he couldn't for the life of him recollect.

"There, that's finished," said Boggs, as he closed his letter. "I am a busy man, Mr. Blundell, and that must be my excuse for receiving you so coolly. It's a poor profession is mine. Great responsibility, and very inadequately remunerated; turf adviser to a lot of young gentlemen who don't know what to do with information when they get it, who back long shots with most injudicious freedom, and take two to one about pretty near a certainty in tenners, bah!" and, disgusted with the picture he had conjured up, Isham threw himself back in his chair and paused.

It is odd, but it is a curious proof of the fascination of the Turf, that belief in these seers of the race-course is never one wit impaired by the exceeding shabbiness of their apparel.

"Who drives fat oxen should himself be fat,"

but that the man who confides Pactolian secrets should himself be wealthy has never been in the least regarded as essential. Why they don't commence with making their own fortune never seems to occur to their credulous clients, and it is curious to notice that the march of education and science never makes the faintest change in human nature. The alchemists of old were, as a rule, badly clad and impecunious, although on the verge of the golden secret, but never wanted patrons; and that many a noble Athenian fell a victim to the confidence trick I have little doubt.

"Now some of my patrons, Mr. Blundell, will be coming over to these races of yours," resumed Isham, "and, of course, they'll want my advice about what they are to do. I don't mind paying a trifle for information, and I should think if any one does know what'll take the Cup it's the trainer of The Cid."

"What might you call paying for information?" inquired Tom sulkily, this not being at all what he had expected from the interview. He had dreamed of an elaborate fraud, and Isham's proposition was a mere picking of pockets.

"Oh! I'm generally pretty liberal," replied Boggs carelessly. "It pays best. It's a small race this, you know, not much to be made out of it. I should think a fiver ought to satisfy you."

"So you sent for me to make me such a bid as that, did you?" said Blundell, rising in great dudgeon. "You manage your affairs, and I'll manage mine, we don't row in the same boat. I can't put a name to you yet, but I've seen you before, I'll take my oath."

" Stop, stop, my good fellow," cried Isham ; " nonsense, we don't part like this. You'll wet your whistle, and we'll talk things over quietly. Sit down, man. You must be pretty green at the game if you fancied I was going to trust you right off."

"You'll have to do it sooner or later if you and I are to do business," replied Blundell sullenly, as he resumed his seat. "You don't suppose a man as was raised at Newmarket is going to make only a fiver out of a chance like this."

" Ah, you were brought up at Newmarket, were you ?" rejoined Isham, and his light blue eyes surveyed his visitor in the keen, stealthy, half-absent manner a cat affects when playing with a mouse. "They rather neglected your education I'm afraid, or you ought to know your master's neither a fool nor a man to play tricks with. Has the name of being liberal, too," continued Boggs dreamily, as if talking to himself ; " upon my word I shouldn't wonder if I made a better thing of it by playing on the square."

" Confound it ! what do you mean ?" exclaimed Blundell.

" Only this—the Major knows me, and if it came to his ears that you had been calling upon me I don't think you'd have much more to do with The Cid or any other horse of his."

" I don't know who you are, and I don't care," retorted Blundell, roughly. " What I came here for anybody's welcome to know. I came to find out all I could about The Mumper. I was told you knew the horse, and wanted to buy him back again from Captain Calvert."

" I look like buying horses, don't I ?" said the other, with a derisive glance at his habiliments.

" You might be buying for other people. I wanted to know what chance that black horse really had in the race."

" That depends upon me," rejoined Isham Boggs quietly. " The Cid's chance depends upon me also, and I haven't quite made up my mind as to which I'll win with."

Tom Blundell's face was a study. " Why, damme," he said, " you don't mean to say that you have anything to say to our horse ?"

" And this to a man," observed Mr. Boggs, addressing once

more an imaginary audience, "who has had twenty-two Derby runners in his pocket out of twenty-four. It would be always rash, my friend, to say that I'd nothing to say to any horse in any race in which I took an interest. With regard to your horse, his winning depends a good deal upon how I think it will suit me. You needn't look so particularly astonished; if you ever *have* been at Newmarket you ought to know that it isn't always the owners who pull the strings; there are occasions upon which they have to take orders instead of give them."

"I know that well enough," rejoined Blundell, "but my master's not one of that sort; nor is a regimental race one worth a money-lender's interference if he was."

"Ah!" rejoined Isham, "what refreshing innocence. If, as I said before, you ever *were* at Newmarket, it is very transparent why you are not there now. Might I be permitted to observe," and the soft, polished speech contrasted strangely with the man's shabby appearance, "that neither you nor any one else in the regiment know much about Major Crymes; further, that anything money can be made over is deemed worth interference with by some people. Me, for instance."

"All right, I've no doubt you're devilish clever, but I HAVE been at Newmarket, although you mayn't think so," exclaimed Blundell, no little nettled at the contemptuous way in which Mr. Boggs was treating him. "I don't know what the blank and blank you sent for me for; but we'll win that race whether it suits you or not;" and so saying, the angry Blundell rose preparatory to departing in his wrath.

"My dear sir, that is just it. No, you decidedly wouldn't do for Newmarket—a little too short in the temper, my friend. Sit down, sit down. You have just told me gratuitously what I offered you five pounds for a quarter of an hour ago; what I sent for you to ascertain."

Mr. Blundell dropped back in his chair dumbfoundered. Who on earth was Isham Boggs? Was he a bookmaker from those torrid climes unnameable to ears polite, and where, oh, where had he seen him before?

"I wanted to know whether you thought The Cid good enough to win, and you do. Now, I've another question to put to you.　How do you propose to turn money over this?　By backing The Cid, I presume, from what you said."

"I don't know.　You carry too many guns for me, and that's a fact," rejoined Blundell.　"I'd like to talk the thing over with you quietly."

"Now you're becoming sensible.　Listen!　I suppose I may assume that there are only three horses in the race, Captain Calvert's two and The Cid; neither that brown horse Mr. Harperley has just bought nor that Herodia of Mr. Strangford's are any good, eh?"

"I should think not."

"Very well, The Mumper will turn out the best of Captain Calvert's pair, and, therefore, the race, bar accidents, lies between him and The Cid.　Now, Blundell, my man, I have about thought this thing out, and you can't pay too much attention to the grey.　It will be a very fair certainty for him.　All you've got to do is to pitch him out right, and put your very shirt on it."

"That's all very fine," rejoined the other; "but, in the first place, there'll be a very limited market, and, in the second, The Cid will be a strong favourite."

"Very sensibly put," said Isham.　"How a young man of your understanding should ever lose his temper and talk nonsense beats me.　But these are little points I'm rather happy in arranging; there will be plenty of professional betting, never fear.　I'll ensure a ring, and, what's more, your horse won't start favourite."

"It's all very well," rejoined Blundell, "but I don't know whether to believe in you or not.　Neither I nor any one of my acquaintance knows anything about Isham Boggs."

"It's a pity the world generally, and especially that portion of it that's addicted to horse-racing, is not in similar ignorance. Though only a travelling name, it would conduce both to my profit and comfort if it were less known.　If you have been at Newmarket, you may have heard of Miles Lane, and if you've ever been racing much, he may have been pointed out to you, although he is warned off the Heath."

"Miles Lane!" exclaimed Blundell, starting from his chair.

"What, him as was one of the famous Running Rein lot? By Heavens! I thought I'd seen your face before. I remember you was pointed out to me some years ago at Ascot," and Mr. Blundell stared at the magnificent spoiler as if he'd been the prime minister of a Liberal administration of these times.

Isham's vanity was touched. He was not insensible to this spontaneous tribute to his misdirected talents, and, like many of his class, he had ability far above the average—ability that would have raised him a handsome income properly applied, but which as it was appeared to profit him little.

"Yes," he said, "I was in that plant, and it took us a deal of trouble to bring off, too; while, as Goody Levi said afterwards, 'What's the use of winning the Derby when they won't give it you.' Can't you trust me how to manage a little matter like this?"

"Ah, that was just what it was," thought Mr. Blundell; "could he trust Isham? As for his capacity for mapping out any conceivable turf villainy, of that Tom had no doubt; he had heard so many stories of Miles Lane's audacious frauds in his Newmarket days that he regarded him as a species of racecourse Rob Roy, as a man who, if in some danger of the gibbet or the prison from the Jockey Club and that section of society, was the pet hero of the free lances. But then, would the great freebooter act fairly by him?"

Isham's keen blue eyes read his face like a book, and solved the question for him.

"What, you're not quite sure I'm going on the square with you? Very well. Now, just pay attention to me. After getting your opinion about The Cid's chance, I might as well have let you go as not. Why didn't I? Because when I square a race, and I've squared a good many in my time, I always like to have the trainer in the swim. Now, if I let a trainer know I have backed his horse, and that he is on at a comfortable price in a small way, and that he needn't be afraid of such and such horses, he understands they are out of his way. He's a fool if he asks questions; he'd much better not know, and I need scarcely add that things of this sort can't be too little talked about. What's my object then in letting the trainer know? Simply this—if anything goes wrong with his horse, I expect him to let me know at once, that's all. Then we arrange the puzzle again for the public. Now, do you understand?"

"I think so; The Cid is to win, but if anything goes wrong with him, I'm to let you have a line here at once."

"Just so, and in the mean time you are on at 100 to nothing about your own horse. If anything goes wrong with him you'll know what we go for—be it The Mumper or anything else. I mayn't look like money, Blundell, and I haven't it, but those who employ me have, and never fail to discharge any obligations of this kind."

He spoke no more than the truth, and it was the wide-spread knowledge of this that made him so dangerous on the Turf. There was always plenty of unscrupulous men ready to find money to carry out the schemes his subtle brain had wove.

Keep money himself he could not; the moment the necessary restraint for its acquirement was abandoned, the man became a drunken gambler.

Mr. Blundell walked home from the Punchbowl in a state of high moral ecstacy. The Cid was to win the Cup, and he had made the acquaintance of the famous Miles Lane, one of the chief manipulators of the great Running Rein fraud.

CHAPTER X

THE RACE.

THE excitement about the race for the Cup had not only risen to flood tide in the regiment, but had gradually simmered up into a very respectable boil in the neighbourhood. A local match in the sporting north-country can put the inhabitants into a ferment quiet citizens of the south little dream of; and, by common consent, this race had come to be regarded in that light. It was true, Strangford avowed his intention of coming on Herodia to look after his money, as he said, but nobody had any belief in his chance, any more than they had in young Radcliffe's and two or three more who declared their intention of having 'a ride' anyway. Neither Crymes nor Calvert made the slightest disguise about which of their respective pairs was the best, and, as Julian Harperley laughingly told his daughter one night, " The Cid and The Mumper were as much in men's mouths round York just now as The Dutchman and Voltigeur had been in the spring of the previous year." Both horses had been out with the hounds upon more than one occasion since the famous day at Askham Bog, but their owners rode them somewhat tenderly, as, with a big race before them, it was only natural they should. Still there was no denying that the Major made much freer use of The Cid than Cis ever ventured to do of The Mumper. This occasioned much adverse comment concerning the black; it was the opinion of many that Captain Calvert's horse could not stay, and that he had a dreadful suspicion of the fact himself; others again opined that he was to some extent infirm, and, consequently, required humouring, while the thorough-going partisans of The Cid pronounced The Mumper a crippled miler, and wondered how any

people could be such fools as to back a horse just because he
could jump, when he was required to gallop three miles or so
besides.   It was undeniable that the weight of popular opinion
was decidedly against The Mumper, not only in the regiment,
but still more so amongst the members of the hunt.   Still there
was a small but staunch division who believed in that veteran
black horse with unswerving fidelity.   In the regiment the men
of his troop, swayed by that devotion to their Captain which in
days lang syne characterized the army, and also by the sanguine
prognostications of Tim Murphy, were ' on ' to a man.   Young
Harperley and a small knot of Calvert's intimates stuck stoutly to
The Mumper, while the banker, from what he had seen of the
horse's qualities that day at Askham Bog, and strengthened
further in his opinion by Cis's confidence regarding him, had also
got a modest wager on the black and crimson sleeves, while as
for his daughter, she was standing those colours for a bale or so
of gloves, and immeasurable quantities of sweet anxiety for her
lover's triumph.

But, on the other hand, Mappin made no secret of his opinion
that there was never a horse in the —th Lancers could make The
Cid gallop, that he had no belief whatever in any concealed
virtues in The Mumper, that the horse was a useful old screw,
especially serviceable up in the cramped Ainsty country, but to
talk of him as a steeple-chaser was simply ridiculous.   Crymes
also expressed, for him, remarkable confidence in The Cid
generally, replying to direct questions by the bland rejoiner, " I
don't know, but I certainly don't see what's to beat him."

At Byculla Grange also raged contention and diversity of
opinion, for while the mistress of the establishment pinned her
faith, and gallantly staked her money to boot, on Major Crymes's
white jacket and violet sleeves, her spouse anathematized grey
horses, and kept persistently piling a little more on the black, in
accordance witl the natural contrariness of his nature.

"Yes, madam," he observed viciously one morning in conclusion
to some slight argument with his wife as to the probable result
of the forthcoming race, " you will be probably broke in purse
and Crymes in neck, and, upon my soul, I can't pity either of
you;" and with a low rumbling about fools putting their faith in

grey horses, &c., Mr. Charrington gradually rumbled himself into the stable-yard.

It is the evening before the race, and Harry Harperley, avid of information, and restless as young ones are wont to be before the first big event which befalls their lives, has hied him into York, and dropped into Harker's Hotel to see if there is anything going on. We all know the old joke about " Paris for fashion, London for wealth, but gie me Peebles for plaisure," and so it was in the capital of the north, the Black Swan in Coney-street for swells, Harker's for sport, and the Punchbowl for devilry. Very busy is Harker's that night, for Mr. Bilton, the big bookmaker from Leeds, and many other sporting men have arrived there for the morrow's races, and discussion concerning them waxes high. Very obstinate and cantankerous is that great betting magnate, Mr. Bilton, showing an animosity to greys that would have warmed the heart of the peppery owner of Byculla Grange. Whether it was too much port, or whether the salmon had not suited him, who shall say? but his ominous six to four against The Cid gradually extended to five to two, and when Harperley entered the smoking-room he had just proffered three hundred to one hundred against the Major's horse. York, as a rule, believes little in a bookmaker being influenced in his business by either irritability or indigestion, and the whisper went about, " What has happened to the Major's horse?" Bookmakers in those days, as bookmakers do in the present, followed the bell-wether like so many sheep, and the smaller fry were as anxious to lay against The Cid, as if they had already attended his funeral; they knew nothing, but they assumed Bilton did, and that was quite sufficient reason for following suit.

There were two or three men present, who looked like small tradesmen, who every now and again dribbled a little on The Mumper, and *les ames damnées*, the backers, who for the most part are just as sheep-like as their adversaries, the fielders, began to nibble freely in that direction. So much did the furore concerning the black increase, that before young Harperley left the room he saw Cis Calvert's horse established a strong first favourite at 7 to 4, while 4 to 1 was freely offered against The Cid. Very elate was the Cornet, as after riding back to barracks with the

intelligence, he burst into the ante-room and published it.
Thereon the followers of the Major were dumbfoundered, while
those of Calvert were proportionately elated. As for the princi-
pals, neither of them happened to be present, so the gathering
men left to muse over the mutability of the equine stock exchange with what equanimity they might.

There was a gathering that night in the bar parlour of the
Punchbowl, and from time to time dropped in divers sporting
spirits, who having previously peeped in at Harker's brought the
news that there was something apparently wrong with The Cid,
as they were laying against him " terrible free in Sampson-square,"
and pasting the money down on that old black horse of Captain
Calvert's, which Mappin, it was well known, had said was of no
use whatever. A small knot of men, of whom Tom Blundell
was one, exchanged meaning glances on receipt of this intelligence, recognizing, as they did, the master hand of Isham Boggs
in the manipulation of the betting market. That mysterious
potentate was not present himself. He rarely was on such occasions, and deprecated nothing so much as the dubious celebrity
of a public character. He had had fame thrust upon him on one
or two occasions, and held it undesirable and inconvenient.
There are walks in life in which it is against one's interest to be
readily recognized of the public, as in the case of the detective
policeman, the burglar, the inquiring philanthropist, &c. Photo-
graphy in those days was barely in existence, or there would
have been nobody to inveigh louder than Isham against the
preposterous vanity that prompted display of one's likeness in
shop windows. He was given to do, if not exactly good, still
whatever he did do by stealth, and quite content to trust that,
like virtue, it should bring its own reward, only I am afraid that
the incorrigible Isham would have expressed infinite belief in
his doings being more profitable than virtue, while it was not
probable that any moralist would confound the two.

If ever there was an adorer of Sheitan it was Thomas Blundell.
The sect of the devil-worshippers is by no means confined to Asia,
but has numberless ramifications in more civilized countries.
Blundell's admiration for a clever scoundrel was always great,
but for a successful leg it was unbounded. He regarded Isham

as other men might a great statesman, a celebrated poet, or a distinguished soldier; he had reverenced the unknown Miles Lane, reputed to have been concerned with every extensive Turf robbery for the last twenty years, but his veneration for this personage since he had met him in the flesh as Isham Boggs was unlimited. The great Boggs having vouchsafed to take this little affair in hand, and decreed that The Cid was to win, why, of course, he would win. Of that Blundell entertained no doubt, and it was in the most jubilant frame of mind regarding the morrow that he walked home from the Punchbowl.

A soft grey December morning heralded the day fixed for the decision of the momentous question as to whether The Cid or Cis Calvert's black were the better animal. Society around York peeped from its windows with no little anxiety as it clad itself in shining raiment, for only let the weather be fine, and the races were bound to be great fun. The Lancers had been profuse in the matter of invitations to lunch, and society had due warrant for supposing itself in for a pleasant outing. Many a fair girl robed herself in fur and velvet that misty morning, in great trepidation as to what the skies might have in store; but perhaps no maiden of them all felt so nervous as Annie Aysgarth. It was a good deal more than spoilt silks or lost gloves to her this tournament, little as she dreamed what it was to be in reality; but she knew Cis had rash and heavy bets upon it, which he could badly afford to lose, and that was enough to make her nervous, let alone the thought that gruesome falls sometimes betide those who ride steeple-chases. She had not been able to conceal her fears from Cis himself only the night before, and he had made light of her anxiety.

"Nonsense, sweet," he laughed, " I know how to fall, never fear about that, and I really do think I shall beat Crymes. Harry and I tried The Mumper and Red Lancer on the Knavesmire the other morning, and over two miles Harry on the black gave me 10lbs. and a handsome beating."

" It is very foolish of me I know, Cis dear; but I shall be wretched till you are safe past the winning-post. In front, I hope, but I confess it will be a relief to me when it's all over."

"You're a foolish young woman," rejoined her lover, as he kissed her; "but mind you've bays with which to crown the victor's manly brow when he returns to your side in the first flush of his triumph; and yes, Annie darling, a beaker of something cooling to assuage his manly thirst. Don't look shocked, there was a deal of thirst about the Homeric period."

"You need not fear my looking shocked; you will be welcomed with jubilant smiles, believe me."

Still, in spite of all this reassuring love talk, Miss Aysgarth felt unaccountably nervous as she stepped into the mail phaeton which was to convey herself and her father to Crockey Hill that 12th of December.

There was a gallant array on the hill when they arrived. A temporary Stand had been erected, and was crowded with the officers and their friends. A large marquee had been pitched at the back, and consecrated to unlimited refreshment, while right and left of the Stand were numerous carriages, tapering off to tax-carts and more humble vehicles, as they receded from that vantage point. In front of the Stand a regular ring had been fenced in, and it was evident that no inconsiderable amount of business was being transacted therein. Mr. Bilton was, of course, the leading spirit, but there were plenty of his *confrères* who conducted business on a smaller scale, the majority of whom were of that class known by the designation of bagmen. 'The Vase,' open to the gentlemen of York and Ainsty, had been run, and produced a capital race, resulting in the triumph of an outsider by half a length; and now the event of the day stood next on the programme. The bookmakers were having a busy time of it, for the Tykes seemed bent on having a bet of some sort on the Cup. Sheer weight of money had brought The Cid once more to the fore in the betting, and he had recovered the position he had lost on the preceding evening in a great measure.

Most of the hunting men and the farmers were backing him, his owner and the majority of the regiment were standing by him, and yet Bilton never tired of laying, and his brethren of the mystic circle followed suit. The Mumper still ruled first favourite, although he had but a small following in comparison with The Cid, and could boast of being little more than half a point before his great rival in the quotations. It was curious to note that he was backed chiefly by the York people and strangers in contradistinction to the country gentlemen and farmers, who, with a few exceptions, went for the Major's horse. Of the other three runners, for the field had dwindled down to five, Mr. Strangford's Herodia was fancied by a few who had seen him go well on her in the hunting-field, and Radcliffe had a few believers in him, who entrusted Gil Blas with their investments for the like reason, but Captain Calvert's Red Lancer, ridden by young Harperley, was friendless. People rarely do back the second string of a stable, and yet it is curious how often the crack succumbs to it. Did not the first favourite for the Derby in the present year canter away from his stable companion at Ascot last, while the owner and his friends only awoke to his excellence after losing their money on the other?

Some little way from the Stand, but still quietly edged into an excellent position amongst vehicles of much more pretension, was a York fly. Seated in it, engaged in earnest conversation, were Isham Boggs and Tom Blundell.

"And your horse, you say, is as well as can be wished?" said the former worthy, sharply.

"The Cid is as fit as I know how to make one. In my judgment, Mr. Boggs, he don't want another hour's preparation. He ought to win right out on his own merits unless The Mumper is a deal bigger horse than I think he is."

"Very good. You must be off now. Your master will be wanting you. Listen to me. Mind you come back here the minute the Major has mounted, and wait for me. There will be fifty pounds into your hand when we next meet; but mind I do find you here, because it's just possible your horse mayn't win if I don't."

"Why, what on earth can I have to do with it?"

"Good heavens, man! is this any time to ask questions?" exclaimed Isham, impatiently. "Your master may be inquiring for you this minute. Go, but don't forget what I have told you."

Tom Blundell said no more, but darted off to where his

subordinate was leading The Cid quietly about, imbued with more veneration for Isham Boggs than ever.

The excitement is rising in the Stand, wherein most of the heroes of the coming fray are now congregated, their gay silken jackets concealed by overcoats.

What devil prompted Horace Crymes it is impossible to say, but he was suddenly impelled to crave Miss Aysgarth's blessing on his cause, knowing though he did that it could be hardly hoped for. " Won't you wish me good luck ?" he said, softly, to the banker's daughter. " I think I should about win if I only carried your good wishes."

"I am sorry, Major Crymes, but both my bets and my sympathies are elsewhere. You can't expect me, you know," she continued, laughing, " to so utterly ignore my own interests as to wish the success of The Cid."

" No," he said, with a mocking smile, "but I also have interests to protect, Miss Aysgarth. I number a large following here to-day, and I am bad to beat when in earnest. I was never more so than I am now ; the result of this race seems somehow to symbolize the result of something else that I have set my heart on, and I can give you no better advice than to hedge. The black and crimson will go down before the white and violet, believe me."

He turned away quickly, before she could answer him, and was making his way out of the Stand, when he was arrested by Mrs. Charrington's voice.

" One moment, Major Crymes, before you go. I must wish you all luck in the tournay ; remember I have pinned my faith on your colours, and, should The Cid fail me, am a ruined woman. Good luck attend you, Horace," she added, in a lower tone, " and don't be rash, if only for my sake."

Both women looked nervously after Crymes as he quitted the Stand, though from not exactly the same motives. Mrs. Charrington really was more earnest than she was won't to be in her flirtations, and did know that bad falls occurred in steeple-chasing, as when out-paced horses are called upon to jump must be the case, however clever they may be, while Miss Aysgarth was much perturbed at the Major's last speech.

She knew, as woman always do know, that devoted though he might be to Mrs. Charrington, he was also an admirer of herself, but she had never pictured his admiration as taking practical form before, and yet, if he did not cherish some hope of avowing it, what could his last words mean? Let them mean what they might, one thing was conclusive, they contained a menace to Cis as regarded the forthcoming race, and she was so anxious that he should be hailed the winner, not only because of the heavy bets he had upon it, but because of some small superstitions of her own that had come to associate it with her marriage very much in the manner Horace Crymes had darkly hinted.

The crowd began now to throng the rails of the 'run in' to see the horses canter before going down to the starting-post, which lay a little to the left of the Stand, and the first to make its appearance was The Mumper; plain and common-looking he was pronounced by the lookers-on, and the north country race-goers know a horse when they see one, but for all that he was pronounced a nice goer when Cis Calvert, after the preliminary march past, brought him back again at a smart canter. Herodia, Red Lancer, and Gil Blas followed. Nice looking hunters, said the talent, but they don't steal over the ground like that old black; and lastly came Crymes upon The Cid. The Major brought his horse down again at a good rattling gallop, and a slight murmur of applause greeted the handsome grey as he swept by with his long, easy stride.

"Not the sort to be prejudiced against, Charrington," said Julian Harperley, "not yet quite the man, from the way we've seen him go."

"I don't believe in The Cid," remarked the other grimly. "Mark me, Calvert will make a mess of him to-day."

The horses walk quietly down to the starting-post, gather together for a few minutes in a group, then the flag falls, and they are away.

"The Mumper leads!" exclaims one of those intelligent race-goers who can never by any accident get the colours into his head.

"Nothing of the sort," retorted Mr. Charrington sharply;

"can't you see that's the second colour—black, red sleeves, and *black* cap; that's Red Lancer, and, by Jove! he's leading them a cracker. Herodia second, in green, and Gil Blas, in the pink and black cap close up, the Mumper's lying fourth (you may know him by the *red* cap), and The Cid's waiting on him."

Harry Harperley meanwhile was fulfilling his mission, which was to make running for Cis Calvert. Strangford on Herodia kept close with him for the best of all possible reasons; he knew his mare could stay for a week, but she was not fast, and her sole chance of winning was to lie in front all the way, and trust to her opponents cutting their throats. If he once let them get away from her he knew she had not speed enough ever to catch them again. As for young Radcliffe, as he frankly said, he meant having 'a ride,' he didn't affect much jockeyship, and prudently held, under these circumstances, he had best keep with the leaders as long as he could, and quietly succumb when he found that no longer possible. He had very slight hope of winning, and had indeed backed The Cid for a pony, though he would have willingly jobbed the last ounce out of his horse to win the Cup.

Red Lancer was a fine fencer, and Harry Harperley streamed away with the lead, jealously attended by Herodia and Gil Blas, while as for the two leading characters in the drama they laid off, watching one another like two practised duellists when first confronted. No change occurred in the order of running till nigh half the course was compassed, by which time the three in front held such a commanding lead, that a cry rose from the Stand, "They'll never catch them. By heavens, the two favourites are out of it!"

The very next fence made a change in the aspect of things, for slipping up at the take off, Gil Blas tumbled ignominiously into the next field, leaving his rider to taste earth and see stars, and enjoy all the luxuries of a regular crumpler. But no sooner had he cleared the jump than it appeared to Cis Calvert it was getting high time to get on terms with his leaders, and gradually he commenced lessening the gap between them, while the dangerous Cid hung tenaciously at his quarters. Still Red Lancer raced away with the command, till as they rounded the flag for home Harry Harperley felt that his bolt was shot, and without a struggle yielded the lead to Strangford. Cool as ever, the latter steadied his mare, and with a quaint chuckle remarked to himself, " Two of them cooked ! but oh, dear, I suppose I shall have the swells alongside directly full of running, and we can't go much faster, can we, old woman ? "

Herodia was doing her best, and her rider knew it. Scant hope of his winning the cup, if he were collared, and just as he arrived at this conclusion he became conscious of The Mumper creeping up on his whip hand. One glance at the black told him he was out of it, for Calvert's horse was striding along, full of running, and as fresh apparently as when he started. Another second and the grey appeared on the off side, also going strong and well.

" A race between you, gentlemen ! " cried Strangford, as they passed him, " but I'll follow on just to see the finish."

Cis had now taken the lead, and was making the pace hot. For the first time in the race the Major's face darkened, and there was a slight nervous twitch of his upper lip. They were fairly in the straight run in, and niggling a little at his horse, and kneeing him a bit besides, Crymes ran up to take a feeler. He set his teeth grimly as the fact dawned upon him that the old black had the heels of him, and his sole chance lay in giving him a fall. There were but three fences now over which to do it, and Crymes deliberately drove The Cid at the next stake and binder with a view to putting his adversary down by rushing him at his fence. But Cis, lying a good length and a half ahead, and finding his horse going strong and well, had made up his mind to come straight away, and stand no more nonsense. He shook up The Mumper, and, to the Major's surprise, went right away from him. Putting him down was out of the question, for the black, when it came to racing, was unmistakably the quicker horse of the two, and catch him Crymes could not. He rode the race out steadily and judgmatically, as usual, on the off chance, but Cis Calvert passed the winning-post a good half-dozen lengths in front of him, and the Major was too good a sportsman to cut up a beaten horse in hopeless pursuit.

" Chucked away ! chucked away ! " exclaimed Mr. Boggs, as

he witnessed the finish of the race. "Why the old black beggar's a stone better than I thought him."

"Yes," rejoined Mr. Blundell, ruefully, "it is as you say, 'chucked away.' Our good thing is about as handsomely spilt as any milk I ever saw handed about. I did think you knew The Mumper's form, at all events."

"You think!" said Boggs, "don't you overheat those precious brains of yours by thinking. There's your fifty in Bank of England notes; and now off with you like a sky-rocket, and hand that note to your master at once. Tell him it's immediate, and to read it before he weighs in. Off with you, quick, if you ever expect to see the other fifty."

That fifty pounds in his hand, and the ascendancy Isham had acquired over him, sufficed to send Blundell best pace in pursuit of his master.

Horace Crymes, very sore at heart, was walking his horse slowly back to the saddling enclosure, when Blundell met him, and handed the note with which he had been entrusted. The Major had lost a biggish stake on the race, and money was money to him just now, but it was not that, he was far too practised a turfite to succumb under a reverse. No prouder man ever stepped than Crymes, and the result of the race had wounded him sorely on that point. Where was his bitter boast to Miss Aysgarth now? How shall he ever bear Charrington's cackle over the proverbial softness of grey horses? He had gone down in front of the ladies' gallery, and his character for omniscience in everything sporting would no longer be a recognized fact in the regiment.

He crushed the note mechanically in his hand as Blundell led The Cid into the paddock, slipped lightly off his horse, ungirthed the saddle, and, throwing it over his arm, walked mechanically towards the weighing-room.

"The note, sir, the note!" whispered Blundell, eagerly. "I don't know what's in it, but I was bid tell you to read it before you got into the scales."

Crymes looked at him for a minute, and then, entering the weighing-room, gazed sullenly at his successful adversary, who, saddle in lap, was going through the crucial test of Turf victory.

He dropped his eyes, and, opening the paper in his hand, glanced over it.

A triumphant smile crept across his dark face as he did so, and no sooner had Calvert vacated the scales than Crymes seated himself lightly in his place. Hardly had the clerk pronounced 'all right' than the Major, rising to his feet, exclaimed, "Is there a steward present?"

"Of course, Crymes. What is it?" replied Colonel Copplestone.

"A somewhat unpleasant business, sir, I am afraid, but I have no alternative. If it was my own money only it might go to the devil, but I have a large following who have staked their money on The Cid, and that leaves me nothing to do but to enter a formal objection against The Mumper as being a well-known steeple-chaser, and as such utterly unqualified to run for a regimental race. Captain Calvert's black horse, The Mumper, is better known as the Black Doctor, and has hit the ring hard many times down Warwick and Worcester way."

"Good God, Crymes! are you sure you have warrant for what you say?"

"It's not likely, Colonel, I should make such a charge unless I deemed I had conclusive evidence."

And in the doorway stood two men, paralyzed by these terrible words, Cis Calvert and Julian Harperley, who had come to congratulate him on his success.

CHAPTER XI.

THE OBJECTION.

FOR a few seconds Cis stood spell-bound by the charge brought against him; then he stepped rapidly back into the weighing room, and, in a voice tremulous with passion, exclaimed—

"Whether this is the case or not, do you mean to insinuate, Major Crymes, that I have wittingly run this horse as The Mumper, being aware all the time that he was a well-known steeple-chaser?"

"I should hope not," rejoined Crymes coldly, "though, considering the manner in which you have backed him, I am afraid the world will perhaps put an ugly construction on your mistake. No, don't interrupt me for one moment, Calvert. I knew nothing about this till the race was run, or I should have told you what I had heard. The information reached me on my way here just now. I have my backers both in the regiment and elsewhere; in their interests I am bound to enter this protest."

"But, good God!" cried Cis, "whether this story is true or no, you can surely not believe that I knew anything about the horse's private history? You know how I bought him."

"I must decline any discussion of the subject, and allow me to point out, have made no sort of accusation against you. This is all matter for the stewards, not for you or me."

"Excuse me!" cried Cis hotly, "you know perfectly well that if you accuse me of entering a well-known steeple-chaser in another name, and my brother officers believe that charge, I am a ruined man."

"As I have already remarked," returned Crymes, with exasperating coolness, "I make no accusation of any kind."

"Liar!" cried Cis furiously; "what else is your objection? what else can it mean?"

For a second a savage scowl darkened the Major's face, and he took a quick step or two towards his opponent, then mastering himself with a mighty effort he turned and said in low, measured tones—"Colonel Copplestone, I put myself in your hands both as a steward and my commanding officer." Simultaneously Julian Harperley secured Cis by the arm, and said, "For heaven's sake, my good fellow, restrain yourself!"

"Captain Calvert, you will return at once to barracks, and consider yourself under arrest," exclaimed the Colonel. "Such language you well know can be tolerated to no brother officer, more especially to one your senior in rank. Your objection, Major Crymes, will of course be due subject of inquiry for myself and brother stewards at once, and you will of course produce such evidence as you consider necessary to substantiate such a very serious charge."

Foaming with passion, it was perhaps questionable whether Cis would have yielded to Julian Harperley's remonstrance, but the habit of discipline is strong, and the curt, pithy order of his Colonel curbed him at once, and touching his cap to the chief he turned to obey his command.

Outside the weighing-room he was met by Harry Harperley and other friends, who had come to congratulate him on his success, but already the ominous whisper of an objection had got about, and instead of felicitations they inquired anxiously what was the matter?

"Trouble's the matter, Harry," said poor Cis, quickly, "trouble more than I can quite understand as yet. I'm in an awful mess, boy. Steal or borrow me a hack, and bring it up here at once. I've to ride back to barracks at once. I'm in arrest."

He had all the audacity natural to the cornet of a crack regiment, but 'arrest' to his youthful mind, having reference to an officer, presented a disturbed vision of pains, penalties, and disgrace beyond apprehension. Not only was he very fond of Cis himself, but he knew instinctively that this would bring sore sorrow upon his sister besides, and he loved her very dearly. If he did not know of her tacit engagement, he, at all events, was quite awake to Cis being what he called ' heavy spoons ' on Annie, and the arrangement met with this young gentleman's unqualified approval. It was with a sad heart he hurried off to find his own horse, and bring it up for his captain to ride home on.

"Mr. Harperley," exclaimed Cis, " I trust you don't believe this infamous accusation ! "

" Bearing in mind that you know nothing about the horse," rejoined the banker, " I am afraid that Major Crymes is perhaps better informed. Remember, I say distinctly that I believe you know nothing about the horse, but you must forgive me adding that, though I can make every allowance for your unfortunate loss of temper, I am afraid it has dreadfully complicated the business. At present, if you will allow me to be your adviser, I think there is nothing for you but to do what you propose ; ride quietly home, and await the upshot of events."

" If he didn't say I was a downright leg, he insinuated it," retorted Cis angrily.

" It was a cruel charge to have brought against one, and that your blood should boil over far from unnatural, but as a looker-on, Calvert, I must testify that Major Crymes brought his objection forward without throwing the slightest imputation upon yourself. He, to divest it of sporting phraseology, denounced a fraud, but he certainly did not denounce *you* in connection with it."

" Perhaps not in words, but he did in manner," rejoined Cis sullenly.

" No, I can hardly bear you out in that. Remember, you were naturally excited, and imagined innuendos that were never intended. Pray don't think I am either deserting you, much less taking part against you, but if Crymes proves his case it is bound to prove an unpleasant business. No one will be more glad to see you triumphantly through it than I shall."

" And you will tell Annie you still believe in me," said Cis in a low voice, as Harry reappeared, followed by his groom leading his horse.

" If Crymes proves his assertion," rejoined Julian Harperley, " that is nothing. As I said just now, he has never alleged that you were cognizant of the imposture."

" Good-bye," rejoined Cis, as he swung himself into the saddle ; then leaning over to young Harperley he said, " Come and tell me, Harry, what they decide about the objection. I can only solemnly declare that if it is so, Crymes knows a great deal more about the horse than I do."

All who have had anything to do with racing know what a stir and confusion an objection creates. The Major's protest was quite in accordance with the usual ordering of such things ; considerable consternation on the part of not only the backers of The Mumper, but also on that of Mr. Bilton and some of the leading ring men, who had been somehow inspired to lay more than was good for them against The Cid. In the Stand, amongst the ladies, curiosity was on tiptoe to know the true state of the case, but none of the actors in the drama reappeared.

" Where was Major Crymes ? " asked Mrs. Charrington. " Where was Captain Calvert ? Mr. Harperley, &c. ? what was the objection ? who objected ? who then had won ? " Such were the questions bandied about, and for the answering of which, no reliable male creature could be found available. At last came intelligence that The Mumper was not The Mumper, but alleged to be something else ; what, rumour was not so clear about. He was a steeple-chaser of distinction, he had won races here, there, everywhere ; he had won the Liverpool, he had won it twice, thrice ; the absurdity of describing such an animal as a hunter ! Could this have been an accident ? Somebody must have known. Somebody must have meant winning money over it ? who ? and then somehow a whisper got about that Captain Calvert had backed his horse for a big stake. First it was told that there had been a violent scene in the weighing-room between the Major and Cis Calvert, and that the latter had left the course in high dudgeon ; and finally it was darkly hinted that Captain Calvert had left the course in obedience to the strongly-expressed recommendation of the stewards, who had pronounced him guilty of practice somewhat sharper than could be tolerated amongst gentlemen in Yorkshire.

Poor Annie Aysgarth sat feeling utterly miserable whilst all these *canards* surged around her. Not a quarter of an hour ago, and, with triumphant smile on lip and brow, she was eagerly waiting to greet her lover as he returned the recognized hero of the day; and now why did he not come to her? How dare these women even hint such foul shame concerning him? Where was her father? Where was Harry? The girl had plenty of pluck, and believed thoroughly in Cis. She would laugh to scorn the suggestion that he could be guilty of aught dishonourable. She would have pledged her life upon his truth and loyalty in any matter, and it was exceeding bitter to her to listen to all these evil whispers concerning him, and not to be able to break a lance in his defence. More than once her indignation nearly overcame her better judgment, and prompted her to flash out and ask fiercely, " You know Captain Calvert most of you ; what have you ever seen in him to induce you to think that he would do anything dishonourable? In common justice give the benefit the law allows, and hold him innocent till he is proved guilty." But then, unluckily, she was not openly affianced to this man, and so shrank, as was natural, from taking up the cudgels in his behalf.

Very right was Miss Aysgarth theoretically, but practically she would have done little good had she given her thoughts words. A man is held guiltless in the eye of the law till he is proved guilty, but in the eye of society ! bah ! we know it is exactly the reverse; he is held guilty till he proves his innocence. It is this at times makes hard the pleasant fictions of society's journals. In the days when The Mumper won the Cup these conservators of the public morals did not exist; it was possible to commit card-sharping at Nice, and not have it advertised the same week in London ; divers peccadilloes might be then freely indulged in, and the world none the wiser, but in these times, good lack ! we must look well to our morals, and—and—well, let us hope at least they've improved.

At last Mr. Harperley makes his appearance in search of his daughter, and has to run a very gauntlet of interrogatories, to which he responds, that he believes the stewards have not yet given their decision, but that he understands The Mumper will be probably disqualified, having won a public steeple-chase or two before he came into Captain Calvert's hands, though quite unknown to that gentleman.

"Come along, Annie," he whispers, "the carriage is at the back of the Stand, and I don't think the Farmers' Race worth our waiting for under the circumstances. I will tell you what has happened, as far as I know, presently, but it is a very unpleasant affair, and has taken all the fun out of the meeting. From Colonel Copplestone down to Harry the —th Lancers are looking glum as undertakers over the result. Winners or losers, it seems to make little difference. Come, child, at once, I want to get away without further questioning."

The girl takes her father's arm, and as they make their way out she catches glances, shrugs, and half-smothered whispers, and knows that they are talking about her, as if it were possible to keep such secrets as that of her tacit engagement with Cis; and once more the indignant blood mantles in her face, for she feels that they are pitying her on account of her lover, and to a proud young woman such as Annie Aysgarth, who gloried and believed implicitly in her sweetheart, could anything be more humiliating? As they drove back to The Firs, Julian Harperley told his daughter as much as he had been able to gather of the affair, but as the banker had not been present at the conference of the stewards, he was not much wiser concerning the racing objection than he had been in the first instance, but he had seen what may be termed the military embroglio, and did not hesitate to tell Annie that he feared Cis, by loss of temper, had very much further complicated an already sufficiently awkward business.

The girl was silent for a second, then she said in clear resonant tones, "Neither you nor I, papa, could imagine Cis doing anything dishonourable, but I am grieved about this quarrel with Major Crymes. It is likely to create prejudice against him."

She would not have realized what such breach of military etiquette as Cis had committed really involved, even if her father had told her, but the banker had described the scene in the weighing-room as "high words passed between Crymes and

Calvert," without specifying that one significant monosyllable which from time immemorial it has been held that no gentleman can pass over.

But it speedily became apparent that all life was crushed out of the company assembled in the Stand. That vague feeling of something having gone wrong, which suffices to so rapidly break up any party of pleasure, was evidently abroad. Neither Major Crymes nor young Harperley reappeared, and, though Colonel Copplestone and some of the officers did their best to keep things going, yet there was a general stampede. It was of course known that The Mumper had been disqualified for having, unknown to his owner, won a public steeple-chase previously; but society, as it made its way home from Crockley Hill, came to the conclusion that there was more to tell than had leaked out as yet.

Harry Harperley, as one of the gentlemen riding in the race, had of course no trouble in making his way into the weighing-room, where the stewards, consisting of two officers of the Lancers and three well-known members of the Hunt, were sitting in judgment. Crymes briefly stated his case, pointed out that his knowledge had only come to him after the race was run, and that, in justice to his numerous backers, he had no alternative but to bring it before the stewards.

The evidence was overwhelming, there could be no doubt that The Mumper and the Black Doctor were one and the same horse, and that under the latter name he had a few years back been a steeple-chase horse of no little celebrity. The Mumper was accordingly disqualified, and the race awarded to The Cid.

Harry Harperley, had only stayed to hear the decision. No sooner was it pronounced than he jumped into Radcliffe's 'whitechapel,' which was waiting for him at the back of the Stand. That young gentleman was his sworn ally, and, like himself, a firm believer in Cis Calvert, and the pair were very seriously concerned about the aspect of things. The insult Cis had passed upon Crymes had certainly not been before all the world, as the saying goes, but still there had been some half-dozen people present, and something of the truth had already oozed out. When six people conspire, one usually acquaints those whom it is most desirable to keep in ignorance with all particulars; though in Ireland I am told six conspirators produce as a rule seven informers, and judging from the *cacoethes loquendi* displayed by Irish members of Parliament, it is easy to imagine so; therefore it was not to be much wondered at that some account of the quarrel between the two men was about.

" I shall be at mess, Radcliffe," said Harry, as the trap pulled up in front of the officers' quarters, " if it is only to hear what our fellows think of all this business. In the mean time I must run up and tell Calvert what the stewards' decision was." Radcliffe nodded. " It's rough on him, but this row with Crymes is the trouble. I don't think any one in the regiment would believe Cis was wittingly committing a fraud, and any horse that has ever won public money is, we know, not qualified to run for the Cup."

Calvert was sitting, looking somewhat moodily into the fire, when the cornet entered, but roused himself immediately, and exclaimed, " Now, Harry, let's hear all about it. I fancy Crymes knows a deal more about The Mumper than I do."

" The Major first made his objection, as you may suppose, laying particular stress upon the point that he knew nothing of The Mumper's history till after the race. Then that Dick Hunsley Mappin told us of appeared, there were plenty there who knew him, and stated he had bought the horse in the spring of last year in Warwickshire; that he knew him as the Black Doctor, and his performances were on record in the ' Calendar '; he had bought him merely to hunt, and changed his name, as he didn't want to be chaffed about riding a steeple-chaser. He told of whom he had bought him, and the groom who had fetched the horse from Warwickshire was there to testify to the fact; but further than that he had fetched the horse from there at the time stated, his evidence was of little consequence, as he did not know the horse's name. Hunsley next produced a letter, dated a few days back, in which William Gurwood stated, in answer to a letter he had received on the question, that he had sold the Black Doctor, by Dicebox out of Ebony, to Richard Hunsley on the 20th of April, '51, for value received."

“And they seemed to think there was no doubt about this story?” asked Cis.

“No; they sent for Mappin, who gave the same account of how The Mumper came into his possession that he had already given to you. The story sounded only too true, and as that precious rascal, Dick Hunsley, said, ‘If I’m not telling the truth, gentlemen, it’s mighty easy to send into Warwickshire and see Gurwood; you’ve got his address.’”

“Yes, it can scarcely be a vamped-up story, but it is hard lines the terrible scrape it has got me into.”

“Well, now there comes a point which I can’t help thinking was in your favour. You don’t for one moment suppose, Cis, that any of us doubt your good faith in the business,” interposed the boy quickly, “but there are some don’t know you as we do.”

“You’re loyal, very loyal, to your captain, Harry,” replied Calvert with a faint smile.

“As if we won’t all stand by you; but what I was going to say was this :—Charrington, a steward, as you know, although he declined to act on this occasion, having, as he said, bets on the race, was present ; suddenly he scribbled a few lines on a leaf of his betting-book, and passing it to the chief, said, ‘I think, Colonel Copplestone, you would find it useful to ask this question.’ The chief showed it to the other officials, and then with their assent inquired :

“‘Why, Mr. Hunsley, knowing all this, did you not interfere earlier ?’

“‘It was no business of mine,’ was the sulky response.

“‘But there has been plenty of betting in York about this race ; there was a good deal, for instance, I understand, at Harker’s last night. You must have known all the time that The Mumper had no right to start. Why did you not let Captain Calvert or some of us know the state of the case ?’

“For a second Dick Hunsley looked puzzled, then a sullen scowl darkened his face. ‘Well, if you will have the truth, gentlemen, you shall. Why didn’t I? Because it suited my book not to do so. I had a score to settle, and money to get by it, and I’ve been racing too long not to collar coin when I can, and cry quits with those who’ve put me in the hole. The man who sold me up was backing The Mumper, and I—well, I backed The Cid.'

" 'Thank you, Mr. Hunsley, I don't think we need trouble you further,' said the chief, and that's how the case stands, Cis."

" I should hope Hunsley's evidence is sufficient to exonerate me from all imputation of knowing The Mumper's previous history," replied Calvert, "but I am in a big scrape besides that. I am in arrest, as you know, and can hardly guess how that matter will finish ; then I've had a baddish race of it besides. I only hope you hadn't much on The Mumper."

" No, I took that two hundred to fifteen from Strangford, and had a tenner on my mount, that's all. I've lost a pony, and that matters little, but I'm terribly grieved about you."

" Pooh !" rejoined Cis, " I shall pull through. Give my love to your sister, tell her what you have told me, and tell her—you can, Harry, can't you ?—that you don't believe I am capable of such a piece of rascality as winning the Cup by a shameful fraud. That I rode and won in all innocence that my horse was anything but the hunter I bought him as."

" I don't think any one of your friends will ever suppose any-thing else," cried Harry, with a slight gulp in his throat. He was cruelly hurt at the foul imputations he had already heard whispered against his captain, and had not learnt to avoid display of his best feelings as we do mostly later on in life. " Now I must run away and dress for mess," and Cis and his cornet ex-changed one of those hand grips into which Englishmen condense a flood of sentimental language.

But when Harry Harperley had left the room, Cis reverted to that very much grimmer view of the situation he had been musing over before the youngster had entered. He knew that his quarrel with Crymes might probably become a serious thing for him, so serious, indeed, as to necessitate his retirement from the service ; then he had lost, for him, a very heavy sum of money, and unluckily the bulk of it to Crymes, all of which had to be forthcoming in two or three days. Two circumstances these to make the victim thereof regard the last twelve hours as an ill-spent day. How marvellously penitent and filled with good intentions I have seen men on the day after the Derby; but to what extent rancorous tongues, combined with unfortunate appearances, can mar a man's life Cis has yet to learn; a very imperfect idea as to what constitutes hard lines as yet seething in his brain.

CHAPTER XII.

EASTWARD HO.

PEOPLE who lose money racing are only too prone to believe that they have met with unfair play, but in this case there could be no doubt that a very serious fraud had been attempted, and the backers of The Mumper, who in a very large proportion hailed from the city of York, were by no means reticent of speech on the subject. At Harker's, indeed, Mr. Bilton, and several minor bookmakers who had followed his lead, and been rather bitten in consequence, were profuse in their denunciations of what they termed another of those military swindles. Something had impressed them with the idea that The Mumper was sure to win, and they had not scrupled to overlay their books about The Cid; not so much by any means to be pitied as those unfortunates who had backed the black, and had to go through that grimmest of all racing experiences, the winning money and not receiving it, but, on the contrary, having to part with their own. To have to pay, say ten pounds instead of receiving thirty, is wont to curdle the milk of kindness in the veins of humanity. Tongues waxed wicked at Harker's and elsewhere as they wagged over the subject, and public opinion was decidedly coming to the conclusion that Captain Calvert had planned an artful *coup*, had been detected, and ought to be made a pretty severe example of.

"I was told this Mumper was sure to win," remarked Mr. Bilton oracularly, "but the man as gave me the tip didn't know what the horse was, d'ye see. I wonder how Major Crymes got hold of it; I suppose that Hunsley told him."

There was a talk, too, about the race at the Punchbowl, and a small knot of the *habitués* might have been observed to wear a

smile of beatitude, little part as they took in the conversation.
As for Mr. Boggs, he was not to be seen, and the barmaid, in
reply to inquiries, announced that he had left, but for where she
did not know. The good man was wont to absent himself after
successful management of little affairs of this nature; whether
he feared the undue curiosity of friends, or deprecated their congratulations, who shall say? It might have been he was tender-
hearted, and disliked hearing the wail of those who suffered sorely
from his astute manipulation of the strings.

At the club in St. Leonard's Place there was, as may be supposed, much talk about the race, and gradually the idea gained
ground that, protest his innocence as he might, Calvert had been
perfectly cognizant of what the horse really was all along, and had
intended a *coup* with him. It was argued that Cis had backed
The Mumper heavily in comparison with his usual scale of betting.
It was pointed out that Harry Harperley had bragged, after that
dinner at Byculla Grange, that his owner knew a good deal more
about the black than the public dreamed of; in short, it was not
difficult to give a very ugly complexion to the matter when you
began to collect evidence.

"Those ring men, too," said a veteran sportsman, who, with
his coat-tails subducted under his arms, was standing on the
hearth-rug, and luxuriating in all the warmth of the coffee-room
fire, " knew something. They went for The Mumper. Now
what put that into their noddles if they believed him a black
hunter? I fancy there was a whisper about that the old horse
had shown himself pretty smart between the flags once or twice
before."

"You're right, Collison," said another. "I happen to know
Bilton pretty well, and when I was backing The Cid for a tenner
with him he said, ' I'm afraid you're on the wrong pea this time,
sir; I'm told this is a real good thing for The Mumper.''

"It certainly does seem most extraordinary that any one can
buy a well-known steeple-chaser without being aware of it. Still
I'm told that Mappin declares he knew nothing about it, and
Calvert bought the horse from him," said a third.

"That might be all a blind," rejoined the first speaker. "That
fellow, Hunsley, we know is a crafty scoundrel. I take it he

bought him, and rechristened him with a view to something of this sort. To put him through Mappin's hands was a clever dodge to disarm suspicion. If Calvert was ignorant of the horse's real character, what made him back it as he did? His own people say he never risks more than a pony on a race, and in this case we know he backed his mount for hundreds. We know the story of his bet with Crymes on the night of the entries, and it is no secret he backed his horse besides on various occasions, this is the most awkward thing against him in the whole business. Heaven knows I don't want to throw stones at a man who is said to be in a pretty big scrape besides, but I think people generally will be hard to convince of Captain Calvert's ignorance concerning The Mumper. As for Hunsley, circumstances not having favoured his committing a robbery himself, that he should seize such a chance of turning money as this offered, is quite in accordance with his general character, and that he should turn round upon his confederates precisely what he might be expected to do. No, if Captain Calvert is innocent in this matter, then he is a most unfortunate man, and victim to a curious combination of events."

The club oracle had spoken, and as all frequenters of the smaller of these monachal institutions are aware, when the Collison of the establishment has taken the hearth-rug, which does duty for a rostrum, and pronounced judgment therefrom, the minds of many men became decided on the point in discussion. Windbag though the oracle may be, and utterly incompetent of forming an opinion on any subject whatever, yet, till he do be pricked, he shall impose upon the weaker brethren who lack his lung power and assurance.

At the mess of the Lancers that night, also, was the event of the day discussed after the cloth was drawn, though in very much more guarded fashion than it had been commented on at the Club. Cis was popular in his corps, and they were very loth to believe evil of him, indeed the majority stood staunchly to the dictum that he was a victim instead of a victimizer, and yet his stoutest partisans were fain to admit that the identical point which so exercised the York Club was difficult to get over. What had induced him to bet so very much heavier than his to a satisfactory conclusion, and then they also followed Crymes's example.

"I suppose you've got something to say to me," observed the Colonel, seeing that Calvert still lingered.

"I have first to thank you, sir, for taking my word about that miserable race, and holding me innocent in spite of appearances; next I have to beg the favour of three days' leave."

"What for?"

"To arrange an exchange. I cannot continue to serve in the —th Lancers under these circumstances. Were we likely to change station very shortly it might be, but I cannot face this neighbourhood as things stand at present. I have thought the whole thing out quietly in the last forty-eight hours. I am perfectly innocent, but presumption is so strong against me, that I run the risk of being cut in the hunting-field, of being requested to withdraw from the Club, &c. This will not only be agony to me, but excessively unpleasant for the regiment: thank God, as a whole, they believe in me, but to champion my cause would be to put themselves on a very uncomfortable footing with the neighbourhood. Further, I have strong private reasons, which I need not enter into; and lastly, I have lost a good bit of money, which I shall recover by exchanging to India."

For a few minutes the Colonel made no reply, but seemed to muse over Cis's speech. Then he said quietly, almost gently for him, "I shall be very sorry to lose you, Calvert, and if it was only the money, I fancy it could be easily arranged, but we cannot control the opinion of Yorkshire, and I am bound to admit that there's a deal of common sense in what you say. Given we were living in the old duelling days, we couldn't call out the biggest county in the kingdom. It's unlucky, but it's no use blinking the fact, the case against you is terribly strong. Take your leave, exchange, if you still think it best, at the end of that time, but remember you are not obliged to go, and that if you elect to stay your Colonel will stand by you."

At the expiration of the three days Cis returned from town, proceeded at once to the Chief's quarters, and informed him that he had arranged to exchange to an infantry regiment in

India, receiving a difference of two thousand pounds, and next day it was known through the —th Lancers that Calvert was leaving them, and on account of the race for the Cup. There was much commiseration expressed among his staunch friends in the corps, men who believed in him despite the terrible circumstantial evidence against him ; but Cis, under pretext of having a good many things to arrange, kept aloof from his sympathizers. There were murmurs against Crymes, but here the Major's guarded tongue stood him in good stead ; his assailants were always confounded with the unanswerable rejoinder " that he had exposed a robbery, but never hinted even that Calvert was concerned in it ; that it might as well be said that he had charged Harry Harperley and all other backers of The Mumper with being participators in the fraud, which was absurd." Cis meantime rapidly concluded his final arrangements. He had said good-bye to the Colonel and a few other of his intimates, and settled to leave York by the night-mail for town. He had nothing left him but to write his farewell to Annie, and as he sat down to do that he dropped his head hopelessly on his hand, and reflected bitterly what a terrible change a short week had made in his prospects. To leave the dear old regiment under such a cloud was sad enough, but ' the crowning sorrow ' was having to resign Annie. What was he to say to her ? He had stipulated that he should be allowed to write this letter, and now his heart failed him, and he almost felt that he would have rather stole silently away.

" I must bid you good-bye, darling," he wrote at length, " yes, leave you with but a distant hope of ever claiming you for my own. That you disdain to think I could have been wittingly guilty of the disgraceful fraud with which I am unhappily connected, is the one comfort left to me in my troubles. It was like your own sweet self to stand by the accused and believe him innocent, black though the allegations against him looked. But, Annie, the chivalry must not be all on one side : I could not ask you to be mine while this stain hangs over my name ; were it poverty and exile only, I would ask you to have faith, and wait for better times. As it is, I can only restore you your troth. If, when I have righted myself

usual habit? When we see a man who habitually plays whist
at shilling points suddenly take to five-pound ones, we seek the
cause of the phenomenon, as indeed in social life we do any
extraordinary increase or decrease apparent in our neighbours'
expenditure. A thing this that would trouble some people seriously, leading to liver complaint and all sorts of disturbances of
the system, till they got to the rights of things. It certainly was
unfortunate that Cis had, so to speak, plunged upon this unhappy
race. But on the other point, namely, his insult to Crymes, the
regiment was very much more divided, and the majority, which
numbered in its ranks most of the senior officers, held that there
Cis Calvert could not be justified, that the objection had been
made in perfect good faith, and with all courtesy; no imputation
whatever had been preferred against Calvert, and that there was
no justification possible for the use of the opprobrious epithet he
had made use of. Those who by seniority were best qualified to
judge shook their heads, and opined it would be apt to go hard
with Calvert, though, as they added meditatively, the Colonel
always stood to a good man in a scrape, and more than one story
of the irascible martinet's good deeds was told round the ante-
room fire that night.

They did their Chief no more than justice. No man in the
county of York, unless perhaps it was the delinquent himself,
was so utterly upset by the whole thing as Colonel Copplestone.
He liked Calvert, and believed in him, but, nevertheless, he saw
at once that many people would not do so, but regard the whole
affair as an iniquitous swindle. The race he foresaw would be
a most unfortunate slur upon the regiment, a thing ever to be
flouted in their face, and very difficult to disprove. Then, again,
there was the military *fiasco* to be dealt with, and that the
Colonel felt must be settled at once. If the Major would consent
to accept an apology there was no necessity for the thing going
further, but if not, well, then, it would be beyond his power to
arrange, and must be referred to higher authority. The first thing
was to send for Crymes: the Major was in his quarters, and
promptly responded to the summons, and the two men talked the
thing over. Crymes was perfectly willing to leave himself in the
Chief's hands, and expressed no vindictive feeling on the subject.

"I don't want to make eating his words unnecessarily hard for him, sir. If Captain Calvert will apologize to me here in your presence and that of the other officers of his own rank, I shall be content to let the thing drop."

"Very good, then, I shall consider that so far settled. You are letting him down quite as easy as is possible, and he ought to feel that. I believe him thoroughly innocent, but it's a doosed ugly story to have against one, and a monstrous unpleasant thing for the regiment."

"I have strictly abstained from expressing any opinion on Captain Calvert's conduct," rejoined Crymes; "but you can hardly expect the York Club and the neighbourhood to be so reticent."

"And you think their verdict will be condemnatory?"

"I think it is very probable that they will find it difficult to believe that a man who backed a horse—what for him was very heavily—almost immediately it came into his hands, did not know something about its previous history. Please bear in mind, Colonel, I don't express these as my views, and that what I am about to say is said to you alone. I think there are many men who will argue that the very robbery Hunsley intended, and which the enforced sale of his horses doubtless prevented, has been carried out by Captain Calvert, and there is usually much incredulity displayed as to *accidental* robbery," and Crymes put a cruel inflexion on the adjective as he finished the sentence. The Major was right; loyally though the regiment as a whole stood to him, and though he had still many staunch friends in the neighbourhood, yet Cis Calvert heard from Harry Harperley and others that the public verdict was against him, that he was held guilty of having committed a disgraceful fraud, which was only betrayed at the last moment through the treachery of a well-known scoundrel who had contemplated it himself.

And then Cis began to realize what this race had cost him. It was a terrible Pavia, he had not even saved his honour. All was lost: his commission, he supposed; the girl he loved; money. He was a man without a future. He would leave York, not a beggar, but a man whose life was broken. No wonder that Harry Harperley told his sister that he never saw a man so cut up as Cis Calvert was by the foul charge under which he lay; and Annie, with eyes half-blinded with tears and half lightening with anger, rushed to her desk and hastened to scribble a few passionate lines of scornful disbelief in the calumny, and unswerving affection on her own part, and bade Harry take it to the poor prisoner with all speed. She had pictured him to herself in a cell when she first heard of his arrest, but rigid cross-examination convinced her that he was merely prohibited from leaving his rooms.

That little note, though torture to Cis, did him good. It braced him up, roused him from his stupor of despair, and made him pull himself together. Yes, the first thing to be done was to write to Julian Harperley, and while pledging his honour to being guiltless of the accusation laid against him, to, for the present, resign all pretensions to his daughter's hand. "Till I have lived down or disproved the stigma under which I at present stand it can scarcely be supposed that you will tolerate me in the light of a son-in-law, and, moreover, I love Annie far too dearly to think of inducing her to link her future with one whom most of her friends regard as a black-leg. Pray thank her for her trust and belief in me. It is a consolation to me in my troubles to know that she still counts me a gentleman. What my future plans may be it is impossible for me to decide until I know the Colonel's intentions. As soon as I can I shall send you word what they are, and though I don't venture to ask leave to say good-bye to Annie, indeed shrink from the pain such an interview would be to me, I do claim the privilege of writing her a farewell letter."

Julian Harperley was meditating over what steps it behoved him to take in the matter of this semi-engagement of his daughter when he received Calvert's epistle. He had no disposition in the world to judge Cis at all hardly, but he could not shut his eyes to the fact that his proposed son-in-law was in a very serious mess just now. As far as the affair with Crymes went, Calvert had lost his temper, and was palpably in the wrong; while about the race, appearances were as black as they well could be. The banker had heard the arguments so tersely expressed by Crymes from more than one person that morning. The Club coffee-room at lunch time rang with them. If innocent of the horse's real character or identity, what induced Calvert to back it as he did ? Julian Harperley was a kind man, and not given to judge his fellow-creatures harshly; moreover, he knew this would be a sad blow to his daughter, but he could not make up his mind to a verdict of 'not guilty.' The best he could do for the hapless man was to mentally bring him in '*not proven.*' Still he could not but recognize the ring of true metal in that letter. The banker was aware that his daughter's was no half-hearted love, and that did he choose, Cis Calvert could influence her strongly through it, even in defiance of her better judgment. He confined himself at present to a brief acknowledgment of the epistle and an intimation that he would reply at length as soon as he received Captain Calvert's next communication.

A little more and Cis was summoned to Colonel Copplestone's quarters, and it was made known to him that he must pass beneath the Caudine Forks. "I like you, Calvert, and believe you as straight a young fellow as ever served under me. By heaven ! sir, I believe you perfectly innocent in this matter; but by George ! there was no excuse for your using the language you did, and you must apologize for it to Major Crymes at once in the presence of these gentlemen," said the Chief sharply.

" You all know with what I stand charged," replied Cis, simply. "I think some allowance is to be made for the indignation with which any man must at the moment regard such a terrible accusation. It has been pointed out to me that Major Crymes made no kind of reflection on myself, and never insinuated that I was party to the scandalous fraud which I assisted to commit. I beg to apologize for the expression I used in my anger, and to withdraw it most utterly before you all."

" I trust, Crymes, you consider that sufficient," said the Colonel, "and that this affair may now be considered as disposed of."

" Certainly, sir ; I am satisfied if you are," returned the Major, and touching his cap to the Chief, and with the slightest possible salutation to Calvert, he immediately left the room.

For a few seconds his brethren in rank lingered to shake hands with Cis, and express their gratification at the affair having come to a satisfactory conclusion, and then they also followed Crymes's example.

"I suppose you've got something to say to me," observed the Colonel, seeing that Calvert still lingered.

"I have first to thank you, sir, for taking my word about that miserable race, and holding me innocent in spite of appearances; next I have to beg the favour of three days' leave."

"What for?"

"To arrange an exchange. I cannot continue to serve in the —th Lancers under these circumstances. Were we likely to change station very shortly it might be, but I cannot face this neighbourhood as things stand at present. I have thought the whole thing out quietly in the last forty-eight hours. I am perfectly innocent, but presumption is so strong against me, that I run the risk of being cut in the hunting-field, of being requested to withdraw from the Club, &c. This will not only be agony to me, but excessively unpleasant for the regiment: thank God, as a whole, they believe in me, but to champion my cause would be to put themselves on a very uncomfortable footing with the neighbourhood. Further, I have strong private reasons, which I need not enter into; and lastly, I have lost a good bit of money, which I shall recover by exchanging to India."

For a few minutes the Colonel made no reply, but seemed to muse over Cis's speech. Then he said quietly, almost gently for him, "I shall be very sorry to lose you, Calvert, and if it was only the money, I fancy it could be easily arranged, but we cannot control the opinion of Yorkshire, and I am bound to admit that there's a deal of common sense in what you say. Given we were living in the old duelling days, we couldn't call out the biggest county in the kingdom. It's unlucky, but it's no use blinking the fact, the case against you is terribly strong. Take your leave, exchange, if you still think it best, at the end of that time, but remember you are not obliged to go, and that if you elect to stay your Colonel will stand by you."

At the expiration of the three days Cis returned from town, proceeded at once to the Chief's quarters, and informed him that he had arranged to exchange to an infantry regiment in

India, receiving a difference of two thousand pounds, and next day it was known through the —th Lancers that Calvert was leaving them, and on account of the race for the Cup. There was much commiseration expressed among his staunch friends in the corps, men who believed in him despite the terrible circumstantial evidence against him; but Cis, under pretext of having a good many things to arrange, kept aloof from his sympathizers. There were murmurs against Crymes, but here the Major's guarded tongue stood him in good stead; his assailants were always confounded with the unanswerable rejoinder "that he had exposed a robbery, but never hinted even that Calvert was concerned in it; that it might as well be said that he had charged Harry Harperley and all other backers of The Mumper with being participators in the fraud, which was absurd." Cis meantime rapidly concluded his final arrangements. He had said good-bye to the Colonel and a few other of his intimates, and settled to leave York by the night-mail for town. He had nothing left him but to write his farewell to Annie, and as he sat down to do that he dropped his head hopelessly on his hand, and reflected bitterly what a terrible change a short week had made in his prospects. To leave the dear old regiment under such a cloud was sad enough, but 'the crowning sorrow' was having to resign Annie. What was he to say to her? He had stipulated that he should be allowed to write this letter, and now his heart failed him, and he almost felt that he would have rather stole silently away.

"I must bid you good-bye, darling," he wrote at length, "yes, leave you with but a distant hope of ever claiming you for my own. That you disdain to think I could have been wittingly guilty of the disgraceful fraud with which I am unhappily connected, is the one comfort left to me in my troubles. It was like your own sweet self to stand by the accused and believe him innocent, black though the allegations against him looked. But, Annie, the chivalry must not be all on one side: I could not ask you to be mine while this stain hangs over my name; were it poverty and exile only, I would ask you to have faith, and wait for better times. As it is, I can only restore you your troth. If, when I have righted myself with the world, I find you still free, then, dearest, I shall once more plead my cause, and fervently trust to a willing ear. Don't quite forget one who can never forget you, and whatever the future may have in store, believe me ever your own,—Cis.

"P.S.—Harry will enlighten you as to my plans for the future."

"Good-bye, Harry," said Cis, as, with a big cigar in his mouth and enveloped in a heavy overcoat, he stood at the open door of a carriage in the railway station at York, waiting for the train to start. "I'd have liked to have given you The Mumper, but it would never do to leave the old horse in the regiment; he would be a perpetual reminder of this wretched race, and you can understand how anxiously I long for it to be forgotten. Tell Mappin he's to dispose of him, but not in these parts, and credit me with what he fetches, less his own percentage; and, Harry, that note's for your sister. You can tell her all about me, and you've got my address, and, and God bless you, my boy. Remember me to—" and here Cis got a little choked in his voice, wrung young Harperley's hand, and sprang into the train.

CHAPTER XIII.

A LITTLE TURN UP.

Julian Harperley's astonishment was great when the next day his son told him that Cis Calvert had exchanged into an infantry regiment in India, and already left York for good. The banker felt a sense of intense relief, for he had been much troubled in his mind as to what was to be the upshot of Annie's semi-engagement. He was loth to believe Calvert guilty, and yet he could not honestly say that he deemed him innocent. He felt that to consent to any betrothal between him and Annie was impossible as things stood at present, and yet he knew that his daughter would fire up at the slightest imputation upon her lover, and hold herself beneath contempt if she did not stand true to him in his hour of trial. They must have come in collision upon this point, and to thwart or oppose the girl in anything would have been very grievous to Julian Harperley. He was compelled to admit that Cis had behaved with great delicacy in the whole business, and felt more inclined to believe in his innocence than he had yet done.

"He was awfully cut up, poor old boy," continued Harry, "and more about Annie than anything else; but, as I said, she'll stand to him and wait till he comes back. When we heard he had gone away on three days' leave we had no idea what it meant. We thought it was something about money; he lost a good bit over the race, you know. He kept it all quite dark the first day after he came back. It wasn't till he came to saying good-bye to his old pals that we knew he was going to leave us, and, by Jove, in a few hours he was gone. I saw him off, poor old chap, and he said I was to tell you everything, and give this note to Annie. It's a confounded shame, and I believe that beast Crymes has something to say to it," and the boy's voice shook a little as he uttered the last words.

"You will be writing to him, of course," said the banker, after a little. "When you do, remember me, and tell him that I am highly sensible of the delicacy and consideration he has shown, and thoroughly approve of what he has done."

But it was hardly to be supposed that Miss Aysgarth would take things as quietly as her father. He had told her that Cis had written to him, and would write again when things were definitely settled. She knew from her brother that the quarrel between her lover and Crymes had been successfully patched up, and she knew that Cis had gone up to town on three days' leave. She was not, therefore, at all disturbed at not having received an answer to her note; and when Harry handed her Cis's farewell billet, she received it with a flush of exultation, and marched off to her own room to peruse it in comfort. No sooner had she read it than her face fell, and the tears welled into her eyes. What did he mean? Surely he would never go without at least saying good-bye to her! He knew she held him guiltless; she had told him so. When was he going? What was he going to do? She did not understand it all; and then the girl's eyes fell upon the postscript, and having hastily bathed her eyes, she descended in search of her brother.

She found him in the drawing-room. The Cornet was so unhappy about the whole business that he had lingered there on the chance of her wanting him, and in answer to her eager questioning he briefly explained what Cis had done.

"And you mean to tell me that he has gone—gone for good?"

"Yes, Annie; I saw him off myself last night. It seems awful hard lines that a fellow who has simply been awfully sold should be accused of being a leg and a robber and all that. I don't understand why Cis should have to go—no, that's not right, because he especially told me to remember that he was not obliged to go; that the Chief had said so."

"Then why has he gone?" exclaimed Miss Aysgarth.

"He thought it best himself, and two or three of the seniors, friends of his, mind, I know think he is right."

"And I know he is wrong," cried the girl passionately. "Oh why, Cis dearest, could you not take counsel with your promised wife? Who ever overcame a scandal except by facing it? To run away from a lie is to endorse it. I don't know, Harry, who his counsellors were, but believe me, he has been ill-advised."

"I don't know about that; there are things you women can't quite follow. I don't pretend to be able to myself. I'd pledge my life on Cis Calvert being straight as a line about anything; but to hear some of those fellows argue the case is enough to drive one mad; and upon my soul, Annie, I sometimes wonder they don't accuse me of knowing all about it too."

"They well might," she replied, sadly, "if you gave vent to half the mysterious hints to others you did to me. I suppose you have Cis's address."

"Yes; and though he didn't say so, I think he'll feel pretty bad if he doesn't hear from you before long."

"Write it down for me. I don't want to give him cause of complaint just now. If he had but put faith in woman's wit instead of man's he'd have been still in his old rooms. The one scrape I was incompetent to advise upon he is clear of; about the other I'd have said emphatically, face it to the last, we'll live it down together."

"You're a rare plucked 'un, Annie," exclaimed the Cornet in undisguised admiration of his sister's thorough-going partisanship; "but I don't think the governor would quite have stood that, you know."

"What do you mean?"

"That I don't think he's likely to consent to any marriage between you and Cis Calvert just now."

"I'll never marry any one else," rejoined the girl quietly. "Still," she continued more softly, "I don't think I could wed any one without the dear old dad's consent. And now good-bye, Harry. Remember I'm always to know everything you hear about Cis; and yes, dear, he'll be your brother some day."

With these words Miss Aysgarth left the room; but when the spirit of prophecy possesses man or maiden on the topic of matrimony, the narrator cannot refrain from smiling as he calls to mind the misogamist, those of his friends who vowed they would marry money, and those more romantic, who vowed they would marry for love, and thinks how seldom man carries out his original intent.

When Horace Crymes became aware that Calvert had left the regiment, he saw at once that 'the something' he had scarce ventured to hope for had intervened in his behalf. He congratulated himself upon the reticence he had maintained throughout the whole business. Far from any one being able to allege that he had ever insinuated aught against Cis, there was the record of their quarrel to prove the contrary. The regiment would testify he had never for one moment suggested that Calvert was a party to the fraud, or had known the horse to be other than he had described him. Miss Aysgarth, in common justice, he thought, could hardly decline his acquaintance on that account, more especially too as she could not pose in the position of being Cis's *fiancée*. She surely would have been the last woman to wish that any friend of hers should unwittingly do anything wrong. He, Crymes, unluckily did not obtain his information in time to prevent Calvert starting the horse, but he was able to stay the consequences of his luckless imposture, and surely no gentleman would wish to win a race fraudulently, or the bets connected with it. The Major could not help laughing to himself as he went over the high moral line of argument he intended to take up with Miss Aysgarth; but he was a shrewd man where women were concerned, and knew that in his own interest he had best avoid that young lady as yet. Specious and unanswerable as his story was, he felt that she would not regard it in that light at present. No, Calvert out of the way, there was plenty of time; he could afford to wait before he commenced the siege.

That the world generally should consider Cis's disappearance a tacit admission of guilt was exactly what Miss Aysgarth foresaw; and stand up for him as his friends might, it was obvious that public opinion ran hopelessly against him.

Known to be a friend of Captain Calvert's, and people dropped speaking on the subject before you, and if you persisted in introducing it, listened with a smile of polite incredulity.

One of the few partisans Cis had outside his old regiment was Charrington. Although he had lost his money over the race, he persisted dogmatically in the Captain's innocence, and vowed he should live to convict the real perpetrators of the fraud yet. He held closely to what we happen to know was the true story, namely, that Mr. Hunsley and his friends had contemplated winning a big stake with the renowned Mumper; but that when they, from force of circumstances, lost their horse, they had jumped at the opportunity the Cup race had afforded them of getting that stake by the objection. His dislike to Crymes, and his persistent habit of taking opposite sides from his wife, had no doubt something to say to his opinion, though perhaps it had little to say to his actions. It was always so—he usually differed with Mrs. Charrington, but the lady invariably had her own way. He always disliked her cavalier *servente*; but that gentleman was, nevertheless, like a tame cat in the house. Hence it happened that while Byculla Grange as a house made mock moan that one of society's favourites should have deviated from the paths of virtue and been convicted of cheating, yet the master himself stoutly declined to believe that it was so.

Thirty years ago, ay, and a good deal later, cheating at cards when detected carried social ostracism with it; in the genial times in which we now live I doubt the offence being considered very heinous. It is devoutly to be trusted that we are getting more civilized, for no one with any knowledge of the world can pretend that we are getting more moral.

That Mrs. Charrington should launch more than one winged arrow in poor Annie's direction was only too natural. She was not the woman to forego an obvious advantage of that nature. Miss Aysgarth's admirer had gone down in the tilt-yard with smirched scutcheon before her own, and she cannot forego some slight taunts upon the occasion, not a little impelled thereto because she had detected signs of wavering allegiance, she fancied, on the Major's part.

But the weeks wear on, and the story of the race gradually fades away. Cis's accusers have long forgotten to babble to his detriment, and it is only in the hearts of a few of his staunch friends that luckless Cis Calvert is remembered. There is little fear he should be forgotten at The Firs, and Annie and Harry Harperley pass many an hour over an enlarged map of India, studying the station in the Deccan which Cis has written to Harry to tell him is his destination.

"I'm told, young 'un," he wrote, " I've exchanged into the very slowest infantry regiment in the whole service. They've been in India the last eighteen years, and have almost forgotten their own language ; the officers speak a species of *patois*, a mixture of English and Hindoo ; the ladies of the corps are mostly more or less dark—begums, I presume, who have forgot themselves, and thrown away their future on the impoverished youth of the Feringee ; but some, I fancy, are of less distinguished lineage. Sport, I am told, in the way of shooting is plentiful of all sorts ; but for society—well, I see I am not to expect it regimentally. What does it all matter to me ? I have come here for a specific purpose, and shall know no peace till the scandal is either lived down or my name cleared, and that I may once more address your sister as her affianced lover."

Cis Calvert might make light of the future that lay before him in his letter to Harry Harperley, but it was with a sad heart that he took his berth on board of one of Green's clippers, and made sail for Madras.

But there was another thing that shortly arose out of The Cid's triumph in the Cup, and that was, that Mr. Blundell's insolence and arrogance became past bearing, and created no little ill-feeling amongst his co-mates. Mr. Blundell, it must be borne in mind, had his pockets very handsomely lined by the result of the race, although Isham Boggs, in strict accordance with the principles that characterized his career, had contrived to decamp without paying quite all the money he had covenanted to do. Still, bets and one thing and another made Tom Blundell more flush of coin than perhaps he had ever been before in the whole course of his life. He was a moderate *viveur* in his way, and when in funds rather enjoyed dispensing hospitality in somewhat patronizing fashion. The grooms and stable-men of the corps were no more averse than their betters to the good things of this world, and a man who was open-hearted in regard to the standing of drinks could naturally depend upon a considerable following.

Mr. Blundell never tired of jeering Tim Murphy about 'the black colt,' as he humorously designated The Mumper, nor of telling the story of how he ferretted out the great Mr. Boggs, and so got at the truth concerning the horse ; and his sycophantic following, as they tossed off their glasses, would indulge in such phrases as—" It was 'cute of you, Tom, there's no denying ; but then, d—n it all, man, you're Newmarket raised," or, " Well, the way you turned that poor devil Tim inside out, and put the puzzle together afterwards, was a caution."

So it came to pass that the myrmidons of the officers' stables were divided into two parties, of whom the smaller faction were headed by Blundell, and the larger sided with Murphy. About what they differed was not so clear. There was bad blood between Blundell and Tim over the race naturally, but why their respective partisans should have established a feud was difficult of explanation. However, so it was, and the taunts of the Blundellites, chiefly instigated by that gentleman himself, served further to embitter it.

" Well, my whistling friend," said Mr. Blundell, as on his way to his own stables he passed Tim strapping a horse, "have you got never another secret to let out ? It was uncommon kind of you to bring me and Mr. Boggs together, it was ; blessed if we should ever have got at the history of that 'ere black colt of yours without his help. You'd better have let me stand in, eh ? "

" Yez'll go a thrifle too far, my jewel, one of these fine days," returned Tim drily. " We knew nothing about our horse, though it seems you did."

Mr. Blundell responded to this by a wink, and singing a verse of a slang popular lyric—

> "The painted bit is in his mouth,
>   They're slating him, oh my !
> Although, my dear, I'm from the south,
>   Susannah, I am fly."

" By me sowl, if you insinuate the Captain knew anything about it I'll spoil your face for a congregation of baboons," retorted Tim fiercely.

" Knew ! " rejoined Blundell, tauntingly, and advancing a step or two nearer to the Irishman. " All serene," he continued. " Knew ! I suppose he didn't back that old black devil as if he knew something. Knew ! oh yes, he knew, which fully accounts for the milk of the cocoa-nut," and Mr. Blundell wound up by snapping his fingers in the Irishman's face, a compliment which Tim promptly reciprocated by knocking him down.

This speedily produced a rush of some half-dozen or more of on-lookers to the spot, and Mr. Blundell, having picked himself up, at once challenged his antagonist to come round to the field at the back of the barracks and have it out there and then. This arrangement was so completely in accordance with the feelings of the handful of gentlemen assembled, that an adjournment thereto was immediately made. No sooner had they arrived than seconds were selected, the two men stripped to the waist and stood up to one another. It was at once apparent that Tim was considerably the bigger man of the two, having considerable advantages in height, reach, and weight, but as a set-off against these it was very soon apparent that the Newmarket man had been taught to use his hands, while Tim, in the old prize ring vernacular, was but 'a countryman.' They fought some half-dozen rounds, and in the beginning Mr. Blundell, thanks to his superior science, had unmistakably the best of it ; but Tim took his punishment doggedly, and came up again and again, and forced the fighting as if having it all his own way. No doubt superior weight and strength served him a good deal, but there was one thing aided him a good deal more, and that was, Mr. Blundell was not a very good plucked one. It was all very well while he was fresh, and having things pretty much as he liked. So long he was bumptious enough, but when it settled down into a ding-dong give-and-take business, Mr. Blundell found himself the recipient of some pretty rough handling, and got too weak to stop Tim's fierce rushes and rather round hitting ; then he got very sick of the job, and speedily announced his intention of giving in, as the Irishman was too big for him. His seconds, their own frontispieces not being in danger, nobly exhorted him to

" Take a suck at the lemon and at him again."

But Mr. Blundell said he had had enough, put on his upper
garments, and scandalized his supporters by declining to be
beaten insensible.

This little turn up had one result—Mr. Blundell came to the
conclusion that chaffing Tim was rather an expensive amusement
if it was to be paid for by such a rough twenty minutes as had
been his lot that morning, and kept his gibes at the Irishman's
expense for the immediate ears of his intimates only.

Thanks to Blundell's babbling and what he already knew,
Tim was now aware that the mysterious Isham Boggs who had
exhorted him to call at the Punchbowl was the source from
which Major Crymes had derived his information as to The
Mumper being in reality a horse called the Black Doctor; and
after much cogitation Tim thought it right that this knowledge should be in the hands of some friend of the Captain's.
But who, was the question. Tim first thought of Harry Harperley, but at length decided he was too young. Then he hesitated a good deal about taking his tidings to the banker. He
thought over this for some time, but finally, he could hardly tell
why, came to the conclusion to tell such story as he had to tell to
Mr. Charrington.

Tim might not arrive at his conclusions quickly, but when it
had permeated his brain that this was the gentleman most likely
to take the cudgels up hotly in behalf of his old master, Tim
took the first opportunity of presenting himself at Byculla
Grange.

CHAPTER XIV.

THE ROYAL DUNBARS.

LOUNGING in one of those low cane easy-chairs with flat elongated arms, so much in vogue both in America and the East, is a man who looks out from the verandah of his bungalow with a jaded, wearied expression somewhat sad to contemplate. He stares listlessly across the dusty road at the sandy, rock-studded plain, while he sucks lazily at his cheroot, and his thoughts wander back to the best fox cover in Yorkshire, a soft November day, and such an afternoon as comes but rarely in the lives of most men. How he loathes this everlasting sunshine, how he detests the country, and how he wonders what is to be the end of it all.

Cis has joined his new regiment at Secunderabad in the Deccan some months now, and though he has honestly tried to make the best of them, is fain to confess they are beyond him. They are a class of men with whom he has hardly an idea in common; promotion has been slow, the corps years in the country, and all the men of his own standing in the service are not only very much older than himself, but so completely Indianized that he fails to get on with them. The younger men take their tone from the seniors, and as Cis mentally remarks, such a fossillized regiment he never supposed to be existent.

The seniors are like so many military Rip Van Winkles, and he constantly expects those stupendous tiger-shooting reminiscences to be varied with some personal experiences of the siege of Seringpatam.

On the other hand, there can be no doubt that Cis had been viewed with distaste from the first. These tough old Anglo-Indians were not prepared to look favourably on a light dragoon.

"We don't mean to stand any of his Lancer swagger here," had been said concerning him more than once before he appeared amongst them; and when he did they resented his youth. That a captain barely thirty should presume to take his place amidst these grisly centurions was in itself a reminder of the inequality with which the prizes of the profession were dispensed. That 'a young whippersnapper,' to use their own term, who had been lounging about Hounslow, Hampton Court, and Brighton in kid gloves and varnished boots, whilst they were fighting and frying, should have attained similar standing in the military hierarchy to their own was in itself a cause of irritation; and then to complete the list of his offendings, Cis openly expressed disgust with the country and its customs, and could not refrain from an occasional smile at the peculiar habits of the veterans by whom he was surrounded.

A more curious living picture-gallery than the seniors of the Royal Dunbars it was impossible to imagine. That it was advisable to live temperately in a tropical climate was a maxim which, if it had ever been brought to their attention, they evidently had no belief in; they were what is termed free livers, and late in the evening their various somewhat obsolete peculiarities came out. Two of the veterans were fire-eaters, with fond memories of the old duelling days, and it was no uncommon thing with either of these gentlemen to leave the mess-room with somewhat uncertain step, and a scowling intimation that you should hear from them in the morning; but of course the menaced one never did, and was met next day without the faintest allusion to the trifling difference of the night before. To say of two or three of them, oh, *splendide mendax*, would be to cast an unmerited reflection perhaps upon them as a whole; but though they had all more or less talent in that way, after the custom of those whose brains have ripened under a tropical sun, yet were there some few gifted beyond their fellows in this respect. Men whose adventures in regard to tigers, elephants, hair-breadth escapes, and matters of gallantry held their comrades awe-struck, and, curious to relate, the venerable stories always elicited the same attention and applause. One of their number indeed was wont to act as fugleman on such occasions, and bringing his hand down with a mighty smack on the dinner-table, direct the laughter and applause. Whatever these elderly Lotharios might have committed in their youth, it is certain that their days of devilment were over; they never went into women's society, and the apparition of a lady would have paralyzed the tongues of the gay old dogs, and eventuated in their slinking off to their respective bungalows in most admirable confusion.

That Cis should feel utterly miserable among associates of this kind may be easily imagined. That the few married ladies of the corps were what he had libellously asserted them to be was of course not the case; but still they were women of little attraction, and whose talk was simply cantonment gossip. He had been six months doing duty with the Royal Dunbars and had not an intimate in the regiment, and had further the comforting reflection that he had attained considerable unpopularity with the seniors. He had failed to be impressed with some of those tiger stories; he had been detected yawning at their repetition. He had even stopped old Jungleton, the champion Ananias, in his crack story about the 'must' elephant with an intimation that he had heard it before. A slightly incredulous smile had been detected on his face when Brevet-Major Lovejoy narrated that little episode of his affair with the collector's wife at Burruncompoota. In short, the centurions of the Royal Dunbars voted Cis a supercilious beast, and fought shy of him accordingly. His life was hideously monotonous— duty and the dulness of a mess dinner, books, and rackets. Friends he had none. In his isolation from feminine society— a bitter thing to men of Cis Calvert's stamp—he had imprudently said that he did not believe there was a woman in the cantonment worth knowing. His remark had been bruited abroad, and was not calculated to make things more pleasant for him.

He was sitting listlessly at mess as usual one night when he heard Jungleton suddenly exclaim—

"I say, Lovejoy, have you heard the news? Daventry is coming here as chief of the Commissariat; there's a chance for you, you dog!"

"Ha, ha !" chuckled the disturber of the collector's peace, "I leave that sort of thing now to the young ones, but I've heard plenty about Mrs. Daventry in the upper province. There'll be a row here, Jungleton, mark my words, before the year is out. Never knew the Daventrys twelve months in a place that result didn't come off."

"I presume the Daventrys are people with a history," remarked Cis.

"I should rather think they are," growled old Jungleton. "It's a thundering shame a fellow like that should be kept on the staff, while men who have seen twice his service are still grinding away at regimental duty. Why, there's hardly a play scandal for the last twenty years he hasn't been more or less mixed up in, and as for his wife—Well, they say, Calvert, the ladies of the cantonment don't meet your approval ; I shall be curious to hear what you think of Mrs. Daventry."

"I'm not likely to see much of them ; play is not the least in my line, and from what you say I judge that forms a prominent feature of the Daventry *ménage*."

"That's a delusion a good many men have fallen into. I tell you what, though I don't suppose you'll think much of my opinion, you may consider you understand women,—all young men do,—but just bear in mind you don't understand tigers."

"I don't understand you," said Cis, laughing. "You surely cannot mean these Daventrys are as dangerous as all that. I'm not in the least likely to make love to the lady or play *écarté* with her husband."

"And immediately the cock crew," muttered the veteran. "If you won't take a hint I've no more to say. I've slain a good many tigers in my time, but when you are not prepared to kill them it's safest to keep out of their way."

Cis' curiosity was somewhat excited, and he would have fain questioned Jungleton further concerning the Daventrys ; but the old warrior declined any longer discussion, and the subject rapidly disappeared from Calvert's memory.

He was cantering home from the racket court one evening, and pulled up at the band as he often did, hovering in darkness on the outskirts of the circle, and keeping well away from the lights of the music-stands on account of some strange ideas the General commanding entertained on the wearing of uniform on such occasions. A carriage drawn up in a somewhat prominent position attracted his attention, more from the men that swarmed round it than from anything he could see of the occupants; that it contained two ladies was easy to make out, but from where he was it was impossible to make any guess at their personal appearance. Twilight there is none in the tropics, and the band in India discourses its harmony in what has been termed 'a dim religious light.' Turning to an acquaintance Cis inquires, "Who is the attraction over there?"

"That? Oh, that is Mrs. Daventry, just arrived. She's a sweet pretty woman, and carries on pretty much as if Daventry didn't exist. I don't know her, but she has the reputation of having brought most of her admirers to grief."

"Thanks," replied Cis. "I shall hope to have a good look at her some of these days; no seeing her just now. Good night."

Weeks passed on, and Calvert thought little about the Daventrys. He heard they had taken one of the best bungalows in the place, and entertained a good deal. Daventry's dinners were said to be 'monstrous well done,' while Mrs. Daventry's weekly receptions were talked about as quite the pleasantest entertainments in the cantonment; but Cis so rarely went into society that he had never come across them, and though, after the Indian custom, whereby the new-comer is expected to take the initiative in the matter of calling, Major Daventry had left a card upon him, yet Cis had never troubled himself to return it.

But if he had thought but little of the Daventrys, the lady felt no little curiosity about him. That she was speedily *au courant* with all the gossip of the station was matter of course, and what she gathered about Cis Calvert piqued her not a little.

This ex-light dragoon who had suddenly appeared in what a woman like Mrs. Daventry knew to be a very heavy regiment indeed was a phenomenon worth investigating. A man who had done that must have come badly to grief in some way. She couldn't help puzzling her pretty head as to what had brought Captain Calvert into the Royal Dunbars. His speech about the ladies of the cantonment, which had excited such indignation when first noised abroad, made her smile. She had not been there at the time, and so could very properly consider herself as not included in the category, and she rather admired what in these days is designated 'side' in a man. That Captain Calvert rarely entered society again interested her when she heard it.

"Don't think Indian society good enough, I fancy," remarked a good-looking youngster to Mrs. Daventry, in answer to some leading questions on this point. "In fact, he's rather too great a swell for us, and we could do without him very well."

"Perhaps you don't know him as yet," rejoined the lady.

"That's just it," cried young Heckington, "we don't; and I tell you what, Mrs. Daventry, I suspect he don't want to know *us*."

From what she had heard of the Royal Dunbars, Mrs. Daventry could imagine that possible of a man who had probably mixed in the London world. Captain Calvert, in short, aroused her imagination. What crime or misfortune had cast this lost planet without his natural firmament? Why was he so far from Hounslow, Ascot, Hyde Park, Belgravia, and the happy hunting grounds? She had slight experience of these in her own person, and could not at times help wondering how she became linked to the plausible gambler who now controlled her destiny. Controlled! The world generally would have said that Lizzie Daventry had taken her life in her own hands, and did as she liked with small reference to her husband. One person knew better, and that was Lizzie Daventry herself. It was seldom her lord interfered, but when he did, no man ever exercised marital authority with more relentless severity. She had plenty of pluck, was by no means deficient in spirit, but she dare no more face the Major's cold, cutting sneers than brave public contumely by running away from him; and she had been sometimes sore tempted to discharge her matrimonial obligations in that fashion. What she might have been under happier auspices it is useless to conjecture. She was now, she might justly plead, what Hugh Daventry had made her. That distinguished officer's career had been a mystery to a good many of his professional brethren; he passed tranquilly from one good staff appointment to another with a halo of scandalous stories surrounding his name that would have sufficed to ruin the prospects of any other man. But there are those gifted with the faculty of skating over thin ice, and Daventry was one of them. His moral character might not stand high, but his ability was undoubtedly great, and in those days perhaps the former was less considered than the latter in official appointments. Hugh Daventry had proved himself a smart soldier more than once when opportunity had offered, and in our restless Indian empire it is seldom a man finds that long lacking; while there could be no doubt about one thing, that wherever the Daventrys might be stationed their house formed a central feature of the cantonment. You might recall many a story you had heard to the Major's detriment, but there was no denying he was an excessively well-bred, agreeable man in his own bungalow. You might have heard tales of the heartless coquetry of his wife, but it was not easy to remember them against the pretty high-bred woman who received you with such a charm of manner. This probably was the secret of their im-munity. Anglo-Indian society has never been accused of being puritan in its morals, and was not likely to hold aloof from the pleasantest house in the station because the host and hostess were talked about. Everything was well done at the Daventrys', and you were sure to meet all the best people of the place there.

Still Captain Calvert had never yet made his bow, nor even acknowledged the courtesy of the Major's card. The two men had met a few times in the racket court, for Daventry had been a good player in his day, and although past his best was no despicable antagonist even now; they had got on very well together on these occasions, but nothing more. The Major was not the least inclined to stand upon ceremony when he wanted to know a man, and he had rather a hankering to know Calvert. He was the sole man in the cantonment that had the slightest conception of the cause of Cis's presence in Secunderabad. An old cavalry friend at Mhow had remarked in a letter—" So you have got Cis Calvert at your station, tumbled down to infantry in consequence of some scrape at York. I don't know the particulars, but fancy he lost a lot of money over some regi-mental race. He was, I think, about the best of that very hard-riding lot three years ago, and if you should want a jockey

I recommend you to cultivate his acquaintance. I don't know much of him myself, but have always heard he's a deuced good fellow to boot." Daventry never threw a chance away, and nothing was more probable than his wanting some one to ride for him at the Ski races in the autumn. Still Cis was not the sort of man you could force an intimacy upon, and Daventry, who had graduated in good society, had quite tact enough to see that.

There was little interchange of confidences between the Major and his wife; but when people entertain there is of necessity some discussion of those among whom they are cast, if it be only with regard as to the issuing of invitations, and in this manner Mrs. Daventry had learnt the little her husband knew about Calvert, and had also been informed that she was not to neglect an opportunity of making his acquaintance. She was not likely to do that, for her curiosity was much exercised concerning him. Accustomed to be sought after, *fêted*, and made much of wherever she went, she felt piqued that Calvert had not sought her acquaintance. If he had been some old Indian misoginist she would never have troubled her head about him, but that the whilome crack horseman of the —th Lancers should be vegetating in an Indian cantonment perplexed her much. What was this scrape that had transferred him to the Royal Dunbars? Was it play, or an *affaire de cœur?* Mrs. Daventry was a woman of some experience with regard to both those thunderstorms of social life, and could have imparted sound advice in such exigency. She had seen Cis on some two or three occasions, and was bound to admit that though well-looking enough, there was nothing striking in his appearance. A fair slight man of medium height, with no particularly good feature in his face, if we except the mouth; that was small, with a well-cut expressive upper lip, which, now the moustache, in compliance with the regulations, had been ruthlessly shorn, was almost too tell-tale. Women, as a rule, read faces they care to study better than men, and, as the physiognomist well knows, the mouth is the index feature. In the few glimpses she had caught of him nothing had struck Mrs. Daventry so much as the weary look that played around Cis Calvert's lips. Hugh might think it a play scrape of some kind that had brought this man to India; Lizzie Daventry felt sure there was a love-story of some sort at the bottom of it, and felt all the curiosity of her sex to be possessed of that tale.

If there is one phase of the irony of fate more striking, though common, than another, it is the way we are constantly compelled to know people we have distinctly made up our minds we never will know. You avoid them successfully for years; the danger has been escaped so long you have ceased to think about it, when lo, at some social gathering, before you can open your mouth to expostulate, some fussy busy-body has brought you face to face with your *bête noir*, and exclaimed, "Let me make two men who ought to know each other acquainted." Nothing for it but to grin and express your delight, and walk home afterwards indulging in ferocious anathemas towards your well-meaning friend.

Cis Calvert had not more particularly avoided the Daventrys than he had society generally, but he had been very successful, as may be supposed, in maintaining the seclusion he desired. You must have the reputation, at all events, of a good deal to bestow before people, finding their first overtures unmistakably rejected, persistently endeavour to cultivate your acquaintance.

Chance, which determines a good many things in this world, at last made Cis acquainted with the Daventrys, and it happened in this wise. A man Calvert had known something of in England arrived at Secunderabad *en route* for Nagpore. He was also an acquaintance of the Major's, and in accordance with the Arabian custom of hospitality prevailing in India in those times, quartered himself without scruple on the Daventrys. Having accompanied his host to the racket court, he there encountered Cis, and greeted him cordially. There were a few allusions to old days, and then the Major chimed in with—

"Come and eat your dinner with us to-night, Calvert, and then you and Wrotsley can have a gossip over old times. I've no party for you, nobody but ourselves, unless Mrs. Daventry has picked up by good fortune a waif or two who have consented at short notice to break the monotony of a family dinner in Wrotsley's behalf."

And not knowing exactly what other answer to make, Cis assented.

CHAPTER XV.

MRS. DAVENTRY.

As Cis Calvert dressed for dinner he cursed the facile disposition that had led him to accept an invitation he would have fain declined. He reflected ruefully, as many of us have often done, why was he not more ready with his lie? It is as well to have a store of such subterfuges handy in case of being asked to join in what we dislike. They are not very hard to improvise, but they are still easier to keep in stock, and yet is anything more common than that plaintive social cry—"I don't want to go, but how could I help it? I didn't know how to get out of it." Cis has no particular feeling against the Daventrys; he has known something of society's black sheep in his time, and feels bound to confess that their folds were usually pleasant places; but he shrinks from all society at present, and the idea of this dinner is exceeding irksome to him. Wrotsley and he were very good friends some five or six years ago, but he does not feel impelled to get enthusiastic about Wrotsley at present. Daventry he knows to be pleasant, and Mrs. Daventry he hears is. He wonders a little what the lady is like, for as yet he has never really seen her. He knows the carriage by sight at the band, but the sun has dipped below the horizon always before that discourses sweet melody, and in the semi-darkness of a tropical evening it is impossible to form much idea of the fair occupant. She, on the contrary, had seen him through glasses on more than one field-day, and is perfectly conversant with his personality.

"They say she is both pretty and pleasant," muttered Cis, as he adjusted his neckcloth, but the fellows here are naturally uncommon liberal in their verdicts to that effect. Any tolerably good-looking woman ought to pass for a beauty in these parts, and as for pleasant, hum, that's always matter of opinion, and a point upon which I and most of my brethren of 'the Dunbars' would hardly coincide."

A few minutes before eight Cis swung himself on to the back of his 'tat,' as those clever slaves of ponies are usually called, and cantered quietly across to the Daventrys' bungalow. If he had been asked what he expected to find his hostess like, he would probably have replied with a smile—"Oh, a bold showy woman, with a rather pronounced manner," and was no little surprised when Daventry presented a slight fragile brunette with magnificent dark eyes to him as his wife. Her quiet self-possessed bow and the rather *trainante* tones in which she welcomed him, were also very much the reverse of what Cis had pictured to himself. Lizzie Daventry's quick eye detected in a minute that she was other than he had expected, and resolved to make the most of the impression she saw she had produced.

" India I am told is all new to you at present, Captain Calvert, she remarked, as she signalled with her fan that he should drop in the chair next her. " I must not therefore ask you how you like it, because I feel sure you detest it. Men always do ; boys who have just escaped from school or college may be delighted with it, but for those who have really known life at home it is a terrible change. Some of us get reconciled to it in time, but it is rather dreary work in the first instance."

" I don't complain," returned Cis ; " I came here of my own free will, so why should I ? The ways of the country take a little getting into, and I've perhaps hardly mastered them yet. One may not like it as well as home, but still make out very well all the same."

" Some do, but not such as you, Captain Calvert," replied Mrs. Daventry with a faint smile.

" Why, what can you know about me ?" exclaimed Cis.

" Not very much," returned the lady, " but still perhaps a little more than you fancy ; but dinner, I see, is announced, so perhaps you will give me your arm. That you have not been asked to a more formal banquet rests upon your own head."

" Yes, it was rash, I know," replied Cis, as they passed on to the dining-room, " to venture within the precincts without having properly salaamed in the porch ; but I'll plead guilty to being bad at calling at any time, and especially upon intruding on a strange country. This Indian idea of the new-comer calling upon the old residents is both a tyrannous and appalling system."

"'The argument hardly applies in the present case, as I think, Captain Calvert, it was our misfortune to stand in that painful predicament as far as you were concerned."

Remembering that unreturned call of the Major's, Cis felt that this was an unprofitable topic to pursue, and could hardly help laughing at himself for having given such a palpable opening ; as if women did not even keep as careful register of those unpaid calls as an Israelite of an unmet bill.

" You are mistress of the situation, Mrs. Daventry," he replied at length. "What am I to plead in mitigation ? Sultriness of climate, sulkiness of man, or simple oblivion of social amenities ? I put in all three pleas, mind, and then further plead I am already sufficiently punished."

" How so ? " she asked, raising the grand dark eyes to his for an instant.

"In having been for many weeks without the privilege of Mrs. Daventry's acquaintance."

" Ah, there's a touch of the *beau sabreur* about that speech," she rejoined, laughing ; " so I suppose I must forgive you. Cut those ducks up for me, please, in token of having taken service under my banner. No, I don't quite mean that, but as sign that there is amity between us."

" I trust so," said Cis, as he proceeded to dissect the couple of wild duck in front of his hostess ; " and now, would you deem me very rude if I ventured to ask what you may know about me ? "

" Very little in truth. It was rather woman's braggadocio than actual fact that remark of mine. All we know of you is this, that you were in the —th Lancers, and supposed to be about the best horseman in that very hard-riding regiment."

" And you never heard why I left them ? " rejoined Cis with a bitterness in his tones that made Mrs. Daventry stare.

"No; but I have all a woman's curiosity," she replied quietly. "Only please bear in mind, Captain Calvert, I am not inviting a confidence. Our acquaintance hardly justifies that sort of thing as yet, nor do I think you likely to be one of those who burns to unbosom himself to the first-comer."

"I'm not given to boring my fellow-creatures with extracts from my biography," rejoined Cis tartly.

"He will tell me the whole story before the month's out," was Lizzie Daventry's mental commentary on this remark.

" A most unnecessary labour, as you will see when you come to understand India. The gossip of the station will supply all details of your birth, parentage, and mis-spent life. Don't think me flippant, Captain Calvert, when I use the word mis-spent. I merely mean that it is the *betises* of your career you will find chronicled, while your good deeds, if you have any, and my experience of men scarce lends itself to the belief, will remain unrecorded."

"Not much good to recount of most of us," rejoined Cis, "I'm afraid; but you speak rather more bitterly concerning us as a whole than I think we deserve."

"It may be I've good cause," rejoined the lady, slightly dropping her voice, and stealing a glance at Cis from under her long dark eyelashes; " but it's time Mrs. Cornwallis and I left you to your wine. She and her husband live in the next bungalow, and when I heard your serene highness, who had so far declined our acquaintance, meant honouring us, not daring to receive you *en famille*, I asked them to come at short notice."

"Am I never to be forgiven ? " said Cis, lifting a chair out of her way as she moved towards the door.

"Yes," she replied, with a little nod, " if you make your appearance in the verandah for coffee within a reasonable period."

Cis bent his head in reply, and then turned to exchange reminiscences with Wrotsley, leaving his host to entertain Dr. Cornwallis. These talks over old times come to all of us, and no one can deny their fascination. Albeit we have a vague remembrance that we detested the place when there, and that the companion now calling up the old scenes to our imagination was one of our special aversions ; yet our heart warms to it all, we express fond desire to see the old place again, and think how mistaken we were in our friend ; that he really is by no means a bad fellow, and we regret we hadn't known him better in those days gone by. All a delusion ! He has presented us with a pair of roseate spectacles, recalled to us the years that are flown, brought back for an hour to each of us

' Ma jeunesse que je regrette.'

Poof ! if we saw the place again we should hate it, and if we saw much more of him we should quarrel with him. Similarly, it is a common weakness of men to implicitly believe in certain cates of their boyhood, in some cake or pudding the equal of which they never have the good luck to meet in mature life. If ever they do once more cross that peculiar pie or pastry, a sad wail over the deterioration of the artist's culinary powers is the invariable result.

But interchange of reminiscences is apt to be rather a prolonged affair, and Daventry, having asked Cis expressly to talk over old times with Wrotsley, could hardly suggest their curtailment, consequently it was some time before they adjourned to the verandah on the other side. Mrs. Daventry welcomed them with a sweet smile, and Cis bethought him of following up his dinner conversation, but in that he was mistaken. Mrs. Daventry chose to play hostess, and dexterously attached Wrotsley to her side, so that Cis was left to make acquaintance with Doctor Cornwallis, a shrewd, pleasant man, with much experience of the country, and who had known the Daventrys on and off at various stations for the last ten years.

"You must find the Royal Dunbars a somewhat quiet-going lot after the —th Lancers, Captain Calvert," remarked the Doctor, sententiously, as he ejected a cloud of smoke from between his lips.

"Why, did you know anything of the —th Lancers?" inquired Cis carelessly.

"Yes, I knew them well enough some twenty years ago, when they were out in this country, and a mighty wild lot they were then, and by all accounts they're not much steadier now. You look astonished at my venturing such an opinion, but remember, India is nothing, after all, but a vast military camp, and then, given to gossip as we are, the doing of our comrades at home have always considerable interest for us. There is hardly a regiment out here that could not be said to have its military correspondent at home in the shape of some one who writes to an old friend in it."

Cis glanced keenly towards the speaker, but in the semi-darkness of the verandah it was impossible to see his face. Was he speaking at random? or did these people already know the history of that miserable race? It did not make much difference, he thought; if they did not now they doubtless soon would. What a fool he had been to suppose it wouldn't follow him to India! His first impulse had been right, namely, to leave the service altogether, as if he remained in it he would be always liable to have it thrown in his teeth; but here his reverie was interrupted by his host, who proffered another cheroot.

"Hope you don't dislike this smoking in obscurity, Calvert," he exclaimed, "but we old Indians rather affect it. We get a little too much of the brilliant sunlight, and learn, like bats, to revel in the nightfall; however, after you've smoked that we'll go in, and I dare say my wife will give us a little music."

"No more tobacco for me, thanks," replied Cis, rising. "We are given to hope, Mrs. Daventry, that you are about to crown your hospitality by playing to us."

"I will either play or sing to you with pleasure, if you are quite sure you wouldn't rather lounge here, talking, smoking, and watching the fire-flies. I *can* sing, Captain Calvert; it happens to be one of the things I know I do well, but pray don't think it incumbent on yourself to ask me because you have heard I do sing."

"I can imagine Mrs. Daventry doing most things well," rejoined Cis, "and trust she will allow us to judge of her singing."

"I don't profess many accomplishments," rejoined the lady, smiling as she rose, "but I possess one given to few of us. I comprehend my *métier*. I know what I can do and what I can't. I can ride, dance, and sing, and have, perhaps, some one or two other gifts, the which I shall leave Captain Calvert to discover; and now reciprocate my candour and unfold your accomplishments."

"Don't know that I've got many," replied Cis, as they entered the drawing-room. "I can both ride and dance a bit, can shoot decently straight, and that's about all. I can't sing, and don't pretend to be clever. I got my commission in the pre-educational days, you see, which was lucky. I was eminently adapted, indeed am still, for a profession in which you were not expected to know."

"Oh, I have little doubt you are sufficiently wise in your generation. What shall I sing you? do you like ballads? There is, I think, nothing so delightful, when properly sung, in the shape of singing as the ballad; but of course you may give it like a musical box, or you may make the water stand in people's eyes."

"I quite agree with you, and it is the former rendering that we more usually encounter in society."

"This is a favourite of mine. A man's song more than a woman's perhaps, but it always strikes me as so unutterably sad," and striking a few chords with practised touch on the piano by way of prelude, she burst into Kingsley's famous ballad of "When all the world is young, lad." The dash of spirit and boyish hope of the first verse were given with exquisite fire and animation, and then the flexible contralto voice sank to mournful regret as the singer commenced the second with "When all the world is old, lad," finally descending almost to a wail of despair as she faltered out the concluding words—

> " Creep home and take your place, lad,
> The halt and maimed among ;
> God save you find one face, lad,
> You loved when all were young."

To Cis, still chafing at his exile, the ballad as rendered by Lizzie Daventry appealed powerfully. He wondered how he should find things at The Firs when he 'crept home.'

It was all nonsense, of course, that a man should be so moved as Cis was by this ballad, but we must remember what had happened to him in the last few months, and further, how he loathed this weary Indian exile to which he as yet saw no end. He felt almost as if his battle of life had been fought, and he had nothing left him but to drag himself sore stricken out of the fray. Annie, his good name, position—all were gone. He stood silent some minutes after the song was finished, but Mrs. Daventry interrupted him never a word. Like a true artist she appreciated this mute acknowledgment of her powers very far beyond the conventional " Oh, thank you's !"　" How delightful !" etc. She saw his lip twitch, and knew that his thoughts were far away. She perceived that she had touched some chord connected with his trouble, whatever it was, and once more she felt curious about the reason of his presence in this country. Lizzie knew enough of the ways of soldiers to know that men don't as a rule leave the light cavalry for infantry in India except under extreme pressure.

" What has driven Cis Calvert here?—play or a woman," thought Lizzie with a toss of her worldly little head. " And I mean him to tell me which before the month's out."

" Shall I sing you anything more, Captain Calvert?" she asked at last. " I am afraid my mournful ballad has leavened you with its own spirit. I ought not to have chosen it, but I had no idea that it would have so depressing an effect on you. No, don't thank me; your silence was more eloquent than anything you can say. Do you know this ?" and Mrs. Daventry dashed off into Kenny's charming ballad of " Why are you wandering here, I pray ?" to which she gave plenty of point and archness.

" What a magician you are," said Cis, as she finished. " Yes, you can bring tears into our eyes, or charm the blue devils away from us as you list. I'll not compliment you further than saying, whatever Mrs. Daventry says she can do, I for one shall devoutly believe in for the future."

" I am really pleased to sing to you. I am so sick of the conventional compliments on my performance. To see that you have made any one feel," said Lizzie, with an expressive glance of her dark eyes, " is a triumph for any songstress."

"I am indebted to you for the one pleasant evening I have passed in this country," rejoined Cis ; "and now, Mrs. Daventry, I think it is time to say good night. The matutinal habits of India are unholy in the extreme ; people are all afoot before my late comrades had gone to bed. It's healthy, I know, to lie kicking at and cursing mosquitoes, but I can't help wishing the Royal Dunbars kept their whist table going an hour or two later."

"Going to bed early don't suit you ? I suppose you haven't got into it as yet."

"No, indeed. I've tried hard to break myself into the habits of the East, but retirement to rest at eleven is usually productive of rising at one and smoking a cheroot with a view to produce sleepiness. But go to bed early or go to bed late, I'm always sleeping the sleep of the just at gun-fire, and feel tempted to strangle that miserable malefactor who, under a pretence of being my servant, calls my attention to the fact that the dressing bugle has gone."

"Ah, I dare say it does come hard. I was broke into it young, and then we women are not so conservative in our habits as you. We have more adaptability. But remember one thing, you have broke the ice, Captain Calvert, and at last cast aside the hermit's robe. I hope we shall see more of you in future, and further bear in mind, that I am 'at home' always on Wednesday evenings, and that when your rubber dies out at the mess of the Royal Dunbars you will always find one here on that night. Neither Hugh nor I are given to lengthy slumbers ; four or five hours always suffices for me, though I plead guilty to persistently indulging in what some people call the fatal habit of the siesta —rubbish ! as if it was not common to all the sun countries. Good night."

Cis clasped his hostess's little palm and made his reverence, and then having shaken hands with Daventry and Wrotsley, and made his adieux to the Cornwallises, swung himself once more into the saddle and cantered home.

Arrived at his own bungalow, he proceeded to mix himself a bucket of soda and brandy, then lighting another cheroot, sat himself down after the manner of solitary man to think over the events of the evening. Yes, Mrs. Daventry was very different from the woman he had expected to see ; he had pictured her a showy, affected woman, full of airs and *agaceries*, betraying an unpleasant consciousness of her charms, with a mouth filled with foolishness, and eyes that challenged all male creatures to flirtation, and he was fain to confess there was not the faintest trace of the vulgar beauty of his imagination about Mrs. Daventry. She was undoubtedly a very pretty woman, but anything more unaffected and unconscious than her manner it was impossible to conceive.   When she said she *could* sing there was no trace of her being vain of that accomplishment.   She stated it as a fact too well established to make a fuss about, just as a man of established position never manifests any anxiety concerning it, and she had certainly good warrant for what she said.   Cis could not but admit that he had never heard sweeter ballad singing, and he had thought Miss Aysgarth highly gifted too in that way. The studied simplicity of her dress too was perfect; but one of the great attractions she had for men was, that under her soft caressing manner she permitted them to divine that she was unhappy, that she was not understood.   It was this lent such magical charm to her music.

" The anguish of the singer made the sweetness of the strain." Ah, how many men have succumbed to these misunderstood women, the titillation to their vanity is so irresistible ; they pity the lady, and think the husband a brute in the first instance ; gradually it is insinuated to them that their society affords some consolation ; had they only met when she was free ; from that to 'kindred spirits,' and the final catastrophe, is but a step, and the *dénouement* is generally in the hands of the lady ; with her it rests whether the fly within the meshes escape with scorched wings or two lives are ruined.

Do not suppose for one moment that Cis Calvert had any wild fancies of this nature. He only thought that Mrs. Daventry was a very charming woman, who sang very sweetly, that it was a house it would be a relief to drop in at occasionally, and so break the deadly monotony of this Indian life.   As far as his slight experience of society in the great Asiatic peninsula went, he had been most unfavourably impressed until to-night.   He had found neither social nor feminine attraction in Secunderabad so far, and if he had turned hermit it was because the solitude of his own bungalow was less depressing than the mild revelry of the station. As he had told Mrs. Daventry, his sole distraction in the evenings was whist, and the whist players of the Royal Dunbars retired betimes. The tossing feverishly on your couch, with a mind thronged by ugly memories, while listening to the war-horn of the mosquito, is a sorry time to look forward to, and so badly did Cis sleep that he quite dreaded going to bed. Again and again to him came that miserable vision of Crymes carrying off his betrothed, or rather she who had been his betrothed, even as he had carried off the Cup; for despite a sweet love-letter, in which Annie told him nothing could make her believe him anything but innocent, and that she was still his whenever he deemed it right to claim her, Cis persisted in considering her free. No man, he held, with such stain on his name was justified in asking a woman to marry him.

At last with a weary sigh Cis threw the end of his cheroot out of the window and proceeded to seek his pillow.

CHAPTER XVI.

A CRITICAL SITUATION.

"Well, Lizzie, what do you think of this excessively shy fish I only succeeded in landing last night, though I've angled for him some little time!" inquired Major Daventry, as he and his wife sat at breakfast.

"He's well enough," she rejoined, languidly; "but I don't think he will be much use to you, whatever he may be to me.　I may find him pleasant to ride or dance with; but I don't fancy he's any taste for cards, except in the case of a quiet rubber."

"Taste of that nature sometimes only requires a little development; besides, it was a gambling business of some kind brought him out here.　Those bitten of the game-cock seldom overcome the fever."

"No, indeed," she rejoined, bitterly, "I can testify to that."

"Ah, well, I don't think we shall trouble you for any evidence on the subject just at present.　Will you be good enough to remember that I want the house made pleasant to Calvert.　I needn't caution you not to over-do him with invitations just at first, because no woman understands better than you how to make a man thoroughly at home in her husband's house;" and the sneering tones in which the speech was delivered were enough to goad a better woman than Lizzie Daventry to practical reprisal.

"I shall do, of course, what you bid me," she replied, in her soft even voice.　"If I have no other virtue, I may certainly claim to be an obedient wife.　At your behest," she continued, with an inflexion of sarcasm in her tones, "I have broken half the laws of the decalogue."

"And transgressed the other half, most probably, for your own satisfaction," rejoined her husband, brutally. "Remember what I have told you. I wish Calvert to be intimate here; if he can't be useful to me in one way he may in another. He's worth making a tame cat of if only for his jockeyship. There'll be races got up here in the cold weather, and first call of a good man will be worth money. You do understand a race when you see it, and you know how very few of the gentleman jockeys in this country have any idea of riding. I'm off to the office; don't forget." ·

For a few minutes she sat motionless, then rose and paced the room restlessly.

"If I'm not a good woman," she murmured, "surely I may plead in palliation that I was married as a mere child to a man like that."

Calvert, in common decency, could not be long before he called upon the Daventrys. Her own inclination coinciding with her husband's instructions upon this occasion, Lizzie exerted herself to please her visitor, and few women when they chose had more fascination of manner. What wonder that the visit was somewhat prolonged; what wonder it was speedily repeated! To Cis, sore from his downfall in England, and utterly bored with such Anglo-Indian society as he had hitherto met, such a house as the Daventrys' was an elysium, while sympathetic Mrs. Daventry was a solace to a wounded spirit past all compare.

The cantonment began to talk,—it does not take much to set a station gossiping in the East,—and speedily it was whispered about that Calvert was gazetted first aide on 'the Daventrys'' staff.

That Lizzie should have her circle of adorers was an acknowledged thing concerning her, and whenever the appointment of senior aide-de-camp was vacant there was much curiosity manifested as to who should succeed to it.

Cis had gradually dropped into this position. He generally rode with her, was often her escort to this, that, or the other entertainment, when duty or caprice prevented Major Daventry fulfilling that obligation. He was now an *habitué* of the house, constantly dined there, and rarely missed one of Mrs. Daventry's Wednesdays.

That what's called a little gambling went on upon these latter occasions was undoubtedly true, and that no more pernicious house for a young man could be possible in an Indian station equally so.

The Major took exceeding good care that such play as there was should be kept within moderate bounds ; but these moderate bounds were quite high enough to suck the life-blood out of the ordinary regimental officer. A steady abstraction of so many ounces of blood a day kills quite as surely as the severance of the jugular. Still, as far as Cis was concerned, he was not hurting himself at cards, nor, although Secunderabad believed the contrary, was he at all in love with Mrs. Daventry ; and what was more, that lady was quite aware of the fact.

It piqued her not a little. She was so accustomed to see men yield to her fascinations almost at first sight, that her conquests for the most part interested her but slightly. There was a novelty in this man who courted her society, who was ever willing to dangle by her side, but who never made love to her ; it was altogether a new experience, and it provoked her. She was used to see men's faces flush at a few soft words from her lips, and knew she had power to make the blood surge wildly through their veins at will ; but she was fain to confess that she did not believe Cis Calvert's pulse quickened one beat in the minute at her presence. He was kind, courteous, devoted ; but Lizzie knew, as women instinctively do know, that he was not in love with her. She quickly drew her own deductions. She had never yet failed to conquer when she had pleased to exert herself ; more usually her victims were at her feet without any trouble on her part. There was but one thing could steel man's heart against her attractions, and that was his love for another woman ; and when she had arrived at this conclusion a smile wreathed Lizzie Daventry's lips, and she vowed Cis Calvert should forget that woman in England before long. Of her own power to teach him such oblivion she never doubted. She had taught others before him as mere matter of caprice. She was in the very zenith of her beauty, just entering her twenty-ninth year, and might well feel justified in believing that no man could

be long insensible to her charms whom she set herself in earnest
to subdue.

"Ah, my dear," she murmured, with a scornful little laugh,
" I don't know who you are as yet, though I shall before long ;
but though you were first in the field you are many thousand
miles away now, and Lizzie Daventry has yet to find a man who
can remain at her side and be constant to a memory of days that
are gone.   We shall see."

The days slipped by, and Calvert might be almost said to live
at the Daventrys'.   There was much talk about his extreme
intimacy there in the cantonment ; but still it didn't affect the
lady, as is sometimes the case.

There are men and women to whom society concedes the
privilege of trampling the conventionalities underfoot, as there
are others whose slightest deviation from propriety's grooves is
visited with prompt retribution.

Lizzie Daventry belonged to the former class.   For years she
had been talked about.   She had always some one as devoted as
Cis Calvert at her beck, and had at last quite established it as a
concession she required from society, that she should be allowed
a cavalier *servente*.   Still, for the first time in all her experience
Lizzie found that post filled by a man who was not in love with
her.   Some weeks had elapsed since she had made up her mind
to effect Calvert's subjugation, and Mrs. Daventry was fairly
nonplussed to find all the artillery of her fascinations powerless.
She felt that this man was a loyal friend, an admirer even ; but
a lover—no.   " But he shall be," she would whisper to herself
sometimes, almost fiercely, as her anger rose at Cis's insensibility.

Did he but know it, Cis Calvert was never in more grievous
jeopardy than at the present.   A beautiful capricious woman,
passionate, untrammelled by principle, and used to the gratification of her every whim, is doubting whether she loves him or
hates him ; but is at the same time very resolute that he shall
in any case be made to love her.

When a woman has this feeling towards a man it can end
only in one way—passionate love ; and if the man fail to respond

to that, it were well for him that he should put thousands of miles between them as soon as he becomes conscious of her preference. Byron's line is too hackneyed to quote; but 'a woman scorned' is no doubt dangerous, and likely to work the culprit's undoing if it lieth in her compass.

Mrs. Daventry had come in from her ride one afternoon, with Cis as usual in attendance, and as matter of course he followed her to the drawing-room for a cup of tea. Whether Cis had shown some signs of developing into the lover, or whether her own feelings were getting more involved than she was quite aware of, who can say? but Lizzie suddenly was seized with an irresistible desire to, in nautical phrase, take soundings. She determined to see as far as might be possible what impression she had made upon this man's heart. The siege had been carried on now for some weeks with much persistency, and she thought it time to take stock of the results.

Taking off her hat, she cast herself wearily on one of the lounges in the drawing-room, and said,

"I feel so tired, though I am sure I don't know why. I am going to reverse the usual order of things, and ask *you* to give me some tea."

"Of course; sit still and rest, I'll do all the tea-making business. You overrate your strength and do too much. Do you know I sometimes think you have been too long in this country. You should take a run home to England."

"England!" she retorted. "Do you know it's ten years since I left home a mere girl? Do you think, in the words of your favourite song,

> ' I'd find one face, lad,
> I loved when all was young ?'

No, Cis, I had few friends or relations, and made a run-away match from a Brighton boarding-school. What would I do in England, even supposing my lord and master consented to part with me ?"

"But Daventry would never hesitate a moment if he thought your health was at stake."

"Not a second," she replied, dreamily. "If he wanted me out here I should be bid stay—if deemed in his way I should be sent home."

"I don't think you do your husband justice. I'm sure he allows you to do pretty much as you like."

"In some points, yes," she replied bitterly. "I've unlimited licence for flirtation, and if I ran away altogether I don't think Hugh would be very much put out. Only you men are so blind, you might see what I mean."

Cis made no reply, but gazed at his fair companion in mute astonishment.

"Ah, you don't comprehend. You should understand something about women too by this time, Captain Calvert. You may beat them and ill-treat them; you may hate them and let them know it; but you may love a woman though you ill-use her,—and hatred may be born of love,—and as long as she believes in the existence of that she will forgive much. There's one sin against her she never forgives, and that is indifference."

The conversation was getting embarrassing, and Cis felt that it was so, but he was not quite a neophyte in these matters, and his answer might have been counted diplomatic by a past master.

"So you may say," he rejoined quietly; "but as you can never have been called upon to deal with it, you can hardly be considered an authority on that point."

"You can never conclude a married woman is not," she retorted quickly. "Ah, well, you see an end to this dreary existence. You are not destined to stay much longer in this land of eternal gossip and sun—a slanderous land, where it is difficult to say if the scandal or the weather is served out to us hottest. I should know," she continued in a low voice, "for they have whispered evil of me for years, from Peshawur to the Deccan."

"Pretty women are always talked about," replied Cis, "and I don't know that there is much more scandal afloat here than at home. If the women weren't jealous of your good looks, recollect, they wouldn't talk about you."

"You will be very glad to return to England, I suppose," she suddenly observed.

"I don't know. I have never thought about it. Why?"

"Why? Surely you know the Royal Dunbars cannot have much longer to serve in this country. They have been out so long that they are the subject of innumerable jests—are said to be mislaid by the authorities, and their whereabouts not even known at the Horse Guards; that they were in reserve at Plassy, and have been in reserve ever since. They will go home next year in all probability."

"Do you know, I never thought of that," said Cis slowly. "When I exchanged, my one idea was to get out of England, and to collar as much money as I could on the transaction."

"Ah, yes, I never asked you, but of course I knew you exchanged out here on account of a scrape of some sort. Money, was it? I have sometimes thought it might be the other."

"The other—meaning—"

"Quite so," interposed Lizzie, laughing; "difficulties feminine or difficulties financial seem to be, if not the whole duty of man, the only one he devotes himself to getting into with any sort of energy."

"No," he replied, speaking in somewhat dreamy fashion, as if more to himself than his companion; "money was the least part of my scrape, though it had something to say to it. I'll not bore you with the wretched story; suffice it to say, I sank under a charge which, though powerless to disprove, I was perfectly innocent of. The regiment as a whole stood by me like men, but it was no use, appearances were too strong, and public opinion undoubtedly against me. I bent to the storm and left England; it was better to do that than wait to be cut."

"You were wrong," she said quickly. "Face it boldly, and one can live down a scandal, even if it be true."

Odd, he thought; in the one letter he had received from Miss Aysgarth since he had left York she had expressed much the same opinion.

"You say so now, but you'll perhaps hear all about it some day, and drop me in consequence."

" Never, Cis," she replied. " You know me better. I have plenty of faults, no doubt, but I am staunch to my friends."

Mrs. Daventry's detractors, and they were pretty numerous, would probably have suggested an amended reading to this speech, and phrased it thus :—" Staunch to her lovers till she wearies of them."

" You think so now, but you may be more hardly tried in my case than you think for."

" As if that would signify.   When a woman believes in a man she does it with all her soul.   She will credit nothing to his disparagement.   Will you tell me one thing ? "

" What is it ? " he inquired curtly.

" Had a woman anything to say to this scrape of yours ? " she answered in a low voice, though the quick anxious look she shot at him from beneath her dark eyelashes showed she was by no means indifferent to the reply.

" No ; the money part which aggravated the business was of my own making, but for the rest it was a sheer caprice of fortune."

" I don't believe him a bit," thought Lizzie.   " I can't go any further just now, but I put my question badly.   She wasn't perhaps the cause, but there was a woman mixed up in it all I'd stake my pet arab to a mango."

" Ah, well, you will go home next year, and twelve months buries most social iniquities.   I shall miss you terribly, and you perhaps may send me one little line from the Cape."

" No, I don't think that '54 will see me home again ; if the regiment gets its orders for England I shall probably exchange again."

" Why, what should keep you out here ? " and the wicked dark eyes flashed subtle provocation to the answering of that question.   She was looking her best she knew, and a tithe of the encouragement she had just given had brought most men to her feet so far.   But instinctively as she felt she had a rival in the background, she could not know how unhappily timed was her attack.   There had suddenly come across Cis a recollection of that other afternoon when he had ridden home to The Firs after the day at Askham Bog, and had tea with Annie

Aysgarth.   She too had been in her riding-habit, and her frank honest manner offered a severe contrast to the somewhat meretricious bearing of his present companion.   He liked Mrs. Daventry much.   She had been very kind to him since he had made her acquaintance, and lightened his lonely life no little ; but at this minute he had one of those clear glimpses into the truth that are vouchsafed most of us now and again.   He saw the difference between the gold and the dross, between the pure honest love of a maiden and the capricious fancy of a coquette. For if not one whit in love with Mrs. Daventry, it could scarcely be supposed Cis was unaware that he was embarked in a strong flirtation with her ; that the station indulged in tolerably strong comment on this little affair he might also be pretty certain of did he ever take the trouble to think about what his world might say ; but concerning that Cis was sublimely indifferent, and yet heaven knows he should have been aware, if any one ever was, how tongues can wag to a man's detriment.

He remained silent for some minutes, his memory still busy with that scene in the fire-lit drawing-room at The Firs.   Lizzie, watching him closely from beneath her drooped eyelids, bit her lip with vexation at seeing how little hold she really had on his feelings.   She recognized that his thoughts for the moment were far away, and it was precisely one of those moments when it was a slight past forgiveness to be engrossed with anything but the woman at his side.   A change came over Mrs. Daventry's face, the dark eyes that a minute before had gleamed with softened languor now sparkled with anger, and though she strove hard to suppress it there was a slight acerbity in her voice which aroused Cis from his reverie as she remarked—

"I little dreamt the attractions here were so numerous that they required thought to catalogue."

"Ten thousand pardons ; but my thoughts were wandering. You were saying—"

"That I am very tired and you are very tiresome, Captain Calvert.   I dare say half an hour's sleep before dinner will put me all to rights.   Good night.   If you have nothing to do come and have tiffin with us to-morrow."

Cis pressed his hostess's hand and accepted his dismissal without remark. He was accustomed to her moods, and not without experience of such curt *congé*, and it certainly did dawn upon him as he rode home that he was getting entangled with Mrs. Daventry in a fashion he had never contemplated. He had not in the least lost his head, I suppose I should say heart, but the former in these matters when of irregular nature is perhaps the more important factor of the two ; still Cis knew there were occasions when the march of events and a reckless woman may snatch the reins out of one's fingers, and the coach of our destiny crash down-hill uncontrolled by either drag or driver. He had no belief that Mrs. Daventry's regard for himself was anything more than a caprice for the moment, but he did know that she had not only no affection for her husband, but that she both feared and despised him, if two such sentiments are compatible. To despise what we fear seems scarcely possible, and yet there are times when the sense of terror seems so lulled to rest, that contempt for the cause of it may become the master-passion of the twain.

CHAPTER XVII.

MRS. CHARRINGTON'S ADVICE.

THERE are few old saws so true as the expression ' a nine days' wonder.' Verily in these times you must have astonished the world to considerable extent if it holds you in memory for a fortnight. The pace gets faster and faster, and whether you paint pictures, compose poetry, write books, steal plays or act them, play the fool politically or æsthetically, if you don't, so to speak, pose continually before the public you will most assuredly find yourself forgotten. In '53 the great movement for the elevation of the masses, and the corresponding increase of ignorance in the middle class, had not as yet begun. That smattering of all the ' ologies,' that affectation of knowledge of everything and solid knowledge of nothing, had not yet commenced. That getting of learning through the medium of epitomes is scarce conducive to solid acquirements.

The spring of '53 has passed away, and the triumphs of West Australian at Newmarket and Epsom have effectually driven all recollection of that luckless race at Crockey Hill out of the heads of York and its neighbourhood. Still the exile, you may be sure, is not forgotten at The Firs, nor have his old comrades of the Lancers ceased to talk about him. Tim Murphy, much exercised by Blundell's taunts, has, after making some unsuccessful inquiries on his own account, carried his story to Harry Harperley, and that young gentleman, with a wise discretion, has in his turn told the tale to Mr. Charrington. The master of Byculla Grange, who had already formed a pretty correct idea of the case, seized upon the clue thus furnished him with avidity, enjoined close mouths upon both the Cornet and Tim Murphy, and then set himself to work to prove Calvert's innocence. Not even to himself would he have admitted it, but it may be questioned whether Mr. Charrington did not look forward a little to convicting Crymes of being aware of The Mumper's identity some time before the race. That Blundell, the Major's groom, had known it Mr. Charrington had no doubt; Dick Hunsley had admitted that he had backed The Cid in accordance with such knowledge, regarding the race as made pretty well a certainty for one of the two horses, and that it was within his power to disqualify the black should he prove the better of the twain. If he could only get at this mysterious Isham Boggs, Mr. Charrington thought he should then be in possession of every detail of the robbery—a robbery of which there could be no moral doubt that the Major's servant was cognizant of, whatever his master might have been. But Mappin, to whom he went in the first place for information, could tell him no more than he had told Cis Calvert some months before, to wit, that he had never heard of him. Then Mr. Charrington made personal inquiry at the Punchbowl, but he did not take much by that investigation. Yes, they knew Mr. Boggs; he stayed there at times. Where was he now? They didn't know. When was he likely to be there again? They didn't know. In fact, further than that Boggs existed, and had a palpable entity, there never seemed living creature of whom it was more impossible to get knowledge.

But the ex-Indian officer had not dedicated the best part of his life to wringing the truth from the subtle double-dealing Asiatic without becoming cunning in ruses and crafty in cross-examination. He remembered while the controversy raged hot, that at the York Club some one had said that Bilton, the great Leeds bookmaker, had told him he was backing the wrong horse, when he, Bilton, accommodated him with the odds against The Cid, and that the ring generally seemed inspired with the conviction that The Mumper would win, and rather peppered the grey in consequence. Putting things together, Mr. Charrington came to the conclusion that the shadowy Boggs had probably played prophet on that occasion, and inspired the leading bookmakers to lay hotly against The Cid. A little thought enabled him to remember who it was that Mr. Bilton had made that remark to, and he easily persuaded the gentleman in question to write to the bookmaker and inquire if it was from a person named Isham Boggs that he had derived his information, and further, who and what was Isham Boggs. Mr. Bilton's reply was soon to hand. He answered the first question in the affirmative; and as to the second, said that Isham Boggs was reckoned about the cleverest tout in England, that he believed he had some rather queer stories attached to his turf career, but they were mostly before his, Bilton's, time. Further, he indicated no suspicion that the information furnished him by Boggs had not been given in perfect good faith, nor did he offer any opinion as to who the concocters of the robbery might be.

Mr. Charrington felt that he had not advanced his case an iota by this last move, but he had come to the conclusion that there were three people who could prove Cis Calvert's innocence, and tell the real story of the race if they would; and it was further his opinion that any one of the three would do so for a consideration. These were Boggs, Hunsley, and Blundell; but the first two had disappeared, and Mr. Charrington reflected ruefully that he could not well either bribe or cross-examine the servant of his intimate friend Major Crymes. Still, though Boggs and Hunsley might be difficult to find, with their tastes it was only a matter of time. The hangers-on of the race-course rarely take to any other vocation, but adhere to their calling pertinaciously, despite the very indifferent living it furnishes them with at best, in spite of its cruel vicissitudes; and no man knew this better than Mr. Charrington. Whatever misfortune may befall these men, even when it takes the form of being for a space of some years in what is euphoniously known as 'Her Majesty's keeping,' they gravitate back to the race-course as ducks to water.

There never was a man more qualified to make the most of winning cards than Horace Crymes. No one was quicker to recognize the turn of fortune in his favour than he, or to back it with more audacity. He had grasped at once all the advantage that luckless race had given him, and played his game since with consummate tact and patience. He was rid by chance, he knew, of a most formidable rival, and had been specially careful never to let a syllable escape his lips to that rival's disparagement. He had more than once pointedly declined any discussion of what he somewhat ambiguously termed a painful subject, leaving his hearers on such occasions not quite clear whether he meant regret that duty to his backers should have required him to make that fatal objection, or that he was lamenting that an officer of Her Majesty's —th Lancers should have so sadly deviated from the paths of rectitude. With regard to The Firs, he had perfectly succeeded in keeping up his acquaintance with its inmates at the same time being specially careful not to throw himself too much in their way just at first. To the banker he had more than once expressed regret at the line he had been compelled to take but always hinted that his delicate position prohibited his expressing an opinion with regard to Calvert's conduct. If he never accused Cis of fraud he most decidedly never upheld his innocence.

Julian Harperley had never been quite able to make up his mind upon this point. He still remained constant to the Scotch verdict of *not proven*, but he was quite decided upon another. He most earnestly desired that such engagement as there was between Cis and his stepdaughter should be considered cancelled, and in this he had been materially aided by Calvert himself. Not only had he reluctantly relinquished all claim upon Miss Aysgarth, but he had solemnly renounced the privilege of writing to her. He not only had called that letter written just previous to leaving York his last, but although sorely tempted by Annie's sweet, womanly reply to continue the correspondence, he had abstained. " No," he said, " I love her far too dearly to hamper her with the correspondence of a broken man. Somebody would get hold of it if we exchanged letters, and that she should be known to still write to me would be flung in her face. You may be innocent of card-sharping, but while the world holds you guilty you are as a chimney-sweep to your friends, and blacken their hands whenever you cross palms with them. I have done the best I could for all who loved me in placing thousands of miles betwixt us. You would stand to me, my darling, if I called on you, I know ; but I'm not so mean as to take advantage of your loyalty."

It may be urged that knowing himself guiltless, Cis Calvert was inconceivably foolish not to stay and live down the accusation against him, but I can only remark that innocent people as a rule are usually so overwhelmed with sudden charges of this nature that they invariably display much less discretion than transgressors, who are, so to speak, naturally prepared for some uncomfortable explosion. Next, we must remember that Cis had lost a very heavy stake upon this race, and that the money had to be found immediately. A thousand or twelve hundred pounds takes some looking up when your income amounts to little more than half of it. Lastly, there was a bit of genuine chivalry in Cis's nature, and he shrank from involving his friends in his defence, nor could he endure the idea of the girl he loved being involved in his disgrace. Anything to save her. Thank heavens, their engagement had never been publicly announced, and if he departed silently to India, that he and Annie had ever been friends would be speedily forgotten. He was weak perhaps to take this view of the case, but men with plenty of sense have been overwhelmed by such scandals before now, and have made the mistake of restoring their troth to women who love them dearly rather than involve them in their own wrecked lives; and the women, who would fain have stood by them an they might, have judged the situation more correctly.

Miss Aysgarth meanwhile might certainly claim to be a hardly-treated young lady. She is a good, plucky girl, loving Cis Calvert with all her heart, and ready to stand by him through evil report in any shape. On the first intelligence of the trouble that had come to him she had written him a loving little note, in which she had expressed her entire disbelief in all this accusation against him; then she had received in her turn that letter in which, while protesting his innocence and unalterable regard, he had released her from her troth. She had replied to that in an epistle full of passionate indignation that people should be found weak enough to credit such foul scandal, and protesting against the idea of being absolved from her pledge.

"I gave myself to you for life," she cried vehemently, " to share your sorrows as well as your joys. Do you think me so foolish that I did not anticipate there were storms for us to weather—storms, dearest, which should serve only to knit us closer to each other. One has burst upon us sooner than we dreamt of, and I claim my right to face it by your side. You did wrong, Cis, believe me, not to stay here. Ah, believe me, we are better judges than you on these points. No woman ever turns her back upon a scandal until she is quite certain it will overflow and drown her. I am afraid there must have been money troubles besides, or you would never have stole away without wishing me good-bye. Still, Cis, remember I am yours whenever you choose to come and take me, and I'll believe nothing they say against you, prate them ever so loudly."

When a young lady does not get an answer to such a letter as this she may be excused for feeling a little uneasy in her mind. Lovers now-a-days may doubtless carry their chivalry a little too far; and I have a hazy idea about Christmas time, when mistletoe was about, some quarter of a century ago, that when young ladies declared they would scream if you *did*, they certainly put you down as a most unmistakable muff if you *didn't*.

It was all very well for Cis to release her, and to volunteer to drop all correspondence till his name was cleared; but then he had no business to keep his word, and Annie had not been woman if she had not fully expected him not only to consider her still betrothed to him, but to let her know pretty frequently that he did so.

But this was just what her lover refrained from, taking credit to himself meanwhile for so doing, and the result naturally was, that Miss Aysgarth chafed a good deal over the ordering of things. Did she not believe thoroughly in her lover's innocence and constancy? Undoubtedly she did, but still she thought that last letter of hers deserved an answer; and moreover, although one may have no misgivings concerning one's betrothed's devotion, still it is comforting to know now and again that he is in the same frame of mind. It was difficult to imagine Cis Calvert's morbid view of his misfortune; and Annie found it hard to account for the sombre strain of his letters to her brother. She was haunted with the idea that they none of them knew the whole truth, that Cis had kept back something, and, moreover, she was hardly satisfied with these messages in Harry's correspondence. Why did not the exile write direct to herself? No positive interdict had ever been placed on their writing to each other, although Julian Harperley had certainly said that he thought it would be better all that sort of thing should cease, and Miss Aysgarth had told her father thereupon that things had gone too far; that she could not desert her lover in his trouble, and that she must write if she were written to ; but then this last as yet had not come to pass. No wonder Annie Aysgarth felt her love-affair was running a little askew.

It is a gorgeous July morning, and Horace Crymes is lounging in Mrs. Charrington's own sanctuary at Byculla Grange, a luxuriously furnished boudoir off the drawing-room, with a large French window opening on a prettily laid-out garden. The Major has just returned from the battle-field of Ascot, and has so far little to complain of in the year's racing campaign. He has identified himself for the present with Yorkshire, and in common with the county generally had a rare turn over the triumph of the 'all black' at Epsom, and has done no harm at the royal meeting to boot. Great days for 'the tykes' were those when Malton and old John Scott culminated in taking the classical triplet, last coruscation of the great stable of the north, ere death claimed its veteran ruler.

"So you still think seriously of wooing the banker's daughter," said Mrs. Charrington, who was making pretence of busying herself with some embroidering. "Not a bad-looking girl, and will come to you with something comfortable in her hand, to say nothing of what there may be, as Mr. Disraeli terms it, 'looming in the future.' You might do worse, Horace."

"I have got to that time of life," rejoined Crymes, "when it behoves us to settle. I must, as you know, marry money; and if you give permission, really do not think I can do better."

"Oh, dear, yes," rejoined the lady, laughing ; "I told you long ago I like to settle my admirers, if possible, in my own neighbourhood. But have you any reason to think you'll win Miss Aysgarth's consent ?"

"Any girl is to be won by a man who has time and opportunity to serve him," rejoined Crymes, coolly. "When I beat Calvert in the Cup I virtually gained a bride as well. I'm not sure I didn't hint as much to her before we started, but that victory disposed of my rival."

"I'd not be too sure of that," said Mrs. Charrington. "I feel pretty sure there was an engagement of some sort between them; and she's just the kind of romantic girl to insist upon sticking to it in defiance of the advice of her people."

"Granted in the first instance; but when she seldom hears him spoken of, and knows that he has betaken himself to the other side of the globe for an indefinite period, that feeling will die out."

"It may, and when you consider that time has arrived, then, I presume, you intend to come forward."

"Just so, unless accident furnishes me with a favourable opportunity sooner. Luck so far has been on my side. Had Calvert won that race, as the hero of the hour and winner of a nice sum of ready money, he would have been hard to displace in Miss Aysgarth's good graces."

"Yes, Horace, I would not have given much for your chance under those circumstances."

"Exactly! One of my maxims is never to throw down my cards, but invariably play the game out, however much it may look against me. It has served me well many a time. There is another should be taken in conjunction with it—'Everything comes to him who knows how to wait.'"

"It may be so," replied Mrs. Charrington, thoughtfully, " and, to do you justice, I think you understand us better than any man I ever knew; but I don't think you have an easy task before you."

"Very likely not, but difficulties rather inspirit me than otherwise. By the way, it is possible you might do me a good turn."

" How so ?" she inquired, with no little astonishment.

"Well, you doubtless have some Indian correspondents. You might ascertain for me what Calvert is doing. I have never been there, but scandal is pretty rife in the East, unless rumour belies it."

" Why, you don't surely expect to hear that Captain Calvert is entangled with any woman out there ?"

" No," replied Crymes, with a cynical smile, " I never expect to hear of any of my friends in such grievous case; but it is wonderful how often I am taken aback by intelligence of that nature."

"I have told you I will help you, and if you really are in earnest your opportunity will come next month. We are going, as are the Harperleys and others of our friends, for six weeks or so to Harrogate. It will be easy for you to go to the same hotel, and that will give you every opportunity of prosecuting your suit. Not to flirt at Harrogate is to make yourself conspicuous; to be really in the fashion you should have two or three affairs in hand at once, and as to conduct those without tangling the strings requires audacity and delicacy, it is not surprising that scenes and situations are plentiful in the vicinity of ' the Stray.' Say you'll join our party and come, it will be sure to amuse you, and, as I said before, offer opportunities you will find hard to make elsewhere."

"Thank you very much," exclaimed the Major, rising. "I shall only be too charmed. You are a woman in a thousand," he added, in a low tone—" one who can take a disinterested interest in an admirer. I shall never forget it, whatever the result may be. Once more, adieu," and, pressing her hand warmly, Crymes bade his hostess farewell.

"Yes," murmured the lady, "he's very nice, and it would be very nice to have him settled in the neighbourhood. We should get on beautifully, and be dear friends always. I think, Horace, if I can manage it, we must wed you to Annie Aysgarth."

CHAPTER XVIII.

HARROGATE.

" Though Shakespeare asks us, What's in a name ?
As if cognomens were much the same,
  There's really a very great scope in it ;
For instance, wasn't there Doctor Dodd,
That servant at once of Mammon and God,
Who found four thousand pound and odd,
  A prison, a cart, and a rope in it."

Tom Hood is right. Shakespeare, you see, on which point he cannot be too sufficiently congratulated, lived before the age of advertising. It is all very well to say, " The rose by any other name would smell as sweet." Quite so; but just call them pink tulips, and you'll discover an astonishing difference in the sale, whether for good or evil no mortal can determine, for the whim of the public on such points is a thing surpassing all human understanding. But if there is something in a name there is a good deal more in a water. I mean a medicated Spa water. You may drink them for gout, rheumatism, what you will; but there is also a moral property in them. As the quaffing of the waters of Spa and Homburg tend to foster an inclination for backing the colour or speculating on the spinning of a ball, so do the springs of Bath, Cheltenham, or Harrogate encourage the disseminating of scandal and all manner of evil speaking.

After somewhat careful observation of the latter place, I agree with the pithy sum-up of a veteran stager who knew the town well—" It's the sulphur as does it." The system, you see, has to be purged somehow, and that gout, rheumatism, and all the ghostly brotherhood should exude under the influence of the springs in scandalous garraulity is a benign form of riddance of one's ailments. Gossip in the pleasant little sanatorium runs high, as is natural. What would you have?—we have only to drink the waters, laze, as poor Mortimer Collins called it, and talk about our neighbours; and how can we talk about people whose history we don't know, unless we embroider? Harrogate, as a rule, displays commendable talent in this art, has been, indeed, noted for it the last hundred years or more. Smollett, in his *Humphrey Clinker*, does it justice on this point, and one wonders how many little differences that grand old common called 'the Stray' has seen settled on a summer's morning. One can picture many a pair of young bloods in their shirts, silken stockings, and buckled shoes, foot to foot and hand to hand, engaged in wicked tilting matches brought about by *les beaux yeux* of Mistress Lydia, or the consequences of indiscreet tattling. The Irish adventurer was a great feature in all such places a century ago, if we may trust the novelists of those times, and is probably still to the fore; but society has so enlarged, and the salient point of the Hibernian have been so rounded off, that he is no longer the prominent figure he once was.

Yet I heard a story of Harrogate within the last few years that shows the Irishman has not forgotten the traditions of his race. It is customary at leading hotels in such places as Harrogate, Scarborough, &c. to appoint a president who sits at the head of the table, and is supposed by courtesy to be invested with some slight authority as master of the ceremonies. That he is president of a pure democracy is, of course, palpable, and that such weight as he may carry must be due entirely to his tact and popularity obvious. At an hotel in Harrogate, goes the story, Mr. O'Bluster was raised to the throne, and at once proceeded to rule the Saxon with a rod of iron. Now there were, I say it with sadness, two pretty contumacious English girls, who declined to bow down to the O'Bluster. That eminent Hibernian had probably detected covert discontent with his rule, and when, the night before they left, they petitioned for a last dance, sternly declined to allow the attendance of the professional pianist usually employed upon such occasions. In vain the young ladies pleaded; the O'Bluster declared he should put down his foot upon this continual frivolity, and that this night his friend Mr. Malony had promised to give them a summary of the Irish question. The hilarity of the evening is supposed on these occasions to commence after tea, and that refreshment satisfactorily disposed of, the O'Bluster commenced arranging the chairs in the drawing-room for the convenience of the listeners to Mr. Malony's lecture. Once more was the Celt outraged by the Saxon, for in defiance of the dictum of their Irish president, one of these English young ladies seated herself at the piano and trilled out the Manola valse, while, dreadful to relate, her sister had actually persuaded some one of her admirers to commit felony, treason, contempt of court, or whatever it may be termed, and dance with her to that music.

There are times when collapse of our authority startles most of us on account of its abruptness. Louis Philippe, perhaps, in our days was the most astonished man to discover the reins had slipped through his fingers and the horses had overturned the coach; but his bewilderment was a trifle compared with that of the O'Bluster. Should his authority pass without a struggle? Heaven forefend! Fiercely he demanded of the pianist that she should cease. She smiled sweetly, but played on. Angrily he called upon the dancers to stop their gyrations; they laughed lightly and continued valsing. He appealed to the community, and the elderly and infirm, whose bed-time hour had well nigh come, followed him into the lobby; but the younger and more energetic scorned to succumb to 'Home Rule,' derided the O'Bluster, and had their dance out. The downfall of the president was complete, typical of the probable result of Irishmen ruling Ireland.

Very pleasant, however, is Harrogate when the gorgeous summer weather comes upon us. When Babylon is sweltering under a midsummer sun, and the paving stones remind one of the good intentions with which those nethermost torrid regions are flagged, it is good to lounge about 'the Stray,' and enjoy the balmy air of the highest table-land in England. There is nothing to do in Harrogate for which one cannot be too sufficiently thankful.   Do we not leave the turmoil of Babylon, wherein we struggle for our bread, for rest? and are not pure air and nothing to trouble our minds sufficient for most of us? But for those restless beings who cannot understand the delights of pure, unadulterated indolence, and as a man of Skimpolian tendencies, I pity them from my heart.   There are endless excursions to be made from Harrogate, ruins to be raved about, sights to be sung about; still these are all superfluities.   The genuine visitor goes in for health, indolence, the waters, and such mild amusement as may come to him without trouble.

Mrs. Charrington was very fond of a month at Harrogate. She affected the Queen's Hotel, where she played the great lady, turning up her aristocratic nose with much magnificence at the wives and daughters of the plutocracy from Leeds, Bradford, Manchester, etc., a demonstration which inspired these good people with no manner of awe whatever, and usually recoiled upon Mrs. Charrington's head, insomuch as the deference so ostentatiously claimed was apt to result in her barely receiving civility from what she contemptously denominated 'the spinning women.'   Manchester might be a little loose in its h's, and Leeds express itself with more emphasis than grammar, but they were pretty shrewd in reckoning up their fellows.   They recognized dollars, they recognized success, and they had all that sneaking reverence for a genuine swell so characteristic of a radical.   Let him say what he will, the republican always grovels before a duke; but they didn't see Mrs. Charrington.   Good family, perhaps so; but who was Mrs. Charrington, and what had Charrington done that she should give herself such airs?   Every year did Mrs. Charrington come to Harrogate, and set up for being queen of the Queen's Hotel.   Every year was her authority fiercely disputed, and every year did she declare that nothing should ever induce her to set foot in the place again.   But the gossip, that curious panorama of humanity's weaknesses and scheming, which watering-place life affords, always attracted Mrs. Charrington back again; and then it suited her spouse admirably.   He was close to home, quite handy for the York races, could slip up to his friends on the moors for a turn at the grouse.   People, too, in the year of grace '53, did not wander so far from home as they do now-a-days. Cook had not as yet inculcated his sublime scheme for the seeing of everything in Zoetrope fashion in the minimum of possible time. Railways were, though in use, still but half comprehended of the public abroad; the national instinctive hatred of the barbarous hordes generically described as Russia, but in reality the wandering nomads of Central Asia, who from time immemorial have swept westwards like a torrent, had enlisted our sympathies in favour of the Turks. 'The sick man,' as the Czar Nicholas described him, might be sick, he might be 'coming up piping,' and all that sort of thing, to borrow the extinct *argot* of the prize-ring; but for all that he was apparently not so easy to be done with—not to be put out of the fortress of Silistria by any means for instance, and yet the Muscovite could not be accused of being chary of life to attain that desirable consummation. There were wild politicians who even hinted that we might interfere in the struggle, at which our rulers were vastly amused. The idea of our interfering with anything after forty years of peace, coupled with the remembrance of that awful debt contracted in the early days of the century. Ah, the magnates who conduct our affairs are destined from time to time to be astonished at the manifestation of the national will running not rightly in accordance with the grooves those eminent legislators have prescribed for it; and though we wonder now what on earth took us into the quarrel, it was unmistakably a war of the nation, not of the ministry. Still I fancy in the summer of '53 few people dreamt that the following spring would see us committed to the biggest war we had been engaged in since the famous death grapple with Napoleon in the Belgian corn-fields.

Mrs. Charrington had once more taken up her abode at the Queen's Hotel, and without any solicitation assumed the *rôle* of leading lady, patronizing some of her sisters from the manufacturing centres to a degree they found barely endurable. Why she, a fairly popular woman in her own neighbourhood, should make herself so unpleasant at Harrogate was singular; but the fact was, Mrs. Charrington never could divest herself of the delusion that it was a great piece of condescension on her part

to dine at the *table d'hôte* and mix with the other visitors,
instead of adhering to the dignified seclusion of a private sitting-
room.   In reality Mrs. Charrington, being perfectly aware that
the sitting-room would be, if stately, insufferably dull, abandoned
it for the more lively general table, but always cherished the
idea that it was very gracious on her part to do so, and that the
guests must be proportionately grateful for her goodness.   People
were more wont to entertain such notions in the days of which I
am writing than they are now.   The astounding biographies
which, from the slenderest facts, Mrs. Charrington was accustomed to construct regarding those with whom she mixed were
always a source of much mirth to Julian Harperley and Miss
Aysgarth, now also established at the Queen's Hotel.   No sooner
had she arrived at any new-comers' names and some two or three
trivial details concerning them, than she forthwith presented her
intimates with a florid picture of their lives, and though how
ill-founded were her conclusions was matter of continual demonstration, that exercised no check upon her imagination.

Horace Crymes too had come over to Harrogate, doggedly bent
upon prosecuting his suit with Miss Aysgarth.   He had kept
somewhat aloof from that young lady since the race, thinking it
more politic to do so for a time ; but he had remained on perfectly friendly terms with Mr. Harperley, and, as he well knew,
had afforded Annie no pretext for quarrelling with him.   No
one could accuse him of bitter denunciation of Cis Calvert ; on
the contrary, he had kept rigid guard over his tongue in that
respect, and the girl was perfectly aware of it.   She had heard
her father and many of his friends speak of how well the Major
had behaved through the whole transaction, and even Harry,
hot partisan as he was of his old captain, was fain to confess that
Crymes was not to be numbered amongst Cis's accusers.   The
Major makes his advances with the utmost tact ; he is most
deferential, and by no means too marked in his attentions to
Miss Aysgarth, indeed, is studiously desirous that she should
not suspect him of such design as yet.   He has taken much
counsel with Mrs. Charrington, and while pretending to act
upon that lady's advice, is steadfastly playing his own game.
He is by no means blind to the advantage of having that matron

on his side, and still more keenly alive to the fact that she could be very awkward in opposition; but he is spared all anxiety on that account, for Mrs. Charrington always shows a disposition to provide for her favourites after the regal fashion of Catherine, ' Russia's mighty empress.'

" You are too cautious," said Mrs. Charrington to him one afternoon, as they lounged in the garden in front of the house.

The idea of having to chide Horace Crymes for being a laggard in love !

" You are, of course, a better judge than I can pretend to be ; but I don't think Miss Aysgarth has quite got Calvert out of her head as yet. Besides, you should certainly understand that, though it may be desirable I should get married, yet I am in no hurry to assume the yoke."

" Ah, yes, Horace ; and it willb e terrible for me to part with such an adorer as yourself; but then, you know, we must think what is best for you. To marry money speedily is, you say, imperative. Very well then, do it—you can, well, you know, go on adoring me all the same, and if you marry Miss Aysgarth will be always in the neighbourhood handy for the purpose."

Mrs. Charrington was somewhat in advance of her age, and and a very practical woman. Such bold views of the relations of the sexes were not generally enunciated thirty years ago, though in these days in certain circles the theory of a species of staff is regarded as quite permissible for a married woman. It is perhaps less to be dreaded than the attachment of a single aide-de-camp.

" Remember, I start under peculiarly adverse circumstances. I have got to make her forget a previous lover, for there can be no doubt Calvert was that, and to further make her forget that it was I who brought him to grief."

" Yes, and it's just that last point that will give you trouble. You may supplant a lover in a woman's breast, and she will well-nigh forget him ; but she will always resent the having been arbitrarily deprived of one."

" Quite true ; but difficulties have always a fascination for me. But heaven preserve us, here is one of your wild acquaintances from Spindletown swooping down upon us—a weird and probably *h*-less matron. Forgive me, but I really have not courage to face the attack."

The lady from whom the dragoon fled in such affected terror was a perfect type of those dames from the manufacturing centres that so often discomfited Mrs. Charrington. A good, honest, homely woman, richly though plainly dressed now, but who could well remember the days when she went about in cottons and prints, when she and her husband had not so many shillings a week as they now had five-pound notes. She had neither h's nor pretence, nor that quintessence of snobbism—ostentatious pride in her wealth. She had her carriage there, and Mrs. Charrington, who really knew a pair of steppers when she saw them, had broken the tenth commandment grievously anent Mrs. Hopperton's bays.

"Can I take you out for a drive, Mrs. Charrington? I am going at four, and 'ave only got those Flirtington girls with me. As for 'Opperton, 'e was obliged to run into town to look after business."

Mrs. Charrington declines the invitation in somewhat stately fashion, which is utterly lost upon plump, good-natured little Mrs. Hopperton. That is the terrible part of it: she never can be brought to a sense of Mrs. Charrington's position, and instead of allowing herself to be patronized, treats the mistress of Byculla Grange with an easy familiarity that makes her almost snort with indignation, and amply avenges several ladies whom Mrs. Charrington's patronizing manner has reduced to a similar state of impotent wrath.

Four o'clock is rather the stereotyped hour at Harrogate for the afternoon ride or drive, and at that time there is usually a tolerable muster of carriages and hacks in front of the hotel; true, perhaps many of these may be simply hired, but there are always a considerable sprinkling of people whose homes being near at hand bring their own coaches and cattle. Mrs. Charrington had re-appeared in hat and habit, and albeit on a somewhat large scale, the lady looked remarkably well in that attire; moreover, she could ride, and sat her horse like a horse-woman. This riding party was a pet organization of Mrs. Charrington's. It took place about every other day, and had been started especially to promote Major Crymes' suit to Miss Aysgarth, for these two and Julian Harperley made up the quartette, mounted on their own steeds, and all looking perfectly at home upon horseback. They were a rather more imposing party than was customary before the *porte cochère* of the Queen, while Crymes, sitting down straight and square in his saddle upon old Cockatoo, was certain to bring feminine heads to the windows. That tall swarthy dragoon on his snowy handsome horse was such a figure as women love to gaze upon. Miss Aysgarth had somewhat chafed at this arrangement in the first instance, foreseeing that, in the order of things, Major Crymes would naturally fall to her lot as companion; but the Major's tact had quite done away with all repugnance on her part. He never alluded to the past, and though she knew that he had at one time bid fair to become a declared admirer he never trespassed on that *rôle* now.

They were sauntering through Knaresborough in indolent fashion when Crymes said quietly,

"Miss Aysgarth, will you allow me to allude to a subject painful in the extreme to myself, and about which you must doubtless have heard a good deal from your brother? He, I know, was very much attached to his old captain, and to this minute cannot forgive my unfortunate share in bringing about his exchange."

"I think, Major Crymes, we had best not discuss the subject. I make no pretence but that Captain Calvert was a great friend and favourite of mine, and that I was very sorry indeed to hear that he had to leave on account of a fraud which he committed most innocently and unknowingly."

"Pardon me, you make a slight mistake to start with. Captain Calvert was not in the least obliged to leave, and had he been well advised would not have done so. To have refrained from making use of the information I received, and did not receive, please remember, until the race was over, would not only have been most unjust to those who had backed me, but might have exposed myself to the charge of connivance. That I should have lost my money goes for nothing—only the year before last a well-known owner of race-horses dropped some thousands over the Cambridgeshire, for which his mare started a hot favourite, and the British public insisted upon it that he had made a very good thing out of the business. I don't want to lecture on horse-racing, but I do want you to admit that I had a very disagreeable business thrust upon me, and that I could do no other than I did."

"I am sure, Major Crymes, I have never even hinted such a thing. All those best qualified to judge, including my father, bear testimony in your favour on this point."

"That is quite sufficient," rejoined Crymes. "You may implicitly rely upon my not alluding to so sad an affair again."

He changed the subject immediately, well content that he had got that preliminary ice satisfactorily broken; he exerted himself to be amusing, and when the Major did that he was usually successful. A man of the world who had seen cities, come across many celebrities, a keen observer and skilled *raconteur*, his shrewd comments and stories were worth listening to, and Miss Aysgarth, despite her prejudice, could not but admit that her ride had been pleasant when they regained the hotel.

CHAPTER XIX.

THE MAN FROM MANCHESTER.

Time slipped pleasantly away at Harrogate, and both the Charringtons and Harperleys were thoroughly enjoying themselves. The delicious coolness of the place was exactly the change the banker wanted, while as for Miss Aysgarth, she saw no reason to parade her troubles to the world; besides, her brother kept up a desultory correspondence with Cis, so that she was not altogether without news of him. It is true she did think sometimes that he was showing uncalled-for generosity in the matter of refraining from correspondence. She knew that had he written to her she would have answered his letters, let her step-father say what he would. He might feel bound to restore her troth to her, but was she not equally bound to refuse it. She could not help feeling at times that this lover of hers was carrying his sense of honour a little too far. Even Major Crymes had endorsed her opinion that Cis Calvert was wrong in not sticking to his regiment. Of course that little difficulty of finding money with which to settle his bets had not presented itself to her mind, though it had borne some share in his decision to exchange. Still Miss Aysgarth had fair grounds for good hope that things would come right in the end as regarded that love affair of hers.

The Charringtons were just the people to keep the Queen's Hotel alive, and though the lady's usurpation of authority and her husband's arbitrary manner produced occasional rebellion amongst the visitors, yet upon the whole they enjoyed a sort of popularity. Mrs. Charrington was perpetually organizing picnics to see this place or that, while her spouse showed infinite tact in the starting of whist tables or the getting up of a quiet pool in the billiard-room. Then again there were county people who came for a few days of Harrogate, mostly known to Mrs. Charrington, and easily persuaded to swell her forces for the invasion of Fountain or Bolton Abbeys, to get up a dance for the yeomanry,—at this time out for their annual training,—or to engage in the charades or other diversions that energetic lady might devise for the evening's amusement ; and if the sulphur wells bubbled, so did the scandal springs, and there was much throwing off of ailments both moral and physical.

Of course they didn't know it, but Mrs. Charrington and her immediate set enjoyed no more immunity than other people, and it was whispered amongst visitors from the manufacturing centres that Mrs. Charrington had been divorced once, and that if her present husband had not happened to be endowed with scarcely credible obtuseness, she would ere this have been divorced twice.

" That poor Miss Aysgarth—handsome do you call her ? good-looking, my dear, is the very furthest I can go—had been engaged to one of the dragoons at York, who had turned out a card-sharper and had to fly the country ; that black-browed Major is in the same regiment ; these soldiers all hang together, you know, and I dare say the corps generally understand turning up the king. No, I'd let him alone as regards card-playing if I were you."

Crymes meanwhile continued to oscillate between his military duties at York and the pleasures of Harrogate, and we may be sure strove steadily to work his way into Miss Aysgarth's good graces, and he was succeeding. I don't for one moment mean that the girl had any feeling for him further than that he was a pleasant acquaintance, but he had undoubtedly established himself upon that footing, and did not despair of changing it into something warmer in due course.

It was at this time there descended on the Queen's Hotel, in the person of a Mr. Fulsby, the self-made man from Manchester —a type which, however you may respect for their energies, become social enormities on account of their narrow-minded ignorance and arrogance. Mr. Fulsby was a loud-voiced man, firmly impressed with the belief that Manchester was ' the hub of the universe,' and that the rotation of the world depended in some not precisely to be explained way on cotton. There were two phrases for ever in his mouth—"Manchester won't have it, I tell you," and " I'm a self-made man myself, mind." No baron to a score of quarterings could have been more proud of his descent than Mr. Fulsby was of his want of it, but the peer would certainly have been much more chary of allusion to the subject.

Now that summer of '53 had brought about one or two things that were much in men's mouths : there was, to begin upon, as far as our army was concerned, the first symptom of what, for want of a better term, I must call ' the great military revival.' The close of the previous year had seen England's mightiest warrior lain to rest in St. Paul's Cathedral, and there had dawned upon his successors that the magnificent parade army might be found a trifle under-armed and not altogether versed in the requirements of campaigning. The camp of Cobham, which made a charming lounge for fashionable London, and the tardy recognition that a rifle really was preferable to a smooth bore when it came to a bullet meeting its billet, was the result of these cogitations, and it is open to question whether some of our warrior chiefs of the bow and arrow school, who alternately thrash and are thrashed in South Africa, have as yet got much further in their military conclusions.

The second topic was the outbreak once more of the eternal quarrel between the Turk and the Muscovite, and upon that subject the nation generally was at that time on a gentle simmer, eventually resulting in a boil that neither statesman, journalist, nor political quidnunc could foresee—none blinder perhaps to the possibility of this outburst of national passion than what may be designated the Manchester school.

To interfere with barbarians in their play, which usually consists in the murdering, plundering, ravishing, and torturing of each other, would hardly seem to be the business of civilized nations, except the barbarians were under their rule.

The reverse of this creed is at present in vogue, and the prevention of atrocities everywhere but within their own precincts the bounden duty of governments. Still whenever that undying feud between the Moslem and the Tartar shall be finished,—and finished shortly in favour of the latter it is bound to be,—the possession of the keys of Europe may lead to rivers of blood, and a death grapple 'twixt the Teuton and the Slav.

It was that matter of jealousy about the keys of Europe, and that fine old traditional phantom called ' the balance of power,' subject to perplexing and perpetual variation as powers got out of one scale into the other and so destroyed all equitable equilibrium, that finally brought the western powers to the idea that it was their bounden duty to take part with the Turk as present comfortably impotent gaoler of Europe. The key of the lock in custody of one within the compass of knocking down by any of the community is naturally re-assuring with regard to liberty.

Now, further than that the chivalry of wóman's nature impels her to take part with the weaker side, I can give you no reason, but certain it is, at that time—and if I again remind you I am talking of the year '53, the permanence and constancy of this quarrel must be my excuse for it—the ladies mostly raised their voices in behalf of the Turk, while men of the Fulsby stamp, though deprecating war as a barbarous and antediluvian way of settling differences that ought to have been long obsolete, cast such sympathies as they had towards Russia, who as the stronger power would probably finish up the business to her own advantage speedily, and who, moreover, did a good export trade of her own in corn, and was not a bad customer altogether to Manchester. It may be easily guessed that Mr. Fulsby did not altogether suit Mrs. Charrington and her select circle. In fact, they all literally dreaded the event of this vulgar, boisterous, and utterly irrepressible man in the drawing-room.

Mr. Charrington was for once in accord with his wife ; he was intense in his likes and dislikes, and he positively loathed the man from Manchester. He shrank from his noise, and although Mr. Charrington was by no means deficient in gad-fly attributes his sting fell utterly innocuous on the pachydermatous hide of Fulsby. That anybody could be hurt or offended at his plain-speaking I do not think ever occurred to this braggadocio child of the spindles, but for all that a Nemesis was awaiting him.

Fond as he was of alluding to the army as an expensive and useless encumbrance, and a thing that might be profitably reduced, if not altogether done away with, he still had a hazy idea that Horace Crymes might be an awkward man to air this theory before. The Major's swart handsome face and keen dark eyes would have made most men hesitate before they ventured on taking a liberty with him; and though Mr. Fulsby was in happy ignorance of them, there were two or three stories of what the Major had done when exasperated past endurance that most thoroughly corroborated that opinion.

One evening, whether it was his evil genius that prompted him, or whether he had quaffed deeper of a peculiar brand of Irroy that he rather affected, who shall say, but joining Mrs. Charrington's circle in the drawing-room, he found that lady expatiating on the cause of those dear Turks, and trusting that Europe would intervene in their behalf. They were called so in those days, although it has been the fashion to call them ' unspeakable ' of late; what that may mean I never met any one able to interpret.

"Nonsense, madam," interposed Mr. Fulsby; "the idea of our interfering in the affairs of our neighbours, ridiculous ! we have thrown all that nonsense on one side for good, I hope. Our business is to develop our trade."

"But I suppose you will admit that nations, like individuals, must shape their conduct by some ideas of right and wrong," exclaimed Miss Aysgarth. " They are surely bound to protest, even by force of arms, against injustice ; and it certainly appears to me that this quarrel is none of Turkey's seeking."

" What have we to do with other people's quarrels ? If they must fight, let 'em fight. Trade don't develop that way ; and if it wasn't for the absurdity of maintaining thousands of armed men in idleness there would be an end to war, not that there's any fear of this country being lugged into it. I'm a self-made man myself, but I know Manchester's opinion, and I tell you, ma'am, Manchester won't have it."

" Manchester's not England," observed Crymes, quietly.

" Not England, sir ! Not exactly, perhaps ; but I suppose you'll admit that Manchester is the mouthpiece of England."

And at that time I think Manchester was somewhat of that impression.

"Place in Lancashire where they manufacture cotton, isn't it?" rejoined the Lancer in his most imperturbable manner. "They're supposed to be rather judges of the price of calico, but I don't think England looks to them for much further information."

Mr. Fulsby literally simmered with wrath ; there was an unmistakable smile on the faces of his audience at Crymes's retort.

"You rather underrate the power of trade, sir. Manchester has set its face against standing armies, and, mark me, as far as we are concerned, standing armies will cease to exist."

"Quite right," rejoined Crymes, blandly. "Didn't know Manchester had a standing army myself; but if Manchester don't want it she's quite right to do away with it."

"You twist my words, sir," rejoined Mr. Fulsby, wrathfully. "I'm a self-made man myself, and can't argue with chaps like you, who woke to find your bread ready buttered for you ; but what Manchester makes up its mind to Manchester does, and I tell you she's come to the conclusion she don't want soldiers."

"But, Mr. Fulsby, the country will never stand that," exclaimed Mrs. Charrington. "We shall never consent to do away with the army because you cotton lords consider it unnecessary."

"A useless encumbrance, madam, simply provocative of war," rejoined Mr. Fulsby tartly.

If this Utopian idea still clings to some people in these days, it is easy to imagine how much more it was the case in '53, when war had not been practically brought home to the mind of the nation for nigh forty years, and when some of the wilder theorists of the Manchester school were actually beginning to indulge in the idea of the millennium, of the lying down of the lion with the lamb, and all those other Arcadian views which mislead folks who cannot bear in mind the one fixed immutable fact, that human nature never changes, that this veneer we call civilization is mightily soon scraped off, and the noble savage, with all his grand throat-cutting instincts intact, lies beneath.

Civilized ! alack ! my setter, whose education has taught him not to rend sheep, is about as much civilized as his master, whose teaching bids him avoid rending men, and the inclination is probably more frequent in the man than the dog.

"Well, Mr. Fulsby," said Crymes, quietly, "I happen to be a unit of that encumbrance of which you complain. I don't profess to know anything about the cotton business, but any fool knows that a big war is bad for the trade of the country that goes into it. You've been kind enough to prophesy our disbandment ; I always like to reciprocate a good turn. Now listen to my words of inspiration. Before this time next year we soldiers shall be probably doubled in numbers, and that we are not thrice as strong will be cause for the nation's regret ; before this time next year Manchester will have learnt she is not the voice of England, and England will be drunk with all the intoxication of having once more thrown up her hat and stepped into the European prize-ring."

" You don't surely mean that ? " exclaimed Mrs. Charrington.

"Indeed I do. Mr. Fulsby and his compatriots have very little knowledge of the temper of the nation, and a very exaggerated idea of their own influence. This sympathy with the Turks, about which I offer no opinion, is growing amongst all classes, and the emissaries of Louis Napoleon do their best to spread it. He knows what he wants,—we don't,—and unless the Emperor Nicholas, about the proudest and most obstinate potentate in Europe, gives in we shall find ourselves engaged in a big war before we know where we are."

" Ridiculous, sir !" exclaimed Mr. Fulsby. " You pooh pooh the power of Manchester," and the irate gentleman's eyes gave symptoms of starting out of his head. "A fig for your British army. Sir, I tell you as a self-made man—"

" For which you deserve twenty-one years penal servitude," struck in Crymes, sharply. " Had you been begotten in ordinary fashion we might have pitied you ; but that you should have had the presumption to construct yourself, should be avenged with the severest penalty of the law."

For a few seconds Mr. Fulsby glared as a titter ran round the circle, then rising, looked as if about to hurl some furious retort at his assailant; but the Lancer's imperturbable countenance and tall sinewy figure perhaps rendered that hardly advisable, and with some muttered remark to the effect that personalities were no arguments, the man from Manchester made what might be termed a florid exit.   If the retort was of the strongest it must be remembered that the provocation was great.   To be told your calling is superfluous, and about to be done away with, is enough to produce irritation in the breast of man, let his vocation be what it may; while that ostentatious vaunting that our prosperity is due to our own exertions, is always likely to exasperate those who have either not exerted themselves or done so inefficiently. Most men who have done anything are, so to speak, self-made, but they don't brag about it.

"You hit too hard, Major Crymes," said Miss Aysgarth, as soon as she had mastered a strong tendency to laugh.

"Pardon me," replied the dragoon.   "Mr. Fulsby is a man who comprehends nothing but the cudgel, while the arrogance of the tail of the Manchester school towards my cloth warrants retaliation on our part to the extent of our ability and opportunity. Besides, I most thoroughly meant what I said concerning their exaggerated idea of their power in the country.   Their chiefs know better, but the mass of the Manchester party really believe they are the arbiters of English politics."

That Manchester is a power in the land, still representing as it does large manufacturing interests, no one would dispute; but it certainly does not claim for itself what it did in '53, when that famous triumvirate of quakers sped to the banks of the Neva, with considerable belief that their intervention might stay the impending war.   Fancy the autocratic Nicholas foregoing his spring at the Moslem's throat on the intercession of an embassy from Cottonopolis.   The last thirty years have dispelled a good many illusions regarding the brotherhood of nations and the decadence of the European prize-ring, things supposed to be quite accomplished previous to that pitching of ' the ropes and stakes ' around Sebastopol.

If Miss Aysgarth had accused Horace Crymes of hitting hard, she nevertheless quite appreciated such hitting, as women always do when done in their behalf; and there could be no denying that Mr. Fulsby had been for some days now a vulgar, noisy, dictatorial bore. He was scarce likely to trouble them again while the Major's sarcastic tongue was at their service, and in fact speedily took his departure, to which the ruffling of his self-importance had no doubt somewhat contributed. That Crymes was steadily advancing in Miss Aysgarth's good graces was transparent, so much so that the sulphur drinking throng already whispered it about as a settled thing; and further, were kind enough to pronounce it a very suitable arrangement, which, in their utter ignorance of all details concerning the pair, showed a large-hearted aptitude for arriving at an opinion past all commendation. But Crymes was no whit deceived by the apparent success, nor was his *ci devant* flame, Mrs. Charrington. He knew perfectly that he had as yet made no real progress with the girl, although it was a good deal to have established himself once more on a friendly footing with her; but to overstep that a hair's-breadth would be, he knew well, to undo all he had taken such pains to build up. No; he felt that he must wait and trust to the cards once more turning up in his favour.

"You progress very slowly, Horace," observed Mrs. Charrington as they strolled about the 'Stray' one morning; "but I cannot say I blame you. To push the siege more vigorously would only be to court defeat, and it is always better to avoid coming to the point until success is tolerably certain."

"You are very good, and have so clear an insight into things," returned Crymes. "News from India may serve my turn, or, on the other hand, news to India. The sulphur is in great blast this year, carrying an ounce or two more to the tumbler than usual, and consequently there is no saying what Harrogate may feel impelled to write or say. We live here in a glass-house, under the eyes of people, who, in very indolence, arrive at all sorts of preposterous conclusions concerning us. Whether they have assigned me to you or Miss Aysgarth, with which of you my elopement is speedily prophesied, who shall say; but to doubt that such rumours are current would be heresy to the old sulphur well. That amongst the crowds that come here many correspond with India there can be little doubt. Harrogate may do me a turn in that wise."

"Nobody can accuse you of not reckoning up every chance in your favour," returned Mrs. Charrington, laughing. "You remind me almost of Mr. Toodles in the play, who bought the doorplate engraved with the name of Thompson on the supposition that he might have a daughter who might grow up, and might then marry a man of the name of Thompson. Yes; Harrogate may write, no doubt, to Secunderabad, and describe you as engaged to Annie Aysgarth; but it's hardly likely to unless you bring it about yourself."

"If you cannot help me it is not to be managed," rejoined Crymes, moodily.

"And I most certainly can't. What is more, I would not if I could. I'll do a good deal for you, Horace—even colour a bit in your interest, if you like; but I'll not pen a deliberate untruth."

A curious illustration this of moral perception. Mrs. Charrington saw no harm in a little embroidery, nor even perhaps in the utterance of a pretty fib; but she refused to place a deliberate lie upon paper. I can recollect a curious story illustrative of this feeling. An old friend of mine was retiring from the army under a warrant which allowed favourable retirement after certain service, conditional upon settling in Canada. The whole thing was an absolute fraud. It involved going out to the Canadas with a return ticket, applying for a grant of land, which was at once ceded you upon payment of a few shillings per acre, with the condition that a certain portion should be cleared—the grant was always in the backwoods—within three years. You then presented yourself to the Governor-General with the certificate of your purchase, obtained from him a certificate of your settlement in the country, and returned home by the next steamer, and obtained your retirement. As for the nominal acres in the backwoods, you thought no more about them, and the required work not having been done in the three years, they again lapsed to the Crown. My friend went through the usual course, bought his acres, and then sought an interview with the Governor-General. "Of course you mean to settle in Canada, Colonel S—," said His Excellency, dipping his pen into the ink preparatory to signing the certificate.

"No, I can hardly say that," rejoined the Colonel with some little hesitation.

His Excellency threw down the pen and said, laughing,

"You can hardly expect me to sign this when you refuse to say it represents your intentions."

It was very absurd; but really the Colonel's conscientious scruples stood in his way for that day, and it was not until he recalled that his military life, guided by the Queen's regulations, had been passed in similar frauds, that for years he had been compelled to frame every application for leave as 'upon urgent private affairs,' whether they meant a month's shooting, a week's racing, or a round of the theatres, that he bethought himself he might yield to one further military fiction. He did so next day, infinitely to His Excellency's amusement.

Mrs. Charrington's conscientious scruples were on a similar par, and it may be equally to be overcome on mature consideration.

CHAPTER XX.

"YOU MUST RIDE FOR US."

To break adrift from the nets of Circe requires much resolve. I wonder how often men, conscious of the danger that surrounded them, have vowed to sever their bonds, and yet, unless aided by accident or the caprice of the lady, have found themselves powerless to throw off the gyves. Cis Calvert felt that his intimacy with the Daventrys was likely to end in trouble of some sort, and yet he did not see exactly how to withdraw from their house. He knew that the gentleman was an unscrupulous gambler; he knew that the lady, though wondrous fair, was an equally unscrupulous coquette, and yet he was on such terms with the latter as made it very difficult to change the footing on which he stood with them. Partly from pique and partly from caprice, Lizzie Daventry had devoted herself in earnest to his subjugation, and Cis found himself installed as a favoured admirer with very little effort on his own part. Day by day the chain grew stronger, and he could no longer shut his eyes to the fact that he was almost Mrs. Daventry's avowed lover, and was gradually awaking to the fact that she could be a somewhat tyrannical mistress.

Conversation was apt to languish when the Major and his wife breakfasted *tête-à-tête*. The lady was scarce likely to provoke it, as she knew by experience the unpleasant tone it was likely to take. Her spouse was generally busy over his last night's card account, notes connected with money matters, and divers private businesses of that description, previous to going down to his office. He was one of those men who find themselves settlers in Hindostan by compulsion, that is to say, they are so heavily involved to the native money-lenders that leaving the country becomes simply impossible to them, and the least hint of such a thing on their part would at once consign them to imprisonment, or would have done at the time of my story; quite possible to become a very grey-headed Sisyphus in trying to get rid of that ever-recurring stone, the exorbitant interest-bearing bills of one's younger days.

"It is no use blinking the question," said the Major harshly at last. "I must go for a *coup* over the races here next month. There's a bill to take up from Chowanders, and here's a pretty tidy account come in against you for dresses and fal-lals of one sort and another from Bombay."

"Let me see it," she remarked quietly, as she extended her hand.

He threw it across to her as he rejoined—

"I don't complain; we can't afford to look poor, but eight hundred and sixty seven rupees is money, you know."

"One can't dress for nothing," she replied, carelessly, "and you'd be cheaply out of it if that were all."

"If there are many more you'd better not have them sent to *me*," he said with a sneer. "You've friends, no doubt, who will see you don't want for frocks."

Her face flushed slightly at the insult, but she made no reply. She had some right to say she was what he had made her. From the first years of her marriage she had been the attraction of a gamester's home, the lure to bring dupes to his net. She had been taught to play the game of flirtation as if it was *écarté*, and instructed that it behoved her admirers for the most part to keep her in millinery. Daventry preferred not actually to know that it was so, but that his wife's admirers should settle her dressmaker's bills was not likely to offend his sense of delicacy.

"Another thing," he continued at length, "I shall want Calvert to ride for me. As it happens there are only some one or two fellows in the place who have any idea of jockeyship in reality, though there are dozens who think themselves within a few pounds of Frank Butler."

"Well, why don't you ask him? Surely that is your business, not mine. I don't suppose he'll make any difficulty about it."

"But that is just what the confounded fool does do," exclaimed Daventry, rising and pacing the room with impatient steps. "He says he has determined never to ride again, that he has got into such trouble about some race at home that he never means to have anything more to do with it. That's what's sent him out here, I suppose. It takes a real artist to pull a horse cleverly, and he probably stopped a favourite a little too transparently, and feels as thoroughly penitent as the rest of us when we're found out."

"And you think that is what brought Captain Calvert to grief in England," she said slowly. "I doubt it; but any way if you want anything of that sort done out here I'd recommend you not to ask him to do it."

"What nonsense you talk," he retorted impatiently. "I want him to ride Red Ronald for me, the best 'waler' in the presidency. They'll put a stiffish weight on the horse as an Australian bred one, but I think he can give it to anything they have here."

"But if he has made up his mind to ride no more, hadn't you better ask somebody down from Bombay."

"No," rejoined her husband shortly. "Woman's mission in this world is to upset man's resolutions. It will be for you to make him change his mind, and to the best of my belief you will find it not an uncongenial task. Be that as it may, remember I expect to hear that Calvert will be quite willing to ride for me if I want him, either from himself or you, in the course of the next two or three days."

"Of course I shall ask him if I am ordered to," she rejoined contemptuously.

"I must trouble you, madam, to do a little more than that," sneered Daventry, "namely, to exert your all-powerful influence that his answer shall be in the affirmative. Men don't usually say no to you when you plead in earnest."

"You at all events have slight cause to say so," she retorted sharply.

"No," he answered, laughing, "that is a necessary acquirement of matrimony; husbands who have not learnt that don't have a good time as a rule. For the present adieu, and don't forget," and so saying Major Daventry disappeared.

For a few seconds Lizzie's features wore a look of unutterable loathing. She could hardly have said whether hatred, contempt, or fear predominated in her feelings towards her husband. He had ruthlessly broken down all womanly pride and self-respect in her breast, and he had done this simply by the jeering tyranny that he exercised over her. If there had been one thing she had dreaded in the early days of her married life, it had been her husband's jibing, mocking tongue; when the first noontide of their passion passed, she found her devotion ridiculed, her fondness derided. She said truly she was what he had made her: he had killed all honest affection in her, and taught her that a heart was an inconvenience both morally and physically; that it was the nature of the sexes to prey upon each other to some extent, and that flirtation was to be made profitable by the more enlightened of their generation; that admirers were a matter of course to every good-looking woman, married or otherwise, and that admirers should be expected to supply all such trifling superfluities as gloves, flowers, fans, &c.

Men found it costly to serve on Lizzie's staff in these latter days, as her views of the superfluities got enlarged, including *bijouterie* and even riding-horses. Nothing very new about this theory of irregular taxation; it was understood as well in imperial Rome as it is in modern Babylon; there are some points the world varies very little about. Civilization may advance, but human nature never changes, and when that is sufficiently moved this veneer we call civilization seldom suffices to restrain it.

But one curious fact marked Mrs. Daventry's flirtation with Cis Calvert—she had never even hinted at a desire for anything from his hands, and concerning her wants and wishes, Lizzie was wont to be extremely candid with her admirers; and, little Bedouin that she was, Mrs. Daventry held that alone should tell Cis that her feeling for him was of a different kind from that which usually characterized her love-affairs. Calvert, unfortunately sauntering through a flirtation in which he was only half in earnest, never even thought about it. He was so bored with this Indian life that he could not forego the society of the pleasantest woman in the station, and although quite aware that to be the accredited lover of a lady who is on very indifferent terms with her husband is equivalent to trifling with dynamite, he consoled himself with the idea that it would all come out right in the long run.

Lizzie mused for a little over her husband's behest. There could be no harm, she thought, in asking Cis to do that much for her sake, and rarely as she was accustomed to dispute her husband's commands, it may be doubted whether she would have obeyed him in anything that threatened to work woe to Cis Calvert. She was by no means sure that she was in love with him,—indeed quite doubted her capacity for being in love with any man,—would have probably remarked that she had done with all that nonsense long ago ; but she was clear, nevertheless, about two points, that Cis should never receive harm at her hands, and that she could not endure the idea of his being in love with another woman.

Mrs. Daventry may not mean her admirer any harm, but there is the brewing of a cauldron of Hecate's own broth on these mixed feelings of hers.

There was little fear but what Calvert would call in the course of the day ; if he did not drop in for tiffin he was sure to look in before the evening ride or drive, in which he was now so constantly cavalier in charge. Some veteran *habitués* of the racket court, who took their exercise there steadily, and abjured all social allurements, marvelled much what had become of such a dangerous man in the left court as Captain Calvert ; but those more in the swim rapidly enlightened them, and told that converse of Hood's ' vagabond count '—

> " How for hope of winning her tender regards
> He'd cut cutting of balls, and the shuffling of cards,
> And could be found all day in her pockets."

And then there was much wagging of heads and sorrowful lamentation over another good man gone wrong, as is usually the case when feminine influence overcomes the attractions of the club or mess-table.

Cis dropped in as was usual to tiffin, and, singularly enough, happened to be the only visitor, for as a rule that meal at the Daventrys' was generally invaded by a considerable sprinkling of idlers, the only man whose absence it was possible in the whole cantonment to calculate upon with certainty being the host. But be it understood that the visitors were invariably of the sterner sex; the feminine element was in a minority, as in a society where the men outnumber the women in the proportion of ten to one it is only natural they should be.

"How nice of you to come and break my solitude!" exclaimed Lizzie, as she extended her hand. "I really thought I was going to sit down by myself. I don't mean to say that my own society is not sufficient for me at times, but to-day does not happen to be one of those times; this morning I yearn for the voice of my fellow-creatures."

"And I," said Cis, laughing, "am by no means so catholic; I restrict my yearnings to the voice of one of them."

"I curtsey, metaphorically, to the ground, monsieur, for so pretty a speech; but in the mean time curry and cutlets are getting cold. Come, let's investigate them before it is too late."

She led the way into the dining-room as she spoke, and had no reason to apologize for her luncheon. Whatever Daventry's circumstances might be, however tight might be the strings of the exchequer, he always kept open house, and was rigid in his dictum that the thing should be done properly; neither slovenly cookery nor indifferent wine were ever tolerated in any *menage* of his, and it was scarce likely that his present home should present any infringement of the rule.

"What were you doing all yesterday that I didn't see you?" said Mrs. Daventry.

"Well, I had an attack of duty, and what with one thing and another, never seemed to have a moment to myself."

"You might have found time to run up to tell me you hadn't time to call," rejoined Lizzie laughing. "I'd an Irish admirer once who never neglected that ceremony."

"Ah, but you must be an Irishman to indulge in such vagaries. 'The bull,' in the hands of the Anglo-Saxon, covers him with ridicule; we lack the assurance and that inimitable appreciation of humbug which distinguishes the Celt. Humbug an Englishman, and when he awakes to it he is wroth; humbug an Irishman, if you *can*, and he not only grins, but warms to you on tumbling to your blarney. Bar whiskey, there's nothing he's so fond of save a political ruction."

"And pray how do you come to be so learned about Ireland?"

"I have been quartered four years in the country, and know this much, that the Celt has been humbugging the Saxon ever since the latter first put foot on the green island; and the Saxon, poor fool, keeps on studying and legislating for him, and goes over to talk to him, and really thinks he understands him. Why can't he leave him to the state of anarchy and discord he delights in? Like the red man of the West, he might gradually improve himself off the face of the earth, then—"

"I brought it on myself, so have no right to complain; but when I confided to you my meek little joke about my devoted admirer in 'the Rangers,' I little thought I was to become the recipient of Captain Calvert's panacea for the woes of that Cinderella of nations."

"A Cinderella that persistently grovels in the ashes. Ten thousand pardons!" exclaimed Cis; "I cannot think how on earth Ireland absorbed the conversation in this way. I have read there was a time in London when 'the dear Poles,' an equally impossible people, similarly permeated discourse. There always seems to be some outraged nationality always irrepressible; it seems to be the 'dear Turks' just now, and judging by the papers, one really might almost think England means taking up arms in their behalf."

"Don't talk nonsense, Cis; you know England never fights except out here; anyway, I detest politics. Do you know, I have heard something about you—why you left England."

"Ah, that story has reached you at last," replied Calvert drily. "Is, I dare say, the talk of the cantonment by this."

"I don't know about that. I should think not at all likely. It was about a race, was it not?"

"Yes; but you can hardly suppose I want to discuss the miserable business over again."

"Perhaps not, but suppose I do?" and Lizzie stole a look at her companion from under her long lashes.

"You!" he exclaimed, with undisguised amazement.

"Just so; I want to know how much *she* had to do with it."

"I told you once before that my trouble had nothing to do with a woman," returned Cis, doggedly.

"Ah, so you did; but then I could hardly expect you to tell me the truth at that early stage of our acquaintance. I have some claim to demand frank confession now, I think."

"I have nothing to confess," he rejoined angrily, as he rose, "and if I had should decline to confess it. If you know my story, and choose to strike me off your visiting list, I can only regret that the pleasantest part of my life here is over, and thank you for having lightened the past."

"Sit down, please, and don't be absurd. You know my house would be open to you whatever might be alleged against you in England. If any one should be staunch to her friends, despite what may be said against them, it should be me; not that they have stood by me altogether as they should have done, but I forgive them," and Lizzie smiled sweetly, as one who, pardoning her enemies, heaped coals of fire upon their heads.

But Mrs. Daventry was not altogether satisfied. Her lover was by no means so malleable as she would have him. She was accustomed to find her victims subservient to her rein, and it was patent to her that Cis Calvert was very capable of breaking his chains. Her feeling towards him was still somewhat mixed, but if there were moments when she, so to speak, raged against him for his insensibility, as she termed it, there were others when she melted in good earnest as she thought about him. She was habituated to see men lose their heads about her, and make mock of it, and it was the knowledge that Cis had by no means lost his balance in presence of her fascinations that so provoked her.

"Do you know that you have never given me anything since I appointed you my adorer in chief," she remarked, after a considerable pause. "I really think you ought to have presented me with some token of your fealty."

"What shall it be?" he replied gaily. "It is so difficult to get anything nice here.   Shall I order you a ring or a bangle from Bombay ? "

" No, you shall give me something of your own for a keepsake. Let me have that locket on your watch chain."

It was a plain gold locket with a somewhat fantastic A graved on one side of it; but it had been the gift of Annie Aysgarth, and contained a small coil of her soft dark hair.   Calvert's face hardened as the memory of his lost love was thus rudely recalled to him.

" No," he replied sternly, "I cannot give you that.   It is a keepsake that I will never part with."

" A *gage d'amour*, of course," retorted Mrs. Daventry pettishly.

" And if it were ? "

" Then all I can say," exclaimed Lizzie vehemently, " is, that it is very bad taste, to say the least of it, to flourish your former love-gifts before the woman you at present profess to be devoted to."

Now this was to some extent an exaggeration, and yet it was one impossible for Cis to escape from.   He certainly was continually at the Daventrys', he was the lady's constant escort, and must have pleaded guilty to being engaged in a tolerably pronounced flirtation, but he certainly had never so far professed devotion to the extent that Lizzie insinuated.

" I can hardly be accused of that," he rejoined quietly ; "this locket has hung on my watch chain for some time, and you never heard me make the faintest allusion to it."

" I wonder whether you care one bit about me," she cried vehemently.   " I wonder whether there's a soul on earth has any real regard for me.   I'm a pretty woman, and it flatters your vanity to be supposed a favourite of mine ; but I doubt whether any man ever honestly cared for me—whether there's been one of you all who would have risked, not life in my behalf, but some inconvenience."

The way in which she totally ignored her husband was, though astonishing, not altogether unwarranted, for that gentleman would have been perhaps the very last man to inconvenience himself on her account.

" You know I care for you, Lizzie," said Calvert quietly,

"that I would do anything for you. I can't give you this trinket, but tell me anything you fancy, and you shall have it."

He spoke as if the lamp of Aladdin were in his possession.

"Oh yes, it is the old story," said the lady disdainfully. "You will give us anything we want, or do anything we wish, and the minute we acquaint you with our wants or wishes, then you formulate your excuses for non-compliance."

"You are unjust, and have no cause to say that of me. When I am fairly tried I don't think you will find me wanting."

"You mean that you would really do something for me if I asked you, even if it was something you didn't quite like?" and she glanced at him somewhat inquisitively, curious to know how far her empire extended.

"Can you doubt it? Prove me when you will, and you will find it so."

"That is the conventional answer you all make, and when we do prove you we see what you mean by it."

"I have done," rejoined Cis; "like you, I don't believe in over much protestation. Should the time ever come you'll find you can depend upon me."

"Good, then you must ride Red Ronald for us in the forthcoming races. There, Cis, you can't complain you've been tried very hardly," and Mrs. Daventry threw herself back in her chair with a light laugh.

In an instant Cis Calvert saw that he was trapped. After his just uttered protestations it was impossible to refuse Lizzie's request, and yet he could not but see that it was prompted by her husband. Sore very about that terrible fiasco with The Mumper, he had determined to have nothing more to do with race riding; he would give the world no further opportunity to accuse him of foul play in that line, at all events, and he had doggedly been deaf to all Daventry's persuasions on the subject. But now there was nothing else for it but to assent.

"I had made up my mind never to ride again, but of course if you want me, I am at your service," he said slowly. "Don't, please, run away with the idea that I am a great artist in the saddle. I can ride a bit, and you may at all events depend upon my doing my best for you."

"Thank you so much," she replied as she bent towards him. "You know we both gamble a little, and I don't mind confessing that, as far as I am concerned, it is necessary that I should win money somehow.   Milliners get exigeant at times, and my lord and master, though quite capable of bitter invective if I am not decently dressed, is very intolerant of their bills."

"Can I be of any assistance?" said Cis, in a low tone.

"No," she rejoined sharply.   "You ought to know that you are the last man I would take help from of that description. Let me enjoy the luxury, Cis, of having for once—well, loved a man for himself, and without thought of what he could give me."

"You do me great honour," said Cis, softly, "but I think you are wrong not to make use of me if you need it.   Never mind, Red Ronald must be driven home triumphant, and then we shall be all landed by Bendameer's stream for the present; and now, good-bye."

"Adieu—ride out with me to-morrow morning, and we'll go up to the race-course, and you shall give Red Ronald a gallop. It's worth doing, for he can stride along.   I rode him myself once, but he pulls too hard, and takes hold of his bit in a way that made me feel insufferably small at the end of two miles. I never was so done."

"Very well, I must try what I can do.   Once more good-bye."

She looked after him for a moment, then gave an impatient stamp of her little foot.

"I don't believe he cares a rush about me," she muttered. "Why can't I bring this man to my feet—I who have turned the heads of so many?   There's a woman in England, let him say what he likes; but I'll beat her if I die for it, and he shall give me that locket, her locket, before many weeks are over."

CHAPTER XXI.

NOW BARABBAS WAS A ROBBER.

Cis had a dim foreboding as he rode home, that he had done a foolish thing in consenting to ride this race, and yet for the life of him he did not quite see how he could have got out of it. Say no to Mrs. Daventry under the circumstances he could not; and after all, he argued, what harm could possibly come to himself over it? The probability was he rode as well as any one he was likely to meet; the horse was well known, and if it didn't win, well, it could not be helped. It was, no doubt, looking to what it had already accomplished, a good horse; but there was no denying it was called on to concede a deal of weight, and, as all those understanding of racing know, that brings the mightiest of turf paragons to grief at last. Still he could only do his best with Red Ronald, and if that slashing brown 'waler' failed to hold his own there was no more to be said.

Conversation becomes limited in the monotony of an Indian cantonment, and anything that breaks the wonted stagnation is hailed with acclamation. The races evoked all the sporting tendencies of the Anglo-Saxon, and men deemed innocent of turf mysteries suddenly became endued with all the shibboleth of Newmarket, and babbled of weights, trials, staying, &c., as do their kinsmen at home before the great October handicaps are decided. The Nizam's Gold Plate Cis was fain to admit was cause of as much talk, ay, and speculation, as that ill-starred cup, for attainment of which such trouble has befallen him the winter previous. This horse of Daventry's was in every one's mouth certainly, but the race carried so many penalties and allowances that it partook somewhat of the nature of a handicap, and there were various maiden Arabs that were reputed to be able to gallop, and were more or less fancied by those connected with them.

Rather prominent amongst these was a chestnut horse called Tippoo, that was always bought up with alacrity at the pool, selling at a certain price, and those who bought him were usually no neophytes at Indian racing. With one of these Cis had got rather friendly, and he, upon one of these occasions, asked him if he knew anything about Tippoo.

"Nothing in the least," replied the other, frankly. "Then why do I so often bid for him, you will ask? Simply because he belongs to Captain Gideon, who is about the knowingest hand on the Bombay turf. I don't even know whether Tippoo's coming here, but if Gideon and his horse do turn up, I can't think he'll have brought him so far for nothing. But you are likely to be more in the way of knowing than any one. Daventry's a great friend of yours, isn't he?"

Cis nodded assent.

"Well, he and Gideon were racing partners once, and though they split, it was quite a friendly dissolution of partnership. He'll most likely put up with Daventry if he comes; and if he tells any one—and that Sim Gideon will open his mouth at all is always doubtful—it will be Daventry. As you're going to ride for him, he's bound to give you a hint if Tippoo's dangerous, for I have seen you back Red Ronald more than once."

"Yes, I generally stand my own mount for a bit, and the old 'waler' is an honest good horse, though it's quite possible he may be asked to give too much weight away this time."

"That is just it. I think it will bring him to grief; but as I don't see what is to beat him, I've back'd the man. Sim Gideon's green and white sleeves are always dangerous if they start; but," said the speaker, "backing them is risky, for they so often don't."

Cis was now riding Red Ronald in his morning gallops, and the way in which the big brown Australian took hold of his bit and strode away with him increased his jockey's confidence, and he felt, despite the weight, it would take something superior in Arabs to dispose of him. Daventry and his wife were usually out to superintend the morning's exercise, and day by day the whole party got more and more enthusiastic over the prowess of Red Ronald.

Coming one evening to a dinner to which he had been asked as strictly *en famille*, he was somewhat surprised to find Lizzie endeavouring to make conversation with a slight, dark, sallow-faced man, whose nose betrayed unmistakable Semitic lineage. The new arrival was evidently no talker ; albeit the keen black eyes most certainly gave the lie to any theory that his reticence was the result of feebleness of intellect. A physiognomist would have recognized the shrewdness of the countenance equally with a man of the world, the latter by the way more to be depended on in judgment than the speculative philosopher. The thin lips were hardly indicative of his race, but they told a tale of quiet determination without much notification of intention. Captain Gideon was essentially not a lady's man ; his manners, like his dress, were quiet and irreproachable, but he had evidently no small talk, and, rarest of virtues, understood the art of remaining silent when he had nothing to say. He bowed when introduced to Cis, and honoured him with a some-what comprehensive stare, but made no attempt at conversation. Even when the races came under discussion, and the Daventrys and Cis waxed eulogistic over the powers of Red Ronald, and dwelt upon the great chance he possessed of taking the Nizam's Plate, Sim Gideon listened in a dreamy sort of way, as talk about a thing in which he could have no possible interest.

"But you have brought down a horse yourself, Captain Gideon," exclaimed Cis ; "and what is more, your chance is fancied by several people here."

"Indeed ! I don't know much about 'Tippoo' myself ; brought him with me chiefly to see what he was like. There's nothing like a good public trial to ascertain if a young one's any good."

"But that's rather exposing your hand," urged Cis.

"You needn't ride him out, you know," rejoined Gideon, sententiously. " I'm not much of a horseman myself, though I get along out here, where so few of 'em know how to sit still. I do know *that*, and so give my mount a chance ; but you'll see in the next two or three days a good many horses have their heads ridden off. More windmills to be seen on any racecourse out here than there are even at Lincoln."

" What do you mean, Captain Gideon ? "   exclaimed Mrs. Daventry.

" Well, you can see more windmills from Lincoln racecourse than anywhere I know, but nothing reminds me so much of a windmill as to see our young gentlemen out here commence finishing about a quarter of a mile from home, ' legs and arms a wallopin', wallopin',' as the old song has it."

" Ah, well," said Mrs. Daventry, smiling, " we don't intend Red Ronald to be ridden in that fashion, do we, Captain Calvert ? "

" I can only promise to do my best ; but please don't run away with the idea that I am anything more than an ordinary performer, who, like Gideon, has learnt to sit still.   I think I can win on the best horse amongst moderate amateurs, but don't pretend to do more."

A few intimates now dropped in, and cards became the order of the night.   Races are always apt to evoke a temporary spirit of gambling in the place they occur, and the whist and *écarté* ran a little higher than customary, although not so far as to be stigmatized as high play.   Cis, who had joined the *écarté* table, and been cursed with a run of persistent bad luck, could not but perceive that Captain Gideon was an expert at the game.

" By Jove ! " he muttered to himself, " if he's as good in the saddle as he is at *écarté* I sha'n't care to see him at my girths the day after to-morrow."

" I am afraid you have had a bad night," said Mrs. Daventry as Cis made his adieux. " Captain Gideon is always bad to beat at cards, and also on a racecourse ; however, I don't think we need be afraid of him this time.   Were Tippoo dangerous I should have heard of it."

" He's an old friend of yours, I suppose ? "

" Mine ! " she replied, in a low tone, while a look of ineffable disdain swept across her face.   " Merci, Monsieur !   No ; he is one of my husband's intimates."

Daybreak the next morning saw half the cantonment out to see the different horses gallop, and none of them attracted more attention than Red Ronald ; and the resolute way in which he galloped the whole of the Trimulgherry course under Calvert's guidance delighted his backers, who were further inspired with confidence by the way in which his jockey rode him, a matter of as much moment as the prowess of the horse.

Tippoo also attracted considerable attention, not so much on his own account as on the well-known astuteness of his owner. He was a neat enough looking chestnut, but somewhat small, even for an Arab, and was ridden in his work by a native jockey, although Gideon was there to superintend, and made no secret that he should ride the horse himself in the actual race.

Another of the competitors that was followed about by a knot of admirers was a handsome iron-grey Arab called Saladin. The Soldan,* as he was sometimes called, had won three or four good races, and although these naturally entailed penalties, his party thought they were no more than he could concede, except in the case of the mighty Australian ; and as a 'waler,' and on account of a long series of victories, Red Ronald had even to give Saladin a good bit of weight. This was the one horse in the race that Daventry was afraid of ; he thought he could beat him, but was fain to admit he had not got quite so accurate a line to go upon as he would have wished ; in short, the race was not quite such a good thing for Red Ronald as the Major liked when he was backing that noble animal in earnest. Money was rather scarce with him, too, just at present, and if the race for the Nizam's Plate should come off wrong, Daventry felt that he would have rather an awkward stile to get over, and he finally determined to save himself on Saladin, and with that view asked Calvert to back the horse for him, not liking, as he said, to do so himself.

The night before the races was always dedicated at Secunderabad to extensive and final pool-selling ; there had been, of course, pool-selling before as well as betting, but the heavier pools were generally reserved for this particular evening. The rendezvous

* "For Saladin the Soldan said,
　Where'er that madcap Richard led,
　Allah ! he held his breath with dread,
　And split his sides with laughing."

for this business was the public rooms, the hour half-past nine, the selling to commence punctually at ten, which enabled those interested to get their dinners comfortably, and it also allowed ample time for speculation and discussion before midnight. When the first pool was put up, the place was thronged with men in every description of mess dress, amidst whom mingled some few in civilian garb. There were many who cared little about the races further than they made excuse for a pleasant picnic, but they knew they should meet every one at the rooms and hear all the gossip of the cantonment. Where could one smoke a cheroot more profitably than in discovering what one's neighbours were saying about each other?

The prominent feature of the evening, as far as speculation went, was the support awarded to Tippoo. His owner personally bought him in pool after pool, and made several heavy bye bets about him besides. The Saladin party stood manfully to their guns, and never missed buying their horse when he went at a certain price, but Cis Calvert, who was executing Daventry's commission, interfered with them a good deal. Red Ronald, the favourite, threatened at first to decline in public estimation, as when put up his owner made no sign, but young Heckington, one of his intimate friends, came to the front, and supported him as boldly as Captain Gideon had Tippoo, winding up by betting an even thousand rupees that Red Ronald beat the latter with Tippoo's owner.

It was towards the end of the evening that Dan Sherston, the general's aide, sauntered into the rooms and inquired what was doing.

A keen sportsman all round, it was singular that he had not put in an appearance before, but, as he explained, the mail was in from England, and the Chief's despatches happening to be of considerable importance this time, getting away sooner had been impossible.

" What has been going on here? "

" You'd never guess, Dan," exclaimed one of his chums. " Gideon has been backing that chestnut pony of his as if the race was a gift to him."

" Hum ! that is startling intelligence after what we saw of the little chestnut this morning ; but I'll back my news to smother yours ! You will all see it in the papers to-morrow morning when you get them. We've declared war with Russia !"

"What ! War ! We're at war ! With Russia !" exclaimed half-a-dozen voices. "You surely don't mean that, Sherston !"

"Indeed I do ; and from private letters hear that all England is on the boil, that drums are beating, colours flying, and the nation mighty unanimous about the humbling of the Muscovite."

"And France goes with us, I suppose," said Calvert.

"Yes, and the siege of Silistria goes on, and the Guards have sailed for Malta ; in short, the ball bids fair to open in right lively fashion. Everybody at home is under orders for the East, horse, foot, and artillery."

"But I don't suppose there will be any actual fighting. Russia would never be so mad as to let things come to extremities with the Western powers. It will all end in a mere demonstration, and a peace with Turkey being patched up," observed Calvert.

"I don't know about that," rejoined a grim old colonel who had served through the Punjaub campaign, and many another tough piece of business. "The Russians are a mighty tenacious people, or, at all events, their rulers are, doggedly pursuing their own purposes, and taking little heed of what folks say concerning them. You see they believe implicitly it is their destiny to rule at Constantinople, and so does the Moslem, but they are always wrangling about the time ; then the two races hate each other, and both are impressed with the idea that it is pious, praiseworthy, and a step towards the attainment of heaven, or paradise, to cut the other's throat. No, you may as well expect to separate a couple of wild cats by expostulation now they have once commenced. I'd back it to require forcible intervention."

"But Russia would surely never risk a war with France, England, and Turkey," said Calvert.

"Why not ?" rejoined the veteran. "It is all very well to declare war against Russia, but it is not so easy to know where to hit her. The first Napoleon found that to his cost. No, mark me, Russia won't desist from her endeavours to worry the Turk until

she's had a pretty severe pummelling. In the mean time the
Moslem seems to take a good deal of worrying, and to be dying
hard."

" We haven't had a bet, Captain Calvert," said Gideon, as he
joined the circle. " Wouldn't you like to back your mount
to-morrow? Tippoo beats him for a thousand rupees, if that
suits you."

" No, thanks ; I don't bet," replied Cis.

" I beg pardon," rejoined the other, laughing. " Delighted
to find you don't fancy Red Ronald ; but about not betting,
surely I've heard you backing Saladin pretty freely this evening."

" That was different. That was not—" and here Cis stopped
abruptly, " for myself," he was about to add, but suddenly he
reflected it was hardly fair to explain that he had been merely
executing a commission for Daventry, as that gentleman had so
evidently desired to keep himself in the background regarding it.
" I had reasons for that," he concluded vaguely.

His inconsequential remark evidently attracted some little
attention from the spectators, but Gideon hastened to reply—

" Pray excuse my stupidity. One is of course not always
bound to back one's vanity instead of one's judgment. Captain
Calvert, you have made me more afraid of Saladin considerably
than I was. If you have tranquillized my nerves somewhat
about Red Ronald, it has only been at the expense of raising a
bugbear in Saladin. I shall dream I can never quite get up to
the Soldan all night."

The lookers-on smiled at this badinage, but Cis felt no little
irritated.

" If you think I have no belief in Red Ronald you are mistaken," he replied sharply, " and to show you that I hold that
opinion you can book the bet you offered. I beat you for a
thousand rupees to-morrow."

" Done," rejoined Gideon quietly, and then lounged listlessly
away.

" What is Captain Gideon's regiment?" inquired Cis of a quiet,
shrewd-looking man, who had been an apparently amused
listener to the foregoing conversation.

" The Royal Rohillas at present, I should assume ; but I

forgot you are new to India, and will scarcely understand me. Gideon has been out of the service some years, and is now simply a leading turf man ; keeps a large stud, and is a bold and dashing bettor. The Rohillas are hill tribes, with predatory instincts, and your regular turfite is of necessity imbued with the same."

"Thanks; good night," and Cis proceeded in search of his 'tat.'

As he cantered that useful animal homewards he pondered a good deal over the night's proceedings. The affair of The Mumper had made him sceptical, and again and again did he curse the mischance that had mixed him up with the Secunderabad races. Still he could see no reason for the vague feeling of uneasiness that possessed him. That Daventry should seek to make himself safe by backing his most dangerous antagonist was but natural; and that an astute racing man like Captain Gideon, who was very sweet on his choice, should endeavour to get every rupee he could on his horse was quite in the order of things, and yet, confident as he felt in Red Ronald's ability to win, he could not shake off a sense of impending trouble. His equivocal relations with Mrs. Daventry might have been deemed quite sufficient to warrant such feeling in the eyes of most men, but that source of tribulation never occurred to Cis.

The fierce tropic sun had scarce begun to relax in its intensity before all Secunderabad was on its way to Trimulgherry racecourse. The burnt-up turf reminded one more of the harrowed American track than the green sward of Ascot or Newmarket; but waggonettes, buggies, and carriages, the classification of which surpassed all knowledge, clustered thickly round the winning-post. In rear of the carriages, on both sides of the course, ran a line of marquees, each of which flew its regimental burgee, after the manner of the drags at Epsom, and where iced drinks, &c. were dispensed *ad libitum*. There was much talk laughter, and flirtation going on amongst the gathering, here and there diversified by the equipage of some sporting rajah from the city of Hyderabad, with the long tails of his horses dyed red, and his snowy turban adorned with an *aigrette* of diamonds, while his dark eyes glittered in anticipation of the fun, for in his indolent and somewhat lordly fashion your Asiatic is a keen sportsman, untroubled by the scruples which oppress his western compeer, and not one that understands why "the gladiator pale for his pleasure" should not draw "bitter and perilous breath." One thing noticeable was the absence of any attempt at a betting-ring; such speculation as was indulged in on the races virtually finished at the Assembly Rooms over-night, and there was little or no further wagering on their result.

Mrs. Daventry was there, looking her best and brightest in a bonnet that awoke pangs of jealousy and curiosity in many a feminine breast. Where did she get it? how could she wear it? and similar interrogatories were sufficient to show that their minds were much exercised concerning it; indeed, Mrs. Daventry was wont to be a subject of much tribulation to her sisters, who were always abusing, envying, and secretly admiring her. Not her beauty, for that they were much given to denying, and wondering what the men could see in her; but her *hardiesse*, whatever they might say, always commanded their respect.

Both Captain Gideon and Cis were lounging at Mrs. Daventry's carriage, lazily looking on at the two or three minor races which, like the preliminary farce at a theatre, ushered in the *pièce de résistance*. Mrs. Daventry looked restless and uneasy. Suddenly she exclaimed—

"I have just heard, Captain Gideon, that you backed your horse for a good deal of money last night."

"I certainly backed him a bit," replied Gideon quietly. "The price was tempting. He was going begging in the pools, and I have more belief in Tippoo than other people."

"But I understood you to have pinned your faith on our horse, and yet I'm told you were backing Tippoo against him for level money last night."

"Happened to suit my book. You ladies never understand the peculiar exigencies involved in that expression, and that one may be backing a horse whose chance we have no belief in, simply as a matter of figures;" and here Gideon swung himself off the box and walked away, ostensibly in pursuit of refreshment, but it struck Cis to avoid further questioning.

"I don't understand it, and I have not been able to see my

husband. I suppose it is time now you went down to weigh in," said Mrs. Daventry, hurriedly; "but whatever you do never take your eye off Captain Gideon. He not only can ride, but is a very tricky rider besides, and he don't back horses as I'm told he backed Tippoo last night without reason. That he should tell us nothing about it would not surprise me in the least. He rarely takes his most intimate friends into his confidence, and twenty-four hours ago professed to know nothing about Tippoo. Adieu for the present, and may good luck attend you."

Mrs. Daventry's last words had put Cis on the *qui vive*, and the first thing that struck him was, that Red Ronald seemed to have lost his fire and go very sluggishly in his preliminary canter. Yes, there was no doubt about it, the horse did not move with the freedom he had shown in his gallops; and Cis wondered whether there was anything wrong with him, or whether it was merely that the afternoon sun had made him lazy. "He'll wake up, I dare say, when he's set going."

"Who the devil's riding Saladin?" asked Gideon, as they walked their horses down to the post; and Cis listened with some little curiosity for the reply, as he glanced at the pale, slim young gentleman, with the mere suggestion of a moustache, who bestrode that redoubtable iron grey.

"Don't know his name," answered Tom Dufton, one of the cheeriest and most sporting soldiers in the presidency, and who was for the moment enjoying the dubious honour of piloting a Persian-bred horse, the property of one of the rajahs patronizing the meeting, which he had irreverently described as all legs and tail when first introduced to it; "but he's a young un staying with the collector, who has come out on the shoot, and 's mad to kill his tiger and all that sort of thing. The collector has got the pieces down this time, Sim, and no mistake, and I don't think you'll find the young un a duffer at the finish. I sha'n't be there to see; this long-legged brute will never get two miles, but I hear he's one of the coming lights of the Bibury Club, and took down the number of one or two of their cracks last year."

"Well, the new importations have it between them. I suppose it lies between the grey and Red Ronald."

"Hum! not quite, Sim, I should think, after the way you backed yours last night. I thought what was good enough for you should be good enough for me, and consequently am standing Tippoo for a trifle—"

"I dare say I shall be near enough to see how the new lights finish, and tell you whether the hope of the Bibury or Captain Calvert is the better jock; but here's the starter."

The despatching of some six or seven horses on a two mile contest is not a very difficult matter; that perilous advantage of getting off in front is not so eagerly snatched at as in shorter races—advantage that so often brings juvenile light-weights to grief in the temptation it holds forth to ' ride their heads off.' The field for the Nizam's Plate is delayed for a moment or two, thanks to the vagaries of Tom Dufton's mount, the Persian-bred one showing a lamentable lack of manners at the post, and then they are away. The running is as usual made by the chorus, as one may designate those that swell the field, but rarely influence the result, while the leading performers lie in a cluster behind them. At the mile post Tom Dufton feels the fractious Persian die away, not gradually, but rapidly in his hands, while at the same moment Cis thoroughly grasps the fact that Red Ronald is dead as a stone. Instead of reaching at his bit, and shaking his head in his usual fashion, he has come this first mile in a dull, inert manner that his rider cannot understand; and it becomes necessary now to shake him up, even to keep him on terms with his horses. As the chorus, including the Rajah's hope, die away, Saladin and Tippoo forge to the front, and Cis takes third place, but with the conviction that his horse will be left as if standing the minute they begin racing in earnest. He is speedily confirmed in his opinion, for, taking the lead, Gideon brings them along a cracker with a view to making the weight tell on Saladin. A cry from the carriages proclaims that the favourite is beat, as Cis is seen to be riding his horse ; it is only for a few strides, however. Red Ronald seems hopelessly out-paced, and without the semblance of a struggle left in him; and his jockey, far too good a horseman to needlessly distress a beaten animal, drops his hands and promptly eases him. Tippoo looks like winning easily, but the rising star of the Bibury Club hangs like a shadow at his quarters, and bringing Saladin with a determined rush in the last half-dozen strides, in spite of Gideon's resolute finish, lands the grey winner by a neck.

The Collector and the Saladin party generally were jubilant, as winners usually are. Sim Gideon wore his habitual look of placid indifference, as if it really was an affair in which he had no concern; but there were two faces that undoubtedly expressed dissatisfaction at the result, although, perhaps, in different ways. There was an angry flush on Calvert's countenance, as of a man who has to call some one to prompt account for his conduct; while Daventry's for once looked no little disconcerted at the result of the race, which seemed the more curious to Cis, when he reflected that he himself had backed Saladin for Daventry to an extent that must have rendered the victory of that gallant grey tolerably innocuous to him.

"What is the meaning of this, Captain Calvert? What was the matter with Red Ronald?" inquired Lizzie, as he joined the little knot round the carriage who were condoling with its fair owner on her defeat in the Plate.

"Too much weight, I suppose," replied Cis, carelessly; "the old horse fairly stopped with me when it came to racing."

Mrs. Daventry looked keenly at him for a moment, and then cried gaily—

"Well, I am ruined, and shall have to wear cleaned gloves and old frocks for the next three months. I am sorry, Captain Calvert, we ever asked you to ride such an impostor."

"You have no cause to say that, Mrs. Daventry. Red Ronald is a good horse, though he didn't show himself so to-day. He'll win many a good stake for you yet. For the present, adieu; I must go and put off my riding toggery."

"Couldn't have been a very bad race for him anyhow," exclaimed Heckington. "He backed Saladin last night to win him a pretty good sum."

"What? Captain Calvert backed Saladin?" said Mrs. Daventry, sharply. "Are you sure, Mr. Heckington?"

"Quite so.   Next to the Collector and his immediate party Calvert was the most prominent supporter of the grey."

On his way to the dressing-tent Cis met Daventry.

"Bad business very.   I've dropped a pot over it myself," exclaimed that worthy.   "I fancied my chance strongly.   I suppose it was the weight that beat him."

"Weight!" ejaculated Cis, contemptuously.   "He was no more the same horse I galloped yesterday morning than a mule's a monkey.   The horse was hocussed, and to get at who drugged him, is your next business.   He hung dead on his bridle before he'd gone half a mile."

"Impossible!" cried Daventry.

"A fact," rejoined Cis.   "I'm as sure the horse was, nay, is still, under the influence of an opiate as if I had seen him take it.   There's a proper scoundrel in your stable, and the sooner you make him out the better."

Cis Calvert is right; and it will be well for him that he also should arrive at knowledge of that scoundrel.

CHAPTER XXII.

A BITTER QUARREL.

DINNER at the Daventrys' that evening was by no means an hilarious business. It had been intended that the triumph of Red Ronald should have been celebrated by a select band of eight; but Cis Calvert and another had sent excuses at the last moment, and the remainder had very little to be jocund about. Daventry had not only lost a considerable sum of money, despite of appearances, but felt convinced that it was due to having yielded to the persuasions of his late racing confederate at the last moment, and pursued a tortuous policy instead of running his horse fairly. Gideon's shifty tactics had more than once in the days of their partnership cost him dear, both in rupees and reputation, and he ought never to have been such a fool as to listen to him. He verily believed that Red Ronald would have won had he been allowed, for although he had no intention of admitting it, none knew better than Daventry that Cis Calvert had reason for the opinion he had expressed concerning his mount. The hostess was indignant that she had been made a cat's-paw of. She did not understand it all as yet, but she felt sure that she had been bidden persuade Calvert to ride a horse which had not been meant to win, and she was exceeding wroth at this. The same queer feeling that made this reckless pirate abstain from plundering him herself, prompted her to guard against any attempt to involve him in her husband's questionable practices. Daventry might have said what he liked, but Lizzie would have been thoroughly loyal to Cis, and never urged him to ride this race for them had she not believed it to be all perfectly honest and straightforward. She did not know exactly what had taken place, but was quite as convinced that Red

Ronald had met with foul play, as had his rider, and it was with no little asperity that she replied to her husband's remark before dinner—" Calvert's very late ; but I suppose we must give him a few minutes more law," with—

" I've a note from Captain Calvert to say he's not well enough to come ; and I don't wonder at it. Such a ride as he had to-day might well make any man sick."

Daventry did not venture upon a reply ; he could cow her when they were alone, but in public she sometimes defied him. He knew that she recked little what she said when her blood was up, and that to attempt to bandy words with her was dangerous—quite capable of washing the family linen in public on such occasions ; and there never was a man more alive to the foolishness of that than Daventry—and rightly too, as some of it was of a hue more sombre than society quite tolerates.

As for Sim Gideon, whose innate love of fraudulent practices had brought about the extremely unpleasant result of the Nizam's Plate, he was as usual unmoved at the collapse of his schemes. This is invariably an attribute of great swindlers : they are as indefatigable in spinning their webs, and as undismayed at the breaking of their meshes as a spider. A thorough ' leg ' of this description, who starts with the status of a gentleman, maintains a precarious position in social circles for a marvellously long period at times, and when at last he is taken so red-handed that all club-land casts him out, accepts his ostracism with philo- sophical stoicism.

Mrs. Daventry had long retired to her room, and the other guests, after a little stiff whist, had at length departed, leaving Daventry and his guest still smoking in the verandah.

" Well, you've made a precious mess of it," observed the host, grimly. " I wish to heaven you and Tippoo had never come near Secunderabad ; left alone, I fancy I should have won right enough with Red Ronald, and landed a good stake ; now I'm stone broke."

" Pooh, you backed Saladin, or rather Calvert did for you, to about cover you. Can't see you're much hurt, anyway," rejoined Gideon in his habitual languid drawl.

" I had to bet it nearly all away again at the last moment.

The Collector challenged me to back my own horse against his, and knowing how Red Ronald would run I daren't refuse. If he'd known our little game he couldn't have had me more neatly."

Sim Gideon gave a low whistle. That any possible regard for his reputation should provoke a man into injudicious betting was simply past his comprehension; but then, it was some years since he had had a reputation worth speaking of.

"Well," he replied at length, "if you were weak enough to be chaffed into backing a horse you had given me permission to settle, you can't be surprised that you've had a bad race. I can only tell you again what I told you before, that Tippoo did not run up to his trial; if he had he would have beaten Saladin far enough. There was five times the money to be made over him that there was over Red Ronald, and the latter was the only horse I was afraid of. You couldn't scratch him, and you daren't hint to Calvert that he wasn't wanted. There was only the one way to put him out of it—that opiate in his water. It's unlucky, devilish unlucky, as I fancy you could have won with the 'waler'; but it's more unlucky for Calvert than any one."

"Unlucky for Calvert! What do you mean?" exclaimed Daventry hurriedly, and as he spoke a white arm gleamed for a second in the moonlight, as a window above their heads, and equally under the pent-house roof of the verandah, was pushed a little more open.

"Why, you see, he backed Saladin a good bit last night, and who has an idea it was for you. He rides against him to-day, and never attempts to take his horse up to him at the finish; the public generally won't understand it was because he couldn't. The public are a very muddle-headed lot, and will probably come to the conclusion that Calvert, having backed Saladin, pulled Red Ronald. I fancy there's a queer racing story against him in England. Shouldn't wonder if you're not a good deal condoled with."

"There is, though I don't know the exact particulars; but his crucifixion won't do me any good. I don't see how I'm to get back my money; and you?"

"Don't mean to be long out of mine. It won't be long before Tippoo and I tackle the Collector again, and mark me, Saladin goes down next time. The trial was right, and he hasn't a lease of his new jockey, that was a few points in his favour this time. But it's getting deuced late, so good night. I've to make an early start of it to-morrow, so if you are not up, good-bye," and Gideon sought his chamber.

Very little of the foregoing conversation had escaped Lizzie's ears. She had gone to the open casement for a little fresh air in the first instance ; but no sooner did she catch the subject of their talk, than she composed herself deliberately to listen. In her excitement to hear why it should be " more unlucky for Calvert than any one," she could not resist pushing the casement a trifle further open, lest Gideon's reply should escape her, and recognized at once the correctness of his deductions. She ground her little white teeth as she got into bed, and perhaps never felt more bitter towards her husband than she did this night. She would have laughed to scorn the idea that she was in love with Cis Calvert, but would have been much puzzled to explain why she so rigidly exempted him from that irregular taxation she never scrupled to levy on her other admirers, and Lizzie had refused to accept any but the most trifling mementoes from his hands. She was very angry to think that he had been robbed, not so much of his money,—though she knew he had lost that too,—but of his reputation, and that it was she who had lured him to his undoing. But for her he would have persisted in his refusal to ride Red Ronald, and been perfectly clear of the whole business, and now, great heavens ! he would hold her cause of it all, and perhaps believe in her complicity with Gideon and her husband. If it was only mere caprice on her part to bring this man to her feet, Lizzie would have exulted in an occurrence that promised indirectly to assist her object. A man who had fled from a racing scandal at home could hardly present himself as rehabilitated by another incurred in India. It would tend to still further part him from that woman in England of whom Lizzie felt so fiercely jealous. But a woman who loved in earnest could hardly endure that the subject of her passion should receive harm at her hands ; and Lizzie was on the verge of dis- covering that, for the first time since her ill-starred marriage, she had fallen genuinely in love. She had run away from school with her husband only to be speedily disenchanted. The moon-stricken Juliets of this world, with their milk-and-water fantasies, little dream of the fierce passions of the Cleopatras; and it is only in their noon-tide at times that even they make such dis-covery, and then—well, we can but wish them well through with it.

"I am afraid your schemes went a little awry yesterday," observed Mrs. Daventry to her husband the next morning at breakfast.

The remark was made in soft, indifferent tones, apparently; but the Major's trained ear detected the covert sarcasm imme-diately.

"You're about right; they did. Money is likely to be scarcer than ever for some little time, so the less you come to me for it the better."

"It had no business to be scarce," she replied haughtily, and in a manner that involuntarily attracted his attention. "If you had not been led away by Captain Gideon's over-cleverness, but simply trusted to a good horse, with a good man on him, to win your money, you would have done well enough. I ventured once to remark when you were partners, that Captain Gideon's habit of invariably going round two sides of the triangle to get where he wanted would infallibly beat him in the end."

If irritated he was somewhat struck by the shrewdness of the illustration.

"You happen to be right in the present instance," he rejoined, sharply; "but great *coups* are not brought off without a little financing. Tippoo didn't come off; but it was the best thing I have been in for years, and it was very near landed."

"Quite so; only Tippoo, having metaphorically to go round two sides of the triangle to Saladin's one, was of course defeated."

"That will do!" shouted the Major. "Unnecessary discus-sion of disagreeable subjects is the most ridiculous waste of time conceivable. I presume you have said your perfectly uncalled-for say."

"I have only to add that I request you will not induce me to lead my friends into such dubious conspiracies in future. Captain

Calvert may be seriously compromised by—by Captain Gideon's roguery."

"Turned moralist by all that's incomprehensible," exclaimed Daventry in blank astonishment. "Let's look at you, madam, in your new character. I suppose you'll be troubled with a mission next, with a big M. Listen to me; I stand no fooleries of that nature. You may dance, ride, and flirt to the top of your bent; but you'll do as I tell you, and not trouble me with moralities."

"I will take no more part in entrapping men to risk their characters in such arrant villanies as this last you and Captain Gideon plotted," she retorted proudly.

Daventry walked across to her and looked down keenly into her face. She met his gaze without flinching for a moment, and then her glance faltered, and her eyes dropped.

"By the gates of Somnath she's in love with him!" exclaimed the Major with a burst of derisive laughter.

"And if I were!" she returned passionately, as she sprang to her feet. "Have I received such kindness and loving consideration from you these past years as should make such a thing impossible? Have I not been openly flung at the head of any man who had either money or interest to serve your ends? Have I not even been bidden take my milliners' bills for payment to those who should have dreaded a further settlement with you for presuming to interfere had you been a man instead of the despicable black-leg you are? Has there been any tie between us save fear of you, and the rending of the last few rags of respectability that covered me on the one side, and the sordid feeling that I was of use to you on the other? Don't suppose that I acknowledge any authority to control me in the future save that of mutual convenience. Separate yourself from me, and see what comes of it. You owe me more than I owe you. More than one of your many scrapes you would never have tided over without my help. Try me too hard, and you will see what it is to have me against you."

She ceased, and overcome with her excitement, threw herself back into a lounging-chair that was handy.

"She's broken loose, by Jove!" thought the Major. "I'm

perfectly right; it's love for this beggar Calvert has put the devil in her. There wasn't a better broke woman in the country, and the idea of her ever caring about a fellow in earnest, with all her experience, seemed preposterous; but, by the Lord! when they fall in love they're all out of hand, and there's no counting what pranks they'll play."

"I'll not argue our mutual obligations," he rejoined cynically, "it's hardly worth while. If you mean running away with Calvert, don't think I am going to interfere. It will be un-pleasant for three people, but before the year's out I fancy Calvert is the one who will be most alive to the mistake. You also may find those 'rags of respectability' garments not to be found in all shop-windows. No, we'll not discuss it further," he interposed sharply, as Lizzie seemed about to rise again; "best not. Go or stay, but in the latter case you'll do as I tell you. Good-bye for the present."

For a few minutes after Daventry's departure Lizzie sat motion-less, but her little hands gripped the arm of the chair as if they would crush it, her eyes glittered with anger and excitement, her breath came short and thick. She trembled with passion, and it was, perhaps, as well no weapon had been to her hand during that last speech of her husband's. Women have stretched men lifeless at their feet for such hideous gibing ere now, and Lizzie was not of a temper to reck consequences under bitter provocation. At length she rose, and stepping out into the verandah, began to pace slowly up and down and think. There had been many a hot quarrel between her and Hugh Daventry during their ten years of wedded life, but he'd never ventured to loose his mock-ing tongue so coarsely as to-day. Previously she had invariably succumbed to his sneers, but was conscious this time of having held her own. Still the more she thought of it the more she felt that the quarrel between them was *à l'outrance*. She might not go off with Cis Calvert, but she could no longer live with Hugh Daventry. She had no woman friend with whom she could take refuge in this emergency, for, as she well knew, Lizzie Daventry, under her husband's protection, and backed by her own dauntless assurance, had hard work to hold her own; but deprived of those, to aid her was simply to swamp the woman rash enough to constitute herself her champion. Reckless freebooter as she was, and merciless as she had been at times in her exactions from her victims, Lizzie had a certain queer vein of chivalry in her.

"No!" she muttered, with a little sharp laugh very different from her usual ringing peal, "those who have been good to me, poor dears, have as much as they can do to take care of themselves. I'll not transfer my troubles to crafts frail as my own, and so drown my friends;" and then once more Lizzie marched slowly up and down, thinking of what she had best do.

Wrong and indefensible it might be, but the idea of eloping with Cis Calvert held a very prominent part in her deliberations. She was rapidly awaking to the fact of how very dear this man was to her, and the more it dawned upon her, so in similar ratio increased the misgiving of whether he had any love for her. What should she do? That she would leave Hugh Daventry before the week was out she was determined—but how? Ah! that was not quite so easy to come to a conclusion about.

"At all events," thought Lizzie, "I must see Cis again. I am bound both to wish him good-bye and to justify myself in his eyes. He shall at all events know from my own lips that I was innocent of the treachery practised on him in the matter of Red Ronald, though I can't think Cis would believe me guilty of having any knowledge of such a thing when I begged him to ride for us. Robbers we are, both of us; but even Hugh never would have so out-Barabbassed Barabbas if it had not been for that detestable Captain Gideon."

But the next day and the day after passed, to Mrs. Daventry's amazement, without Cis putting in an appearance, nor did they bring a line from him explanatory of such an unusual circumstance. With her husband she hardly exchanged a word, and even he was as yet unaware that Gideon's prediction had been fulfilled—that already a murmur was running through the cantonment that Red Ronald had been unfairly ridden, and that Captain Calvert had won a nice stake over Saladin's victory; such head, indeed, had the scandal arrived at that on the third day the colonel of the Royal Dunbars had sent for Calvert to his bungalow and acquainted him with the story. That Cis should repudiate it in most unmeasured terms was but natural; but he avowed frankly that in his own opinion the horse had been, in racing parlance, "got at."

Now the Royal Dunbars had the mischance to be commanded at that time, as has happened to divers other distinguished regiments in turn, by a vacillating, irritable old woman, keenly jealous of his own power, and wonderfully afraid of those in authority over him; not the man this to stand up for one of his officers in trouble, but, on the contrary, certain to abandon him for fear of offending the authorities. In Cis's indignant denial —and that it was made with some warmth be sure—he thought he discerned want of respect for himself.

"Want of temper, Captain Calvert," he spluttered, "will not rebut a rumour of this sort. It will be more to the point if you write me a letter to denounce Major Daventry, so that I can forward it to the General."

"I don't denounce Major Daventry, sir. I say in my opinion the horse was drugged; I don't for one moment assert with his owner's knowledge."

"Ah, well, if you will mix yourself up with people like that, a man is judged a good deal by the society he keeps."

"That is somewhat hard on him, Colonel Milkinson, when he belongs to the Royal Dunbars," retorted Cis, now thoroughly angry.

"What do you mean, sir?" stammered the Colonel, dimly conscious of hidden sarcasm in this rejoinder. "By heavens, I am not the man to tolerate disrespect. You have not got on with us since you joined. You're bringing a scandal on us now; in short, sir," continued Milkinson, churning himself gradually into a state of much wrath, "the regiment does not like you."

"And that is by no means the worst of it," replied Cis, who was getting cooler in proportion to the other's rising choler.

"Not the worst of it! By the Lord, sir, what can be—"

"I don't like the regiment," interrupted Cis, blandly.

For a few seconds Colonel Milkinson was literally dumbfoundered. That any one should presume to consider service in his regiment anything short of Paradise was inconceivable; then he spluttered out in a voice that trembled with passion—

"Under those circumstances, sir, the sooner you leave it the better."

"Quite so; I am glad to find we are of one mind on that point. I will make my arrangements with all possible despatch, and presume, Colonel Milkinson, I may reckon on you to facilitate them."

"They cannot be too quickly made, Captain Calvert, for both the credit and comfort of the Royal Dunbars."

Cis flushed angrily, for he felt that old Milkinson had "scored one" to wind up with, and a fierce retort rushed to his lips which for once he had the prudence to swallow. "I shall send in my papers to-morrow. Good-morning, sir."

When Cis reached his own bungalow and began to reflect, he speedily came to the conclusion that he had veritably "done it" this time. He had made up his mind to abandon his profession, and distinctly told Milkinson so. To withdraw from that position would be excessively humiliating, and it was possible the Colonel might demur very much to such retraction even if he himself wished it, which he did not. No, better quit the service at once; he could not go from regiment to regiment, leaving always an ugly story behind him. And then he thought grimly what would they think of him at The Firs? What would York and his old comrades of the Lancers say when the news came home that he had had to leave the Royal Dunbars on account of another racing scandal? and as he thought of Annie Aysgarth listening tearfully to the story, and perhaps even crediting it, his lip twitched a little. The minute Milkinson had pointed out the rumour afloat concerning him he recognized at once how terribly against him appearances were. People cannot believe in a man being always wrongfully accused. A man may be charged with roguery wrongfully, and his friends believe that it is so, but when a few months later he is once more cited for the same offence their belief in him is bound to be considerably shaken. Brought up twice in six months for stealing watches, and the odds are, the man is a professional pickpocket, and not the victim of untoward circumstances. Cis saw all this clearly, and the more he thought of it the more convinced he was that the service had done with him. A man with two such stories tacked to his name could not continue in a profession in which they would meet him at every step. What he was to turn his hand to next he didn't know, but at all events he should get clear of a country he detested, and would have the proceeds of his commission at his disposal while he looked round.

He turned to the table for a match with which to light a fresh cheroot, and suddenly became aware of an English letter lying there—sign that another mail was in. Those were stirring times, and the mails eagerly looked for. A glance showed him it was from Harry Harperley. He tore it open; it was dated Woolwich, April, 1854, and ran as follows :—

"DEAR CIS,

"We are just off for the East, have been swinging our horses all day, and sail to-morrow. We were rather in a funk we should be left behind, as we saw so many other regiments go before we got a hint we should be wanted. The excitement is intense, though there is any amount of difference of opinion about how things will turn out. The general opinion I think is, there will be no fighting, and that the Russians will cave when they find we are in earnest. At all events, nearly all the infantry and artillery have been pushed on to Varna, a place on the Black Sea, of which no doubt you never heard. We are all getting so learned about Turkey, and do nothing but read about her, and study maps of her, and dream of seeing Seraglio Point, the Golden Horn, the Sweet Waters, and smoking our chibouqes in the big bazaar at Stamboul. The governor has behaved like a brick—paid all my ticks, and gave me *carte blanche* for an outfit, but that is not, of course, a very big affair. He came up to town to see the last of me, and will run down here to-morrow to wish us all God speed. It's worth being a soldier now, I tell you; as Strangford says, the public is only just beginning to appreciate us. All the bands are perpetually playing 'Cheer, boys, cheer,' I presume with a view to exhort the nation not to be quite heart-broken at our departure. Hang it all, Cis, how I wish you were with us; and if not exactly with *us*, you can be with the army if you like. All sorts of fellows are volunteering, and I heard the Chief say last night,—he'd just come back from having a last few words at the Horse Guards,—'It don't look as if the Government thought it would all end in smoke ; the military bigwigs there are besieged by volunteers, and, sign of the way the wind blows, I hear, accept the services of all who are worth their salt. Any man who has served for a few years is sure of employment. They are going to raise all sorts of Turkish auxiliary corps.' Good-bye, and God bless you. Annie told me to give you her love when I wrote, but she would send no further message, although I rather pressed her.

" Yours ever,
" HARRY HARPERLEY.

" P.S.—Wild rumours that the allies really mean striking a blow, which I presume in our less stilted vernacular means have a cut at the Ruskis. *Viva !* May we arrive in time."

Cis read Harry's letter through twice, and then throwing it down sat smoking and musing for a good half-hour ; at the end of that time he rose and muttered, " That's what I'll do. My papers go in to-morrow, and I'll be off to Bombay in three days. The General's sure to give me leave under the circumstances, and from Bombay I'll make my way straight to Constantinople. What to do next I shall find out there. Yes, when a man is like me ' *sans six sous sans souci*,' it is about time, like the black Mousquetaire of the legends, to remember there is active service as a distraction. I know nothing about it, but if it *is* a fight, I should think the chances are there'll be plenty of it. Anyway that's settled."

Mrs. Daventry never entered into Cis's calculations, and yet, as a man of the world, he ought to have known she was not exactly to be left out of them.

CHAPTER XXIII.

"GOD BLESS AND GUARD YOU, DEAREST."

CALVERT kept his intended departure from the Royal Dunbars as quiet as he had kept his premeditated flight from York some eighteen months previously. He had very few debts in the cantonment, and had not lost anything over the race to signify, so that his arrangements were soon made. He sent his papers to the Colonel, with an application for leave home pending their acceptance, the ratification of which leave he pledged himself to await at Bombay, while the paymaster of the regiment promised to look after the sale of his effects and all minor money matters. Then he wrote to Daventry, as Chief of the Commissariat, requesting him to lay a *dâk* for him to Bombay, as he was going up there on leave, but mentioned no word of his abrupt retirement from the Royal Dunbars; and then he thought that he must go and say good-bye to Mrs. Daventry. He intended to neither mention his selling out nor the scandal about Red Ronald, which had in some measure led to it; in some measure only, because, had he liked either the corps or the country, the charge against him was of no such nature as to have compelled him to retire. It was easy to prove that he had backed Saladin for Daventry, and though Red Ronald had certainly run very badly in his hands, still jockeys cannot be held accountable always for the vagaries of the animals they bestride.

But there were too many people necessarily cognizant of Calvert's intentions for them to remain a secret many hours, and it was not long before the news of his retirement from the regiment reached Mrs. Daventry. Young Heckington of the Royal Dunbars, who was a pretty constant frequenter of the house, brought her the intelligence, and she further drew from him that

Cis Calvert's riding of Red Ronald had been severely commented on. He did not venture to insinuate that it had been more than found fault with, but Lizzie understood him thoroughly.

"Fools!" she said, indignantly; "they don't understand a race when they see it. Nothing could be more palpable than that there was something wrong with the horse. He went very different from the way he galloped the morning before."

"Pity he backed Saladin over-night," said Heckington.

"And if he did it was for my husband," Lizzie was about to burst forth; but suddenly she reflected that was not altogether a satisfactory rebutting of that unfortunate fact, insomuch as it merely proved Red Ronald's owner backed the winner, and might have given corresponding instructions to his jockey.

"I have yet to learn, Mr. Heckington," she replied coldly, "that because a gentleman fancies the chance of another horse more than his own, and in consequence backs it, he cannot be depended on to do his own mount justice."

The way she said this was superb. She might have spent her days in strict and high-principled circles, instead of having been for ten years the wife of an unscrupulous gambler. As for young Heckington, he was taken completely aback, although he certainly might have known better. He knew Cis Calvert was a great favourite of Mrs. Daventry's, and he should have known that to say anything to a man's detriment before a woman whose particular friend he is lays you open to assault always.

At this juncture Captain Calvert was announced, and Heckington thought it a favourable opportunity to make his adieux.

Lizzie's pulse quickened a little as she came forward to welcome Cis, and it well might. She knew that he had come to say good-bye, and she had just awoke to what that meant to her. The vital question as far as she was concerned was, did it mean anything to him? This interview must show; and if he did care for her, what then? To a woman stung to madness by her husband's insults that was a rather critical thing to determine, and one in which passion was like to supersede prudence as far as she was concerned. As for Cis, although not altogether blind to Mrs. Daventry's capricious preference, he was far from having any idea of the stormy passion that lady had conceived for him.

There were so many forces at work of which he knew nothing, foremost of which was her husband's brutality, and, secondly, pique at his own indifference to her fascinations. That is hardly the correct term either, for Cis showed himself very sensible of her attractions, although he was resolute not to succumb to them. It had seemed to Lizzie almost due to herself to subjugate this man who hesitated to hold her chains. What she had begun as a matter of sport had resolved itself into earnest before she was aware of it; and she who had queened it so many years had suddenly been conquered in her turn. *Væ victis!* Cis, did he but know it, is avenging some numbers of his fellows who have experienced dour times at the hands of Circe.

"And so, Cis, you are going to leave us," said Mrs. Daventry, as their hands met. "I told you you would some little time back, but I thought you would wait till the Royal Dunbars went home, at all events. I hear your papers are in; is it true?"

"Quite true; they went in the day before yesterday."

"Sit down here—this low chair, and tell me all about it," said Lizzie, as she seated herself on the couch.

"There's not much to tell. You know I am very weary of this country, and that, except yourself, I care for nobody in it. I found a letter the other night from a friend in the Lancers, telling me they were ordered to the East, that all the army was going there, and urging me if I couldn't get away from here to sell out and volunteer. Any man with a few years' experience of the service is pretty certain of employment."

"And that is your sole reason for this sudden step?"

He nodded assent.

"Loyal as ever," she murmured. "Cis Calvert, don't tell lies to me," she suddenly exclaimed; "I know better. I have heard the whole story, and how the fools dare to throw mud at you for your riding of Red Ronald. I wish, Cis, I had bitten my tongue out before I had ever persuaded you to ride him; but with all my experience of Major Daventry," she continued, in mocking tones, "I never dreamt that he was capable of such deliberate villainy. I told you there was something wrong just before you went away to dress. I know all about it now: they arranged the race for Tippoo, and as for Red Ronald, he was stopped in the stable."

"I knew that," rejoined Calvert; "but of course," he continued, in very marked, deliberate tones, "*without* Major Daventry's knowledge."

Lizzie understood him. She saw that, though he knew pretty well what had happened, he intended no admission to her that he believed her husband cognizant of it.

"And do you mean to tell me this had nothing to do with your sudden resolve ?" she asked, incredulously.

"Next to nothing. My losing my temper with old Milkinson had infinitely more. Indeed, except in indirect fashion, I may say the race had little to say to it. I must tell you about my interview with Milkinson; it was rather rich;" and then Cis proceeded to recount his little but lively spar with the Colonel, which he did with inconceivable gusto, not even omitting Milkinson's parting shot.

Mrs. Daventry was much amused, and laughed no little at the narration.

"You must have nearly given Colonel Milkinson a fit, I am sure ; and one thing, Cis, I must say, surprises me—that he didn't put you in arrest. He is so very fond of exercising his prerogative in that direction, and you seem to have given no little provocation."

"Not liking your regiment is punishable by no military statute," remarked Calvert, sententiously.

"You treat it lightly," replied Lizzie, suddenly recalling to mind that their conversation was not couched in the serious vein to which she wished to restrict it, " and it is like you to do so ; but I know very well, Cis, that it is this race that is the cause of your quitting the service, and that I, miserable that I am, induced you to ride. Yes, I who would have cut my right hand off sooner than bring you to grief."

"Now, pray don't distress yourself upon that point," rejoined Calvert, who was not altogether unprepared for a slight scene in saying good-bye to Mrs. Daventry. "You haven't brought me to grief in the least, and if you had, upon my soul, I think I should thank you. I ought to have sold out of the Lancers, and then I should have got an appointment, and been in Bulgaria by this time. I have done no good out here, and with the exception of your friendship shall have not one ray of light to look back upon in my Indian experiences."

"Friendship, Cis! and is that *all* you have to give me?" murmured Lizzie in low, tremulous tones.

"All I have to give any woman now," he replied quietly. "I thought you understood long ago that I was a broken man when I came here. If I'd been a Frenchman it would have been the Zouaves and Algiers, as an Englishman it was the Royal Dunbars and India."

"As if I cared one straw about that!" she replied passionately—"I who have belonged to *les enfants perdues*, as they call the marked companies of the Zouaves, all my life."

"And as such we have met, recognized each other, and shall be sworn comrades always. My love is given, as you know, hopelessly. I never hope to claim the woman I once thought to marry now."

"You told me," hissed Lizzie between her teeth, "that there was no woman concerned in the scrape that brought you to India."

"Nor was there; but the scrape separated me from the girl I was engaged to. I suppose you'll admit that was a very possible circumstance."

"And how dare you make love to me then?" exclaimed Mrs. Daventry, utterly oblivious of the queer morality formulated in her question.

That he should dare to make love to her as a married woman seemed of no account; but that being infatuated about a girl in England, he should presume to make love to her, Lizzie apparently considered as a crime of the deepest dye.

"I don't think I ever did exactly," replied Cis, slowly. "You know you're so awfully nice, fellows can't help themselves, and do it almost without being aware of it."

"And you class yourself with the rest!" she replied contemptuously. "And you think I treated you as I treat them? You lie—you know better."

"I don't think you are quite fair," he replied. "You have

treated me with great kindness I'll admit; but, Lizzie, I have never been your lover—an admirer if you will, a *bon camarade* amongst the free lances, I acknowledge, bound to stand by you in your need even; but your lover—no."

"You admit you are bound to stand by me in my need," she exclaimed, rising and standing opposite him with her hands lightly clasped in front of her, "and I never was in greater need than now. My husband's insults have become more than even such a woman as I can bear. Cis Calvert, I love you very dearly; save me, save me from myself, take me away with you. I will work, beg, nay lie, steal for you if needs be. You are going to the war, to rough it; don't think that would have any terrors for me, or that you would find me a clog on your movements. I can both ride and use a pistol if needs be; but oh, Cis, don't leave me behind."

"My dear Lizzie, this is madness. I have told you I have no love to give you in return for your devotion. I cannot accept all when I have nothing to give in return."

"You say you will never be able to marry that other woman. Oh, Cis, why cannot you take one who loves you so truly? I ask so little. I am content to be your mistress," she exclaimed, as the blood rushed to her temples, and she fell at his feet. "But oh!" she continued, as her voice sank to a whisper, "I am so weary of all this mock love-making."

Her hands were clasped together on his knee, and the dark eyes flashed up in his face from beneath the wet lashes with a passionate eagerness that might have well turned any man's head. Cis was no Joseph, and though he had no intention of running away with Mrs. Daventry when he called to bid her good-bye, it was just possible she might have run away with him but for one thing—she stung Cis by alluding to Miss Aysgarth as 'that other woman.' In total ignorance of Annie's name, it is difficult to say what else she could have called her; but that slight circumstance steeled Calvert's heart.

"Impossible, my dear Lizzie," he said gently, as he raised her to her feet. "If I had love to give you it might be different. Point out any way in which I can be of use to you, and it shall go hard but what I manage it for you."

“ Fool that I am,” she exclaimed, as she dashed the tears from her eyes. “ Kiss me, Cis, for once, as a sign that my madness of the last ten minutes is forgotten. There,” she continued, as he touched her cheek lightly with his lips ; “ now we are friends once more. Sit down and don’t speak to me for a little ; ” and Lizzie began to pace the room with rapid steps.

Calvert sat silently waiting for the concluding act of the drama. What would be her next proposition ? In good truth he could not help wishing his final valedictions said, and himself on his route to Bombay. It was impossible to guess what this exasperated woman might propose doing. The Daventrys kept up appearances very fairly before the public, but Cis had been too intimate not to have had occasional glimpses behind the scenes, and was quite aware that there was considerable friction in the workings of the domestic machinery. He had little doubt that an irreconcilable quarrel had taken place between the pair, and that Lizzie was capable of proceeding to extremities she had just afforded pretty positive proof.

Suddenly she stopped opposite him, and said fiercely, “ My mind is made up. I have been his slave for years, but I’ll be so no longer ; I’ll bear his ill-treatment no more. No, Cis,” she cried hastily, in answer to a low ejaculation on his part, “ he does not beat me. A man who understands it can punish a woman more with his tongue than if he took a dog-whip to her. You say you will stand to me ? ” and she looked straight into his face.

“ Most certainly.”

“ Then I want you to lend me two hundred pounds. Can you do it ? ”

“ I should fancy so, with very little trouble. I have all my commission money to fall back upon, and I’ve no doubt between our paymaster and a native sheroff I could let you have it in the course of a few hours.”

“ Thanks, so very much. What do I want it for ? You’re dying to know, but don’t like to ask. Ah, well, to pay my milliner’s bill, say. My husband would tell you, no doubt,” she continued, in sneering tones, “ that the use of your purse will always console a woman for the loss of your love.”

Suddenly Lizzie's voice faltered, and without further speech she burst into a fit of hysterical weeping.

For some few minutes Cis tried in vain to soothe her. She repelled him angrily; while her convulsive sobbing shook her violently. Gradually the storm wore itself out, and at last she motioned Calvert to come near the couch upon which she had thrown herself.

" Don't despise me utterly, Cis, because in my misery I say hard things. I tell you no lie when I say I have never loved man as I have loved you. It is all over, and we must part. Another minute, and you shall lay your lips to mine in a final farewell. But I cannot stay here. You must find me the means for escape ; it will be easy to find the opportunity if I only have money. We may never meet again, and yet I have a presentiment we shall, and before very long. Good-bye ; God bless and guard you, dearest." And as Cis bent over her, Lizzie threw her arms round his neck, pressed one passionate kiss on his lips, then rapidly releasing him, motioned that he should leave her.

That evening Lizzie received a small bag of rupees, and a draft on a well-known banking firm in Bombay, and the morrow's morn saw Cis Calvert on his way to Constantinople.

CHAPTER XXIV.

" BOOT AND SADDLE."

SOME months have elapsed since Major Crymes so differed at Harrogate with the man from Manchester on the probabilities of war. There is no question about it now, England is AT war. True, not a shot has been fired; but the bray of martial music is incessant in her seaport towns as her soldiers hurry to the ships awaiting them; the hammer clangs ceaselessly day and night in her dockyards and arsenals; patriotic songs ring from every ale-house parlour, and her people are filled with the lust of carnage.

Amazing this to the Manchester school, who deemed the millennium commenced, and the art of throat-cutting falling into desuetude; destined later to discover that production of cotton is not the chief end of life, nor calico the main luxury of nations.

All the vast mercantile marine of the Western Powers is laid under embargo, and other industries stand aside while the more important exportation of iron, humanity, and saltpetre is in hand. Where it is to go and what is to be done with it has not yet been determined in any way; the plan of campaign not so much an object as to impress upon the Czar that England will not have it, that France will not have it, and that the sooner he and his Cossacks recross the Danube the better. Could the Emperor Nicholas have been made to understand this in the first instance, the Crimean war might never have been; but the Czar had as much belief in the power of the Manchester school as Mr. Fulsby. Later it was not likely that the Emperor of Russia could go back, and fighting became inevitable.

Radicals make wars and revolutions from failing to understand that the man who will not fight runs infinite danger

of getting kicked, and that anarchy is not kept in check by
verbiage.

If there was a man enthusiastic about the turn things had
taken, it was Mr. Charrington. Like most anglo-Indian officials,
he had much antipathy to Russia, and infinite jealousy of the
steady manner in which she was extending her sway through
Central Asia. Like most men who have held high office in
India, he was well up in her past history, and knew that
whenever a born leader of men appeared among them, the hordes
from Turkestan gravitated to the banks of the Helmund, and
from thence swept down like hawks on the rich plains of
Hindostan, the looting and ravaging of which was ever a tempting bait with which such a captain as Nadir Shah might attract
men to his standard. That it was Russia's destiny to lead such
an invasion Mr. Charrington had no doubt whatever, and
therefore considered any crippling of the Muscovite most desirable—an impression not altogether out of date in the present
day.

It was one of those chill, grey March evenings, with a keen
nor'-easter sweeping down the Ouse; the fall of one of those
days when, as Kingsley sings :

> "Chime, ye dappled darlings,
> Down the roaring blast ;
> You shall see a fox die
> Ere an hour be past."

The York and Ainstey had " carried a head " that morning, and
the gallop been both fast and far ; and in the billiard-room at
Byculla Grange were now gathered many of our old friends who
had taken part in the fray, enjoying all the luxury of tea, a pool
before dinner, and a good gossip. Standing in front of the fire,
and still in his boots, although he has doffed his red coat for a
plain velvet smoking-jacket, is Horace Crymes, engaged in conversation with his hostess. The house is full of guests, and
Crymes and one or two of his brother-officers have come to dine
and sleep ; for, as their hospitable host says, this is no weather
to turn out after dinner, save in case of necessity.

"A life off blue!—who's blue?" cries young Harperley, as

still in his pink he leans over the table, and drops that cerulean-tinted ball artistically into the top pocket.

" I am.   What a shame, Mr. Harperly ; I was regularly sold by yellow," cried a pretty, fair-haired girl, laughing as she put down her sixpence.

" Perfectly true, Miss Danvers.   Who's yellow ?   Why, Stratford !   Tell him he must advance you a florin to go on with, or you'll be in the Bankruptcy Court.   It was his reckless attempt to cut in the black left you over the hole.   All right on the white."

" You don't hold me for half-a-crown, Harry," cried Mr. Charrington, the proprietor of the ball in question.

" Done at once, sir, and in you go," rejoined the Cornet, suiting the action to the word.   " I'll trouble you for three shillings—half-a-crown, and a tizzy for the life.   Serves you right, Mr. Charrington, for trying to make a child like me nervous on his stroke."

" It strikes me, Master Harry, you're not likely to suffer much from that complaint," rejoined his host, laughing as he handed over his money.   " But where's your sister ? "

" She's a wee bit tired after her gallop, and thought she would lie down till dinner.   She had her tea sent up to her,—thanks."

" It's a fact, I assure you," said Mrs. Charrington.   " I had it in a letter I got yesterday from an old friend of mine who is in that presidency, and knows all that Deccan country well."

" It seems almost incredible.   He seemed so thoroughly in earnest fifteen months ago.   I can hardly believe in his forgetting Miss Aysgarth so soon," replied Crymes, quietly.

" Can't you indeed," said his hostess, with a mocking twinkle in her eye.   " I could imagine you, for instance, forgetting most of us in the same time.   But joking apart, I have heard of this Mrs. Daventry before.   I never saw her, but I am told she is a very pretty woman, and that anyhow she is one of those women your sex all go mad about.   That is a thing that has puzzled me as it has puzzled many of my sisters, and doubtless will to the end of time.   I have seen you all wild about women who were certainly in my eyes neither good-looking nor well-dressed.

Clever, I presume, they were, but wherein their fascination lay was hard to see. I believe you are a good deal like sheep, and bow down in adoration because some bell-wether of mark has thought fit to kneel at the shrine. There are men in London, I fancy, could establish a Hottentot in such place did they choose."

"There is something in what you say," rejoined the Major, laughing; "but is Calvert very deeply smitten with this Mrs. Daventry?"

"He's never away from her side. Daventry is a complaisant husband, who takes his own way, and recognizes his wife's privilege under such circumstances of doing likewise. She, from all accounts, is a woman who takes care never to be without an *attaché* to administer *les petits soins* for which she can't depend upon her husband. At least such is what my informant tells me, and I have heard strange stories of Mrs. Daventry and her triumphs before, mind."

"There is nothing very strange in a man becoming the slave of a pretty woman," rejoined Crymes; "especially in India, where the monotony of life notoriously disposes men to fall in love with other people's property."

"Ah," replied Mrs. Charrington, laughing, "it's a country would have rather suited you. But I shall leave you; it's pretty nearly time to begin dressing for dinner."

"Well, Crymes," said the host, as, billiard-cue in hand, he lounged up to the fire-place, "I wish you could tackle our Manchester friend of last year now. By Jove! he'd put you down with Ezekiel, Jeremiah, and the rest of 'em. You'll come off as a prophet, and no mistake. If you are good to open your oracular lips with regard to Epsom, I for one shall pay much attention to your words of wisdom."

"Yes," said the Major, smiling, "I should like to catch Mr. Fulsby again, and ask him where Manchester opinion is now. As for Epsom, all I know is, there will be a great falling off in attendance as regards the military element."

"Yes, I suppose so; and we shall then, unlike Fulsby, admit we could have better spared better men. There was wont to be a surrounding of lobsters, prawns, champagne, and strawberries about the soldiers that was very genial in hot, dusty times, when one was backing losers," said Mr. Charrington, almost plaintively. " I've had many a good lunch on the drags opposite the stand."

" And washed down many a reverse, no doubt," rejoined Crymes, as the dressing-gong rung out its demoniacal strains.

Now it was not to be supposed that such a piece of gossip as Mrs. Charrington had come by would be long before it pervaded the whole house. The hostess had honestly, as she said, received the news in a letter from India, but the story was not likely to lack colour in her hands, and, as we know pretty well, warranted any embroidery Mrs. Charrington could give it. That it should not only come to Miss Aysgarth's ears but be openly talked about before her was only natural. More than a year had elapsed since Cis Calvert had left York; and though his flirtation with Annie Aysgarth had been currently spoken about at the time, it was now pretty well forgotten, while those who fancied there was considerably more in it than mere flirtation were few, and had kept their own counsel.

That Annie listened outwardly unmoved to the idle chatter about how Captain Calvert had fallen into the toils of a celebrated Anglo-Indian siren, need scarcely be said; and in the first instance it was with tolerably tranquil incredulity. But that constant dripping which wears the stone extends also to our beliefs. It has been said that if you have only the opportunity to drum any plausible story continuously into the heads of your fellow-creatures, you must be exceeding wanting in eloquence if twenty per cent. of them at least, in a short time, do not place implicit faith in your recital. Similarly, however much you may disbelieve a bit of gossip in the first instance, if you find it constantly repeated and generally accepted as true, it's odds, unless you are more strong-minded than humanity generally, that you also assent to it. Gradually Annie began to feel excessively unhappy over this story. Once more she recalled to mind that Cis had never answered that letter of hers, and argued that if he really loved her he had no business to consider her released from her engagement to him when she had distinctly told him she would stand to it, and disbelieved all that was said against him. She thought, and justly too, that if she had courage to write to him, the least he could do was to gladly accept such correspondence. It was impossible she could conceive the morbid view Cis had taken of his own misfortune. Not one man in a hundred would have been so keenly sensitive to the slur cast upon his honour as Calvert; few regular racing men indeed have not at some time or another in their career had to stand the brunt of some such unfounded attack. Cis was no regular turfite; had he been so, he'd been less sensitive to unjust accusation. Men whose turf life has been summed up at its finish as irreproachable have nevertheless passed through the time when mud was thrown at them—thrown at them for no just cause, but simply by an unreasoning crowd who had lost their money, as had probably the luckless owner who kept horses for their amusement. Then again, Harry had not heard from him lately, and to a girl in Annie Aysgarth's frame of mind, that offered additional corroboration of Mrs. Charrington's story. How the girl wished this visit was over; for although they lived but a few miles off, they had come to spend the week, after the cheery north-country fashion. As for her brother, Major Crymes, and one or two more of the Lancers, they oscillated between the Grange and the barracks, sleeping in these latter when exigencies compelled, or occasionally spending the morning there under similar compulsion.

Prepossessed though Annie had originally been against Horace Crymes, she had most undoubtedly overcome that feeling now. She had seen a good deal of the Major of late, and nothing could have exceeded his tact and deferential courtesy. His attentions were never so marked as to alarm her, but still he never failed to accord her that pronounced homage which men rarely pay except to women they both admire and esteem. He had commenced his pursuit of the banker's daughter a little from pique, but far more because his affairs were in such desperate case that he saw no hope for him but a wealthy marriage. The outburst of war made things still more critical in that respect. Creditors had already shown themselves wondrous keen for a settlement before their military clients departed in pursuit of glory, and Crymes knew that soon as the regiment was under orders the pressure would be overwhelming. But it must be also said in his behalf, that with whatever motive he had commenced his courtship—if such it can yet be called—he was now honestly in love with the girl for herself, and nervously anxious for the success of his suit. Rarely when a man is, so to speak, with his back to the wall, does fortune befriend him. She is a capricious jade, more wont to smile on the well-to-do than interfere on behalf of the gambler playing for his last stake. But though she has deserted him of late, Horace Crymes had ever been one of her favoured children, and she comes to his aid once more in curious fashion.

One morning, at Byculla Grange, a letter with a broad black border is brought up to the Major's room, by which he is informed that an uncle from whom he had really no expectations had departed this life, and left him between three and four thousand a year. The old gentleman happened to be of a most tetchy, irritable, dictatorial disposition. He had quarrelled with all the nephews whom he had to stay with him on probation, owing to their utter inability to tolerate his unbearable temper. Disliking the nephew he had never seen somewhat less than the nephews he had, and impressed by the fact that the Major had never either wanted anything from him or evinced the slightest disposition to cultivate his acquaintance, the old man determined to make him his heir—fortified further in this resolution by the thought of the surprise and heart-burning it would create among the rest of the family.

" By heaven, what a piece of luck !" muttered the Major as he mastered the contents of the letter, and sprang out of bed. " How right I was never to go near old Tom Dowling ! I always told my cousins visiting him would be neither profitable nor pleasant ; that the contents of his will, like a pawnbroker's shop, would consist chiefly of unredeemed pledges. However, I must leave this at once ; it's a bore ; but when a man leaves one near on four thousand a year, the least one can do is to attend his funeral."

Breakfast over, Crymes briefly explained to Mrs. Charrington the necessity for his immediate departure, and the good fortune that had befallen him, and then proceeded at once to barracks to arrange for a short leave.

"Best cut things as short as you can, Crymes," said the Colonel. "I take it the ball's begun in earnest, and it's not likely we shall be left out of the dance."

"I trust not. I must go down to this funeral, and shall probably be detained a few days on other business connected with my inheritance, or else I wouldn't ask you to spare me now; but you may depend upon my not taking an hour's more leave than I am obliged."

"Good-bye," replied Copplestone, as he shook hands. "This time next year may you command the regiment and I a brigade."

"Oh *vive la guerre, cigars and cognac*," rejoined Crymes, quoting the refrain of a popular ballad of those days. "Good-bye, sir."

The late Thomas Dowling had lived in a pretty villa residence, close to Tunbridge Wells. He was no landed proprietor; some thirty acres of grass and ornamental grounds constituting his lordship; while the remainder of his property was comfortably invested in stocks, railways, and such securities. No inheritance could have been more convenient to a man in Crymes' position, as it was easy to realize almost at once sufficient to extricate him from his difficulties. He mused, as he sped southwards, much over his change of position, but chiefly how it would affect him with regard to Miss Aysgarth. He knew, of course, that there was not a soul at Byculla Grange by this time unaware that he had come into a considerable property. He had no motive for imposing secrecy on Mrs. Charrington, and if he had, would have saved her from temptation by not telling her of his good fortune. Miss Aysgarth would be at all events compelled to regard him as perfectly disinterested in seeking her hand, and that when you're in earnest is something. The difficulty he foresaw was the war. He was far too keen a soldier not to hail with exultation the prospect of at last seeing the "real thing" after fifteen years of garrison life in the United Kingdom, but he was also much too good a judge of the situation not to know that England would have to put every regiment she could lay her hands on in the field. This of course meant that the —th would speedily get their orders for the East, and then came the question —What was he to do? To speak now he felt would be premature ; and yet he did not like to start on this campaign without having at least made Miss Aysgarth clearly understand he was a pretender to her hand. As he had forecast the war the year before, so did Crymes now believe that it was no insignificant struggle to which the allies were committed. History told all who loved to read what tremendous power of resistance Russia had invariably displayed when put upon the defensive. Formidable in attack, she was trebly formidable when the object *of* attack, and could point to a long record of those who had driven their heads against the wall when venturing on violation of her territory. No ; war with Russia meant no mere summer campaign, but probably a couple of years' hard fighting or more once she and the allies really came to blows, and it was evident now to all clear-headed men that England was iu no more humour to receive concessions than Russia to make them. Individuals made war in the past—monarchs, ministers, ambassadors. It is nations make war in these days, and Louis Napoleon had no more to do with the Franco-Prussian war than the late Czar of Russia with the last fierce spring of the Muscovite at the throat of the Moslem.

Horace Crymes, however, was a practical man, and knew that his immediate business was to bury his uncle, settle all law business connected with his inheritance as far as possible, and hurry back to York. Quite time enough to make up his mind about what he was to say to Miss Aysgarth when the “ rout ” came ; for that it behoved him to postpone speaking till the last moment was a point on which Crymes felt very clear.

He ran up to the Colonel's rooms to report himself on his return, and found that warrior much exercised in his mind.

“ It's devilish odd, you know ; but why we don't get our marching ticket, Crymes, I can't make out. D—mme, if we're not fit to go I should like to know the corps that is ; and it is a thundering shame if we're to be left kicking our heels about here when they must know, if they know anything, that they haven't half cavalry enough with the army.”

Copplestone was a grand enthusiast about his own branch of the service, and believed implicitly that he could take his own regiment anywhere, and that Russian infantry squares would collapse like brown paper if ridden at by British dragoons.

"Deuced little fear of our turn not coming," replied Crymes. " I've made arrangements while away to get rid of all my racing stud, and mean to clear out all I've got here except old Cockatoo, my second charger, that brown horse, and the Cid. I sent the latter into the school a month back."

" Yes ; and a rare charger he'll make you. Take my advice and leave old Cockatoo behind ; a good horse, but a terrible colour for campaigning : kill your best man to keep him decent for parade."

Colonel Copplestone was not long kept in suspense, for ere the week was out arrived the order for the regiment to proceed to Woolwich, from whence they were to embark for the East, and the —th Lancers were jubilant as their brethren before them at the idea of a turn of active service. Little they reck as they gather round their mess-table for the last time previous to the plate being sent to the custody of their bankers what gaps there will be round the board when they next reassemble, and that, the Queen's health once disposed of, they will be called on to drink silently to their comrades sleeping peacefully on the plain of Balaklava.

CHAPTER XXV.

"A DIPLOMATIC QUESTION."

THE —th were given scant time in which to say "Good-bye." Farewell visits had to be paid hurriedly, and proffered "God-speed" entertainments had to be declined.

At the time of which I am writing the army was in great repute. It was a very long while since we had indulged in the luxury of a big European war, and the nation generally was a little delirious over it, so that not only private persons, but public corporations were keen upon entertaining their soldiers. I can remember the landlord of a famous Bristol hostelry drawing his crack bin of equally famous old port for our delectation as we passed through on our way to the war, and indignantly declining the idea that it should be noted in the bill, and think sorrowfully to this day how thrown away it must have been upon palates accustomed to that fiery fortified combination that did duty as such around the hospitable boards of the army. It is melancholy to reflect upon, one of those anomalies that make one suspect a flaw in the ordering of things, but the appreciation of port comes to us just as the capability of indulging in it has departed. The best judges of that grandest of wines are those who dare no longer drink it. Inexcusable digression you call this! Not altogether. The days when you could drink port, or you liked it, were those in which "all the world was young, lad," and if we are not allowed to sorrow over that past spring-time, about what is it worth while to make moan?

Crymes knew now that his tale had to be told; there was no help for it. Premature it was in his judgment to speak as yet, but he thought it would be still more hazardous to leave York without avowing his hopes; and then he pondered a little on

whether he had best speak to Julian Harperley or his daughter.
Under other circumstances it would never have occurred to
Crymes to hesitate upon such a point. "Get the girl's yes to
your love-tale," he was wont to say, "and a fig for all parents
and guardians; it's want of starch in your own system if you
can't infuse sufficient obstinacy and insubordination into a
woman who loves you. The weakest woman will show plenty
of determination given two things—a lover with a strong will,
and opportunity to see him frequently." But the difficulty here
was, would he get a yes to his love-tale, and albeit little given
to lack of confidence in affairs of this nature, Horace Crymes felt
very dubious on that point. No man had more implicit reliance
in the doctrine of *il faut se faire valoir* than himself, but there
are times when we feel intuitively that we shall fail to command
the top price in the market, and this it was made Crymes muse
over whether it would not be prudent in the first place to open
the trenches with the banker himself. Parental sanction might
count for something, he thought; and situated as he was now,
he might fairly reckon on Julian Harperley's approval; but
then he reflected that Miss Aysgarth was of an age when a
young woman usually takes her fate into her own hands, if she
has any character at all, and he thoroughly comprehended that
Miss Aysgarth both could and would think for herself in such a
matter. No; he thought he must speak to Annie, and if possible
avert a positive rejection. That Horace Crymes was very earnest
in his love is sufficiently obvious by his being apprehensive on
this point; for there was never a man more given to confidence
in his wooing than he.

One afternoon in the early April weather he sauntered over to
The Firs on old Cockatoo, to say good-bye, and put, as he said
to himself, his fate to the test. He had turned it over in his
own mind with much deliberation, and resolved that unless
things looked most decidedly adverse he would speak out to
Miss Aysgarth.

"Odd," he muttered, as he dropped the reins on the old
horse's neck, "I've done plenty of love-making in my time, and
my tongue never faltered; yet here I am, going to avow the
honestest love I ever felt, and standing in a worldly point of

view in a much better position than I have ever so far done, and I feel as if speech would fail me. But what is there in this girl that I should dread tell her I love her? Yes, that is just it; I *do* love her, and never was thoroughly in earnest before."

Crymes sent in his name, and was duly informed that Miss Aysgarth was at home. He found her seated in a low chair by the fire. On a table by her side were spread out a couple of maps, and some books and papers lay strewn on the carpet at her feet. She smiled as she welcomed him.

"Oh, Major Crymes," she exclaimed, "you remember the retort of one of my sex to the great Napoleon, when he told her women had no business to study politics : ' Excuse me, General, but when you men cut off our heads, we may be pardoned for feeling curious to know why you do it.' Like her, now you men have determined to fight, we women are anxious to know *when* you mean to do it."

" Are those our maps of the Principalities, Crimea, European Turkey, &c. ? "

" Yes; and here," she said, placing her finger on Varna, "is apparently where you will eventually all collect. I beg pardon, concentrate is the correct word, is it not ? "

" Yes," replied Crymes, gravely. " I don't pretend to know where the fight will ultimately come off, but rest assured, Miss Aysgarth, that it will not be there. The Russian is already foiled in his spring at Constantinople, and will wait now for us to take the initiative. At what our military directors will hurl us no one can say ; but they are bound to try something. Spite of appearances, it can never all end in demonstration, or the bombardment of Cronstadt. Land fortifications always should beat ships, and the navy are little likely to do much harm to either that or Sweabourg."

"Odd," she replied, " I never regarded it in that light. I thought you were all assembling here," and once more she placed her finger on the map, "and that Russia would have to beat you before she continued her march on Constantinople."

"No, Miss Aysgarth ; without the slightest disparagement to the Muscovite, I fancy he will content himself with standing on the defensive. It is simply ordinary prudence to await the assault when you deem yourself weaker than your adversary."

"And that we shall proceed to extremities you don't doubt?" she inquired.

" I certainly think we are on the verge of a big war. We are the one nation in Europe that always shuts its eyes to that possibility. The long peace since the wars of Napoleon has been simply the result of utter exhaustion. All this talk of an appeal to arms being impossible in these days of advanced civilization is mere balderdash. Men and nations are as quarrelsome as ever they were. Humanity is unchangeable, civilization a mere fashion; and fashion, when the masses are stirred, has about as much to say to it as packthread would have to the guidance of whales."

" It will be weary times for us women who have those near and dear to us away in the strife. I hardly realize it as yet; a twelve-month ago, when Harry got his commission, that I should feel uneasy about him seemed a very remote possibility; and now we shall be shortly watching for every mail with feverish interest."

" I hope that you will not feel quite indifferent to the fate of the rest of us, Miss Aysgarth," observed Crymes in a low voice.

" No, indeed," she replied quickly, as her eyes flashed full on him. " I know you all, and most of you intimately. I should be terribly grieved to hear evil tidings of the regiment, or that any of you individually had come to any sort of trouble. No one will follow your fortunes with keener interest than myself."

" I am going to ask you to take special interest in me," rejoined Crymes. " I have a superstition that those you watch over and care for will come home safe and sound again."

" You superstitious, Major Crymes!" she replied, laughing. " I should never have thought that of you. But," she continued, more seriously, " I know very well if this turn out such a war as you anticipate, some of you will never see England again. You and I have been great friends of late, and I'm sure you cannot doubt that I should be sincerely grieved to hear that any harm had befallen you."

" Great friends ! and is there no possibility of our being more than that to each other ?   You must have known—because women always do know these things—that I have loved you for the last six months or more."

" Hush !" interposed Annie, quickly.   " Do not fall into any mistake, Major Crymes. Friends of course we are ; staunch ones ; and I shall always follow your fortunes with the greatest interest, believe me."

" I would be something more than that," he rejoined, in quiet resolute fashion.   " Stop ! hear me out before you make any answer. It is little for a man to ask that you should listen to his tale, and more might never have been told you did I not think there was strong justification for my speaking. I have loved you very dearly for some time, but feared to put my fortune to the test. You may guess perhaps why. What was current scandal a fortnight ago at Byculla unsealed my lips. The reason I left the Grange, of which you are doubtless aware, gave me full warranty to speak to any woman of marriage. I came into a good three thousand a year by my uncle's will, and consequently am no longer compelled to sue like most of us soldiers —*in formâ pauperis.*"

It might have been fancy, but Annie could not help thinking that she could detect a covert smile at Calvert's circumstances in the concluding words of Crymes' speech, carefully as he had avoided bringing Cis's name into the conversation. If she was angry and mistrustful of this far-away lover of hers, she was not prepared to hear him run down by others, and quite ready to champion him when she could do so discreetly. She snatched at the opening Crymes had given, and bending her head haughtily, retorted :

" You do me too much honour, sir ; but this poor hand is not for sale as yet."

" You know that is not what I mean. You are wilfully misunderstanding me," he replied quietly.   " Men of the world are bound to assure the ladies they hope to make their wives that they can maintain them in all the ease and comfort they have been accustomed to. I know you much too well to think that my banker's account would influence your decision.   I know that I am asking prematurely perhaps, but I could not leave England without telling you this."

"And why would you ?" she cried vehemently. "I tried to prevent you; to tell you it was—"

"There will have been a good many such stories told these last few weeks," he interposed quickly. "Men always do speak out just when they ought not. And yet I don't know. I heard of a girl the other day, who, when her relations were angrily abusing a luckless admirer for declaring himself under the circumstances, flamed out, and said it would be a consolation if anything happened to him to know that he had loved her. Miss Aysgarth," he continued, rising, "I have come to say good-bye. I don't ask for an answer now; I may never ask for an answer; but it will be a comfort to me in time of need to remember that I have told you my story."

"But, Major Crymes," she exclaimed, "I cannot let you go under any impression—"

"I go under no impression that a word from your lips could alter," he interrupted. "Good-bye." He pressed the hand warmly and was gone.

He had told his love-tale, and Annie Aysgarth, unwilling as she had been to listen to it, was fain to confess he had told it well. She did not care for this man, but she felt that his love was not to be scoffed at. With his tall, wiry figure, and dark resolute face, he was the *beau idéal* of a *sabreur*, and she was conscious of a dogged determination about him that made it rash to assume he would fail in anything he had set his mind upon. She had seen one or two instances of her own sex succumbing in the end to men of this stamp, much as they had ridiculed the idea to begin with; and these successful wooers had been neither as good-looking nor well-endowed as Major Crymes. Was she faltering in her allegiance? If she was, who could blame her? Not a line had she received for months from Cis Calvert; and such tidings of him as had reached her ears were hardly calculated to strengthen her constancy. This Indian scandal, which, though not directly told her, was continually buzzed into her ears, was hard to fight against. A girl strong in the assurance of her lover's truth, with letters occasionally from him to show that she still holds the first place both in his heart and his memory, can endure much; but when her letters are unanswered, and the rumour comes to her from afar that this admirer of hers is enthralled by another woman, her belief falters. The sex are wont to be a little merciless to one another upon these occasions; it may not be deliberate malignity, but women are not specially considerate of a sister's feelings upon these occasions. No one told Annie Aysgarth outright of her lover's inconstancy, but over and over again during that wretched week at Byculla Grange it was discussed, though perhaps unintentionally, in her hearing. Every now and again she was doomed to suffer that deep humiliation to a proud, passionate woman—the commiseration concerning the way her lover had treated her, and only a woman can understand the bitterness of tasting of that cup. That her love affairs may go wrong is hard enough to bear; it means so infinitely more to the woman than to the man.

"Love is of man's life a thing apart; 'tis woman's whole existence."

Let this story be true or let it be false, the one fact remained —Cis Calvert had returned no reply to her last letter. Her father had thrown cold water upon the idea of her marriage, but she had stood resolutely by her lover. Surely if she firmly refused to give up their correspondence, it was not for him to renounce it! The plea that he could not allow her to link her fortunes to a broken man, if she chose to waive, hardly became him, if he loved her, to advance. She had told him that her belief in him was unshaken, that she would stand by him in his hour of trouble as a true woman always does; and God help the man who cannot believe in such! But it was hard—ay, infinitely hard—to have the precious spikenard rejected; to find that this man, upon whom she had lavished all the wealth of her love, had so soon forgotten her that his infatuation for another woman was already a current Indian scandal. And now, strange to say, another lover was at her feet, a man who much more nearly represented her *beau ideal* of that possible husband of whom every young girl dreams. They don't marry these shadowy phantoms, any more than men marry the visionary perfection which sweeps across their boyish imagination. Fitzgerald's ballad perhaps describes these withered leaves of youthful fancy as well as anything :

> "There are names that we cherish, tho' nameless,
>   For aye on the lips they may be ;
> There are hearts that, tho' fetter'd, are tameless,
>   And thoughts unexpress'd, but still free !
> And some are too grave for a rover,
>   And some for a husband too light ;—
> The ball and my dream are all over—
>   Good night to thee, lady, good night !"

It must not be for one moment imagined that Annie Aysgarth actually wavered in her love for Cis, but when a man to all appearance completely neglects his *fiancée*, and all she can hear of him is that he is dangling at the skirts of another woman, and when another suitor, not only good-looking but well-to-do in the world, presses himself on her acceptance, she may well ask herself whether this former lover was really worthy of the affection she had bestowed on him. And that was precisely the feeling that began to steal into Annie Aysgarth's mind as she looked sadly back at the march of events. The idea of wedding Major Crymes never crossed her mind, and yet she knew that many a girl in Yorkshire would gladly welcome that swart, handsome Lancer, with his three thousand a year, as a wooer. He was good-looking, and emphatically a man, and could undoubtedly give a right good home to whatever woman he led to the altar. Nobody could see all this more readily than clearheaded, practical Annie Aysgarth. She knew, as has happened scores of times before, that from a worldly point of view she had much better take the well-to-do lover who knelt at her feet, than the broken scapegrace whose very passion for her seemed now open to question. But our feelings are not always under our own control. Human nature is about the one thing upon the immutability of which we can rely; and love has upset prudence since the world began.

Annie Aysgarth was in truth having a hard time of it just now. She might not want to marry Major Crymes, but he and several others of the —th Lancers had been intimates at The Firs ; and though she as yet hardly realized it, she had gathered quite enough from Crymes to know that this was no mere military promenade they were embarked upon. Women cannot help feeling a little heartsick on such occasions. Granted he is no more than a favourite ball-room partner, the thought that they may be pressing his hand for the last time makes their hearts wondrous tender to those who are going forth to do battle for England. Besides, had she not an actual brother going forth in their ranks, a brother of whom too she was very fond, and from whom this was to be her first separation in earnest ? She had of course lost sight of him for short intervals in his public school days, but since he had buckled a sabre it had been his luck to be quartered within a mile or so of his own home, and she had naturally seen him continually. But when those starting for the East might return was a very open question, and one about which no sensible man would even venture a conjecture. There were not wanting those who at this moment did not believe that a shot would be fired on either side ; plenty of people about only the other day pooh-poohing the idea of the bombarding Alexandria, or the despatching the army to Egypt. These things always are so. Nations, like men, don’t quarrel deliberately, but drift into their differences ; and nothing is perhaps so conducive to the arguments of violence as the persuasion of one combatant that the other will not fight.

In fact, Annie Aysgarth had nothing before her but the prospect of that weary waiting, destined to be the lot of so many women during those days. Happy were those whose dear ones came safe back to them, and who were spared the finding of their name in those ghastly returns of killed and wounded only too frequent in the columns of the *Times* before that little matter of the Chersonese was decided !

CHAPTER XXVI.

" THE SWAGGER OF WAR."

ATTIRED in braided pelisse, from beneath the top of which peeped out a gold-laced collar, while below it were to be seen gold-laced overalls thrust into high riding-boots with armed heels, and with a cavalry sabre under his arm, Cis Calvert might be seen one November day picking his way through the dirty streets that led from Tophana to Pera. He looked jaded and wearied, and as if so far he had met neither the excitement nor the oblivion that he craved for. He had no regret for the Indian career he had so abruptly abandoned; he did not like his regiment, and bitterly resented their not standing by him in his hour of need; and then again he remembered the complication with Mrs. Daventry was getting almost beyond his control. There are no doubt men impassive to the fascinations and avowed love of a pretty woman as there are cabbages; but I fancy these stoics will have but a gloomy record to look back upon, and that the memories of twenty love scrapes are better than that of the ledger which shows no such entry. Cis had sought to dissipate his *ennui* by a flirtation with Mrs. Daventry in the first instance; but the lady had apparently caught the spirit of the land of her adoption, and intended a love affair with all the volcanic violence of the East.

As he steamed away from Bombay, ruefully reflecting that he was once more the hero of an ugly turf scandal, Cis could not but call to mind that far sadder day when he had left the station at York. His old Lancer brethren had stood to him like men in his first trouble, but his new corps had looked askance when scandal waxed wicked with his name. Cis did not reflect that in the —th Lancers he was both well known and popular, while in the Royal Dunbars he was neither. Yes ; leaving the latter and the fierce love of Mrs. Daventry was a relief ; the saying adieu to his old dragoon brethren and sweet Annie Aysgarth had been an agony. Should he ever see her again? Better not. With his wretched Indian story on the top of the Yorkshire offending, how could he ever hope to approach her again? It was hard that he should always be the scapegoat. Still it was possible to make some sort of name, show there was stuff in him, and clear the smirched scutcheon which he at present bore, however innocently, in the great drama about to be enacted.

When Cis arrived at Constantinople the main body of the allied army was round and about Varna, while the cavalry were using up their men and horses in that useless promenade in the Dobruska ; but it was evident to every one that the allies were bound to do something, and, in fact, had only concentrated their forces preliminary to striking a blow, though in what direction that blow would be aimed was as yet a profound secret. Cis's anxiety to get military employment at once was such that he jumped at a commission in the Bashi-Bazouks, that "refuge of sinners" as it was often laughingly called in consequence of numbering amongst its officers no inconsiderable number of "the broken brigade," who, like Martha's husband in Faust,—

> " Loved women too, and had for wine a thirst,
> Besides their passion for those dice accurst."

Most of the friends who might have helped him were away in Bulgaria, and afraid to be out of the fray, he was glad to take the first thing that offered. Beatson, of Beatson's horse, was a name of mark in India, and Cis had fair reason to suppose such a well-known leader of irregular cavalry would be speedily found work for his command. Whether the material he met with proved past his kneading, or what might be the reason, the writer knows not, but certain it is, that the Bashi-Bazouks, from whom at one time great things were expected, were never heard of in the Crimean business after the work began. It was curious too, for in their early days they were pronounced just the fellows to tackle the Cossacks. It was true that the experts who then so freely expressed their opinion had never seen a Cossack nor a shot fired in anger, but there was a period of enlightenment before them, and before many months some of these critics had cut their way through the children of the Don at Balaklava and witnessed the red rain of Inkerman. Since Cleopatra led the stampede of Actium the Egyptians have always run away, but the Russians were made of very different stuff, and the Crimean men won their scanty laurels in very different fashion from the triple-crowned heroes of the twenty-five minutes' fight at Tel-el-Kebir.

Poor Cis, he chafed with impatience when the news came down of the landing in the Crimea and the defeat of Menschikoff on the Alma. When were they to get their orders? When were Beatson and his wild troopers to take their part in the dance? Then came the terrible account of Balaklava, and the well-nigh annihilation of the Light Brigade. Surely they must be wanted now. Every sabre that could be raised must be required at the front after such a disaster as that! Splendid as the charge was, famous as it is still, and will be for all time in song and story, that it was one of those costly deeds of derring-do which it is not meet to exult about there was no denying. Yet no order came for the Bashi-Bazouks to embark for the front. Cis's heart sickened. He had come here for "the real thing," to take his share of the work, and found himself knocking about Constantinople and its vicinity much as a man quartered at Aldershot might be seen about London and Greenwich in the season. Every time he went up from Gallipoli to the capital he felt ashamed of his gaudy, untarnished splendour as he encountered the many weather-stained uniforms which characterized the invalids from the front; men wounded at Alma or Inkerman, or to whom the wet, cold, and severe starvation of the trenches had tried past endurance. Cis might well look faded and wearied as he picked his way through the mud and filth of Galata on a louring day towards the end of November; he could not but feel that the cards were running persistently against him. As if the York scrape had not been black enough, he knew he had left the Royal Dunbars with the reputation of having stood in with two of the most notorious "practitioners" in the presidency in about as shameful a turf robbery as the presidency had ever witnessed. He had himself endorsed his fault in the second case as he had in the first, by flying from the scandal, although influenced by very different motives. His own thoughts were torture to him; he felt that Annie Aysgarth was further removed from him than ever. If her father had deemed that miserable steeplechase cause to demur against him as a son-in-law, what would he say when the distorted story of the Nizam's Plate reached his ears? Poor Cis, he longed for work; he longed to be where shot were flying and sabres ringing. His blood had tingled, as every soldier's of England had, when he read Russell's soul-stirring accounts of the death-ride of Balaklava; of the long, stubborn, dogged stand at Inkerman; and here he was kicking his heels about the camp at Gallipoli or the dirty streets of Constantinople. He might as well, he mused grimly, have been listening to the band on the Meidan at Secunderabad.

Full of his own sad thoughts, despite being once or twice nearly knocked down by hamals, trotting blindly along under their monstrous burdens, Cis reached the top of the hill, and turning into the main street was making his way towards Misseri's Hotel when he ran across a stalwart man of medium stature, bearded like a pard, and habited in a rough pea-jacket, long boots, and a forage-cap, the scarlet band of which had acquired a tint that could be likened to nothing but the skirts of a hunting-coat at the expiration of a second wet season. The inhabitant of the pea-jacket stopped, gazed steadfastly at the gaily-attired warrior who confronted him, and then exclaimed:

"Cis Calvert, by all that's whimsical! How are you, old man? And what on earth induced you to enrol yourself in the 'Pillagers'? Rather rough to dub them so, ain't it, considering they haven't had a chance yet!"

"Jerry Arkwright, isn't it?—though a fellow may be excused having doubts about your personality behind all that hair. How are you, old man? I saw your name was mentioned in despatches about the Inkerman day, and d—n it, every one of you deserved it. By the way, you were hit, weren't you?"

"Yes; that's the reason you see me down here now. It wasn't much, but our doctor shipped me off sharp, saying, 'You'll come round quicker below than you will up here, if only because you can get decent food and bottled stout.' I shall be going back in another three weeks or so, and in the mean time there seems a lull. Inkerman has pacified both sides for a little, just, Cis, as in our old Harrow days a good stand-up fight kept two fellows who were always jarring quiet for the half-year."

"Ah, both sides too exhausted to go on, I suppose?"

"Well," rejoined Arkwright gravely, "it is to be hoped *they* are, but there's no doubt whatever about us. I don't, from what I know, think we've another Inkerman left in us just now. The only comfort is the loser in such an awful slogging fight as that was don't usually want any more for some time. But here we are at Misseri's; come in and have some dinner."

"Just what I proposed doing. A talk with you'll do me good, Jerry, although I'm almost ashamed to be seen with you."

"Well, I'm not much to look at," grinned Arkwright. "I hardly look up to the mark for a *levée* at St. James's, I know; and don't you think I've got any evening togs to get into, old man. I'm not proprietor of much more than I stand in, and the essentials are more looked to than the ornamental up there, I tell you."

"You misunderstand me," replied Cis bitterly, and with a contemptuous glance at his own gay attire. "I'm ashamed of all this tinsel being paraded alongside a uniform stained with the smoke of Inkerman."

"The Crimea's bad for clothes," replied Arkwright, sententiously; "but hang it all, why ain't you with us up there instead of kicking about here got up for a Queen's Ball?"

"It's a little rough," rejoined Cis. "You know, or perhaps don't know, I left the —th Lancers and joined the Royal Dunbars in India. I sold out of that regiment and came straight here to volunteer for anything might be going. I was offered a troop in these Bashi-Bazouks of Beatson's and jumped at it. I thought they'd be safe to send these fellows to the front, but they don't seem to fancy 'em somehow. I'm not sure but they're right ; still when it comes to looting I'd back our fellows against any corps—ah ! or any brigade in the army."

" Well, you see," said Arkwright, " their proficiency in that respect alone is sufficient to condemn them to inaction. There happens just now to be no scope for their peculiar talents at the front. They could only loot our side, and, upon my soul, we've so deuced little to lose we couldn't stand any petty abstraction, to say nothing of its not being worth their while. But here, Cis, if you mean business, take my advice and chuck that corps. This thing mind's got to be fought out in the Crimea at present, and those fellows will never be sent there. Erzroum, Kars, or up that way, will be their destination, if ever they are sent to the front in any direction. The Crimea, my boy, is the cockpit in which the first main between the Muscovite and the Western Powers is to be decided. We're bound to go on there till we've got Sebastopol. About what is to follow then this prophet's dumb. It's not necessary to speculate on at present. We are very much outside at present, and shall be quite content to just hold our own till the spring."

" But surely we've reinforcements on the way out ! " exclaimed Cis.

" A dubious blessing," rejoined Arkwright, diving into a mysterious *salmi*. " We can't quite feed those we have there, and a multiplication of mouths means an extension of that difficulty."

" But we must have more men," cried Cis.

" Get me another pint of stout, waiter. Of course we must, but we hardly want them till the spring. John Bull is just waking up to the muddle we're in. Grub and transport is a mere matter of money now, and England, when it comes to that, is bad to beat ; two, three, or four thousand navvies would soon make a road to the front, and there's no fear of our having plenty of everything unless it's men next year. We must win in the end. It's water carriage against land unmitigated by railroad. The Russians have the best of it now, but they won't have six months hence ; but there'll be a power of stiff fighting before we get Sebastopol. The Muscovite has shown already that he yields never a yard without a good stand-up tussel, and is always good to try till daylight to recover anything he lost at sunset. 'The Ovens,' in the taking of which poor Tryon of the Rifles lost his life, gave them a rare lively night in the left attack. They were seized with a cheer and a rush with the bayonet; but the Russians came on again and again till sunrise to dispute possession."

" Yes, it was a fine thing that," said Cis gloomily, " and to think of kicking about here in all this tawdry"—and here he glanced contemptuously at his lace-dizened uniform—" while such chances as that are going on at the front ! "

" Well, poor Tryon's chance came off the wrong way, like many another good fellow's since we landed at Old Fort ; but we can't all win whatever the game is, and there will be more deuce aces thrown than double sixes no doubt by those gambling with death around Sebastopol. Nevertheless, Cis, I say, resign your commission in ' the Pillagers,' sink that gilded splendour, and come back with me in three weeks. There's plenty of work for all of us, and a volunteer of the right sort, like yourself, won't find himself out of employment long, I'll warrant. If you don't mind taking a subaltern's berth there are regiments at the front woefully short of officers."

" I'd take a non-commissioned officer's appointment sooner than knock about here in this peacocky garb," rejoined Cis curtly.

" Well, old man, if that's your temper you needn't be down-hearted; never fear but what you'll find a place amongst the commissioned after a week or two. Now, let's go and smoke."

The two adjourned to that ante-room off the *Salle-a-manger*, which was dedicated to the Nicotian goddess ; literally, at that time, the high change of travel and the hot-bed of *canards*. It was more thinly occupied than usual, and conversation languished, like the operations of the Allies. There was little indeed of a cheerful nature to be got out of Crimean talk at that time. The sufferings of those engaged in the Sebastopol leaguer were no secret at Constantinople, and the long aisles of the big hospital on the opposite side gave appalling corroboration of the truth of these stories. It was well for the besiegers that the besieged were as exhausted as themselves, and left the annihilation of their foes to those grim Generals, January, February, and March. It was an anxious time ; raise the siege the Allies could not even if they wished. To disembark was an impossibility. No ; they were in " the ring " now, and the battle between them and the Muscovite had to be fought out then and there. Grant's famous struggle in the wilderness during the great American rebellion, bore the nearest resemblance to the Crimea of all later warfare —a slogging, dogged fight, with very little strategy in it.

And it was about this time, while they were still waiting for Arkwright to recover his health and strength so as to be once more able to face the trying and dreary trench work of those gloomy winter months, that the news came down to Constantinople of that awful hurricane in which the ' Black Prince,' one of the few ships laden with warm clothing, of which the authorities actually had knowledge, foundered, and went down with every sock and blanket,—to say nothing of her crew. 1 am not going to dip any further into that miserable muddle ; there was plenty enough said deservedly, both at the time and afterwards —albeit that the army, like the serpent, moves upon its belly, has never been, nor is yet, an admitted fact amongst our military administrators. The necessities of life, by the way, seemed as scarce amongst the pursuers of the light-footed Egyptians as they were with their forbears who fought so hardly for the possession of the famous fortress of the Chersonese. Singular, we place the last hero of Egypt on the pedestal of public opinion, just as we take the hero of the Peninsula down from his pedestal of stone. Can satire go further?

A world of gammon and spinach, my masters, in which it is only the new lamps that sell. An age of cant and humbug, in which it is only the new *culte* that goes down. Æstheticism has pretty well had its day. Shall we resort to gladiatorial exhibitions and the fierce sports of the arena? A man at bay for his life has much attraction in the law courts, and to see one of these miserables wrestle against condemnation will cause much influx of silk and satin to our modern arenas, and endless applications to the Judge who has the disposal of seats. The barbarian battling out his life with the wild beast, or the murderer contesting his existence with the hangman ; is there much after all

T

in this advanced civilization we are so apt to brag about? Very
little, I trow.

But to moralize is to bore. Reflections on the past are of no
more account than regrets over the spilt milk, while speculations
on the future usually expose the prophet to ridicule. Let us still
continue to sing " Cock-a-doodle-do " to the amusement of conti-
nental nations, and be duly thankful that ten thousand Osmanli
of the sort that confronted the Russe at Plevna were not behind
the lines at Tel-el-Kebir, instead of the " light-footed " fellahs of
the land of the Pharaohs.

CHAPTER XXVII.

OLD COMRADES.

BUFFETING her way slowly through the waters of the Euxine, hardly yet apparently settled down after the savage tempest of St. Andrew's Day, was a small passenger steamer, threading her course to that rugged promontory, which, crowned by that Genoese fort on its summit, was once more destined to become famous in the history of Europe. Since the days when Xenophon and his Greeks escaped from Central Asia to take refuge on the waters of the Black Sea, the Chersonese had pretty well faded out of the minds of Western Europe. Through the long struggle of the nations against Napoleon, the Crimea had never been hinted at as a battle-ground, but now all who cared to read knew that a bitter quarrel, nominally between the Osmanli and the Muscovite, albeit in reality the stern protest of France and England against the Russian eagles entering Constantinople, was there to be determined.

Standing on the bridge of the steamer and peering through the scud and haze, somewhat characteristic of Black Sea weather in December, are Cis Calvert and his Fusilier friend, Jerry Arkwright.

"There you are," exclaimed the latter; "one can make it out distinctly now. There's the old fort, and another two hours will see us in Balaklava. Ha! and there's the old music."

And as he spoke, a low sullen boom was wafted across the seething waters, which even Cis Calvert, whose ears were not attuned to the melody, recognized as a growling defiance from the leaguered fortress.

"I suppose," said Cis, "that sound is incessant?"

"Well," replied Arkwright, "as you know, I've been out of

it since the Inkerman business, but I don't think that there's much firing done upon either side for the present. We of course exchange a shot or two at intervals, just to show the fight is not over, and we mean to be at them again before long; but you know, as far as we are concerned, getting ammunition up to the front is a very serious difficulty, and when once got there, we can't afford to throw it lightly away. As for our friends inside, they are simply defending their own arsenal, and probably have both unlimited guns and ammunition, judging from what I saw before I left, and the awful reports that have come down from the front of late. I fancy just at present they are leaving the wet and cold of the winter to settle us. They may fairly argue, "You can't get in; and half of you won't be about when the spring comes."

Cis gazed with rapt attention at the grim, rugged cliffs as the steamer rapidly closed upon her landfall. This, then, was the scene of the famous duel, to join in which he had made every sacrifice, and yet, did he but know it, even at this very moment bitter tongues were busy at his expense up in the Yorkshire wolds, as well as in the sandy plains of the Deccan, marvelling how any soldier could have resigned his profession when his country was engaged in the biggest war she had waged since Napoleon's final downfall at Waterloo. It was "hard lines," but the fates were against Cis. He was innocent, but yet he persistently appeared in the blackest colours to his friends and acquaintances; and moreover, his hot temper had prompted him to scant patience when he found men ready to believe things to his detriment. Instead of following Annie Aysgarth's advice and living such scandal down, he had invariably fled from it; and though the mere fact that he had volunteered for the Crimea, albeit he had sold out in India, was quite sufficient to clear his reputation in that respect, still neither in York nor the Deccan was this latter circumstance known. So far it had never occurred to him what comment might be made upon his abrupt retirement from the Royal Dunbars; but this he did know, that twice he had hurriedly left a regiment on account of a great scandal. Was he to clear all stain from his name before Sebastopol? Was the chance to be vouchsafed to him? Would he get employment of any kind ? Surely, as Arkwright said, there must be room and work for all who could grasp a sabre. Still as they glided through the narrow entrance of the land-locked harbour of Balaklava, Cis could but reflect sadly that he should shortly be shaking hands with all his old comrades of the —th Lancers and yet not be of them ; talking to men whom he had known since he first donned sword and spur, men who had driven their horses through the death-ride of the " Six Hundred," and that he was not with them.

Calvert gazed with amazement as the steamer crept into the berth allotted to her, in that unfortunately little understood chaos which Balaklava at that time presented. Ships were packed close as herrings in a cask, close as the yachts in the Granville Basin at Dover previous to the race week. Boats shot about in every direction through the gloom, bearing the British officer, clothed at that time principally in hair and griminess, ravenous for food or liquor, or anything that might mitigate the monotony of salt pork and rum. It was not of course so much that the things were not there, although that was, perhaps, a subject not to speak too confidently about, but that nobody knew in which ship to search for cargoes. What might be termed quite the superfluities of life lay close along the walls ; boots, warm clothing, and the essentials lay far out, with no record of their valuable freight to guide those on shore only too anxious to come by such things.

The two men were not long in making their way on shore, and Arkwright speedily ran across a young gentleman of his own corps, who was down foraging, and who promised to bring ponies to convey him, Arkwright, and his baggage to the front next day. Striding through the mud, for to pick your way in Balaklava would have been quite a work of supererogation, Arkwright led the way to Oppenheim's store—a philanthropist, who sold well at a price pretty well everything that reached the shores of the Crimea. You paid well—why not? Men had little to think about but the keeping of soul and body together in those days. The great ganglionic centre becomes the god of our idolatry in such times, and I'm afraid the possessor of a couple of ducks would have been deemed more desirable as a host than the greatest humourist in the Crimean army. Half a score of hands were stretched forth to welcome Jerry Arkwright, a popular man, and one who had been out from the beginning till knocked over on that misty Inkerman morning. Jerry, as may be supposed, had a very large and numerous acquaintance; but with Cis it was different. The ex-Lancer had by no means the catholic acquaintance of the Fusilier. Big camps did not exist in the pre-Crimean days, and excepting in such places as Dublin, or it may be Limerick, the cavalry by no means saw so much of their infantry brethren as they have done since; but a big war, and more especially when an army is destined to be concentrated, as was the case with the English in the Chersonese, of necessity draws them closer together.

Suddenly a slight boyish figure, the gold band of whose forage-cap bore tokens of the wild, wet weather the allies had recently experienced, pushed his way through the throng. His uniform was not only frayed, but bore, sad to say of a light dragoon, unmistakable signs of patching and darning. Though healthy, his face bore a somewhat worn, haggard appearance, characteristic of those who had gone through the discipline of those first three months' Crimean campaigning.

"Cis Calvert, by all that's unfathomable! Cis Calvert, by all that's glorious! Good Heavens! old man, do let me shake hands with you, if it is only to feel certain that it is yourself and not your wraith that I am speaking to. Good Lord! Cis," continued young Harperley, as he wrung his old captain's hand, "why we all looked upon you as in India, miles away; but of course now you're coming back to take a turn with the old corps?"

"I only wish, Harry, that it may be so," replied Calvert sadly, "but you must know I am no longer a soldier. It's too long a story to tell now, but I came to worse grief in India than I did at York. I left the Royal Dunbars in a fit of anger. I was just as wrongly accused of having a hand in a racing robbery there as I was after that miserable ride over the Crockley Hill Course this time two years. In the first case, dear old Copplestone and my brother officers stood to me like men. Whatever any of you might think about my quarrel with Crymes, you all absolved me from any knowledge of The Mumper's previous name and history. In the Royal Dunbars it was otherwise; they neither liked me nor I them. They at once took part against me, and a sharp ten minutes' interview with the imbecile who commanded them, resulted in an exchange of shots on both sides that left so little chance of cordiality again between us as to make my leaving the regiment in some shape almost a necessity. I was mad to be with you all out here. It was misery to think that my luck had thrown me out of the dear old corps just before they were destined to see service; and when, Harry, I read the glorious but terrible story of that day in the valley of Balaklava, the tears rained from my eyes, not only for those whose hands I should never clasp more, but also to think that I had not been riding, stirrup to stirrup, with all my dear old pals of the last ten years in that supreme hour of grief and gallantry."

"Well, it was roughish, you know," rejoined the cornet, whose amazement at his late captain's somewhat high-flown language was visible in his face. He could not understand it. Men engaged in the real game of war indulge very little in these sort of flights; their talk is essentially curt and prosaic, that is to say amongst our own people, who are wont to feel ashamed of the Victoria Cross when they have won it, and deprecate nothing so much as an explanation of how they obtained it. "We rode straight, Cis, and we rode fast, though, upon my soul, we can't take much credit for the latter. We had to save those guns if we could, and considering what a cross fire it was, a man would have been pretty tired of life who didn't bustle through it; and when more than half of us were down, and the remainder of us all broken, the man who had a horse under him and didn't hurry back must simply have lost all his ideas."

"You had a terrible 'return' after the fight," replied Cis, "but yet not quite so bad as was the fate of some of the other regiments in the Brigade. Poor Strangford, I saw, was killed."

"Yes," replied the cornet gravely, as his voice sunk. "He was riding not six lengths from me, and threw up his arms with a shriek that I seem to hear even now and again in the night-time, before he pitched from his saddle. We brought him in next day and buried him; but the doctor said he'd been shot clean through the heart, and was probably dead ere he touched the ground. Radcliffe too was awfully knocked about—had indeed to be sent away—and has not as yet come back to us; while your old opponent, the Major, rode as he did that day when he led the field from Askham Bog across the Rufford Drain to Red House. By heavens! Cis, he did terrible work during that ride. Stern, hard, and relentless we all knew him. His sabre was red to the hilt when he saw our lines again, and there must have been many a wail of woe from beyond the steppes when the record of the Major's savage handwriting was published."

"Did he come through scatheless himself?" asked Cis.

"No, indeed. He had three or four sword-wounds, while his clothes were torn to ribbons, and they at first talked of sending him also down to Scutari, but he said grimly that nothing ever hurt him, and he would be d—d if he went except in a coffin. You can't think what a changed man he is since out here. Few of us liked him in the old days—few of us indeed knew him. I assure you that he's now not only quite popular, but is looked forward to amongst the cavalry as one of the rising men. But of course you're coming out to see us all, and I suppose you'll hang on to us, at all events till something suitable turns up?"

"You forget, Harry," replied Calvert, "that I am no longer a soldier. Until I have got a berth of some sort I am simply a useless encumbrance, a consumer of rations which I can do nothing to earn; and from all accounts rations are by no means too plentiful."

"That they ain't," replied Harry with a grin. "We don't lose our temper because there's no fish, nor turn up our noses at anything as long as it's fresh in this country, old man. You can either eat anything, or nothing; and in the latter case the sooner you clear out the better. But, Cis, you're not going to let that old Mumper story prevent your taking a turn with us. The whole truth came out before we left York, and we all know now, including Crymes, that you were the victim of a most craftily-concocted plant. That old black horse had been bought to perpetrate precisely the fraud which he eventually did in your name. The planners of this precious robbery lost the

Mumper owing to a compulsory sale by the sheriff, but to their great satisfaction suddenly discovered that you meant to race him, and were consequently going to play their game for them. The manipulation of the betting market was of course easy, and nothing could be safer than to bet against a horse which they knew they could disqualify should he chance to win. To back The Cid and bet against The Mumper were obviously their tactics. They looked upon the race, as we all did, as lying between the pair. Had The Cid won they would have said nothing, but of course when The Mumper came in first they objected. Old Charrington found the whole thing out two or three months after you left, got hold of the name of the chief actor in the rascally business, and then communicated it all to Crymes. The Major's turf lore stood you in good stead there, Cis. He recognized the man at once, and said, though it was a big thing to say, he didn't believe there was a greater scoundrel unhung. He had gone under a score of aliases, and that he had evaded so far the clutches of the law only showed what a cunning knave he was."

"Well, thank heavens, my name stands thoroughly clear in the eyes of all of you, and I presume I may add in the eyes of the Yorkshire people too ?"

"Bless your soul, yes. Old Charrington wasn't the man not to send the story around ; besides, Cis, you know you had plenty of good friends, and my father amongst them, who were only too glad when they could refute the scandal against you."

"Yes," rejoined Calvert, gravely ; "I am glad that your father should know that I was blameless in the matter. And Annie, what of her ? "

"Why, you know she never held you guilty any more than I ever did. Nothing could have made either of us ever credit a thing like that of you."

Bitterly did Cis now think of the complication that had happened to him in the Deccan. Almost at the same time that Fortune was working for him, and, with the assistance of his friends, clearing his name in Yorkshire, his malignant star had plunged him into a still more serious scrape in India. Cis Calvert does not know it as yet, but in the Madras presidency that Mrs.

Daventry has left her husband is well known, and it is generally believed in company with Captain Calvert.

"I have heard nothing of her or any of you for so long that I felt almost afraid to ask."

"Why, good heavens! surely you and Annie correspond still. She said nothing to me about you just at last, but of course it is now months since I left home; still I always supposed that she heard regularly from you."

"No; I suppose it is my fault. I can only say that I did what I thought was right. A man lying under such a stigma as I did was not justified in holding a girl to her troth."

"Pooh!" rejoined Harry Harperley contemptuously, "that is all cleared away now; besides, my sister is a girl in ten thousand, grit to the tips of her fingers, and I fancy you might have depended upon her sticking to you, if all that was hinted against you had been really true."

All that story about Cis Calvert's flirtation with Mrs. Daventry only reached Byculla Grange just before the —th Lancers got their route for the East. That it should reach Miss Aysgarth's ear promptly was but natural. There are always women who never spare a sister in her agony. But people generally are not given to hint that a man's sister has been jilted before his face, so that in the very few days that elapsed before the regiment left, it is no great matter for astonishment that that Deccan story should never have reached young Harperley's ears. That a proud girl like Annie Aysgarth would mention such a thing in her letters to her brother was little likely. She, who would have stood by him to the last, had reluctantly come to the conclusion that he loved her no longer. Had he done so he . would never have failed to answer her letters. Infatuated by that Indian woman, he had doubtless forgotten all about her. All must be over henceforth between them. After that last letter she could stoop to no further overtures; and yet there were times when Annie Aysgarth, in the loyalty of her love, wondered whether that story she had heard at Byculla was really true, or the result of Mrs. Charrington's "embroidery." Anyway, it was months now since she had heard anything of Cis, and not only did she marvel much when she should be destined to hear of him again, but dreaded it too not a little.

"Well, you see, it's a good bit since I left India, and then I've been kicking about wasting my time with those Bashi-Bazouks. I thought they were safe to put those beggars in the front, on the same principle that our gallant allies yield the *pas* with their Zouaves to *les enfants perdus*."

"Ah, old man, I don't think our people think as highly of Beatson's fellows as the French do of their Zouaves. They've real rum 'uns in their ranks, of all nations, according to rumour; but there's no doubt they're real gluttons when it comes to fighting, and they ask for nothing better than to be put in the thick of it. But look here, old man, you must come out and shake hands with what's left of the old lot. I shall come in to-morrow with a spare pony. We'll meet you here at twelve and take you out to lunch. You needn't come out ' a watering for the flesh-pots.' *Entrées* are what you call scarce with the bipeds, and as for the horses, poor brutes, they literally are, in the old show-man's vernacular, a gnawing of their tails for very hunger. And now, good-bye. I've just collared a couple of bottles of Oppen-heim's particular. He's right not to give it a more definite name, because further than being d—d strong, I should hesitate to put a name to it."

Cis and his friend Arkwright speedily made their way back to their ship. Afternoon closes in early in December, and the majority of people in Balaklava had to make their way up to the front; and it was very easy in those days to lose your way after sundown, and spend hours wandering about strange camps before finding your own. All their fellow-passengers had landed and dispersed, and the Fusilier and Cis passed a very dull even-ing, broken only by the low jabbering of strange tongues in the adjacent vessels, for Babel was not more prolific in languages than Balaklava at that time, and the low, sullen boom from the besieged fortress, which told that the Bastion de Mât, or Redan, still hurled defiance at the foe.

"Well, Jerry," said Calvert, as he knocked the ashes out of his pipe, "it's pretty dull work here, even with you to talk to.

You're all right,—will be amongst your own people to-morrow, and no call to complain of idleness, I'd dare swear ; but to live down here on board ship will just send me wild. If I can't get employment in a few days I don't know what I shall do."

"Don't be a fool, Cis. Deuce a fear but what the chance of being shot will be speedily provided you, but your highness can't come bustling up here and expect to find a general's commission waiting for you on the beach. Now, look here. Our chief's a regular brick, and I, in consequence of my manifold virtues, naturally an eminent favourite with him. I know, sad to say, that the dear old corps is terribly short of officers, and when I've told him your story I feel pretty sure he will apply for you as a volunteer. He stands well with the authorities, and they are not likely to refuse his request, and if you are not in the way of your full share of kicks for the minimum of half-pence, by the Lord, I can only say they've just awoke to the value of the Fusiliers. There's been no disposition to keep us in lavender so far. I'll see about it as soon as ever I get up there, and if the chief only says yes, shall come down and fetch you up bodily the day after to-morrow. You can live with me, you know, and come down and take a turn or two in the trenches as an amateur until an appointment of some sort is made out for you. And now it's time to turn in, so good night."

" Thanks no end, old man. By Jove, if you can only manage that I'll ask no more. Give me but that start, and I know the rest is in my own hands," and the hand-grip Cis exchanged with his chum was of that sort that serves the Anglo-Saxon so much better than words in his emotional moments.

The next morning Arkwright took his departure, and at noon young Harperley duly kept his tryst at Oppenheim's with Calvert, and the pair rode leisurely away to the lines of the Light Brigade, behind Kadakoi. The cornet had already acquainted his brother officers with Cis's presence in the Crimea and his reason for it, consequently there was quite a crowd to welcome him in what was not the mess tent, for in that gloomy winter no regiment indulged in such a luxury, but a sort of lounging tent, where the —th Lancers met to gossip, smoke, and drink their ration rum, or whatever other potable they might come by. Foremost to welcome him was stalwart old Copplestone.

"Ah, Calvert, my boy," exclaimed the Colonel, "if I'd only guessed the work before us, I'd never have let you leave us; not that I've any complaint to make against your substitute, but I'm fond of the whelps of my own rearing."

And then the others crowded round him, shook him heartily by the hand, whilst they murmured their regrets that he was no longer amongst them. And then the talk fell into that grave, earnest mood to which it at times gravitates in such scenes, when men have to recall for the benefit of some new-comer how So-and-so made an end of it. Cis had to listen once more to the story of poor Strangford's death, and that of half a score more in his own or other dragoon regiments with whom he had lived on terms of the closest intimacy. There is an ever-growing callousness in all campaigning, but still men speak sadly, and with bated breath, of their comrades who perished in the strife. It was at this juncture Crymes entered the tent. For a moment Cis looked embarrassed. He could not but remember that day when he had to humble himself before the Major, and apologize for his too reckless tongue; but Crymes grasped the situation with his accustomed *sang froid*, and extending his hand said,—

"Will you shake hands with me, Calvert? It is my turn to apologize now, for I plead guilty to having wronged you, though only in thought,—I went no further. The whole miserable business, as I am aware Harperley has told you, was all cleared up very shortly after you left. There is plenty of scope for quarrelling out here without quarrelling with one another. Ah!" he continued, with a faint smile, as Cis cordially responded to his overture of amity, "we wanted you and hundreds more of you the day they sent us up the valley yonder," and here the Major jerked his head in the direction of the valley of Balaklava. "It was as lively while it lasted as anything we ever had with the York and Ainstey, and the worst of it is it was all a blunder. It's little use wrangling about whose, but there was a sore loss of light dragoons, without any corresponding result that day; in fact, except myself, I don't know any one who got much satisfaction out of it."

"You! Major," exclaimed young Harperley; "why, except that clip on your head, and I don't know how many more disagreeable prods about you generally, I can't for the life of me see what you got out of it."

"Listen, young 'un," replied Crymes, as a slightly ironical smile played over his face: "I'm a horrible pagan, I'm afraid; and, sad to say, my gladiatorial instincts have led me ever since I became a dragoon to wish for my wicked will with my sabre for half-an-hour. Well, they let us loose that day, though I only wish it had been with more purpose."

"It's bad for the other side," muttered young Harperley, "when the Major gets his wicked will with his sabre, that's all I can say."

"And now, Calvert," continued Crymes, "what are you going to do? I'm sure the Colonel, like all the rest of us, will be glad if you elect to take a turn once more with us."

"You're all very good," rejoined Cis, "but the fact is I came up with Jerry Arkwright of the —th Fusiliers, and he has promised to get me attached to them if possible. You see they're at the front," continued Cis, half apologetically.

"And we're not," broke in Crymes, sharply. "You're quite right, Calvert; there's not likely to be anything for us to do, unless it's bury our horses, until the place is taken; and if I know anything about it that won't be for some months yet. No, the infantry fellows are likely to gather all the laurels that are going for the present. You'll see fighting with the Fusiliers deuce a fear before long. I half envy you your chance, as I'm sure it offers the best opportunity of seeing service."

A little more desultory conversation with his brother officers, and then Cis made his way back to Balaklava on foot, there to wait on board ship till he heard what Jerry Arkwright had managed to do for him.

CHAPTER XXVIII.

THE REAL THING AT LAST.

Cis Calvert was not destined to remain long in suspense, for the next day brought not a note, but Jerry Arkwright himself.

"It's all right, old man," he exclaimed, the minute he gained the deck. "I've brought down the ponies; pack up your traps, and as soon as I have collared a ham we'll make the best of our way to the front. The chief's a trump, as he always is. 'Captain Calvert!' he exclaimed; 'yes, I know him by name. Not a bad sort, considering he's only a cavalry man, so I've heard; with rather less side and a trifle less wax in his moustache than those fellows generally affect. However, the beggars rode straight the other day there's no denying, and I should think, like the rest of us, are more concerned about filling their mouths than twisting their moustaches. We are awfully short-handed in officers, and a fellow who's come all the way from India to take his share in the fighting don't deserve to be disappointed. I'll apply for him at once. Go down to Balaklava and tell him so yourself, and that he'd better come up here at once and employ himself in learning his way about the ditches, till I receive an acting commission for him from head-quarters.' So now, old man, as soon as ever you get your traps collected meet me at Oppenheim's. I shall have got the ham by that time I hope, for my two subalterns will be both savage and grumpy if I don't come back with that at my saddle-bow."

A dull, black, dreary time was this in which Cis Calvert was about to commence his campaigning experiences. The Chersonese, or at all events that corner occupied by the allies, was a sea of mud, and for the half-starved animals, insufficient as they were in number, to carry the food absolutely necessary to the front was an impossibility. That regiments should sometimes be a day without rations was a contingency scarce possible to provide against. That they should have now and again, in rough military metaphor, "to eat their cartridges," is an experience common to all campaigns ; but that the commissariat, which during forty years of peace had faded away into almost the shade of a service, when suddenly called upon to resuscitate itself and perform the most arduous duties, should fail, was surely only what might have been expected. Whether it is in a more satisfactory state at the present is, I fancy, open to question, and the glories of Egypt somewhat testify to their short-comings in that respect.

The capture of that ham apparently proved more difficult than Jerry had anticipated, or else his active mind had aspired to the attainment of further luxuries, for it was not till considerably past the hour of tryst that Arkwright made his appearance.

" Here, out with the ponies, quick, Mike," exclaimed the Fusilier. "There's a fellow just told me there's a beastly Black Sea fog rolling down over the monastery, and, by Jove, if we're caught in that we shall be bothered to pick our way home. The roads, my boy, are very imperfectly defined in these parts, and you're off them and into a kitchen, hut, or stable before you know where you are. There's a monotony too about our architecture that's puzzling. The over-grown umbrella under which I live is exactly like your or any one else's umbrella; and we've no time to go into high art in the shape of fancy paintings with which to distinguish them one from another. But here comes Mike with the ponies. If you think, just because it's only seven or eight miles, we can canter it in forty minutes you'll be speedily undeceived. There, that's your mount. Don't turn your nose up because he's only thirteen two and you can see his ribs. We call them in pretty good condition out here when you can't see clean through 'em. Now that animal," continued Jerry with a wink, as he swung himself into his saddle, " could about do his seven miles in an hour and a half on Newmarket Heath, but I fancy he'll be nearer three than two carrying you up to camp."

There was a very great deal more earnest than jest in Jerry

Arkwright's chaff. The poor half-starved "garrous" that were at that time slaves of the regimental officers or the commissariat, could go little faster than at a foot's pace through the sea of mud it was their daily lot to travel. Nothing but the rare strain of Barb blood in their veins pulled through the survivors; and about the poor brutes that perished over that weary seven miles the spring, when it came drying up the mud and bringing forth the primroses, made terrible revelations; grimmer revelations yet came to light too with the violets over the scrub-clothed slopes of Inkerman and the blood-stained turf in Balaklava valley; for there was exposed many a poor fragment of wrecked humanity, sacrifices to the grim Moloch of war, who had perished uncoffined, unannealed.

Jerry's prophetic friend unfortunately proved to have fore-casted the weather only too accurately. Before they had got a couple of miles out of Balaklava the white, misty Black Sea fog began to envelope them. As long as they kept the main cause-way this was of little consequence. The poor ponies no doubt were over their fetlocks in mud; the road was full of holes, which would probably have settled the springs of the strongest-built provincial carriage that ever ran in England in about a quarter of an hour; but still it was a road, and was useful insomuch as it kept them in their straight path to the front. But shortly after leaving Kadakoi came the place beyond which the road had not been carried, and where the trails—I can use no other word for them—diverged in different directions across the plateau to the various divisional camps. And now their difficulties began. To follow these trails with plenty of light, when one could take note of the surrounding landmarks, was of course not difficult, but when verging on sundown, and enveloped in a Black Sea fog, which, though never attaining the density of that sulphurous, unimpenetrable vapour that in winter time enshrouds our own metropolis, it became embarrassing even to men who, like Arkwright and his henchman, were conversant with every yard of the ground.

" We are off the line, Mike," suddenly exclaimed Arkwright. as he pulled up his pony. " Where the deuce we have got to I'm blessed if I know. We surely ought to have passed in rear of the left attack siege train before this, but we not only don't see that, but not a sign of tents of any kind. A horrible suspicion has come over me that we've wandered up the wrong side of the ravine. Just where it begins, you know, it's a mere gentle dip there, and very easy to make a mistake about. If so the first thing we shall strike will be the French lines. What do you think, Mike?"

" Well, yer honour, it's just my opinion we've lost our way."

" As if there was any doubt about that, you idiot," rejoined Jerry, laughing; " but where do you think we are?"

" Upon my sowl I don't know; but sure av we continue our wanderings we'll hit lines of some sort—our own, the French, or it may be the t'other people's. Annyhow it's a mighty mane night to lie out in the open. The bhoys 'll have a bad time to-night of it in the trenches."

" Well," said Arkwright a little petulantly, " there's not much chance of getting a hint what's to be done out of you."

" 'Deed, Captain, I know my place betther. Is it for the likes of me to presume to be thinking what's best to be done when yer honour's to the fore?"

" Well, there is something in his philosophy after all," said Arkwright. " It's an ugly night to lie out, and we must come across lines of some sort at last, and they'll give us shelter if they can't give us supper."

Once more the trio proceeded to blunder along through the mist, and after another fifteen minutes' riding Arkwright suddenly exclaimed :—

" Come, we're close upon tents of some kind."

The words were scarcely out of his lips when the sharp rattle of a firelock as it came down to the charge, was followed by the "Qui Vive?"

"Ami, officier Anglais," rejoined Arkwright hurriedly. "French, by Jove, Cis," he continued, "and there's no time to be lost answering these fellows, they let go upon monstrous slight provocation."

The result of this exchange of civilities was a polyglot and some-what incomprehensible conversation, in which French, English, and Mike's Milesian brogue alternately mingled. At last the sentry passed the word for his officer, who it so happened had a slight smattering of English, and between his smattering and Arkwright's similar smattering of French, they at last ascertained that they had wandered into the lines of the Chasseurs d'Afrique, having, as Jerry had shrewdly conjectured, diverged to the left of the ravine instead of to the right, which they ought to have done shortly after passing Kadakoi; but that this was the camp of the Chasseurs d'Afrique to an old hand like Arkwright was explanation of where they were. Thanking the French officer he bade him a courteous good night; and then turning to Calvert exclaimed,—

"It's deuced awkward, Cis, but we've got all away to our left, and shall have to cross the ravine close by the Naval Brigade camp. Hitting off the road there will be uncommon awkward in this sort of light, and it's rather a queer place to get the ponies down if we miss it. Once pass that and it is pretty plain sailing. I shall know my way then."

But the hitting off of the edge of the ravine proved by no means an easy matter, and again and again did Arkwright come to the conclusion that they had once more lost their way, and that they had by no means come the straightest path to where they were aiming for was more than probable.

"Here's the ravine just to our right, glory be to God!" suddenly said Mike, "but it's a mighty quare place we've hit it off at. It'll be as well, Captain, to thry for the road before attempting to get down."

But ride up and down the ravine in either direction much as they liked they could discover no signs of a pathway leading to the bottom. The zigzag descent could only be designated as a mountain track, and was consequently not quite so easy to discover as a turnpike road. Now except here and there the descent was by no means precipitous—an awkward place to ride down no doubt, but with one of the surefooted Turkish ponies in broad daylight by no means a desperate undertaking. The difficulty at present consisted in picking your way. The party could see so very few yards ahead of them that they might be selecting one of the almost impracticable places.

"It's awkward, Cis," exclaimed Arkwright, "but we can't

spend the night looking for this confounded path. We must
get off and lead down, and if destined to tumble down trust to
not being broke in the process. I'll give you a lead," and so
saying Jerry Arkwright swung himself off his pony and slipped
the bridle through his arm. "Mike, you scoundrel," he added,
"to break your own neck you're quite at liberty, but remember
you're in charge of the commissariat, and the breaking of a bottle
represents a general court-martial. Now, come on. The trenches,
old man, are not half so dangerous as this."

Their descent was slow, and could most decidedly not be
deemed wanting in interest. There was either a man or a pony
down every few yards,—still they had achieved what Arkwright
and Mike deemed about two-thirds of the descent, when suddenly
Arkwright's pony placed its foot upon something which gave
way with him, pitched forward on its head, and rolled heavily
down the ravine.

"Hold hard," cried Arkwright, as a hideous exhalation spread
around them, "bear a little to the left; I know where we are
now. We are right opposite the Naval Brigade, and have got
amongst that mass of corruption which once were horses.
Well to your left, Cis," he shouted again. "We are really
very few yards off the path, and though we have achieved that
bit of knowledge too late to be of much good to us in getting
down, it will be very useful to us in getting up the other side.
I wonder how I shall find poor old Sambo when I get to the
bottom. One comfort is, a Turkish pony takes a deal of
killing."

On arriving at the bottom the wiry little steed was found
shaking his head in a somewhat aggrieved fashion, and looking
disconsolately round for his companions, and apparently very
little the worse for his roll; barring a broken bridle there was
really no great harm done, and to knot that was of course the
work of only two or three minutes. The ascending path the
opposite side was easily hit off, and after passing through the
Naval Brigade camp, now that they had got their bearings the
way to the second division was plain sailing.

"And now," said Arkwright, as they handed their ponies
over to the bâtman, "come across and let me introduce you to

the chief. He's as good a fellow as ever lived; but if there's one thing would make him edgy it would be an addition to the ranks of the battalion without his knowledge. He's about right too. Short-handed as we are now, a colonel ought to know the whereabouts of even an available drummer."

Colonel Hamilton welcomed Cis with all that *camaraderie* which I verily believe is only known in the services, and perhaps never even then so thoroughly seen as when they are face to face with the "real thing."

"Known you by name, Captain Calvert, for some time. A man who, having sold out, volunteers to come here, is worth having; and at Arkwright's suggestion I had great pleasure in applying for an acting commission for you. I have no doubt I shall get it, and in the mean time I'm sure all my officers will have much pleasure in showing you the ropes, and of course if you like to take a turn or two with us in the trenches pending your appointment, you will familiarize yourself with what is rather an intricate country to a new-comer. However, you've had a long ride up from the front, and I've no doubt will be glad of something to eat as soon as you can get it. I can only say I shall be very pleased to have you with us, and leave you for the present to Arkwright's care."

A queer feeling was that first night at the front in that dismal winter in '54. It was the chances were so utterly different from what people pictured it. Imagination led one to conjure up in their mind's eye incessant salvoes of artillery, the continual whizzing of rockets, and an incessant spattering of musketry. But from the failure of the October bombardment to the spring-time, barring the episodes of Balaklava and Inkerman, both besieged and besiegers confined themselves to the sullen defiance of an occasional shot or two, that is, as far as the artillery duel went. True the Russians ever and anon beat up the trenches of the allies in right reckless, resolute fashion, and when the crash of musketry was heard in the night-time all Crimean men knew there was a sharp and wicked bit of fighting going on somewhere along the line. There was a noted leader of these sorties well known by sight to the Second and Light Divisions, for the trenches at the right attack seemed to constitute this hero's happy hunting-ground, a tall, dark, daring fellow, clad in Albanian costume; he was a marked man both from his dress and gallantry. And when he eventually fell with his face to the foe in one of his dashing assaults, there was a feeling of relief amongst those engaged in that attack, and a conviction that they were well rid of a most dangerous assailant. But the dull, depressing monotony of trench duty at that time was almost inconceivable. Sitting for hours in a cold wet ditch, waiting for something which did not take place, is about the only simile one can give of it. No doubt every now and then, as I have just said, the Muscovite would make things lively enough for the most exigeant fire-eater. Men might have no special gluttony for fighting, nor have any greater love for " villainous saltpetre " than Bob Acres, but there is a monotony connected with all big sieges which languish wont to make even those with very little stomach for fighting long for something that should break the dull daily routine.

The next night found the Fusiliers in order for the trenches, and as Arkwright said—

"There is no more fighting about it, Cis, than there will be in camp, and it's a little more damp and disagreeable; but I think, old man, it would be good policy to follow the chief's tip, and just have a look round the blessed ditches we're taking care of."

"Of course," replied Calvert, "a man don't come out here as a volunteer unless he means work, and of course when anything does happen a man ignorant of the ground can be of comparatively little use."

"All right, then down you come with me to-night and study the ways and windings of the trenches."

A dull, grey evening. The sun had sunk to rest some two or three hours before the trench guards paraded on one of well-nigh the shortest days in the year. Clothed in their worn, grey, patched overcoats and common fur caps, there was a marvellous similarity about the British soldier of those times. All distinction of regiment seemed lost, and it really was by no means impossible for an officer strange to these haggard, half-starved bands to mistake the one for the other. And this was precisely what happened to Calvert, as with half a score more of what were called the covering parties, he threaded his way to that mystic ground pictured in England a scene of romance, in reality the dull scene of prosaic suffering.

Scenery, romance, ay! scene of bitter misery to many thousands of miles off, if one can be allowed the expression. One, I recollect, who fell in that last grisly struggle which terminated in the triumph of the allies, and the general orders of the night contained unwittingly the ghastly mockery, " Captain ——, of the Connaught Rangers, has leave of absence to England from the eighth of September, 1855, pending his retirement from the service."   His leave had come, but lying cold and stark in front of the great Redan, his lifeless face turned skywards, little wrecked he of leave or license at Her Majesty's hands.   Dead; with his face to the foe, and cheering on the company he had long commanded, he had gone down like scores of others that bitter day.   It was hard, after enduring all the chances of the campaign.   He retired from the army at his mother's urgent request; he " was the only son of his mother, and she was a widow."   For her sake he resigned his profession; it was the very irony of fate that rendered it forty-eight hours too late.

But to return to Cis Calvert and the Fusiliers. As they wend their way to the trenches the different parties, as may be easily imagined, got a little entangled as they made their way to their different positions.   To the old hands this was of course nothing, but to a neophyte like Cis Calvert it proved unexpectedly embarrassing.   As before said, there was nothing to distinguish one regiment from another in their attire; it was pretty dark, and even had it been light Cis of course could know none of his new comrades by sight.   Getting somewhat uneasy at last, he suddenly addressed the man next to him, exclaiming,—

" You belong to the —th Fusiliers, my lad, don't you?"

" Nae, nae, sir.   You joost gotten amaingst the Hielanders this time; but if you're seeking your way into Sebastopol, if ye'll gang our gate ye'll get as near as is possible the noo I'm thinking."

For a few minutes Calvert's sensations were unpleasant in the extreme.   He had lost his party, and after the terrible " hard lines" that seemed to dog his career, was horrified at what construction might be put on it. A man going under fire for the first time being suddenly discovered missing, certainly runs the risk of being hardly judged by those associated with him. He had no fear of Arkwright conceiving an unfavourable opinion, but Cis had served too long not to know how terribly such a thing might be misconstrued by the men of the regiment. With the British soldier to have the faintest doubt of his officer being genuine "grit" is fatal. He can forgive incompetence, harsh treatment, or abuse, but the man who flinches himself he will never trust to.

Do you remember that famous Indian story of that stern and rigid disciplinarian who commanded one of Her Majesty's regiments, and being perfectly aware of his own unpopularity thus addressed his soldiers? It was, I think, before the storming of the Sikh entrenchments at Sobraon.

"Men," he exclaimed, "you don't like me, I know, because I keep your necks pretty tight to the collar. I've even heard it hinted that I run a chance of being shot down by my own people the first time I lead them into action. I don't believe there's such a cur amongst you, but if there is, he's going to have his chance now, only mark me, by God, I recommend him not to do it this time. We're in a pretty tight place, and there's no one but me to get you out of it."

It flashed across Cis Calvert's mind at the present moment that not only were all these men new to him, but that he was coming into the regiment by what might be denominated a side door. He was not getting his commission in the usual order of things, but receiving a mere acting lieutenancy pending official confirmation from home. He hadn't even got that as yet, and to be suspected of shirking on this his first night of soldiering with his new corps would, he knew, take a lot of living down. His anxiety was so obvious that the rugged old Highland sergeant whom he had addressed noticed it and remarked—

"Dinna be fashed, sir. Ye'll be new to the work I reckon, but we'll soon pass ye along to the Fusiliers the once we get doon."

The grim old Scotchman spoke truth. Once they had gained

the trenches Cis found very little difficulty in discovering Jerry Arkwright and his following.

A duller, drearier, more monotonous night than this promised to be perhaps the " covering parties " never looked out upon. Still it was all new to Cis, and it was with no little interest that, leaning his elbows upon the parapet of the advanced trench, he peered through the murk at the dim outline of the great Redan and the long line of earthworks that connected it with the Malakoff Tower. Little to be seen—but he was gazing, it must be remembered, as men did who found themselves face to face for the first time with the famous fortress. It is an old world story now, but in those days people had been reading the thrilling stories of Inkerman and Balaklava, mixed with the half-pathetic, half-humorous stories of Crimean camp life, for weeks and weeks, and curiosity concerning it ran very high.

Not a shot, not a sound, save ever and anon a dull, monotonous roar, that presaged the shower of grape that every fifteen minutes, as if regulated by a stop watch, the Russians sent up the Woronzoff road : terribly jealous ever was the Muscovite of that joint in his armour, albeit by no means a weak one. Still, quiet as the evening had begun, no old trench-goer would have augured that it might finish in that wise. The storms of the trenches, like the white squalls of the Mediterranean, gave slight warning of their approach, and just as even the experienced mariner has occasionally bare time to close reef his topsails, so those who kept the trenches had scant time to spring to their feet and snatch at their arms before the foe was upon them.

" They look like leaving us to smoke our pipes in peace tonight," said Arkwright, " but one can never be quite sure here, Cis. An ominous calm is of course often the presage of no end of a row down here," and even as he spoke the Flagstaff Battery far away to the left broke out into angry violence, and the fierce angry flashes of its guns showed that the Russians and the French were differing violently in opinion. Another moment and the quick crack of musketry broke upon the ear, but the distance was too far for the cries of the combatants to reach their ears. " Hottish work on the extreme French left," continued Arkwright, " though which side is making the sortie it is impossible to conjecture."

Suddenly from out of the darkness cracked the rifles of the advanced sentries, followed by a wild yell from the Russians as they chased those flying scouts pell-mell over the parapet.

" Stand to your arms ! " thundered Arkwright, and the hoarse cry echoed from end to end of the right attack. " The Albanian, by heavens ! " exclaimed Arkwright, as through the mist dashed a tall, dark, handsome man, waving a sabre, habited in broidered fez and the snowy picturesque kilt of his country- men.

Another moment and the grey-coated, flat-capped Russians were engaged in a hand-to-hand struggle with their English foes. There was little shouting now ; fierce, smothered execrations and savage bayonet thrusts, mingling with the occasional crack of musket or revolver, alone marked such stern contention as now went on in the advance parallel. That the bayonet is ever of use in large battles may perhaps be a question, but there can be no doubt about it in the storming of entrenchments. Through the whirlwind of the carnage the Albanian flashed like a meteor, and gallantly did the stubborn soldiers behind him respond to his lead. Wildly did Arkwright fight his way through the *mêlée* towards this gaily-habited chief, but the result of a furious blow dealt on the shoulder of an old Muscovite grenadier apparently did that grim warrior no harm, while Jerry's foot slipping in its delivery, he rolled over on his back in the mud. No matter to laugh at, absurd though it may sound, for shortening his firelock, the veteran would probably have closed Arkwright's account in this world with a bayonet thrust ; but ere he could use it Calvert's revolver rang sharp and true, and the Russian fell face forward across his intended victim.

Cis had craved to see " the real thing," and was so far in luck. There was certainly no nonsense about his first experience in trench duty. The Russe had come on in earnest that night, with the fixed intention of scouring the trenches and spiking every gun in the third parallel ; and if the fighting was destined to be short, as it usually was in these cases, there was no mistake about it being sharp while it lasted. The fierce, murderous instinct latent in all men, the savage lust of carnage, was now thoroughly aroused in Cis. Unheeding such wounds as fell to his share, he had now lost pretty well all feeling but the desire to kill, and it was in this mood that, amid the fierce imprecations which fell from the lips of his followers, the Fusiliers, he found himself with the blood streaming down his cheek face to face with the Albanian. War is not made with rose-water, and the twain struck at each other at once. Again the blood poured down Cis's face in response to a back-handed stroke of his adversary's sabre. Reeling back he half mechanically parried another furious cut of the Albanian's, and with his left hand fired his revolver, which luckily had yet a chamber unemptied, and the Muscovite leader dropped in his tracks like a stricken deer. His followers seemed to lose all heart at his fall, and a few more minutes saw the Russians once more scrambling over the parapet in the direction of their own lines.

And then there was time to count up the cost, and see who would never again answer to their names at muster. One of the first to gain his feet was Jerry Arkwright, who, after a few muttered maledictions at the frivolous weapon supplied to their customers by army tailors, fell in his men, and proceeded to that grim sequel of battle—the calling of the roll. Some half-a-dozen killed and a score of men more or less wounded constituted the casualties of the Fusiliers, and then it occurred to Arkwright what had become of Cis Calvert.

"Who knows anything about the gentleman who came down to us as a volunteer? What's become of Mr. Calvert, does anyone know? He was talking to me when the attack began."

"They're a bringing him along now, sir," replied a tough old corporal, who was busily engaged in staunching the blood which flowed from more than one reminiscence of the evening's fight. "'Twas he shot down the white petticoated fellow that led them just before he fell himself. There was a pretty bit of hammer and tongs work between them before they both went down; but here they come, and the doctor with them."

Anxiously Arkwright hurried forward to learn his friend's

fate, and it was with no little relief that he heard the surgeon's cheery verdict of—

" All right ; a bit knocked about, lost a little more blood than's good for him, and hasn't quite come to himself as yet, but there's no real harm done.   As for the white-kilted fellow who led our opponents, he'll trouble us no more.   You've been away of late, Arkwright, and don't quite know what that means ; but that man," and he pointed down at the dark face of the Albanian, now set calm and immovable in death, " was a soldier every inch, and one of the most dashing leaders they had. There'll be quieter times for the right attack now he is gone, poor fellow."

CHAPTER XXIX.

A LETTER FROM THE CRIMEA.

At last England had realized the fact that after the long peace she was once more committed to a European war. The country hardly realized it at first. Dumb with the exultation of the dashing victory of the Alma, it was only those who had to make moan over their dead who thoroughly realized the cost of the game they were engaged in. But the triumph of the Alma was speedily followed by the fierce struggle of Inkerman, and though that might be called a victory, yet it was evident to all that such costly glories as these were little better than defeats. Through the house of the peer, as well as the cottage of the peasant, the story of that terrible Sunday morning sent a wail of despair. The nation at last understood that a struggle with the Muscovite meant a good deal more than the clang of bells, cheers, fireworks, laurels, and salutes. And now slowly commenced to leak out the grim story of the misery and suffering of the army before Sebastopol; how that they were more besieged than besieging; how that they were perishing by hundreds, not from shot and shell, but from cold, wet, hunger, and exposure; from lack of clothing, from want of tents,—from want, in short, of the bare necessities of life.

Then England turned in her wrath, after the manner of the old Athenians, with the savage disposition to throw these short-comings on some one, and to rend him there and then. But what would you have? Sift the thing as you might it was no one's fault in particular; it is simply the error that exists to this hour of believing that organization can be done at the last moment. A country that declines the expense of maintaining a commissariat and transport staff in times of peace cannot be astonished at finding that they are not to be improvized at the last moment. Men are no more made organizers than they are poets or roasters, and that a scanty staff, to whom no practice has been vouchafed, should display want of knowledge of their vocation should excite surprise in no one. But the nation did not understand this, and after the manner of a great constitutional country, hungrily demanded a victim. However, since the days when we shot an admiral, we have usually confined ourselves to clamouring for the culprit, a matter in which we have certainly shown more wisdom and discretion than our gallant allies of the Crimean days, who during the time of their own revolution not only demanded that some one should suffer for shortcomings, but took remarkably good care that a good many did.

That all this story of muddle and misery should make a great impression in Yorkshire is needless to say. When the Charringtons, Mr. Harperley, Miss Aysgarth, and others, read the tale of Balaklava their hearts stood still, and they felt a strange sensation of choking in their throats. It was natural. Some four or five careless young fellows, who only a few months ago had been hunting, dancing, and laughing with them, were gone, and they should see them no more; and though Harry Harperley was as yet unscathed, yet every one saw now that there was many another life to be forfeited before the quarrel between Russia and the Western Powers was to be brought to a conclusion. Harry was a fair correspondent as things went, but writing letters on your knees with chilled fingers, in a soppy bell tent, is a performance that requires some fortitude. At the best of times the British subaltern is not a prolific correspondent. Observation tends to show that, except with reference to ways and means, he regards letter-writing as a somewhat frivolous waste of time. They were certainly so far justified, insomuch as there was nothing satisfactory to tell. They were having "hard lines," and like the Anglo-Saxon generally were doggedly making the best of it. "This thing has got to be soldiered out, and of course we shall pull through in the end, but life at present ain't all 'beer and skittles,'" was pretty much the language in which most of these young philosophers would have summed up the situation. However, one February morning a letter, with the well-known Crimean post-mark, came, as a friend of mine used to describe it in those troublous times, "like a thirteen-inch shell." Miss Aysgarth pounced upon it at once, while her father, looking across at her, said,

"Thank God, at all events our boy is all right. Tell me what he says as soon as you have made it out."

"Light Brigade Lines, Camp before Sebastopol.

"DEAREST ANNIE,

"You and the dear old father like to hear, and so like the exemplary son and brother that I am I write, although I have nothing to say. I remember in my school-boy days perusing, probably under compulsion, in the works of some great authority, that when a man had nothing to say he most distinctly had better not write, but if I wait for that, judging from appearances, you wouldn't hear from me for some time. We neither get on or go on; we don't even keep pegging away. As for us horse-soldiers, we seem well out of it for the present, and indeed till they get some more of us out the picket work up the valley is about as much as we're fit for. We are not only terribly short of men, but if anything even worse off for horses. It's cold, and there's no doubt those poor fellows in the front must be having a pretty rough time of it: but although we are told that the Czar relies upon Generals January, February, and March, I can't help thinking we're through the worst. A few weeks and we shall come to spring weather, and the springs here we are told are not of the bleak pattern that we are accustomed to on the Yorkshire wolds. Lots of reinforcements too are all ready to come along. The 10th Hussars and the 12th Lancers are on their way from India. Strong regiments both, and we are told that their Arabs will stand this work much better than our big horses. One thing is certain,—the Turkish ponies will pick up a living where an English thorough-bred would starve.

"Now I *have* a bit of news for you. Who do you think turned up here a few weeks back? No other than Cis Calvert! It seems he quarrelled with his Colonel in India, sold out of the Royal Dunbars all in a hurry, and then came out here as a volunteer; and for once, Annie, his luck really seems to have changed. He got attached to the —th Fusiliers, threw in for a rattling sortie his first night in the trenches, had the luck to shoot down the Russian leader, and, in fact, generally distinguished himself. He got knocked about a bit, but there is no real harm done, and the Fusiliers are uncommon proud of their new recruit, dear old Cis, the very best of all our lot, and that's a big word. The Colonel said only the other day when he heard the trench story, 'We must have him back again as soon as he gets his company,' and promotion, Annie, runs pretty quick amongst us all now. Thanks to old Charrington, we of course all know the true story of that luckless business on Crockley Hill. Crymes made up with Calvert the minute he saw him, saying he felt that he owed Cis an apology on his side, although in his ignorance he could hardly have acted differently from the way he did. I never felt half so jolly about anything in my life as when, having heard of his exploit, I rode up to the front and found he was not seriously broke. He will doubtless experience plenty of opportunities before we get inside.

"By the way, the Fusiliers had a good story going the day I was in their lines, of which Arkwright was the narrator. They had a court-martial it seems on a man for what was supposed to be an attempt at desertion. The joke consists in the absurd wording of the charge. The man was arraigned 'for attempting to enter Sebastopol,' a thing we have been all trying to do for the last four months? Good-bye. Tell the father he'll have to rig me out all again in horseflesh, as my sole surviving equine anatomy I really couldn't show on in the streets of York. Kindest remembrances to the Charringtons. Tell her she will have to give a series of dances 'when Harry comes marching home' to enable him to recover 'his steps;' and further inform the master of the Byculla that I shall expect to be allowed five lives at pool for the first twelvemonth in consequence of the demoralizing effect this prolonged residence in uncivilized parts has produced in my billiard science. Once more, Annie dearest, good-bye. I—and all the rest—are very fit, always excepting those who you know from the papers have not been with us since that sad October day.

"Ever your affectionate brother,
"HARRY HARPERLEY."

Miss Aysgarth could not refrain from a slight start as she read of Cis Calvert's presence in the Crimea. Her father marked her cheek flush and her eye sparkle as she perused the record of Cis's doings, and then he saw that unbidden tears were trembling in the lashes. It was with a slight mixture of sob and smile that she handed her letter across to the banker as she finished. The triumphant smile which always wreaths a woman's lips when she hears that the man she loves has distinguished himself, mixed as it must ever be in listening to such stories as the above, with a slight shiver at the dangers he has passed through. Cis Calvert in the Crimea? Where then, she thought, was this Indian siren, in whose toils he was immeshed? Was that rumour at Byculla Grange mere Anglo-Indian gossip? It might be, she thought. She was no child, nor ignorant that scandal was ever prevalent in the land. She had heard, moreover, that our Eastern empire is much addicted to what they term "gup," whereby they mean gossip, scandal, or by whatever other equivalent the taking away of one's neighbours' characters may be designated. At all events there was one comfort. If her lover had been entangled he had at all events now broken his chains. If he had temporarily wavered in his allegiance there was at least good hope that rumour had much exaggerated his defection. This Mrs. Daventry could surely not be with him in the Crimea? Ladies as yet, so far as she knew, had not ventured further than Scutari, where, if half the reports that came home were true, there was only too much for them to do, and the papers teemed with sharp remarks on the shame and sin of even allowing the few soldiers' wives to participate in such rough work as was now going on.

Mr. Harperley read the letter gravely and with no little interest. He knew now, as did every one else round York, that in the race at Crockley Hill Cis Calvert had been the victim of a fraud, of which he was as innocent as any looker-on. But he had, as was very natural, heard considerably more about Cis's flirtation with Mrs. Daventry than his daughter. He was quite prepared, that business satisfactorily explained, to welcome Cis as a son-in-law, but he did think that things had better remain as they were between them for the present, that is to say, without any positive engagement, and without their corresponding until such time as the war should be over. He liked Cis, and was conscious that in his judgment about that unfortunate race he had wronged him. He was anxious not to fall into a similar mistake a second time, but he loved his daughter dearly, and was disturbed at the idea of handing her over to a man who did not really care for her. Cis's Indian flirtation might be mere gossip, unfounded rumour, easy of explanation, but he deemed it a thing best cleared up before the old relations were renewed.

Having finished the letter he handed it quietly back to his daughter and said, "That all who knew Captain Calvert will be pleased, though not surprised, at his distinguishing himself is a matter of course; there are plenty of his friends round here that this news will delight. He left us under a grievous misconception, and the majority of us know that we did him scant justice on that occasion; but, Annie, although this Indian matter has never been touched on between you and me, still I know very well that it must have reached your ears, and I think for the present it will be wise to let things stand as they are. If he clears himself in your eyes on his return I shall give you to him with as much pleasure as I can give you away at all. Let us be of good hope that things will come all right in the end, and in the mean time, like hundreds of others, be content to wait."

When she gained her own room, carrying, one may be certain, her brother's letter, Annie sat down to think. She had been all but trying to steel her heart to think no more of this man. And now she did not feel sure but what all this Indian story might turn out to have been grossly exaggerated, should there even be any foundation for it. True, there was usually a suspicion of truth at the bottom of Mrs. Charrington's stories, but in this case it was only what she had heard from a country which, in those days, was practically very distant. Still flashed across her mind that thought which instinctively wrings every woman's heart, Why had he not answered her last letter? And such a letter! She was conscious that she had poured forth all the depth of her love for him in that epistle. If she refused to give him up, and showed herself desirous to continue correspondence, surely it was not for him to decline; it might be all very chivalrous to say that with such a slur upon his name, as a man of honour, the only thing he could do was to resign all pretensions to her hand; but like most women she could not, and she did not, think it was for him to decide upon that. Surely she was the best judge of a matter so nearly concerning herself, and when she elected to stand by him, let him have committed what crime he might, was it not for him to thankfully accept the sacrifice. Another thing she knew now, that no stain attached to his name; and it was evident from her brother's letter that Cis also was now aware of that fact. Surely he ought to write to her now; he could hardly expect that she should humiliate herself by writing to him again whilst that last letter remained unanswered. And then she too came to the same conclusion as her father, that there was nothing left for it but to watch the papers and wait. If he had really ceased to love her then she should hear of him no more, and it were best so; if on the contrary he remained true to her, a letter would come at last.

And then, like a true woman, she began to make excuses for her lover. She had not liked that chivalrous view; she had held it was not for him to take it. And yet it was very noble of him too, and of course first arriving at the Crimea it was all strange to him, and he must have had a great deal to do. Had not her brother pointed out the difficulty of carrying on correspondence in the plight they then were; and now in consequence of his heroic conduct—of course it was heroic in her eyes—he was lying wounded and mangled. True, Harry said it was nothing serious; that " he was not badly broke;" but then that's just the way men talk of these things. She could recall accidents in the hunting-field in which the sufferer had been reported " all right," nothing much the matter, he has only broken his arm, two ribs and a collar-bone. How could she expect him to write when he was probably so badly wounded as to be in the hands of a sick nurse? And now her thoughts travelled round to the opposite point of the compass, and she began to ask herself whether it was not unkind, almost unfeeling, not to despatch a little note of sympathy to this man in his hour of agony. Even if he was no longer her lover he had been very near and dear to her only a twelve-month ago: and at last Annie Aysgarth finished up by doing what would be the natural end in such a case in a woman's reflections, that is, she sat down and cried her heart out.

At Byculla Grange, I need scarcely say, there was much discussion concerning Cis Calvert's gallantry. The exoneration of his character with regard to the steeplechase had occasioned a great revulsion in his favour. He had always been a popular man, and now people recollected his dashing horsemanship. If he had been one of the first flight with the York and Ainstey, it was evident now that he meant to hold the same place when there was work to be done. Members of the York Club were conscious now that they had been a little unjust to Cis Calvert; that, although there were undoubtedly strong grounds for suspicion, there had been hardly sufficient evidence to pronounce a verdict against him; and then a man's previous character and social status should always plead for suspension of judgment in such a case. They were one and all only too anxious to make amends, and every one now spoke enthusiastically concerning him. There were of course plenty of such stories going in the journals in those days, but this sortie happened to create rather more sensation than usual from the fact that it took place at a time when the exhaustion on both sides had caused active operations to languish. Then again the picturesque costume of the Russian leader had made him quite a man of mark—no more persistent scourer of the right attack trenches than he—and therefore it naturally came to pass that the man who had slain the Albanian became to some extent a man of mark in his turn. Through the Second and Light Divisions Cis Calvert's name and story were now pretty generally known.

"I always said I knew it all along," exclaimed Mr. Charrington, as he threw down the *Times* at breakfast, containing an account of that night skirmish ; " I always said Calvert would come out all right. Was it likely a fellow who rode as straight as he did to hounds wasn't likely to run straight all through? He's a glorious fellow, and the banker's daughter hardly showed her usual good sense when she allowed him to go packing off to India. I used to think at one time that she really meant to take him for good and all, and I've no hesitation in saying that I think she was a fool not to. Whether he did or did not ask her of course I don't know, but I'm pretty sure he would if she had chosen."

"Don't talk nonsense, Robert," replied Mrs. Charrington a little sharply. "Miss Aysgarth had, or at all events I fancy will have, the opportunity of doing a good deal better for herself than that. You must recollect Major Crymes came into all his uncle's money just before he left for the East, and Annie Aysgarth can be Mrs. Crymes when he returns, I have very little doubt."

It may not be a very courteous or yet a very polished fashion of replying to a lady's speech, but Mr. Charrington simply gave vent to a prolonged whistle.

"You'll be kind enough to explain that, Robert, although I know pretty well what it means."

"Oh, nothing," replied Mr. Charrington, with some slight hesitation, "only I did think—that is, I was under the impression that he admired some one else."

"Meaning me," replied the lady with the greatest calmness. "Of course he did; some of them" (by them Mrs. Charrington described the male sex generally) "always do, but you know very well he couldn't marry me, and that I'm a true wife to you, although I plead guilty to the womanly weakness of a love for admiration. If you had ever noticed anything, which of course you men never do until we point it out to you, you would have seen that I always provide my admirers with suitable wives,— a purer philanthropist never existed. Having ascertained by personal experience that a man understands how to render those *petits soins* so dearly loved of my sex, I then do him a good turn, and marry him off to the most eligible young lady on my list."

"Good Lord! and to think that I have been living for the last fifteen years with a professional matchmaker and never knew it."

"No," replied the lady with a smile; "your unobservant sex only awake, as a rule, to our virtues and perfections after you have lost us."

But this was a little too much for Mr. Charrington. He was
fond of and quite satisfied with his wife, but he also knew that
she had occasioned him many a paroxysm of jealousy; that
there were times when she could not restrain a certain crispness
of temper, and that, though not altogether the unmitigated
blessing she represented herself, they got on very well together;
still there was that occasional crumpling of the rose-leaves unavoidable when two people make up their minds to dwell
together in unity. He didn't whistle this time, but thrusting
his hands in his pockets muttered something indistinctly about
a cigar in the stables, and strolled out of the room.

He was wise in his generation, for to get into argument with
a woman on the subject of her own perfections is, to put it
mildly, unadvisable in the eyes of a sensible man.

But if Cis Calvert's late doings were discussed at the York
Club, Byculla Grange, and The Firs, there was also a more
humble place in which they were talked over, and that was at
the Punch Bowl Tavern in Stonegate. The great Isham Boggs,
who had not been lately seen in York, had once more arrived at
that hostelrie. Isham had come up on one of his touting
expeditions. That Mr. Popham had got a flyer for Epsom in
Wild Dayrell was pretty generally known, but it was also
rumoured that there was a colt in the north country stables
which would take a deal of beating, and it was to inquire about,
and if possible get a sight of, this animal, that was the object of
Mr. Boggs' present mission. He was sitting in that bedroom on
the first-floor, which he habitually used on his visits to the Punch
Bowl. He was engaged, moreover, in that solace to his lonely
hours which he specially affected, to wit, the consumption of gin,
tobacco, and the perusal of the racing calendar. But he was not
alone upon this occasion. Mr. Blundell, since the departure of
his late master for the Crimea, had relapsed into a mere hanger-on
on the outskirts of the turf. Isham Boggs might fairly claim to
be the biggest scoundrel that had ever come within Mr. Blundell's
personal knowledge, and from our previous acquaintance with
Major Crymes' late groom we can easily conceive that his admiration for Isham was unbounded. To a man of Mr. Blundell's
perverted morality Isham's villainies were simply strokes of

genius : he had as much admiration for Isham's talents as if they had been employed in a laudable and legitimate vocation. Still it was not altogether his own choice that he had become what he was—the mere shadow and assistant of the unscrupulous Isham.

When the —th Lancers got their orders for the East the Major, as we know, got rid of all his race-horses, and had, of course, no further occasion for Blundell's services. Mr. Blundell, it must be remembered, had borne a very shady character when Crymes first engaged him, and when the truth concerning the disqualification of The Mumper was, thanks to Mr. Charrington's exertions, brought to light, it became evident that Mr. Blundell had been, more or less, in the secret of the fraud. That he had called on Mr. Boggs at the Punch Bowl more than once, that he had actually been in the trap with him to witness the race, and had brought the short note to his master which had led to the Major making the suggestion, transpired during the inquiry. There was no tangible offence with which to charge anybody, but it was quite clear that Boggs and Dick Hunsley had contemplated an elaborate racing plant. What Hunsley's embarrassments had prevented their carrying out in one way accident had enabled them to carry out in another. That Mr. Blundell lent himself to the carrying out of Isham's scheme admitted of no manner of doubt; and under these circumstances it was little likely that the Major's late stud-groom would get employment in Yorkshire. He was a man who had no fancy for working harder for his bread than was absolutely necessary. Like many others he had much hankering for the flesh-pots, but preferred their being filled with as little exertion as possible. To obtain a precarious living by assisting the great Isham in his continual villainies was much more in accordance with Blundell's disposition than seeking for honest labour ; and that gentleman, who had always employment for two or three tools in connection with his nefarious schemes, had munificently appointed Mr. Blundell to that dubious position.

"I only wish we had that Mumper game to play over again. We didn't get half enough out of it."

"Didn't we ?" replied Isham, contemptuously. "I made a

very good thing of it; and as for you, it was the easiest earned seventy-five pound ever you picked up. It's mighty little you was asked to do for it."

"Yes, but you know you said I was to have a hundred, and it really is dead low water with me now."

"Said you were to have a hundred? Ask any one who knows Isham Boggs if you wer'n't devilish lucky to get three-fourths of it? Folks don't as a rule care about discounting my promises to pay. Dead low water are you? Do I look as if I was going about in my private carriage? That's just where it is. Whenever I plan a little bit of successful—well, say industry,—and make a bit of money by it, I never can keep it. Most of what I got over that steeplechase I dropped at the back end over the October handicaps. Well, he was a rare good horseman was Captain Calvert, and it was 'hard lines' that he should have been hunted out of the country when he wasn't even in the swim."

"Well, I see by the papers," rejoined Blundell, "that he's gone to the Crimea, and been in among them Russians. You think it was hard for him. We none of us know what is quite good for us. Who knows if he'd been with the regiment that Balaklava day whether he'd be alive now?"

"Now look here, my friend. I'll trouble you not to bother me with any more of your philosophy. If you think losing your money is good for you do it by all means. I know it don't suit me half so well as winning other people's."

"I don't want to quarrel, Isham, I'm sure. When do we leave this?"

"In two or three days most likely, but it all depends on what news I get. We've got this horse to see about, mind, and find out whether he's really any good or whether it's all gammon."

Mr. Boggs' mission was destined to turn out somewhat disastrously. He was fascinated by the north country colt that he had come up to see; put his faith in him instead of the favourite, and the end of May saw him and Mr. Blundell completely beggared upon Epsom Downs. No very new experience to either of them, but more so to the former. Both of these worthies now fade from our pages. Their subsequent career shows how

unevenly justice is served out to us in this world. Mr. Blundell
became a mere jackal of the race-course; but as for Isham Boggs,
like many other illustrious scoundrels, he made no edifying
finish on " Tyburn tree," or, to speak more prosaically, in front
of Newgate, but having come once more, unexpectedly, through
an exceedingly well-concocted robbery, into what was for him a
bit of money, he succeeded in persuading a well-to-do widow,
proprietress of a sporting tavern, to marry him. Isham had
remote dreams of betting lists and unlimited gin; but his con-
sort, before he could get the former on a comfortable footing,
took an evangelical turn, sold out of the business, and rumour
says that the mighty Boggs turned teetotaller, and, deaf to the
war-cry of the fielders, has been actually seen in his advanced
years holding a plate in a " Little Bethel " or Low-Church
chapel.

CHAPTER XXX.

THE TAKING OF THE QUARRIES.

IT is an early March morning, and standing in the Quarries in rear of the left attack are a group of men, busily scanning the Russian lines through their field-glasses. Bearded, unkempt, and unwashed, it would have puzzled their dearest friends to recognize those dandy warriors wont to lounge in the park, a flower in their buttonhole, so often in the season.

"We don't seem much nearer getting in," observed a dashing officer now gone to his rest, but who lived to be a General before he died; "and mark that green hill that lies in front and a little to the left of the Great Redan. What can our engineers be about? If we don't occupy it, depend on it the Russians will before many days are over."

It was probably more the business of the French engineers to take possession of that hill than our own. Our engineers might certainly have retorted that they had not sappers enough to trace the lines, nor could the infantry furnish either the working parties necessary to make the entrenchments, nor the covering parties requisite to defend them when they were made. If our gallant Allies were not quite in such straits as ourselves they at all events had their own troubles to contend with, but they kept them to themselves, whilst we proclaimed our sufferings to the world generally, including the enemy.

The first impulse of every Englishman, as we all know, is to write to the *Times*, whether his train is late, whether he is overcharged by his cabman, or whether he has quarrelled with his wife; and not only did the accredited reporter of the *Thunderer* send home his fair and unbiassed statements of the wretched state the army was in, but all sorts of correspondence in the shape of private letters from men in the Crimea, were published by their imprudent relatives, and the Russian Generals as they read these statements might well feel good hope of hurling the invader once more back into the sea. It became at last more a game of endurance than anything else : it was a question simply of which side could pour the greatest amount of men and material into those few square miles of the Crimea in which the struggle was destined to be decided. Steam water-carriage of course in the end beat waggon-carriage across the steppes, as it was bound to do. The soldiers of the Allies were at all events landed in the Crimea with practically no loss, but the Russian reinforcements wasted terribly during that long and terrible march from the north to the southern extremity of her empire ; and, as was said, when the spring-time came, the navvies arrived, and the railway was laid down from Balaklava nearly up to the front, it at all events looked as if *we* meant to stay.

The prognostications of that member of that grimy group on the Quarry Hill were speedily verified. A week or two afterwards and the eyes of the Allies were greeted with the first outlines of the Mamelon, destined to occasion considerable trouble and much loss of life before it fell into possession of the French. As the sap rises in the trees with the spring-time so was fresh life infused into the campaign. Both sides had received reinforcements of men and ammunition. That the stagnation of the winter had disappeared, and the work was once more to begin in earnest, was obvious to the most careless spectator, and that the first step must be the taking of the Mamelon by the French was apparent to every one. One night the Zouaves burst over their trenches, hurled the Russians out of the Mamelon, and, carried away by their national *élan*, followed their flying foe to the very foot of the Malakoff; intoxicated by the elation of victory they actually meditated the taking of that work by a *coup de main;* but there the fugitives were promptly reinforced, and turning fiercely upon the somewhat disorganized victors, not only hunted them back to the lost entrenchment but retook it, and defied all attempts to dislodge them during the night. Pellissier, the French commander-in-chief, was, however, the last man to abandon a point upon which he had once set his mind. Once let him determine that the carrying the position was necessary, and he was ruthless of life in effecting his object, and that the Zouaves would have another opportunity afforded them speedily, was a thing of which there was little doubt.   One afternoon it was whispered about that the French were once more going to assault the Mamelon, and the dying rays of the April sun saw an anxious knot of British officers once more gathered on the Quarry Hill, with their glasses fixed on that irritating earthwork.   Too far off to hear the yell with which the Zouaves once more sprang at the throat of the foe, one could just catch the faint notes of the *pas de charge* as they swept across the open, for all the world, as a sporting subaltern exclaimed, "like a pack of hounds being thrown into cover." The fierce, angry crackle of the musketry raged for a few minutes, and then the flat-capped Muscovites could be seen falling back on the Malakoff, and it was obvious that the work was in the hands of the French.   This time their leaders succeeded in keeping their men in hand, and instead of following the beaten foe turned their attention to throwing up an entrenchment in the gorge of their new conquest.   Rapidly that little group on the Quarry Hill break up and tear down to the respective covering parties to which they belong, already falling in, for a hint has been given that they might be required to make a demonstration on their side, with a view of harassing the foe and securing the French in their new position.

From this the siege progresses rapidly; the allies advance steadily, and the approaches are pushed closer and closer. Every inch of ground is fiercely contested, and the Muscovite will fight stubbornly the whole night to recover any loss of position. The French have in this instance an easier task than the English, insomuch as the latter are working on rocky ground, which of course makes the construction of the sap difficult, while the French in softer soil can not only run their trenches more easily, but can obviously get much closer to the enemy's work than our own people.   In the left attack, when they reached the crest of the hill overlooking the Barrack battery, further advance was impossible, and that a main assault should be delivered from that point had never entered the head of any of the chiefs of the Allied Army.   The French had for some time believed that the way into Sebastopol was through the Flagstaff Battery, but the verdict of the English engineer, who if he could not see a joke was at all events a *connoisseur* in fortresses, was now pretty generally accepted, and that whenever the Malakoff fell Sebastopol would be virtually in the hands of the Allies was now usually conceded. As the French pushed on it became absolutely necessary that sundry of the Russian advance posts in front of the Great Redan should be taken by the English. From these positions the enemy's sharpshooters were able to enfilade the French trenches. The two most conspicuous of these points were a set of rifle-pits, subsequently called Egerton's Pits, and the Quarries, by no means to be confounded with the Quarry Hill, in rear of the left attack. Stone quarries were somewhat numerous on the plateau, most of the materials for the building of Sebastopol having doubtless been obtained therefrom, and that these should at times be available as natural defences is evident.

That the siege was going on in grim earnest now there could be very little doubt. Hardly a week passed without, in the slang of the army, "a row in the ditches." From the obstinate fight the enemy had made for the retention of the Rifle Pits it was rightly augured that the Quarries would be a stiffish nut to crack. Poor Lempriere, although reputed the smallest officer in the British army, had shown that pluck is no matter of inches, and had died gallantly at the head of his company in the rush with which these pits were carried. His Colonel had picked him up in the first flush of their success, and carried the lifeless figure out of the turmoil, rejoining his men only to be in his turn also carried away a corse before morning, victim to one of the fierce onslaughts made by the enemy in the course of the night for the recovery of lost ground.

A few evenings later and Cis Calvert, now gazetted a lieutenant, is parading with a strong party of the —th Fusiliers for trench duty. There is a rumour that we mean having the Quarries shortly, and to-night—

> "A whisper's caught up through the ranks as they form,
>   A whisper that fain would break out in a cheer,
> How the foe is in force, how the work will warm :
>   But steady ! the chief gallops up from the rear."

"Gentlemen," said the field-officer of the trenches, addressing the group of officers lounging in front of their respective commands, with as pleasant a smile as if about to ask them to supper, " the honour of taking the Quarries has been deputed to us. Of course we shall get in, but remember we have got to *stay* in, and the enemy are not likely to leave us in the enjoyment of a tranquil evening. All I have to impress upon you is this,— keep your men well in hand, and don't be tempted to follow up the first success. Remember your business is only to take the Quarries and keep them, and should you allow yourselves to be run away with by the idea that we can carry the Redan besides, we shall be likely to fall into the same mistake the French made in their first assault on the Mamelon." Touching their caps the officers were about to fall in, when the Colonel bending from his saddle said, " Oh, Arkwright, you're in command of the Fusiliers, are you not ? "

"Yes, sir," replied Jerry.

"That's all right," continued the Colonel cheerily. " You know every inch of the ground, and you and your fellows will lead the attack ; remember we must have the Quarries, and we must keep them. I'm promised plenty of reinforcements, and, by Jove, you know, we can't afford to have those Frenchmen grinning at us. If we're not still there by sunrise to-morrow I for one shall be most likely past praying for."

"I dare say it will be a lively night, sir, but you can rely upon our fellows. We have got a good many old soldiers in our ranks still," with which words Arkwright turned and rejoined his men.

And now the covering parties wound their different ways steadily down to the trenches, threading the intricate maze of *boyaux* and parallels till they reached their respective stations. Jerry Arkwright halted his men in a species of *place d'armes*, formed in rear of the advanced parallel. Calling his brother-officers to him he said pithily:

"Look here, you fellows, we've got to rush this place as soon as we get the order. It's not far to go, and let's have no stopping for shooting till we get in. The men may use their firelocks then anyhow, but to fire prematurely is simply to call attention to the fact that we are coming,—that's all I've got to say. Another chance for you, Cis," he answered, as he gript Calvert's hand; "there'll be promotion on Cathcart's Hill for some of us before daybreak."

Never a man understood better the old saying, "the more you look at a fence the less you like it," than the dashing chief in charge of the attack. Not the man he to keep his bulldogs in the leash. Not a quarter of an hour after they got into their places, when his voice rang low and clear through the trench,

"—th Fusiliers! forward! charge!"

Jerry Arkwright, Cis Calvert, and three or four more sprang over the parapet, and like a wave their soldiers streamed behind them. Almost before the Russians had fairly discerned them they were into the Quarries. A fierce ten or twelve minutes' *mêlée* and the enemy were falling back pell-mell on the Great Redan, while the victors set to work under the auspices of an officer of the Engineers and his sappers, who had accompanied the attack, to entrench the reverse of their new acquisition.

"Well done, Fusiliers," cried the chief; "though I'm afraid, Arkwright, we can't call it altogether a bloodless triumph."

"No, sir, indeed," replied Jerry; "poor Matlock is killed, Lieutenant Wilkinson I've sent back badly wounded, to say nothing of a good many of my men."

"I'm sorry to hear poor Matlock's gone, though when you play with the china you must expect to break plates. Ha! we have woke them up at last, and I fancy have ensured a hottish night all along the line."

And as he spoke the Russian batteries open fire from the Malakoff to the Flagstaff, producing speedily retort from the lines of the Allies. Anon amongst the fierce roar of the artillery came the spattering of musketry, not necessarily indicative of an attack upon either side, but acute suspicion of it. Again and again on both sides did the lines blaze with the quick flashes of the rifles, simply from the alarm that the foe was advancing to the assault. In one place alone was there an ominous silence, and that was from the newly-taken position and from the Russian entrenchments that faced it. Suddenly the Great Redan thundered forth with increased vehemence, shell after shell hurtled through the air, carrying more or less destruction through the right attack.

"Steady, lads, steady," cried the Colonel in clear resonant tones. "Keep your men well together, Captain Arkwright; this is only the overture; the play will begin again shortly. They are coming on again before many minutes are over, and in real earnest."

"Yes," rejoined the Engineer officer cheerily, "the Russians are not quite the boys to take an action of ejectment quietly, and, by the Lord! here they come."

"Let them have it all you know," cried Arkwright. "Use your rifles freely, men. Remember the more you stop before they get to the parapet, the less trouble you'll have afterwards."

Covered to some extent by the thunder of their own artillery, and despite the withering fire of musketry relentlessly poured upon them from the position they had just lost, a dense Russian column came steadily on. But the English on their side had by this time been heavily reinforced, and a fierce hand-to-hand struggle of some ten or fifteen minutes only resulted in the enemy's reeling back shattered and discomfited. Another officer of the Fusiliers was carried campwards after this last sortie, finishing up his military career by what eventually proved the loss of a leg. Arkwright's prophecy that "it was destined to be a hottish night" was amply fulfilled. No less than five times did the foe come on and furiously endeavour to recover the lost position. The thunder of the big guns was well-nigh ceaseless on either side, and in the last sortie but one, Arkwright, who had handled his men with great skill and gallantry throughout the struggle, fell, and was carried away apparently dead. When the sun broke, the ground between the Quarries and the *chevaux de frise*, that covered the salient of the Great Redan, was dotted with little grey heaps, interspersed occasionally with scarlet, that, when the sun had set, had been living men. Black with powder and his eyes bloodshot with the smoke and carnage of battle, Cis Calvert mustered the shattered ranks of the Fusiliers, sole surviving officer of that party.

"We have got them and we've kept them, Calvert, though it has cost us dear. The relief will be down directly, and it will be for others to see the position is not lost, but, good Heavens! are you the only officer left of the six of you there were last night?"

"That's all, sir. Poor Arkwright fell in the last sortie but one, and I very much fear that, except carrying him to Cathcart's Hill, there is nothing more left for us to do for him in this world."

"Down on your faces, men," suddenly thundered the Colonel, as the shrill whistle of a shell fell upon his ear, albeit not showing the faintest intention of following his own prescription.

Another moment and a thirteen-incher had pitched into the group, but when the dust and smoke of the explosion had cleared away Cis Calvert and three of his men were down, though not the least in compliance with the Colonel's orders. The shell had issued a mandate on its own account, which had taken precedence of the chief's, to which, indeed, there had been no time to give effect. It was the last sacrifice to the holocaust of the taking of the Quarries.

CHAPTER XXXI.

A FAREWELL SHOT.

"They had sharpish work at the front last night," said Crymes, as he entered the semi-mess tent of the —th Lancers. "I hear the —th Fusiliers got terribly mauled. Rumour says that every officer they had down in the trenches was killed or wounded. If you have nothing to do, Harperley, I'm good to ride up to the Second Division in the afternoon and inquire if Calvert is all right."

"What was it?" inquired Harry, "a sortie?"

"No; we took the Quarries, but the Russians, as usual, made us fight for them all night. I fancy the butcher's bill is pretty heavy this time."

"I'm your man," replied young Harperley. "Not only shall I be in a fever till I know if dear old Cis is all right, but I happen to have a good many other pals in the —th Fusiliers whom I should like to inquire after. But how did you happen to hear all this?"

"I was field-officer you see last night, in charge of the pickets, and the roar of the big guns and the rattle of the musketry left no doubt about their having stormy times at the front. Nothing of course came our way, nothing ever does. Cavalry are, I suppose, always out of it in a big siege. We have had our day, and until the d—d place is taken I don't suppose we shall have it again. Since the reinforcements from India arrived and the drafts came out from home we are strong enough to do something if we only got the chance."

"I'll ride up to the Second Division with you after lunch, Major, with pleasure. Can't say I heard anything of the row myself. I had spent the night before on picket in the valley. It was my turn in bed."

That afternoon saw the Major and young Harperley riding into the lines of the Second Division. They found the Fusiliers something "like the dog that has fought, licking their wounds." Even if triumphant there can be very little feeling of exultation when a regiment gets cut up as severely as they had been on the previous night. The survivors cannot help feeling a little sad for those comrades who died by their side. One of the first who came forward to welcome them, with his head wrapped up in bandages, was no other than Jerry Arkwright.

"I'm awful glad to see you, old man," exclaimed young Harperley. "We heard on our way up that you were amongst the fallen. I can see you have been knocked about a bit, but I do hope that there's nothing serious?"

"No; I feel pretty generally earthquaky at present, and had a mighty close shave. I was picked up for dead, but a quarter of an inch in these cases makes all the difference; the bullet went through my forage cap, and just grazed the skull; but our doctor says that, owing to its natural density, there's no material harm done; however, it's been a bad business. Matlock was killed outright; Griffith and Bradshaw are very severely wounded, one must lose an arm and the other a leg; while poor Cis Calvert is knocked about all over."

"Good God!" exclaimed Harry Harperley, "you don't say it's as bad as that? Where is his tent?—we must see him."

"They won't let you do that; the doctors allow nobody inside there," rejoined Jerry, in husky tones. "As the greatest friend he has in the regiment, I petitioned just to go in for three minutes, but I was told gruffly that looking after my own head and nerves was quite enough for me to do at present, and that, moreover, poor Cis is still only half conscious. It was a shell, you see," continued Jerry, in low tones, "and the doctor won't as yet confess the extent of his injuries, but there's no doubt, poor fellow, that he's pretty bad, and that if they get him round sufficiently to send down to Scutari to be nursed, they'll be lucky."

"Well, I'm very sorry indeed to hear about Calvert," said

Crymes, quietly; "I'm sure if you can let his old regiment know how he is going, we shall be only too grateful."

"No, thanks, Captain Arkwright; we won't get off," continued the Major, in answer to the mute interrogatory of Jerry's *bâtman;* very glad to see you came safe out of the *mêlée* yourself; but you must expect hottish times during the next few weeks."

Young Harperley said nothing for some little time, as they jogged leisurely homewards. The boy had not only strong personal affection for Calvert, but all that admiration that we only give to our beau ideal in those early days. He had felt the sharp severance from some of his comrades already acutely, and now it seemed that not only was he to lose the brother-officer to whom he had most looked up, but the lad knew that he would have his story to write to Annie.

Brothers, especially younger ones, do not as a rule know much concerning their sisters' love affairs, but Harry had been the confidant of both sides on this occasion, and was quite aware that Annie had parted with her heart in serious earnest. The two people he loved most dearly on earth were Cis Calvert and his sister, and to see those two married was one of the things he looked forward to with the greatest satisfaction.

Crymes, too, was thinking a great deal over the situation. That there was every probability of his rival being swept from his path in real earnest he knew this time, and a few months back he would have ruthlessly reckoned up this as so many points in his favour in this love-chase he was pursuing. But the grim earnest of war had brought out in Crymes, as it did in many another such similar hard and worldly character, all that was best in him. He had always admired pluck, and Cis Calvert had shown a reckless daring in the trenches that the Major fully appreciated. He would have said now, with reference to Miss Aysgarth, "Let the best man win her." A few months back he would have remarked with a sneer, "All is fair in love or war; don't suppose that I'm going to neglect such chances as fortune sends me." Now it was in tones of genuine regret that he turned round to young Harperley, and quietly said, "That's a poor account we heard of Calvert; he must be badly hurt when they

don't let his brother-officers see him; and the hot weather we are
now having, it's desperate odds against a man pulling through.
Give him the best care they can at the front, both the food and
the attendance must be rough. The ordinary hospital orderly is
a very poor substitute for a woman's hand about a sick man's
pillow; the sooner they can get him down to the banks of the
Bosphorus the better. The sun beats through the tents now with
a strength which is very trying to a man with all the fever of
his wounds on him."

"Well, Major, considering the way you were knocked about
at Balaklava, there's nobody entitled to speak with more
authority; not, after all, that you were much troubled with
the sun during your convalescence."

"No, by the Lord," said Crymes, with a low laugh; "there
were days at that time when I think I would have paid a hundred
a-piece for extra blankets. But look here, young 'un, you ride
up and see Arkwright as often as you can; never mind what
Calvert says, but ship him down to Scutari as soon as he can
bear the journey."

"Come," rejoined Harperley, "you took a pretty different
view of things in your own case; your language was pretty
strong and emphatic when we talked about shipping you down
there."

"Never mind," returned the Major, shortly, "I wasn't half
as badly hurt as I fancy Calvert is. If you care about him, do
as I tell you."

The next day was mail day; all letters for England had to
be in the hands of the letter-serjeant by five o'clock, and that
afternoon, any one who had peeped into the cornet's tent might
have seen Harry in his shirt-sleeves, struggling desperately with
pen, ink, and paper. He was writing to his sister, and knew
that he had to tell the story of Cis Calvert's last misadventure.
He had a pretty fair inkling of what bitter sorrow this news
would be to her. He didn't in the least know the rights of it,
but he had somehow gathered since he met Cis in the Crimea,
that there was a screw loose with their correspondence. He
thought it was possible that pending the clearing up of the
Crockley Hill scandal his father had sternly prohibited it; but

of that Cis was now proved innocent, and as soon as this
business was over they would all go home and set the bells
ringing in York minster. That had been his impression, but
the boy's face grew very serious as he recalled what Crymes
had said on their way homewards. He himself had been
gambling with death too long not to recognize the truth of what
the Major said. What a lot of his friends had been returned
badly wounded, and before three weeks were over he had stood
by their graves either on the plateau or by the quiet hill-side,
while the big guns of Sebastopol and the trenches sounded their
solemn requiem.

Harry's letter would have been the cheery letter a young
fellow like himself might have been expected to write. The
hardships of the winter were over, provisions plentiful—a very
important factor in all campaigning, more especially at nineteen,
when the appetite is healthy; and yet when Miss Aysgarth
read it some fortnight or so later, she felt instinctively there
was a want of real cheeriness running through the preamble.
Harry knew that in spite of all this fencing the real gist of the
matter was to come as yet, and he " craned " at it as he never
had yet at a big fence.

"You will, I know, be very sorry to hear that poor Cis
Calvert is badly hurt. He was the last officer left (in the
morning) of the lot that went down to the trenches over night
of the covering party of the —th Fusiliers. One of the toughest
bits of work they have had at the front for some time ; and
poor Cis's luck was real hard. He had escaped untouched
through the whole business, and while mustering the remnant
of his men previous to marching homewards, and after the hot
cannonade which had been carried on the whole night had
virtually ceased, a stray shell splashed into the midst of them
and knocked over poor Cis and three or four of his following.
I am afraid, Annie, it's a bad business, for the doctors refuse to
let either me or any other of his friends see him, saying, ' Indeed
it would be no use as he is only semi-conscious.' We must
hope for the best ; but I shall be awful glad when I see the
dear old fellow shipped off to Scutari. Crymes says it's not

good for any one badly hurt to remain up here ; and poor dear
Cis I feel sure will do no more soldiering this year. He may
not have been out very long, but, by Jove, he has done his
share ; and our Colonel vows that he will have him back in
command of a troop of ours as soon as ever he is fit to be about.
As I told you before, we never found out what a good fellow
the Major was till we got on service. He rode up to the front
with me to ask after Calvert only the other day, and seemed as
distressed about it as any one of us. He told me only this
morning that it was a great satisfaction for him to think that he
and Cis had shaken hands before this business. Good bye ;
love to the dear old father, and remember you need none of you
feel the least uneasy about me ; us cavalry swells seem quite
out of it for the present ; nor till the fall of Sebastopol is there
much probability of there being any work for us.

" Ever your affectionate brother,
" HARRY HARPERLEY."

Not much in such a letter as this, you will say, and yet the
Crimean mail-bags in those days were plentifully sprinkled with
such epistles, which brought hot tears into many a woman's
eyes, and gave even strong men a choking in the throat when
they found that either Tom, Jim, or Dick, would never again be
seen on Ascot Heath, or help them through a magnum of claret
at the Rag. And as this letter sped homeward through the
Mediterranean it was destined to cross another letter bound for
the Crimea, which did not reach Cis Calvert for many a week
later than it should have done. Annie Aysgarth after a sharp
struggle had swallowed her pride on the receipt of her brother's
letter. She could not hear of Cis in the midst of the strife
without writing him one line of passionate sympathy. She felt,
if anything happened to him, that she could never forgive herself
if she did not give him one more opportunity of reconciliation,
and then after that cry in her room was over she sat down and
wrote one of those letters such as were penned by scores of
women in those days—days be it remembered before the art of
letter-writing was lost—now we talk through a telephone, scratch
what we have to say on the back of a post-card, or condense

it into the twenty words that can be sent by telegraph for
a shilling.

"My dearest Cis,

"Although you have never answered my last letter,
and I did think that it at least merited a reply, I must write to
you once more. They tell me that you have forgotten me, but
I'll believe it only from your own lips, or from your own hand.
Still, even if it were so, I only know that you have once been
all the world to me; and I know from Harry that you are now
in the Crimea, and in the midst of all that dreadful fighting. It
is hard to have both you and Harry there, and the mail, as you
may imagine, makes me like many another woman turn sick for
fear of the news it may bring us. If all is to be over between
us, I at least deserve a kind letter of farewell at your hands. I
dare not say more; indeed I am afraid I have already said too
much. If my letter to Secunderabad ever did reach you it was
cruel of you, Cis, not to have vouchsafed me a reply. Farewell
my own; yes, even if it is for the last time I claim the right to
call you so. You were my own once; yes, all my very own
that evening we sat over the fire at tea when you gave up the
run of the season to ride home from Askham Bog with

"Yours ever,

"Annie Aysgarth."

Cis in the mean while is bothering the doctors not a little.
They shake their heads over him, and concur generally that it
is a very ticklish case, and that it is desirable to get him down
to Scutari, where there are many advantages not procurable in
those sun-smitten tents of the Crimea, as soon as may be. But
that is where it is; he is so desperately knocked about they
cannot as yet patch him up sufficiently to stand the voyage
down; Cis continues in a comatose state that rather puzzles the
faculty; they cannot arouse him. When in their desire to awake
the brain-power once more they permit the visits of Jerry Arkwright and one or two more intimate friends the result is still
more disheartening. Cis gazes at them with lack-lustre eye,
and it is difficult to understand whether he even knows them.

Now and again he will open his lips, but it is very sparingly, and even then very little to the purpose. He apparently has but slight understanding of where he is, and his wild utterances refer more to his Indian days, or the time at York, than his later experiences. True, ever and anon he would revert to that fierce evening in the Quarries, the feverish light would gleam in the lack-lustre eyes, and in a broken voice he would say, " Steady, men, steady! here they come again ! Hold your fire till I give the word," and then sink back on his pillow exhausted.

Endless were the kind inquiries made about him from the gallant Colonel, at whose feet it may be said he fell, and whose own escape was almost miraculous to all his particular chums in the army. Harry Harperley " bucketted " ponies unmercifully between their lines and those of the Second Division for news of Cis. Old Copplestone himself made more than one visit of inquiry. That he, Cis, had distinguished himself, I need scarcely say, he had no comprehension of. He hardly seemed even to recognize those few intimates who were allowed to see him, and at length the doctors decided, dangerous though they admitted the experiment might be, to ship him down to Scutari. His soldier-servant was to go with him, and the doctor of the —th Fusiliers and Jerry Arkwright saw him on board ship. Harry Harperley, with something amazingly resembling an apple-core in his throat, was also present in the Balaklava harbour upon that occasion; but utterly exhausted by his journey down from the front, Cis apparently recognized none of them.

" Shall we ever see him again, Doctor ?" inquired Jerry Ark-wright, as they descended the ship's side.

" That's more than any one of my profession could honestly tell you," replied the surgeon ; " I firmly believe I've done my best in getting him away, but it's no use disguising that it's a dreadfully touch-and-go case. I like and admire poor Calvert as much as either of you, but it's no use mincing matters,—his life hangs on a thread.

CHAPTER XXXII.

SISTER ELIZABETH.

It is a good many years now since the great drama of the
Crimea was played, but there must be many who recollect one
of the first tragic scenes in that history, and can call to mind
the burning of the 'Europa,' and how Willoughby Moore, after
having seen the last of his Inniskillen Dragoons into the boats,
perished in the blazing transport; pretty well the first sacrifice
of life that, in our fierce struggle with the Muscovite. But
there are many who do not know how quietly and unobtrusively
his widow took up the cross that he had been fain to lay down,
and did his duty to her country. Miss Nightingale and her
nurses constituted an army of strength to whom the soldiers
of the Crimea could never be sufficiently thankful. But Miss
Nightingale's mission was avowedly more to succour the soldiers
than the officers; these latter, as might be well supposed, had
more opportunity of taking care of themselves in their hour of
tribulation than was enjoyed by the rank and file. Of course
they took their place in the long aisles of the Scutari hospital,
and shared the lot of their humbler comrades; but there was no
special building set apart for their accommodation. It occurred to
Mrs. Moore that this was a want she could well supply. With
no little trouble she organized a band of nurses, and opened a
convalescent home for officers on a lovely site some two or three
miles from the big hospital, and many an officer, worn out by
sickness, wounds, or the nervous tension involved in the perpetual trench-work, felt most sincerely grateful for the careful,
gentle tending that enabled him once more to take his place with
his comrades at the front.

Leaning at an open window, gazing sadly over the blue waters of the Sea of Marmora, was a woman, still young, but whose worn, handsome face told a tale of trial and trouble. The dark hair was coiled quietly away under a plain mob cap, and the prim grey stuff dress and white apron were as rigidly divested of the faintest sign of coquetry as the garb of the early Quakers. Whether the lady at the head of the establishment knew the history of Sister Elizabeth or not was pure matter of conjecture; but what *was* well known to every one about the place, Lady Superintendent and under nurses, was that no more unflinching worker than Sister Elizabeth had they in that hospital. Zealous and untiring she moved from ward to ward, with her soft voice and almost caressing manner, whispering words of strength and consolation, winning confidences, and melting strong men of the world sometimes to tears in their hour of weakness. She wrote letters for them to those dearly loved at home; ah! and took down dying behests too at times, and, save when she bade good-bye to some patient, who had for weeks caused her serious anxiety, no one ever saw a faint smile wreath the lips of Sister Elizabeth; no one of the numerous sufferers whom her unremitting devotion had nursed to health could have been made to believe that the woman to whom he in the main owed his recovery had, not a twelvemonth before, been the most reckless flirt between the Himalayas and Cape Cormorin.

Suddenly the door opened, and one of the assistant nurses gliding into the room, said quietly:

"The directress wishes to see you in her room for a few minutes, Sister Elizabeth; there is a very bad case just come down that will require the most unremitting attention if he is ever to recover; you are the cleverest and most untiring of all of us, and the directress, I fancy, means to hand him over to your charge."

" I will come at once, and only trust that Providence will be as good to me as it has been before, in like cases. Did you happen to hear his name?"

" Yes; Mr. Calvert of the —th Fusiliers; it is the officer of whom all the papers talked so much about in the winter; it's the man who killed the Albanian in that great sortie about Christmas."

Lizzie Daventry turned white to her very lips, and her fingers gript the sill of the window in a manner that would have left livid marks had they touched flesh instead of wood. For a few seconds she turned sick, and felt in deadly terror of swooning. Her teeth were clenched, and it was only by a desperate effort that she succeeded in recovering herself. As if she didn't know the whole history of that wild night's trench-work! As if the fullest report that she could possibly lay her hands upon was not one of her most cherished possessions! As if her cheek had not flushed and her eye sparkled as she read it, and murmured to herself, "Loved him, yes! the only one of them all I ever really loved. Loved! Yes, and loved in vain; but, Cis, my darling, it's a consolation to know that at all events I loved a *man!*" And now she was called upon to battle with death over this man's couch. Could she do it? Could she command her feelings? Could she trust herself? She had nursed, and successfully too, several cases probably as severe as this. Her heart had been filled with infinite compassion and pure womanly sorrow at the sufferings of her patients; nerve, hand, nor watchfulness had ever failed her as yet; but this was different. She had loved this man—nay, did love him, cared for him as she never had and never should care for another; and experience had taught her that an emotional nurse is decidedly not good for a patient."

"I will try it," she murmured; "I cannot bear to think that other hands than mine should tend him here, and if I feel it is beyond my strength I will make a clean breast of it, and request to be relieved of my task."

"Tell the directress," she replied, as soon as she could master her voice, "that I will be with her in two or three minutes."

She had purposely kept her face averted, and gazed seawards from the window while overcoming her emotion. This had occasioned no surprise to the assistant nurse, as alert though Sister Elizabeth was when on duty she was notoriously absent and dreamy when not occupied. A few minutes' interview with the directress, and Sister Elizabeth found that she was indeed to take charge of the man she loved. No sooner had she received her instructions than she glided down to the ward in which he had been placed. She paused for a moment at the threshold to compose herself; she had never seen his face, she had never set eyes upon him, since that afternoon at Secunderabad, when she had dismissed him with her passionate kiss still clinging to his lips. She had doubted whether she should ever see him again, but it was probably the wild hope of doing so, mingled with the feverish desire to bury the past in oblivion, that had brought her to Constantinople. The real earnest work had done her good. The strange contrast it offered to the frivolous life she had previously led took her out of herself. For the first time this woman was living for others, and not for herself, and then where she was now she got the very earliest intelligence of what took place in the Crimea, and her heart was as much there as even Annie Aysgarth's.

Another moment and she was standing by Cis Calvert's bedside. She had looked upon a good many shattered specimens of humanity since she had commenced her duties in that hospital, but this was the first time it had fallen to her lot to tend any one whom she had previously known. Cis's pale haggard face and fever-lit eyes shocked her dreadfully. She knew from experience that this man was sorely stricken. He was still in the semi-conscious state, which was the furthest the doctors at the front had been able to advance him on the road to recovery. He gazed apathetically round him as if entertaining the very mildest curiosity as to who might be about him, or what they were doing. He rarely spoke, and was very patient except in one respect—his dislike to any exertion was very pronounced; the mere fact of being called upon to take sustenance seemed to irritate him. A surgeon was standing by his bedside when Sister Elizabeth reached it, his fingers on the wounded man's pulse, and an empty medicine glass in his other hand.

" The moving him from aboard-ship has taken it out of him a good deal. I've just given him a strong dose of ammonia," said the doctor in low tones; "and now I must talk to you about him for a few minutes. It's about as bad a case as we have had. He is awfully knocked about, but it is not altogether hopeless. An immensity depends upon the nursing. There is nothing, you see, to absolutely kill him if we don't let him slip through our fingers from exhaustion. He must have perpetual food and perpetual stimulant,—beef-tea soup, brandy, champagne, and ammonia must be always handy, and never leave him, if awake half an hour, without one or the other. You must exercise your own judgment about which it is most judicious to use. Pull him through the next week, and I think the chances are he'll pull through altogether. I'm thoroughly aware of your great value as a nurse; but this case will tax all your energies, and the minute you find it too much for you, you must let me know, and I will of course see that you are relieved."

"You may trust me," replied Sister Elizabeth, in quiet, resolute tones; "if my nursing can save him it shall be done; and the minute I feel that the strain is too severe you can thoroughly rely upon my studying the best interests of my patient, and handing him over to some one else."

From this time Cis Calvert became Sister Elizabeth's sole charge. She no doubt did her share of nursing three or four of the unfortunates in the adjacent beds; but even the other assistant ladies and under-nurses who shared her labours in that ward were astonished at the unwearied devotion she bestowed upon Mr. Calvert. A few hours' sleep she was fain to snatch at times; but as far as endurance permitted Cis received neither food nor drink from any hand but her own. He never evinced the slightest sign of recognition; but still, purely mechanical though it was, Sister Elizabeth's presence seemed to soothe him. A slight gleam of satisfaction would steal over his face when, after an unavoidable absence, she returned once more to that chair by his bedside in which she had passed so many vigilant hours of late. As for Lizzie Daventry, the control she exercised over herself was something marvellous. Again and again had it seemed as if the slender thread of life must snap; and often had the yearning to press her lips to his forehead proved almost irresistible. It was well perhaps that the presence of other patients in the ward helped her to restrain this impulse. Slowly, but, alas! very slowly, did Cis struggle back from the confines of the grave. The week the doctor had stipulated for had passed, and at the end of it he could only shake his head and say:

"Care, Sister Elizabeth, unwearied care, such as he is getting, may pull him through, but he is very far from out of the wood yet. You never deserved more credit for untiring attention than you have shown to your present patient; but do recollect, my dear lady, you over-tax your strength. If I did what was right I should order you a week off duty; but that poor fellow, I'm told, seems to miss you so terribly that I haven't the heart to relieve you for a few days as yet."

"Never mind me, doctor; I make no pretence that the work isn't hard, but I can *bear* it so far, and will readily confess as soon as I break down."

"There's nothing like a woman for pluck," retorted the doctor. "And if ever a man ought to be a judge on that point it's a doctor who has taken a turn in the Scutari hospitals; but remember, confess in time both for your sake and your patient's."

Doctor Barry was a shrewd observer, and although not a word had passed between him and Sister Elizabeth, he had some idea that Cis Calvert had been known to her in former days. I don't mean that he for one moment dreamt that there had been love passages between them, but merely that from having had some previous acquaintance with him she took a strong interest in her patient.

Although Cis Calvert at last began undoubtedly to regain strength there was one thing that puzzled the doctors, and that was that it seemed impossible to arouse him from the apathy into which he had fallen. It seemed as if the mainspring of his life was broke: he ate and drank mechanically; he sat at the open window, for he was strong enough now to sit up for a few hours each day, and gazed over the blue waters of the Sea of Marmora with a far-away gaze that looked as if he barely took in what was passing before his eyes. Nothing puzzled Doctor Barry more than Cis's lack of interest in what was going on around him, and the question was whether the severe shock he had received had not affected him mentally. Still there were numerous cases on record in which the body had recovered before the mind, and it might be that it was so with Calvert.

"If we could only rouse him it would be either very much for his benefit, or we should know the worst; but while he remains in his present state it is impossible to know the extent of the mental mischief."

As for Lizzie Daventry, she had good reason to apprehend the worst. That this man had never loved her she knew; but then, considering what had been between them, he should still fail to recognize her seemed almost incredible. True, she was dressed in very different fashion from what he had ever seen her, and she had never allowed him to suppose by either word or gesture that she had ever seen him before; and yet she felt sore at times, that all the care and patience she had lavished should not only go unrequited—that she was prepared for—but even apparently unrecognized.

The fact was, that all Cis's mental faculties had been utterly unhinged by the injuries he had received : he lived in a stupor. To this minute he rather imperfectly comprehended where he was. They had told him he was in the hospital at Scutari, but the whole thing was vague and undefined to him. He spent hours endeavouring to collect his scattered thoughts. How did he leave India? How did he get into the midst of that *mêlée*, where shot and shell hissed so angrily; where rifles cracked, and sword and bayonet-thrust were so fiercely distributed? Who was this woman who watched so tenderly over him? He had seen her somewhere before, but where? And then he would give the whole thing up as a riddle past understanding. After all what did it matter? as to whether he lived or died, he felt quite indifferent. Dr. Barry was right; Cis required something to stimulate his well-nigh dormant mind.

Still as the weeks slipped by, and he gathered physical strength, there could be no doubt that Cis's mental faculties were also recovering ; very slowly, it is true ; but close observers like Dr. Barry and Sister Elizabeth could see that day by day he began to take more notice, that the dazed expression was fading from his face, and although still very languid and spiritless, his perceptions were evidently awakening. One morning there came a packet of letters from the Crimea addressed to Captain Calvert, Scutari Hospital.

They had been taken in the first instance to the big hospital, from whence they had been sent on to the branch establishment for officers, where Cis was slowly battling his way back to life.

"There is news come for you from the Crimea, Mr. Calvert," said Sister Elizabeth in her sweet low tones, as she glided softly to the window at which Cis was seated. "As they are directed 'Captain Calvert,' I can only trust they tell you your late gallantry and sufferings have been recognized," and so saying she placed the packet in his nerveless hand.

He gazed vacantly at them, but made not the slightest effort to open the packet. She stood looking at him for some minutes, and then calling to mind that Dr. Barry had said what benefit a stimulus of some sort would probably be in the arousing of Cis's mental faculties, said quietly :

"Should you like me to read them to you?"

She was so much accustomed to do this for those in her charge who were badly wounded, as well as to write letters to their friends at home for them, that there was nothing in the least out of the way in her volunteering to do it in Calvert's case. She knew how he had sold out, and, volunteering again, had joined the Fusiliers as an Acting-Lieutenant. She had followed his career closely since, sometimes through the papers, and sometimes patients that she nursed had given her news of him, for Cis had made his name in the Second Division as one of the most dashing juniors in the trenches. She hoped these letters contained the news that his gallantry at the Quarries had been rewarded by restoration to his old rank. Lizzie Daventry was a plucky woman, but if she had suspected what was before her, it may be doubted whether she would have volunteered this service.

"Thanks," he murmured, "if you will be so kind. Stupid I know, but attempting to read makes my head spin."

Sister Elizabeth broke open the packet, which contained three letters, one of which was unmistakably the hand of a woman. Sister Elizabeth selected one of the other two, and breaking it open commenced reading its contents.

" Camp before Sebastopol,
August 10th, 1855.

" DEAR CIS,

"Grouse shooting just about to begin, and they can't make it very much hotter on the moors on the 12th than it's getting here. Every one says we are pretty near the final go-in now; in fact the waste on both sides is getting too severe to continue. The ordinary trench casualties are upwards of forty a day,—that's of course without counting sorties or other like dissensions. The French have got within about thirty yards of the Malakoff, and amuse themselves by pitching soda-water bottles charged with gunpowder, and a slow match run down the neck, into the Ruski trenches. And I hear if you're tired of life you've got nothing to do but to look over the parapet and you are in the next world in no time. A fellow who was round their advance trenches the other day told me he saw one of their officers just raise his kepi on a ramrod above the parapet, and there were three bullets through it before you could wink. And now, old man, how are you getting on? We all want to know, because you were a terribly broken affair when we sent you away. Do scrawl us a line just to say you've pulled through, or if you don't feel up to it yourself, ask either your nurse or your doctor to write for you.

" I've one bit of glorious news for you—I say *you* advisedly, because all our fellows, like myself, are very sorry about it, but we know you will be pleased, and we are not such a selfish set of beggars as to grudge you your well-earned promotion. The field officer in charge of the attack spoke most highly of your conduct. The chief strongly recommended you for promotion, and old Copplestone applied for you to fill a vacant troop in your old regiment. And, Cis, my boy, you've got it. We all congratulate you most heartily, but hope you'll not forget the turn you did with the Fusiliers, and I'm bid tell you by every one that when we all get home you must remember in future that you have two regimental dinners to eat instead of one.

" Ever yours,
" JERRY ARKWRIGHT."

A faint smile played over Calvert's countenance as the letter was finished. He knit his brows and looked curiously at the reader, and Sister Elizabeth suddenly awoke to the consciousness that he was paying far more attention to her than to what he had been listening to. She doubted indeed whether he had quite taken it in; still that interest of some sort had been aroused in him was evident. She picked up the second letter and commenced to read that to him. It is not worth while to give this *in extenso*. It was from Harry Harperley, and was jubilant with congratulations over Cis's coming back to them as a captain, winding up with anxious inquiries about his health, and an earnest request for a few lines as soon as ever he was able to write them.

And now there only remained that third letter, and Sister Elizabeth's usually cool, steady hand trembled slightly as she broke the seal. She knew intuitively, as women do know these things, that letter was from that girl in England, the love for whom had steeled Cis Calvert's heart against her fascinations. And she was right; it was Annie Aysgarth's letter she held in her hands; and then she did what few of the men who had known Lizzie Daventry would have given her credit for. As Lizzie Daventry Cis Calvert would never have heard or seen that letter; as Sister Elizabeth she nerved herself, and read it through unfalteringly to the end. And then, as she recognized the wealth of love that was in it, and that *she* had nursed this man back to life, only to restore him to her rival, she gave way, and could no longer restrain a slight sob. She was weak, it must be borne in mind, with the watching and hard work she had done of late; and then through the whole of her frivolous life, be it remembered, this was the one man for whom she had ever had a pure affection.

Suddenly a smile flickered round Cis's mouth. Annie's letter had rekindled the dormant memory, recognition gleamed in his face, and in a low voice he exclaimed,

"Lizzie!"

CHAPTER XXXIII.

CONVALESCENT.

DR. BARRY was struck next morning by the change in his patient. "Why, you are a different man, Captain Calvert, from what you were twenty-four hours ago. Only go on like this and we shall soon have you in the saddle again."

The doctor had heard in the convalescent house of Cis's promotion, and knew that he was about to be restored to his old rank and his own regiment.

"Wonderful what the intelligence of promotion does for them; that bit of news was the very stimulus to his mental faculties we wanted. It has brightened him up no end—eh, Sister Elizabeth?"

"That had nothing to do with it," rejoined the Sister, quietly. "I know, because he was so weak and dazed that I read the letters to him, and more indifference than he displayed at hearing of his promotion was simply impossible. But you are right, Dr. Barry, he did get the stimulus, though it was in another form: he got a letter from the girl in England he is or was betrothed to, and that did for him what neither you nor I could effect."

During the silence of the night Lizzie Daventry had once more become master of herself. There was no quiver in the soft voice this morning; no one could have guessed the sharp agonies she had gone through but yesterday. She had not seen Cis this morning as yet, having been in reality so worn out by her late long vigils and the violence of her emotions for sleep to have become a positive necessity, only arrived at by resort to a soporific. Now, however, she once more stepped noiselessly to his bedside.

"Lizzie," ejaculated Calvert, as he saw her.

"Sister Elizabeth, if you please, Captain Calvert," she replied quietly; "remember I have buried my past; I will say no more than that you assisted at its funeral. From the day I set foot in Constantinople I began a new life. We have crossed each other's paths for a brief space, and shall part shortly, never to meet again. I am glad that I have been of some use to you in your hour of need."

"Use," returned Cis, "I know that you have saved my life; I know that but for your unwearied watching and tireless care I should have died. I am too weak to say more, too weak to thank you at present, but, bear in mind, I know it."

"I have done no more for you, Captain Calvert," rejoined Sister Elizabeth, in low, measured tones, "than I have for many others. If I have watched perhaps rather more carefully over you, it was simply that we have rarely had a case that required such vigilant nursing. You have rewarded me by the only means in your power, namely, becoming convalescent—I trust to be able to add, well again, before long."

She lied, and she knew it. Done no more for him than others! She had nearly killed hersels from pure jealousy that another should hand him cup or smooth his pillow, but he must never know it; his heart belonged to that woman in England. And then she wondered if any of those men she had fooled in India had ever suffered as she was doing. She thought of that young dragoon up at Simla, whom she had lured to his ruin at her husband's bidding; she remembered all the story of that gun accident on his way down to rejoin his regiment, and she knew that rumour said there had been very little accident about it, and that young Goring had deliberately taken his own life. She could recall now the agonized face with which he bade her good-bye, and begged her to keep a ring he drew from his finger as a remembrance. But for her fatal smiles she knew that he would never have frequented her husband's play table; and as she became conscious of the dull aching at her own heart she marvelled did men suffer like this? Suddenly she experienced a strange giddiness, and had to catch at the balustrade of the landing to save herself from falling. She had had one or two of these little attacks of late, and knew in reality she had been taxing her strength too highly; but she was resolute to complete her task, though she had not as yet considered what a crowning trial might yet be in store for her.

One morning, a day or two after this, she entered the ward, and found Cis Calvert with a pen in his hand, sitting dreamily over a sheet of paper.

"I am glad, Captain Calvert," said Sister Elizabeth softly, "to see that you are strong enough to write; I should hardly have thought you were, and, as your nurse, hope you will make it brief."

Cis turned to her with a puzzled expression; the pen was shaking in his feeble fingers, and it was evident that the concentration of his ideas was a matter of much difficulty.

A sharp spasm shot across Sister Elizabeth's face, but it was gone in a moment. She knew now what she had to do.

" Would you like me to write that letter for you, Captain Calvert?" she asked: "you are still too weak to write it for yourself; and I've served as an amanuensis to many of your comrades under similar circumstances."

"I'm afraid I must ask you; I don't seem able to rightly recollect things somehow, and don't feel able to make this pen go straight."

"I will say all you wish," replied Sister Elizabeth, as she seated herself at the little table. " I must say it in my own person, because, of course, whoever I write to will know it is not your own handwriting. Who is it to be to?" and Sister Elizabeth's head was bent low over the paper as she asked this question.

" Miss Aysgarth, please; tell her how ill I have been, and all about me; say my name is clear, and that I have never ceased to love her."

" Convalescent Home, Scutari,
August 15th, 1855."

And here Sister Elizabeth paused. How was she to begin this letter? She felt she could not write "Dear Miss Aysgarth."

She thought for a moment, and then resolved to commence without the usual formula.

"I write this at Captain Calvert's request, who, I regret to state, although slowly recovering, is still as yet too weak to hold a pen himself. He was very badly wounded, and when we first got him here we entertained the gravest apprehensions concerning him; but I think I may safely say all that is past. And now for his message: he bids me tell you that his name is cleared, that he loves you, has never ceased to love you, and looks passionately forward to seeing you again when the work here is over. If I do not write at greater length, Miss Aysgarth will, I am sure, excuse it, for our hands are always full, and time is a most valuable commodity with us.

"Sincerely yours,
"SISTER ELIZABETH."

Had poor Cis been capable of much thought he would have felt a little curious as to how his letter would be signed, but he had never quite known the extent to which scandal had coupled his name with that of Mrs. Daventry. He was in ignorance that in the Madras Presidency he was very generally supposed to have eloped with Lizzy, although they had not gone away together. This bit of gossip, however, had never reached Yorkshire, or else Annie Aysgarth's letter would never have been penned.

"I'll read it over to you," said Sister Elizabeth, "and then you will be able to see if I have said exactly what you wanted. Will that do?" she asked, as she finished reading.

"So many thanks," replied Cis feebly; "but I want you to put in a postscript. Add that it is to your devoted care that I owe my life, and that I am as grateful as I have strength to be."

Sister Elizabeth made no reply, and then with firm hand and unfaltering pen wrote her postscript. What she said was this:

"Captain Calvert has covered himself with glory. We are all very proud here of our soldiers in the Crimea, as no doubt you are also in England, Miss Aysgarth; but of none are we prouder than him."

Her hand never trembled, her pen never faltered, and yet can crueller trial be meted out for woman than to have dictated to her by the man she loves a letter containing the avowal of his undying passion for a more favoured sister? But though Sister Elizabeth showed no outward sign, it could hardly be imagined that her heartstrings were unwrung.

Three or four more days and Cis misses his nurse, and misses her sadly. Men sore shaken in nerve and body are wont to lean to an unlimited extent upon those who watch over them; more especially do they succumb to the kindly presence of a woman near their sick-bed. In answer to his inquiries he was informed that Sister Elizabeth was not well, and needed rest; the days glided by and still he saw nothing of his late nurse; but Cis was gathering strength rapidly now, and by persistent cross-examination of those about him he soon extracted the truth, namely, that Sister Elizabeth was seriously ill, and he was not likely to see her by his bedside again. Poor Cis, he puzzled in his still somewhat benumbed mind as to what he could do to show his gratitude for all she had done for him. It was difficult to say; but at last the inspiration came, and from that moment every morning there arrived for Lizzie a basket of flowers, the choicest money could purchase, with Captain Calvert's anxious inquiries about her health. And this perhaps was the brightest hour in Sister Elizabeth's day; for her turn of prostration had now come, and she was struck down with low hospital fever induced probably by over-work and the violent emotion she had of late gone through. Dr. Barry from the very first did not like the aspect of his new patient.

"She has overdone it," he said, "in spite of all my cautions. I warned her not to overtax her strength, and what the result would be of so doing. Now she has got this low fever, and a very limited amount of vitality with which to fight against it, I hope and trust she will pull through; and mind," he said, turning to the attendant nurse, "she *must*. We cannot afford to lose her. Should she go the wrong way she will have died for England as much as any of those who fell in the Crimea."

One afternoon came down that long deferred despatch which announced that Sebastopol had fallen; how that the French had carried the Malakoff with a rush at mid-day, and had spent the whole afternoon in savage fighting in the Karabalncia suburb. How that the English got into the Redan only to be driven out again; and how about midnight the Russians had blown up all their magazines and sullenly retreated across the harbour to the north side of the city, leaving an hospital full of wounded behind them. There was much jubilation in Constantinople, as may be supposed, and now the guns had ceased to boom in the Crimea, the cannon like the bells were resonant in London and Paris, and well might the Turk and Western Powers rejoice. If we had got Sebastopol at last we had undoubtedly paid pretty heavily for its possession.

Cis Calvert is limping along the terrace in front of the convalescent house two or three days after the news of the fall of the famous Chersonese fortress had reached Scutari. Although it was three months since he had been wounded he was still very lame, and could only walk with the assistance of a stick. He had been what is technically termed "hit all over;" and in addition to his crippled leg had but very limited use of his left arm. He reaches a bench, when with a salaam the young Greek, whose duty it is to bring him flowers, comes up to him and submits the daily offering he sends to Sister Elizabeth for his inspection. As he turns his head he sees two figures at the end of the terrace that makes his heart jump. He passes his hand hastily across his eyes—is it all a dream? for he is aware that his head is still a little confused at times. No; a second glance, and surely it *is* Annie Aysgarth and her father who are coming towards him. Cis grips the back of the bench hard. Crippled as he is he moves with no little difficulty; and in the present whirl of ideas occasioned by the sudden appearance of his *fiancée*, feels simply incapable of moving a step. Another minute and Annie has sprung towards him; her arms are round his neck, and her lips laid to his.

"My dearest Cis," she exclaimed, as she withdrew blushingly from the embrace in which he had held her, "it is something to find you still alive, although your poor face shows only too plainly all the suffering you have gone through."

"I can't say how glad I am to once more shake you by the

hand, Calvert. There are so many of the cheery lot I used to dine with in the old barracks at York whose palms I shall never clasp again. More than once I feared that it might be the same in your case, and that I might never be able to tell you how ashamed I, like many others round York, felt that we should ever have doubted you for a moment. You are still terribly crippled, the doctor tells me."

"Yes," returned Cis as he shook hands; "but the doctor tells me that I shall be all right in time."

"Yes, Cis, dear," said Miss Aysgarth; "and papa and I have come out expressly to take you home with us. You can be of no good here till you are well again. We have had a talk with Dr. Barry, and he says total change of air and scene would be the best thing for you. And that, moreover, after such a terrible time as you have gone through it would be simply useless your attempting to go to the front again for some months."

"Another thing, too," chimed in Julian Harperley; "now Sebastopol has fallen, the general opinion is, after our late bitter experience, that it is too late in the year for further operations; and I hear the probability is that we shall winter where we are, and not commence the game again before the spring; besides, you must remember that you are now back again in the —th Lancers, and those who should know at Constantinople tell me it is in serious contemplation to send all the Cavalry down here for the winter."

Miss Aysgarth seated herself on the bench beside Cis, when the Greek, who had been an impassive observer of the meeting between Cis and his friends, quietly inquired,

"Me take flowers as usual, sar?"

"What lovely flowers!" exclaimed Annie. "Who are you sending them to, Cis, dear?"

"They are going," replied Calvert, gravely, "to Sister Elizabeth, the lady who wrote to you for me, and to whose devoted care I'm indebted for being alive at this minute. I am sorry to say that she is very seriously ill, and cannot help thinking that the unceasing vigilance with which she watched over me may have been in some sort the cause of it."

"Do you think they will let me see her, Cis?" exclaimed

Miss Aysgarth. "Do you think they would let me watch over and nurse her, and so endeavour in some shape to slightly repay the large debt of gratitude we both owe her?"

Cis thanked his sweetheart by a glance. "I can only say, Annie," he rejoined, "that the utmost you can do for Sister Elizabeth will never repay what she has done for me. As a man and a cripple I can only feebly express my profound sympathy with her in her illness by daily offerings of fruit and flowers, but you may be able to do more."

"And if I can, Cis, it will be done, never fear. I have got to look after you a bit, my own, of course; but the woman who has put her life in jeopardy to save you for me deserves every bit of strength and love that lies in me."

"Excuse me, Annie," interposed Julian Harperley, "but I think our unexpected arrival has been a little too much for Calvert in his present state of health. If you are to turn nurse you must bear in mind the weakness of your patients."

"Oh, how stupid of me! Of course. Thanks, papa. Cis, dear, you must take my arm, and don't think that I'll spare myself about Sister Elizabeth if I am allowed to help. I am not always so foolish and inconsiderate as I have just been; thinking only of my own pleasure in once more seeing you, instead of your shaken health. Come, papa, beef-tea and perfect quiet is what he requires now, isn't it?"

And the faint smile with which Cis responded to the suggestion showed it was not made before it was needed.

CHAPTER XXXIV.

SISTER ELIZABETH'S FAREWELL.

DR. BARRY began to be seriously uneasy about Sister Elizabeth. "Her weakness is extreme," he muttered, "and she seems to have no strength or vitality left with which to battle with this low, wasting fever." There was no light-headedness —simply utter prostration; but she seemed to grow feebler daily, and her life, like the sands of an hour-glass, seemed trickling steadily away. Miss Aysgarth was incessant in her inquiries, and begged hard to take her turn in nursing the patient.

"My dear young lady," said the doctor, "if we were short of help I would accept your assistance with the greatest possible pleasure; but this is a very critical case, and you must forgive me if I prefer leaving it in skilled hands to trusting it to an unpractised person like yourself. I am sure, Miss Aysgarth, you would be unwearied, but, you see, you lack experience. Her noble devotion has been such that if anything happens to her I shall feel that I have lost the most precious life confided to my charge since I left England."

"If I may not nurse her will you tell her that I am here? She wrote to me in England about Cis—Captain Calvert. No; why should I be ashamed? I mean Cis. I am going to be married to him, you know."

"Well, I thought it looked a little like it when I saw you on the terrace with him the other day. Pray accept my hearty congratulations, Miss Aysgarth."

"Thanks very much, doctor; but it was Sister Elizabeth saved him for me, as you know well, and as Cis knows also. Can you not understand how very anxious I am to help her in her hour of trial? Don't think for one moment that I wish to intrude my incompetent self when there are abler, but none more willing, nurses at hand. But, doctor, I do claim the right to be made unsparing use of, should you ever see the opportunity."

Day after day Sister Elizabeth grew weaker and weaker, and each morning brought not only fruit and flowers, but sweet, loving notes of sympathy from Annie Aysgarth to the broken woman: unknown heart-pricks that, could she have dreamt of, Annie would have cut her right hand off sooner than have written. But of course neither the doctor nor Miss Aysgarth could have the slightest idea of the petty stabs the latter was unwittingly dealing; while as for poor Cis, Sister Elizabeth's perfectly calm, collected manner had made him utterly forget that she had once entertained what he would probably have described as a *penchant* for himself; and yet if he had only recalled that last scene with Lizzie Daventry in India, he must have been compelled to admit that a *penchant* rather inadequately described the feeling she had for him.

But the idea came now to Sister Elizabeth that she should never more leave the bed in which she lay, and with it a sense of relief and contentment that her weary battle with the world was so soon to cease. What had she to look forward to in this life? And she felt that the efforts she had made of late for the sufferers from the Crimea were some atonement for her previous career. Do not for one moment imagine that she was dying from a broken heart. She was sinking, as many another noble woman has fallen before and since, from low, wasting, hospital fever. But if hearts don't break, a heart-ache goes far to aggravate such complaints; and it makes a terrible difference to the doctor's skill when his patient shows no desire of clinging to life. As the conviction possessed Sister Elizabeth that her days were numbered, there suddenly came upon her a strange desire to look upon this woman who had been preferred before her. The impulse to see Annie Aysgarth grew stronger daily. It would matter nothing to her now—the fierce jealousy that had once torn her breast was gone; she felt she could see this girl now, and place her hand in that of Cis's with a smile. Surely Miss

Aysgarth would not grudge her one kiss of his lips before she died.

Sister Elizabeth's mind was at last made up, and on Dr. Barry's next visit she told him of her wish. The doctor fumed and fidgetted not a little ; if there was one thing he particularly did not wish for his patient it was anything like emotion ; and yet, only he was quite unaware of the fact, it had been administered to her of late in matutinal doses. To see a stranger at any time he would have pronounced bad for her just now. But the doctor had some experience of womankind ; he knew that she had taken considerable interest in Captain Calvert, and what seeing a man's acknowledged *fiancée* means to any woman under these circumstances he could pretty fairly conjecture. Still Sister Elizabeth was so persistent in her wish, that he came to the conclusion at last, refusal might do her more harm than an interview with Miss Aysgarth could possibly do. He knew how invalids sometimes fretted, and thought to himself that he should be able to caution Miss Aysgarth to exercise the greatest control over herself, so that, albeit somewhat reluctantly, he at length promised that Annie should pay her a visit about noon the next day, the period at which invalids are usually at their best.

" I have only one stipulation to make," said Dr. Barry, " and that is, I must limit the length of this interview ; you really, in justice to yourself, cannot afford to talk to any one for long, and shall caution Miss Aysgarth, and shall depend upon her adhering strictly to my injunctions."

Miss Aysgarth listened attentively to the doctor's admonitions, and promised to conform with them to the very best of her ability.

" Don't allow her to indulge in emotion, nor permit yourself to do so either. That you should feel strongly with regard to the woman who has saved your lover's life is only natural, and that Captain Calvert owes his life to her I tell you admits of no doubt whatever ; but, Miss Aysgarth, you must remember her life hangs upon a thread, and I should never have acceded to her request only I think that denial may possibly do her more harm than letting her see you. No woman in Scutari has done nobler service, no more precious life will have been sacrificed than hers if she dies ; her tenure of existence is so frail that much emotion may kill her ; and, therefore, I must look to you to preserve a composure you will probably not feel, and to restrict your interview to a quarter of an hour."

Thus sternly cautioned, Miss Aysgarth was the next day ushered into the quiet room on the upper story where the stricken woman lay. Annie gazed with no little surprise on the pale, worn features which, if they had lost that majesty of beauty which had characterized Lizzie Daventry when we first encountered her, were perhaps more lovely now than ever, in consequence of the spiritualized expression gathering over them as she neared her rest. The dark hair was drawn loosely round the well-turned head, for her illness had been such as necessitated no despoilment of her tresses, and Miss Aysgarth stood simply amazed at Sister Elizabeth's appearance. No one had ever hinted to her that this woman was beautiful, and yet Annie thought that she had never seen anything more lovely than this sick nurse. On a small table by the bedside were a bunch of grapes and the flowers which Cis Calvert had sent that morning.

"Miss Aysgarth," said Lizzie, in a low tone, "will you come and sit, please, by my bedside? I have wanted so much to see you, and had to plead so hard before Dr. Barry would allow it. He meant it for the best, but I have a presentiment that nothing will make much difference to me now. Don't think for one moment that I have any wish to die, but I feel quite resigned to death should Heaven please it."

"I trust," interposed Annie, "that though you are doubtless very ill you are destined to be saved, even as you have saved so many others. Dr. Barry knows that I am at his disposal should there be any question of extra nursing."

"Thank you, no ; every possible care is taken of me, my slightest wish attended to ; I wish to see you, Miss Aysgarth, because I wanted to see the woman for whom I had saved Captain Calvert. No man ever loved a woman more dearly than he loves you. He is true to you as steel. But a year ago and I was counted handsome. It is over, and I can tell it you all now. If I could have won your lover from you, Miss

Aysgarth, I would, but he never wavered in his allegiance, and I, who had never failed before to bring any man to my feet I wished, was fain to confess myself defeated. Can you guess now why I sent for you?"

"I think so," replied Annie, as the tears gathered in her eyes. "I can understand your wishing to see me, and from the bottom of my heart I am grateful to you for affording me the opportunity of thanking you for all you have done for me. I shall owe to you what I hold most precious in this world." Here her voice faltered, and she paused for a second before gasping out—"Cis."

Oh Annie, Annie! is this complying with Dr. Barry's injunctions about not giving way to any emotion?

"No," replied Sister Elizabeth, "I want more than that from you; I have told you that in the insolence of my beauty and the madness of my passion, I did my very best to win your lover from you. I have told you that I failed utterly. I have endeavoured to honestly make what atonement I could for trying to wrong you. Can you lay your lips to mine and say that you forgive me this attempted wrong? Remember I ask it as one who must shortly kneel before Him by whom all sins are forgiven."

Dr. Barry's injunctions were scattered to the winds. Annie Aysgarth with the tears streaming down her cheeks had fallen by the bedside, and pressed her lips passionately to those of Sister Elizabeth.

Dr. Barry, whose anxiety about Sister Elizabeth had caused him to hover restlessly in the vicinity of her room, began to glance impatiently at his watch.

"Seventeen minutes," he murmured; "I really can't allow any more; I was a fool to allow it in the first instance. That Miss Aysgarth will get to thanking Sister Elizabeth for saving her lover's life is a matter of course, and then they'll both begin to cry about it. And that poor lady, with only about enough strength to keep her alive, and not a particle to spare for scenes. I shall go and interrupt them at all hazards. If they haven't got their talk over by this time, at all events they ought to have."

Dr. Barry's sharp tap at the door made Annie Aysgarth spring quickly to her feet, and it was hopeless for Annie to conceal either her tears or the emotion under which she laboured.

"Miss Aysgarth," said the doctor in a very determined voice, "you have broken your promise; I must insist upon the immediate termination of this interview. What you two women have been saying to each other of course I can't conjecture, but this conversation has done my patient no good I'm quite certain."

Annie did not trust herself to speak, but pressed Sister Elizabeth's hand and mutely left the apartment in obedience to the doctor's behest.

"It's too bad," growled the doctor as he approached Sister Elizabeth's bedside; "if there's one thing, my dear lady, that I want, it is that you should husband the little strength you have left. Scenes take it out of one, and that's just what you two ladies have been indulging in."

"Doctor," replied Lizzie, as she stretched out her hand to him, "it matters very little now; all that can be done for me I know has been, and will be, done by you, but don't deceive yourself; I know when I leave this bed it will be only for that colder and narrower one in which we must all some day lie. I'm sure you would wish your poor assistant's last days to be spent as tranquilly as possible. You must be good to me—I want to see Miss Aysgarth daily—to know her as well as my brief stay in this world will permit. Promise me I shall have my way in that."

"The devil's in the women," muttered the doctor, not without a suspicion of tears in his own eyes at hearing his favourite nurse endorse a terrible thought which he had for days been struggling to combat, namely, that she was destined to succumb to the low fever from which she suffered. "My dear lady, you know I wouldn't deny you anything except for your own good. Still it is my duty as your physician to say that the quieter you are kept the better."

"Quite so, doctor," replied Sister Elizabeth, in a voice which if low was perfectly resolute. "Still you will do as I wish, and I say emphatically I must see Miss Aysgarth every morning. No one can be more sensible of all the care and kindness you bestow upon me than I am, but you will do as I ask, even if it is against your own convictions. There, leave me now; you will do what I tell you I know: I am tired."

Dr. Barry walked down-stairs more sad than perhaps he had ever left any patient's bedside previously, but from henceforth there were no further restrictions on Miss Aysgarth's visits, and not a morning passed that Annie did not spend some time in the room of the dying woman.

But the mornings, alas! were few, and even sanguine Dr. Barry could no longer shut his eyes to the fact that his patient was doomed. Ere ten days had come and gone, when Miss Aysgarth took her accustomed place by the bedside, Lizzie whispered in reply to her kiss of greeting:

" It is very near the end now, and if you don't mind I should so like to say good-bye to Cis; you won't grudge me one last interview."

" Grudge you," returned Annie ; " think of what I owe you. I believe from the bottom of my heart, and I know all the people here would say the same, that you would have given your life for his. Cis, believe me, would have come to see you long before had he been allowed."

Only another morning or two and Annie leads Cis up the staircase, and conducts him to Sister Elizabeth's bedside. The stricken woman greets him with a faint smile as she stretches out her hand.

" I could not go, Cis, without wishing you good-bye. Your betrothed has been an infinite solace to me during the last few days. Women have been jealous enough of me in days gone by," she continued, with just a spark of the old coquetry ; " but no one, I think, can feel that of me now. You won't refuse, Annie dear," she added, turning her eyes wistfully towards Miss Aysgarth, " to allow me to say good-bye to him alone."

Miss Aysgarth's sole reply was simply a pressure of the thin fingers, and then she silently left the room.

" It's been a hard world to me, Cis," murmured Lizzie, as she stole her hand into his. " I know I've not been a good woman. I don't want to justify myself altogether at the expense of others ; but, as you know, I was thrown a mere school-girl into Anglo-Indian society, and that is rather a thorny road for any one as young as I was to travel under such guidance as was vouchsafed me. My husband caught my fancy, but no one ever touched my heart till I met you. To have won you I'd have staked everything. My fair fame, position—but why repeat the old story ? You can remember what I said at Secunderabad ; and I would have done it without a second thought. It's far better as it is, Cis, dear. I'm going home fast, and it is a comfort to me to think that this one true love of mine was pure and unstained. Indian scandal travels home, we know ; and whether Annie Aysgarth ever heard your name coupled with mine I can't say ; but she knows from my own lips that you never swerved in your allegiance, though I confess to having done my best to win you from her."

"You know, Lizzie, that when we met I had no love to give. You were the greatest solace to a sore-tried, broken man amidst a community he disliked, and in a country he detested. What you have done for me here, I, as well as all the hospital, know. But for you and your unwearying care I should probably not be alive at this minute, and my bitterest thought at present is that you may pay the penalty of that devotion."

A sweet smile stole over the dying woman's face as she murmured :

"Never call it a bitter thought, Cis. I should like your wife to say in days to come, Sister Elizabeth gave her life for him, and would have given ten if she had had them. Now kiss me once, dearest, and then say good-bye. I am very weary, and shall be glad to be at rest."

Cis leant over the bed and pressed his lips to those of Lizzie Daventry.

"Good-bye," she murmured, "for ever. Send Annie to me for a little while."

Cis walked into the corridor and motioned silently to Miss Aysgarth, for the brine was in his eyes, and there was a strange choking in his throat, which forbade him to trust his voice.

And when the sun rose next morning Sister Elizabeth lay cold and still, locked in the dull apathy of death. If her past life in India was not good to look back upon, surely she made ample atonement by the noble work she did in the Scutari Hospital.

CHAPTER XXXV.

CONCLUSION.

THE dark-blue waters of the Bosphorus danced in the October sunlight as they swirled past the Seraglio Point, and hastened to pour themselves into the Sea of Marmora, which glistened like a silver lake 'neath the golden beams. On a small grassy plateau at a little distance from the hospital, which was already decorated with a sad sprinkling of memorial crosses, stood bareheaded a little knot of people, who had come to bid Sister Elizabeth a final farewell. Julian Harperley was there, as was also Miss Aysgarth. Cis Calvert also stood there with moist eyes. He had managed to hobble to that grave-side with the assistance of his *fiancée's* arm and a stick. He believed implicitly that the dead woman had given her life for his. Dr. Barry also stood by that open grave with a twitching of the mouth as he listened to the solemn words of the Burial Service, highly unprofessional, but indicative of the high esteem in which he had held Sister Elizabeth. Ten or a dozen bare-headed men and boys were also present, and the tears stole from the eyes of more than one of them as they thought of all they owed to her who was gone. Several of the staff of the hospital were also present to pay this last tribute to their friend.

A handful of mould drops upon the coffin as Sister Elizabeth is laid to her rest—" Earth to earth, ashes to ashes."

Sadly did the little group of mourners disperse, and Julian Harperley would fain have given immediate orders for the handsome marble cross destined to mark the grave; but he speedily found that he was not to be allowed to do this by himself. Many of Sister Elizabeth's old patients insisted upon contributing towards a stone to her memory, and finally, a very handsome granite obelisk marked the last resting-place of poor Lizzie Daventry.

There seemed no reason now why Julian Harperley and his daughter should not at once take their invalid home with them. He was quite well enough to bear the voyage, and Dr. Barry even said it would be beneficial to him; but the banker lingered in the faint hope of catching a glimpse of his son. He had ascertained from undoubted authority that the cavalry were to be sent down from the Crimea for the winter; and this resolution once come to it was not likely the authorities would delay putting it into execution. The winter was fast closing in upon them, and the bitter experience of last year had shown that the traditional turbulence of the Euxine was no exaggeration. So he and Annie had secured a ramshackle house in the vicinity of the hospital, and there, with the assistance of some servants picked up in Constantinople, they managed to bivouac somehow.

Miss Aysgarth was sitting lost in day-dreams, an unheeded book lying open in her lap, when a pair of arms were suddenly thrown round her neck, and a boisterous kiss imprinted on her cheek.

" Oh, Cis, dear," she murmured, " how did you manage to get up-stairs without help ? "

" Cis dear," replied her brother's laughing voice ; " it's some one infinitely dearer and more precious than Cis. My dearest sister, look round and then return thanks to Providence that your brother is restored to you."

" How glad I am to see you, Harry," replied Annie, as jumping up she turned round and warmly reciprocated her brother's embrace. We have been lingering here just to have a peep at you before returning home. Papa will be so pleased!—have you seen him ? "

" No ; we only got in about two hours ago. Should never have known you were located this side if it had not been for a jolly old cock of a doctor. He came on board as soon as we anchored, and as soon as he found out we were the —th Lancers he told us Cis was all right again. Then he asked for me, and told me you and the father were living this side. I thought, of course, you were living on the other. I got leave from the chief to come off with Dr. Barry as soon as he had finished business. The regiment don't land till to-morrow."

"How bronzed you have got, Harry," said Miss Aysgarth; "and you really have a moustache now."

"That's like your sisterly impudence," rejoined Harry; "just as if I hadn't when I left York."

"A girl would never have discovered it, though you kissed her," said Annie, laughing.

At length Mr. Harperley made his appearance. He had been on board ship to look for his son, only to ascertain that his son had gone on shore to look for him. But they had met at last, and now the three indulged in an unrestrained gossip, during which Harry gave his opinions about the course of the campaign with a confidence and freedom that would have electrified the Allied Generals, could they have heard him.

"Get in!" said the boy; "of course we could have got in when we first came up there; all the infantry fellows say so, only the Generals couldn't make up their minds to try it. Balaklava, of course, was a beastly mistake, except for one thing."

"And what was that?" inquired his father, not a little amused at the crowing of his own cockerel.

"Why, we cavalry chaps would have been right out of it but for that; it is the only chance we have had. Dash it," he continued, "we always are out of it. Here they are, having dog-hunts, private theatricals, steeplechases, rides through the Baidar valley to the Poros Pass, and all sorts of fun, and here we are sent down to this disgusting old graveyard."

Again the banker laughed; his sense of humour was tickled by the boy's off-hand criticism; but at the same time he felt no little fatherly pride in the idea that this saucy son of his was one of the famous Six Hundred.

Suddenly Harry stopped in his military criticism, and exclaimed:

"But look here, I must see dear old Cis! Upon my word, if I go back without having seen him, I believe the fellows will run me up at the yard-arm. Walk down to the hospital with me, won't you?"

"All right, Harry," exclaimed Miss Aysgarth. "One moment, while I get my hat, and then we will walk down and see Cis. He is still very lame, you know, and has by no means recovered the use of his bridle-arm, but he will be awfully glad to see you."

"Not so glad as I shall be to see him, for, as I dare say you can guess now, when Jerry Arkwright and I put him on board ship we felt very doubtful whether we should ever see him again in this world."

So the trio walked down to the hospital, where Cis was most unfeignedly glad to see his old comrade. He thoroughly enjoyed the long chat about the doings at the front, and the story of the fall of Sebastopol. There were old friends to ask after, and to inquiries about some of them came the sad response that they were quietly sleeping on Cathcart Hill. At last Harry Harperley sprang to his feet, and exclaimed as he wrung Cis's hand :

"Well, good-bye, old man ; it's awfully jolly to see you becoming your old self again. I must be off, and get on board at once, for we disembark to-morrow, and the chief, as you know, don't stand over-staying leave, under such circumstances. The fighting all done with for the present, we are going to have a real gentlemanly winter this year, if only in contradistinction to the one we passed last. Like Julias Cæsar and all the other ancient military swells, we have gone into winter quarters, and mean to refrain from punching each other's heads till the primroses are about again. But I fancy things will be lively enough when the spring comes round. And now, once more, good-bye, old fellow."

They all shook hands with Cis, and Julian Harperley and Annie walked with the young Lancer to the landing-place, saw him jump into a caique, and recede rapidly in the brilliant moonlight, on his way to the transport. They stopped for some few minutes watching the glittering showers that fell from the oars of the sturdy Greek boatmen, and then turned and walked happily home. For the present the banker and his daughter had cause for much heartfelt satisfaction ; had they not got the two near and dear to them safe out of the hurlyburly for the present ?

A week passed pleasantly away, while Mr. Harperley and Harry did all the lions of Constantinople and its neighbourhood. Miss Aysgarth devoted herself to taking the greatest care of Cis, who she was still sure required the utmost attention. At the end of that time the banker and his daughter and Calvert embarked for England, leaving the young Lancer behind them in a by no means depressed state; a cavalry race meeting was already in active organization, and that consoled Harry in some measure for the lost dog-hunting delights of the Crimea.

Dr. Barry proved right, and thanks to the fresh sea-air and the thorough change of scene Cis picked up strength rapidly. Still he was very lame, and bore unmistakable tokens of the severe illness through which he had passed, when his *fiancée* carried him triumphantly home to The Firs with her. No sooner was it known round the country-side that Captain Calvert was engaged to Annie Aysgarth, and staying with the banker, than all his old acquaintance hastened to call upon him. The country was proud of her heroes in those days as these, and not only was this one who had distinguished himself, whom they had all known, who was about to take himself a wife from amongst them, but to whom also they owed some little reparation for having doubted him concerning that unfortunate business at Crockley Hill. Annie was at first made supremely happy by the revulsion of feeling in her lover's favour, but soon she began to get much disquieted about the state of his health. A man does not go so near the verge of the grave as Cis Calvert and recover in a few months. The cold of the winter tried him severely, and as is so often the case, the maimed limbs were very susceptible to rheumatic affection. The arm he was slowly recovering the use of, but the doctor said that he would assuredly limp to his dying day.

Nobody had welcomed Cis home more cordially than the Charringtons. If the lady was an embroiderer she was at all events not a malicious one. And though she had been only too willing to believe in both the York and Indian stories to Cis's detriment, yet she really was glad to find they were un-founded. Then she had all the interest a woman invariably feels in an engagement, albeit Miss Aysgarth had not plighted her troth to the man she, Mrs. Charrington, had selected for her. As for Charrington, he would sit and talk Crimea with Cis as long as he could induce him to descant upon the subject. He even buried his jealousy of Crymes when he heard how ruddily gilt was his sabre when he returned from that terrible ride up the valley of Balaklava.

But as the spring-time came round Cis began slowly to recover the lee-way he had lost in the winter, and at the same time the papers teemed with rumours of peace. There could be very little doubt about it now; an armistice had already been agreed upon, and the remainder was pretty well a matter of detail. That the evacuation of the Crimea and the return of the army would be a mere matter of time was certain.

And now Julian Harperley began to urge upon his son-in-law, that was to be, a desire that lay near his heart. He could not quite bear the idea of parting with his daughter, and what he was very anxious for was that Cis should leave the service, make The Firs his home, and come into the bank as his partner. He knew that it was not good for a man to have nothing to do, but the war was all over, and though Cis was not incapacitated from resuming his profession, still he was undoubtedly lame, and so at a considerable disadvantage in it. He could ride fairly, but not as he once did: and, moreover, although sufficiently at home in the saddle when he got there, he could not at present get up without the assistance of a horse-block or some such aid. Annie strenuously supported her father's arguments; her heart had lived too much in her mouth during the last year not to make her wish that Cis should have done with the service. So at length it was settled that as soon as the regiment came home Calvert should send in his papers, and the wedding-bells be set a-ringing.

With the early June days the Crimean army began to swarm home. Transport after transport poured alongside the dock-yards of Portsmouth and Devonport, and discharged their living freights. As much as could be collected of the infantry, at all events, bronzed and bearded, paraded in the drizzle at Aldershot to receive the thanks of their Sovereign. And a perfect swirl of spray flew from the bear-skins of the Guards as they cheered

Her Majesty in response. That once got over, leave was granted pretty freely to the officers of the Crimean army, and Harry Harperley speedily made his appearance at The Firs. They had been only waiting for this, and a fortnight after his arrival Cis Calvert and Annie Aysgarth were duly united in the Minster.

One of the handsomest presents that the bride received upon the occasion was a diamond-and-cat's-eye bracelet, presented by Major Crymes. The Major has never married, but hunts pretty regularly with the York and Ainsty, and there is no more valued or constant guest at The Firs, when he is in the neighbourhood.

THE END.

BUNGAY: CLAY AND TAYLOR, PRINTERS.   S. & H.